F
MAT

Matturro, Claire
    Hamner, 1954-

Bone valley.

$23.95

DATE			
6-19			

BONE
Valley

Also by Claire Matturro

Wildcat Wine

Skinny-dipping

BONE Valley

Claire Matturro

WM

WILLIAM MORROW

An Imprint of HarperCollinsPublishers

This is a work of fiction. The characters, incidents, and dialogue are products of the author's imagination and are not to be construed as real. Any resemblance to actual persons, living or dead, is entirely coincidental.

HarperCollins books may be purchased for educational, business, or sales promotional use. For information please write: Special Markets Department, HarperCollins Publishers, 10 East 53rd Street, New York, NY 10022.

FIRST EDITION

Designed by Nicola Ferguson

Printed on acid-free paper

Library of Congress Cataloging-in-Publication Data

Matturro, Claire Hamner, 1954–
    Bone valley/Claire Matturro.—1st ed.
        p.   cm.
        ISBN-13: 978-0-06-077324-3 (acid-free paper)
        ISBN-10: 0-06-077324-3 (acid-free paper)
            1. Cleary, Lilly (Fictitious character)—Fiction.   2. Attorney and client—Fiction.   3. Sarasota (Fla.)—Fiction.   4. Women lawyers—Fiction.   I. Title.

PS3613.A87B66 2006
813'.6—dc22   2005044910

06 07 08 09 10 JTC/RRD 10 9 8 7 6 5 4 3 2 1

To the Peace River, struggling, like the Florida panther, for survival.

The Peace River was eighth on a list of America's Most Endangered Rivers, released in 2004—the reason: proposed expansions in phosphate-mining operations in and near the river's watershed, which have already both depleted and polluted the water in the river.

Bone Valley is also dedicated to the people, organizations, and politicians who fight the good fight trying to save Florida from the phosphate miners, including, though by no means limited to: the late Gloria Raines; Manasota-88, its leader, Glenn Compton, and its members; to the *Sarasota Herald-Tribune* for its decades-long coverage of phosphate issues, and staffers, editors, and writers such as Tom Tryon, Waldo Proffitt, Tom Bayles, Victor Hull, Allen Horton, John Hamner, and all those others who do not let us forget what phosphate mining does to Florida; the people and board of county commissioners of Charlotte County, Florida, who fought so long, so hard, and at such an economic cost to try to save the Peace River (the source for Charlotte County's drinking water) from expanding phosphate mining in its watershed; and to friend and inspiration, the tireless Becky Ayech.

Acknowledgments

Folks, I had a lot of help on this one.

Right off, let me tell you that Boogie Bog, its CEO, and its shady cast of characters are entirely and wholly fictional creations. However, an abandoned phosphate-processing plant in Manatee County, Florida, called Piney Point, is real. When its owner went bankrupt in 2001, it left 1.2 billion—yes, that's billion—gallons of toxic waste waters stored in holding ponds roughly equal to a five-story building for the state of Florida to clean up. At Piney Point, seventy-foot-high ponds, called gyp stacks, contained phosphogypsum, the waste product of processing phosphate into fertilizer. This gyp waste is radioactive, highly acidic, and unquestionably deadly when spilled into natural waterways. The state of Florida as of mid-2005 had spent $95 million to treat and then dump more than a half-billion gallons of this toxic waste into the Gulf of Mexico. Work is still under way, and the final cleanup bill may be as high as $170 million.

Fortunately, unlike the fictional Boogie Bog, the earthen dams around the Piney Point gyp stacks did not break, nor did the stacks flood in heavy rains. Nonetheless, the damage to the Gulf of Mexico and the economic hit to the state of Florida as a result of Piney Point are enormous. And continuing.

The threat of a catastrophic spill from Piney Point was very real. Cavities and cracks in the earthen dam, the only thing holding the toxic waste waters back, appeared, but the Florida Department of Environmental Protection heroes sealed those cracks before any spills occurred. But it wasn't just the cracks in the dam that posed a continuing danger, it was also the rain. In Florida, it rains a lot. These ponds trapped the rain. An article in the *Sarasota Herald-Tribune* quoted a Florida Department of Environmental Protection spokesperson as saying that rainfall in one year alone added 331 million gallons of water to Piney Point's stacks, and that water became toxic when mixed with the waste. Heavy rains in December 2001 brought the stacks to within a few feet of overflowing. And, at a similar gyp stack near Tampa, Florida, high winds and torrential rains from Hurricane Francis on September 5, 2004, ripped a chunk from its earthen dam and 65 million gallons of highly acidic wastewater escaped into Tampa Bay. According to the *Sarasota Herald-Tribune*, Florida currently has twenty-five gyp stacks that contain an estimated 1 billion ton of phosphogypsum. More toxic gyp wastes accumulate every year, posing a continuing danger to Florida and its waterways.

My gratitude to the people who helped me understand the phosphate issues is great. Tim Ohr, a freelance writer and author of books on natural Florida, including *Florida's Fabulous Canoe and Kayak Trail Guide*, *Florida's Fabulous Trail Guide*, and *Florida's Fabulous National Places*, selflessly walked me verbally through the basic issues concerning the phosphogypsum stacks left at Piney Point, and gave me a thorough lesson in the basics of phosphate mining. It was Tim's task to teach me such things as the difference between a slime pond and a gyp stack. His primer course in phosphate mining laid down an important foundation for *Bone Valley*. Tim didn't know me from Adam's house cat when I first contacted him after reading several of his articles. Yet he shared his time and knowledge most graciously and generously with me. Thank you, Tim.

Sarasota Herald-Tribune environmental editor and writer Tom Bayles, another stranger, took time out of his busy workdays to answer what seemed like a hundred questions via e-mail and phone about Piney Point, phosphate mining, and the science and numbers involved. Tom in person and Tom's articles were a vast source of information and inspiration. And Victor Hull and Allen Horton, though we never talked, your articles in the *Sarasota Herald-Tribune* were another great source of information on Piney Point and all things Florida and phosphate. Thank you all.

My father, John Hamner, retired journalist, and friend Mike Lehner both ran unofficial clipping services for me, mailing me articles on phosphate, gyp stacks, Piney Point, and other such things when I was outside the range of the *Sarasota Herald-Tribune*. All the reporters who have covered phosphate and gyp stacks in Florida helped greatly—you should see my Piney Point and phosphate files!

Three Web sites also proved so helpful I wish to mention them, not only to thank their contributors, but to refer them to any of you who wish to read more on phosphate issues. These are: www.manasota88.tripod.com, www.thephosphaterisk.com, and www.fipr.state.fl.us (from the Florida Institute of Phosphate Research).

Please let me thank the animal-rehabilitation people I met in researching this novel. These people do work that is both hard and heartbreaking—and sometimes dangerous—and they do it with great love and generosity. To Zannah in Georgia, for sharing the story of Bob the doomed squirrel, for her good, big heart, and for teaching me something about raising baby squirrels, thank you. To Bill in Georgia, for his love of our winged creatures and answering all the bird questions, especially the feeding ones, thank you. To Loraine in Thomasville, for the story of the bobcat who attacked her in a cage, the goats, for all the animals saved, and for sharing her animal sanctuary with my husband and me one Sunday, thank you. Your animal sanctuary, where I watched the deer and the coyotes and the fox all cohabit peacefully, gave me a glimpse of what I think the kingdom of heaven might be like.

To Jane in Tallahassee and the people at St. Francis in Gadsden County, thank you for teaching me about the care and feeding of orphan birds, patching up tortoise shells, and all other things such as that. Oh, and a word about what to do if you find an orphan baby bird or other animal, or a wounded animal: contact a certified wildlife rehabilitator. It's often pretty complicated, and you can make things worse in a hurry if you don't know what you are doing. If you can't find a wildlife rehabilitator listed in your phone book, try calling your local veterinary offices; they can refer you.

Mike Peel, certified Rolfer in Bradenton, took the time to enthusiastically teach me about Rolfing, both by word and example. The fact that the Rolfing scene ended up on the cutting-room floor, so to speak, didn't devalue your lessons—thank you, Mike.

Dan McNicol showed me the Peace River, up close and personal, from a canoe and a tent on its banks. It's a glorious river, and it should be protected and cherished, not mined and exploited, and I thank Dan for introducing me to it in a whole new way.

With great delight, let me thank Jan Heffington, friend and Florida neighbor, for sharing her trained cats, Cleo and Bailey, with me whenever I needed a kitty fix while writing, and for having one of the best ideas in *Bone Valley* and generously letting me use it. Thank you, Jan.

Always, always: Thank you to my editor, Carolyn Marino, and her assistant, Jennifer Civiletto, for not only making me a better writer, but for adding an element of grace to the whole process; to my publicist, Samantha Hagerbaumer, who keeps track of me even when I can't; and my agent, Elaine Koster, who makes the maze and fine print far less scary, and is an excellent sounding board and wholly honest in her critiques.

And finally, though by no means lastly, to Bill, Deborah, and Peter, who teach by example that it isn't the slogan on your T-shirt, or the bumper sticker on your car, but how you live each day that makes a person an environmentalist. These three are rare examples of people who live lightly on the earth with tremendous respect for nature, and they helped to inspire the character of Lenora.

Thank you all. And, if I didn't get it exactly right, then it's my fault, not any of these generous people's.

Now, a word to the people and officials of Charlotte County, Florida: As of this writing, it looks like you are losing the battle to save the Peace River, one of America's Most Endangered Rivers of 2004 and your source of drinking water, from the phosphate miners. I hope by the time this book comes out, your story has a better ending. Keep up the good fight.

BONE
Valley

Chapter One

The practice of law is best performed by lunatics. That way, they don't mind that much of the law is lunacy.

For example, in Florida, insulting an orange can land you in court.

One may be sued for defaming a little, round fruit. Sued and required to pay money. If not to the orange grower suing you, then certainly to the lawyer defending you.

I, Lillian Belle Rose Cleary, defense lawyer, sat in my office at Smith, O'Leary, and Stanley in Sarasota, with the Florida statutes book opened to section 865.065, titled "Disparagement of perishable agricultural food products," and tried to absorb the concept of fruit libel. As I read, my putative new client, Angus John Cartright, a rough-and-ready young man wearing jeans and cowboy boots, sat across from me whistling what sounded like a slow version of "The Yellow Rose of Texas."

Because I didn't like what I was reading in the statutes, I put down the law book and picked up a copy of the complaint filed against Angus John, a legal document that said he had willfully and wantonly and maliciously given speeches in which he claimed certain, specific oranges "glowed in the dark" and were unsafe to eat.

"Is this true?" I asked, holding up the complaint. "I mean, that you said all this about these oranges being too dangerous to eat?"

"Yes." He had stopped whistling and stared at me with big, hazel eyes.

"The complaint also alleges you did so without having any reliable evidence to support your claims. Did you have any scientific studies to back up your statements?"

"It's a matter of common sense."

Oh, so, okay, in other words, no. Well, as much as Angus John's admission of the key facts in the complaint against him might simplify drafting an answer and pursuing discovery, it didn't make his case too enticing to defend. I mean, where's the fun in litigation if the did/did-not spat wasn't there at the get-go to run up thousands of dollars in attorney's fees arguing about who said or didn't say what, not to mention revving up *that* dog and pony show before a jury.

"The plaintiff is suing you because you publicly said its oranges were—"

"I have an absolute First Amendment right to speak my mind," Angus John said, and then grinned big, as if he'd just told me a small joke, which, in a way, I guess he had. "They can't sue me."

Okay, so spank me, I'm no constitutional scholar or anything, but I've been a lawyer for over a decade and one of the lessons I've learned is that there are no absolute rights. Especially absolute First Amendment rights.

Just as I was fortifying myself to explain the underlying basic premise of the American litigation system to Angus, that being that anyone with the $250 filing fee can sue anybody else, I heard an insistent tapping of fingernails on glass. Angus and I both turned to stare out my office window, which looks out on our back parking lot since my office is on the first floor, in the back corner, right by the exit.

A thin, older man grinned through the glass panes.

I sighed. Jimmie Rodgers, my handyman, the man who had single-handedly and largely on his hands and knees restored my home's terrazzo floors to their former glory, rebuilt my back porch after one of those hurricanes, and done countless other home projects, all working roughly at an inch of progress and two bottles of wine an hour. He liked to quote poetry of all kinds to me, and had slipped me small paperbacks of poets I'd never heard of who wrote stuff I didn't understand. Then Jimmie would explain it all to me over a couple of bottles of wine. He was, of late, particularly fond of Anne Sexton and Sylvia Plath, and could recite long poems about suicide by either or both of them at length and by memory. This explained why he was erratically employed. The man does good work, but don't hire him if you're in a hurry, or a hard-shell Baptist, or don't like poetry.

Jimmie tapped and grinned and I made my face form a kind of smile back. On top of being my handyman, he was also my client in what I considered the stupidest case of my entire career.

Ignoring my orange-defaming potential client, I jumped from my chair and aimed myself for the back door to let Jimmie in.

When Jimmie came into my office, he smelled a bit gamey, but before I could say much to him about washing up before his court appearances, he beamed, hugged me, said a quick, "Hey, Lady," then took center stage in my office. Spreading his arms wide, he said in a singsongy voice: " 'I danced through the shards with no visible wound. The night I risked tequila and Seconal to stop you both, I woke.' "

Great, another suicidal poet.

"That's from this book"—Jimmie pulled a beat-up chapbook from a pocket in his baggy painter's pants—"I found at Brant's Used Books on Brown Avenue. Only paid a quarter for it."

Angus John made a production of standing up and grinning and offering his hand.

But Jimmie, caught up as he was with poetry and gift giving, didn't fully focus on Angus and thrust the book at me. "It's for you, Lady."

Politeness required me to take the used book, but I tried to hold it with my fingernails as if it were hot, and I made a quick memo to my internal file to disinfect my hands as soon as possible and to put the book somewhere safe, like a trash can.

Angus, having been ignored by both Jimmie and me, cleared his throat. I was too busy trying not to actually touch the book I was now holding to acknowledge Angus, and Jimmie apparently hadn't yet realized someone else was already in my office.

"I know I didn't have an appointment," Angus said in a tone that suggested this was a grievous breach on my part, "but I did hope to at least have your attention."

"Mr. Cartright," I began in the tone I take with the rude and idiotic. "Olivia O'Leary brought you in here not ten minutes ago and asked me to look over the complaint with an eye toward possibly defending you. I was not expecting you." And I would not have even remotely entertained the notion of allowing him in the door under such circumstances but for the fact that Olivia, also known as the Scrub Jay Lady, was the wife of named partner number two and a close friend of mine despite the fact I once thought she had murdered one of my clients.

"Normally I schedule an appointment," I explained, "so we won't be interrupted and so that I might review the law and the complaint well before an initial meeting, so you see that you are a rare exception"—that being lawyerese for rude interruption—"to my standard practice."

Before I could continue with my lesson in office protocol, my secretary supreme and secondary therapist, Bonita, stuck her head in the half-opened door and said, "*¿Como esta, señor?*"

"*Moo-ee be-in,*" Jimmie said, and grinned like a fool at her while I flinched at his Spanish. Though he is more than twice her age, Jimmie is sweet on Bonita. But then, most men are.

Bonita finished greeting Jimmie and then flitted her eyes toward Angus John, and I said, "Olivia snuck Mr. Cartright in while you were in bookkeeping. And Jimmie came in the back door."

Bonita started to make gracious noises toward Angus John, but my phone intercom came alive with our receptionist's prim little voice. "Lilly, please pick up the phone."

I did. "There's a woman sheriff's deputy out front, demanding to see you. Something about M. David Moody. She says that they found him dead. Pulled him out of one of those . . . excuse me a minute, Lilly . . . a what?"

In the background I could hear a woman talk, but I couldn't make out the words.

The receptionist came back on the line. "A phosphogypsum stack. That's like a big lake full of toxic waste, behind a seventy-foot wall. Least, that's what the detective says. You got me. Anyway, Mr. Moody was floating in one, dead, up at Bougainvillea Bayou in Manatee County. Shall I send her back?"

Whoa.

Time out.

M. David was dead?

Drowned in a lake of phosphogypsum in Manatee, our neighboring county to the north, at the defunct phosphate-processing plant the locals had dubbed Boogie Bog?

Pushing aside the wholly uncharitable idea that sometimes karma works itself out in one lifetime and didn't require reincarnation as a roach, I flashed for a moment on M. David Moody before he was a newly dead man. M. David the ardently elegant, M. David the brilliant, M. David the perpetual chair of some well-publicized charity-fund drive, M. David who had enriched himself on underground rocks in the phosphate-rich region of Florida known as bone valley, leaving in his wake a slew of radioactive sludge.

So the son of a bitch was dead.

Maybe that made us even.

But why would a deputy want to talk to me about M. David? I hadn't spoken to the man in ten years, and had, in fact, gone pointedly out of my way to avoid doing so.

"Lilly? You there?" our receptionist asked. "Shall I send this deputy woman back?"

Back to my office, where the ignored Angus John was glowering, Jimmie had started his old-man flirting, and Bonita was trying to gain order.

"I better come up front," I said.

"I'll go with you," Angus John said.

No doubt he was trying to escape Jimmie and get a few moments of undivided attention from me. But my mind was already hopscotching around the newly introduced topic of M. David.

As I walked down the hallway toward our reception area, Angus kept pace beside me. "There's some other people who are being sued under that stupid food-libel law," he said. "Do you think you should put together a class action to help them?"

"A class action is only for plaintiffs. That is, people who want to sue others. Defendants, that is, people like you who are being sued, can't form a class action."

"Why not?"

"Neither the federal nor the Florida rules of civil procedure allow it."

"Have you ever tried it?" Angus asked.

"No, because it can't be done."

"Why not?"

"Trust me, okay? I'm a lawyer. I know these things."

"But have you actually ever tried to form a class action for defendants?"

I sighed. It was Friday afternoon. I had to be at the courthouse for Jimmie's stupid car-case hearing in half an hour. I'd skipped lunch. With all the city concrete, it was hot as blue blazes and still only late May. And I had absolutely no interest in spending time discussing with some woman from the sheriff's office the illustrative history of M. David Moody and my diminutive but unpleasant part in it, though

I had much curiosity about how the man came to be dead. But mostly I didn't want to give a discourse to a cowboy zealot on the mysterious ways of the Florida civil-litigation system.

"Angus, I apologize." Smile, smile. "I am sorry, but you've caught me at a bad time. Please let me make you an appointment. We'll talk," I said, applying one of the cardinal rules of client relationships—procrastinate politely.

So spoken, I pushed at the door separating the hallway from the firm's lobby, but Angus rushed out in front of me and held the door open for me. On the other side, a tall blond woman stood waiting.

She held out a perfectly manicured hand, French tips and all, with a sapphire-and-diamond ring that reflected the artificial light of the reception area in a small dazzle. "I'm Manatee County Sheriff's Office Investigator First Class Josey Henry Farmer."

I took the perfect hand and looked up, and up, into her eyes, which were a bright blue. "Lillian Cleary, attorney first class. Pleased to meet you, Officer Henry-Farmer."

"Just Farmer."

"Pleased to meet you, Farmer."

"Investigator," she said. "Investigator Farmer."

Title clarifications aside, I was taking in her height. Next to her, Angus looked like a puppy. I fared better, but was still about eye high to her nose. Feeling reduced, I tried to stretch my back and neck but couldn't approach her tallness.

In any crowd of women, I'm always the tallest. No question. It's been that way since I hit my full growth back in tenth grade and I liked it. So therefore I didn't like it at all that Investigator Josey Henry Farmer beat me out.

"I'm six feet," I said.

"I'm taller," she said. Then she glared at Angus. I couldn't read her expression, though it appeared to me to be something between irritation and suspicion.

When nobody spoke, I glanced at Angus, who was looking back at Josey with a similarly weird expression.

So, okay, what gives? I thought, then realized I didn't really care. Quickest way through this was to introduce them, and ask Angus to leave.

"Officer Investigator First Class Josey Henry Farmer," I said, "please meet Angus John Cartright."

Angus John grinned and stuck out a hand, which Investigator Just-Farmer took, flashing the ring again.

"Fine. Now, go away, Mr. Cartright," Officer Josey said.

As Angus ducked around the corner, toward the conference room, I began the usual professional introductory chitchat stuff, but Investigator Farmer interrupted and asked, "Did you know M. David Moody?"

"He was a prominent member of the business community."

"Did you know him?"

"I knew him. He was a prominent member of the business community," I repeated, already edgy.

"Did you know him? *Personally?*"

"What, like biblically?" I retorted. "I knew him, okay?"

"How did you know him?"

"I told you, he was a prominent member of the business community."

"Were you his lawyer?"

"No, I'm not a business lawyer per se. I specialize in defending people who've been sued, civil suits, not criminal, defending them usually in the tort field, like malpractice and—"

"Were you close to Mr. Moody?"

Close to M. David? Not hardly. I doubted, frankly, that anyone had been close to him. "No, ma'am," I said.

"You don't need to ma'am me. Any reason why Mr. Moody would have a file on you?"

"No reason I can think of."

"Any reason he would have your firm brochure with a note on it to make an appointment with you?"

"No."

"Any reason you know of that he would have told his secretary to make an appointment with you as soon as possible, but ended up facedown in a phosphate gyp stack at Boogie Bog instead?"

Uh-oh. I definitely didn't like the sound of any of this.

"No, ma'am, no reason at all. I don't even use phosphate, not as fertilizer or detergent."

While I pondered what I considered a remote possibility that M. David would have the nerve to try to see me even in a professional setting, Investigator Farmer stared at me as if she had X-ray vision. Then she scoped the perimeter and turned back to me.

"Perhaps we should go to your office and pursue this further," she said, no doubt having noticed that Angus was hovering in easy hearing distance and our receptionist was apparently listening to us with some interest.

Bonita was probably ready to be rescued from Jimmie by now, and I nodded. "Come on back," I said, and held open the door to the hallway for Investigator Farmer, noting as she passed how buff her legs and arms were.

In a fair fight, this woman could pin Angus in the first round without damaging her manicure.

Chapter Two

The judge was rubbing his eyes and stifling a yawn before I finished my first sentence in the Parrot versus the Bikini Top case. Okay, it was late afternoon, it was warm inside the courtroom, but come on, pay attention, I thought.

As I concluded my introduction and mentally geared up for my argument, the newest judge on the bench, a man at least five years my junior, gave into his yawn, and then said, "Counselor Cleary, why don't you refresh me on the facts?" Translation: The good judge had never read my impeccably organized and excessively detailed memorandum of law in support of my motion for a summary judgment that Bonita had personally hand-delivered to the judge. A motion based upon the notion that when a well-endowed woman takes her bikini top off on a busy street because a parrot is pecking in it, the chaos and injury that naturally follow are all within the confines of the act of God doctrine. That is, it wasn't my client's fault there was a car wreck, and he doesn't have to pay anybody any money.

"Yes, Your Honor. My client, Jimmie Rodgers—"

"Good afternoon, Your Honor," Jimmie said, rising slightly from his chair.

Rather than chastise me or my client for that slight breach of etiquette—clients weren't supposed to talk at hearings, that's why they hire lawyers—the judge nodded toward him.

"Yes, Your Honor. Mr. Rodgers was driving his automobile down Siesta Drive on a Sunday afternoon," I said, in an overly animated voice, hoping to wake the judge up. "Being a cautious driver, he observed a young woman wearing a bikini and riding a bike along the side of the road. A large green parrot was sitting on her shoulder. Naturally Mr. Rodgers slowed down and took notice of her so that he would not endanger her in any way with his large automobile."

"Um, objection, Your Honor, I . . . she's not, um, supposed to . . . editorialize," my opposing counsel said with a squeak in his voice. I hadn't bothered to remember his name, though he had said it only five minutes before. Though he was a big guy, he looked about eighteen, a novice who didn't even know lawyers don't object over stuff like that in a hearing.

"Young man, this is a hearing on a motion. Not a jury trial. I assure you I can tell a fact from an editorial without your help," the judge said.

Pretty arrogant, I thought, for a man who hadn't been a judge more than a month and who hadn't even been practicing law when the governor appointed him to the bench. But the fact that he'd taken a break from lawyering to work on a Ph.D. in history hadn't interfered with his rise to the judiciary because both his brother and his father were Big Republicans duly elected to Important Offices and his aunt owned about a fifth of the southwestern part of the state of Florida and made large and regular campaign donations to the right people. After all, this was Sarasota, hometown of the woman heiress who selected our president for us back in the year 2000 and then not surprisingly rose from secretary of state to go on to greater political glory.

Putting aside my momentary resentment of the easy success of the well-connected, I said, "Thank you, Your Honor. As I was explaining, while Mr. Rodgers was driving down Siesta, the young woman pulled her bikini top off and shook—"

The judge looked over his glasses at me. Okay, got his attention. "Shook . . . what? The bikini top or—"

"Both. You should've—" Jimmie said, jumping up out of his chair as I tried to pinch his leg inconspicuously to signal him that he should shut up.

"Sit, Mr. Rodgers," the judge said, cutting him off. "Continue, please, Counselor Cleary."

"The young woman shook her bikini top out, Your Honor. As she explained later, the parrot had flown off for a moment and captured a lizard, then it dropped the lizard down her bikini top. That was bad enough, but when the parrot went pecking in her top after the lizard, well, naturally, she needed to shake her top out before the parrot bit her while chasing its . . . lunch. Mr. Rodgers was so surprised by her taking off her top and shaking it out, he naturally failed to notice that the car in front of him had slammed on its brakes."

"My client, Your Honor, sir, did not, er, 'slam on his brakes,' he just slowed down. Her client was the one who did the slamming, right into the back of my client, knocking him from behind, when my client, er, was doing exactly what he was supposed to do, and . . . like, he got hurt," said my earnest opposing counsel in triple-speed speak, complete with squeak.

"Young man, please stop interrupting Counselor Cleary."

"My name is Jason Quartermire, sir, not 'young man,' Your Honor, sir."

"Young man, stop interrupting."

"Yes, sir."

I paused a moment to make sure it was still my turn, then I said, "The plaintiff, who was driving in front of Mr. Rodgers on Siesta Drive, testified in his deposition that he too noted the young woman disrobing on her bike, and he braked. Page twelve of his depo, Your Honor." And that same plaintiff was now suing poor Jimmie Rodgers with litigation-lottery fantasies of the big bucks, upon spurious allegations that the minor rear-ender had caused him to suffer a double spinal subluxation that was so painful only daily chiropractic treatments, and, oh, say, a quarter of a million bucks, could ease his suffering.

"What happened to the parrot?" the judge asked.

"It lost the lizard, sir, but recovered its position on the young woman's shoulder," I said.

"So what was the act of God?" the good judge asked.

"The parrot, Your Honor. The proximate cause of this whole accident was the parrot dropping the lizard into the young woman's bikini top and then going after it. That, sir, was an act of God. And it is a well-settled principle of law that where the proximate cause of damages is an act of God, and not an act of negligence on the defendant's part, that there is no cause of action. Accordingly, as the proximate cause of the plaintiff's *alleged* damages was a natural act of God and not Mr. Rodgers's negligence, he is entitled to a summary judgment and there is no need to tie up judicial time and expense in a jury trial."

"I don't think so, Counselor Cleary," the judge said.

"If you'd seen that girl's titties, you'd've known it were an act of God for sure," Jimmie said, rising from his chair again.

I slapped my memorandum of law against Jimmie's stomach and said, "Sit down, Mr. Rodgers."

"Counselor Cleary, I do not condone lawyers battering their clients in my courtroom."

"It's awright, Judge, sir. It didn't hurt me none and she did fuss at me not to say titties."

"Then stop saying it," his honor said. Then he turned and looked directly at me. "Nice try, Counselor Cleary. Motion denied."

"You mean we lost?" Jimmie asked.

"Don't you want to hear my argument?" the big kid with a new law degree asked.

"You won, young man. Relax. Notch your gun. And, no, I do not want to hear your argument."

"Thank you, Your Honor," I said. "I'll prepare the order for your signature." Then we all stood and the judge left the courtroom.

While I tried to hustle Jimmie and my memo of law out of the courtroom in a hurry, young Mr. Quartermire waylaid me.

"This was my first hearing. I was really nervous."

"I would never have known," I said, mistakenly thinking my sarcasm was obvious.

"Really? That's so nice of you to say," Baby Lawyer said. "I mean, I've heard a lot about you. You're kind of . . . you know, like a legend around here."

Flattery wasn't going to console me, so I barely nodded and started walking. I didn't need any more child-lawyer devotees. Smith, O'Leary, and Stanley, my law firm, had a library full of law clerks who filled that bill. What I wanted very much to do was get back to my office, send Jimmie on his way, and rehash with Bonita my strange interrogation by Investigator Farmer regarding the gypsum-stack death of M. David. Oh, yeah, and document my time for the hearing and go home before dark.

Not reading my body language, Mr. Quartermire tagged along beside me. "In fact, I was really surprised that a lawyer of your . . . er, stature, would take this case."

Yeah, well, me too.

As a partner with a healthy number of years of experience, I had moved well beyond stupid car-crash cases. Normally I would have spent about thirty seconds passing this file down to a first-year associate. Ultimately, a Smith, O'Leary, and Stanley associate as young and untrained as young Mr. Quartermire would have practiced budding lawyer skills in a series of meaningless legal thrusts and parries with the opposing side until Jimmie's insurance company decided on a proper settlement amount.

But just my luck, Jimmie Rodgers was not only the man who had done all the odd jobs around my house, but he reminded me of my grandfather, who also drank more than was sociably acceptable. Given our relationship, I wasn't about to turn Jimmie down when he asked me to defend him in his stupid car lawsuit, even though the case was far beneath my standing in the hierarchy of Sarasota lawyers. Friends don't leave friends at the mercy of the vagaries of the Florida tort system.

So, there I was—stuck handling the kind of case that dumb kids like the nervous Jason Quartermire cut their teeth on.

What with a parrot-induced fender bender and a defamed-orange case to live down if word got out, I knew I needed a page-one lawsuit. But the legislature had made it so difficult to sue doctors in Florida that those million-dollar med-mal suits I was locally famous for successfully defending were drying up. At a point in my career where most lawyers looked forward to coasting on their laurels and having their associates do the hard stuff, I was looking at developing a new legal specialty.

Seeing no need to explain any of this to Quartermire, I simply said, "Good day," in a voice that signaled the end of our conversation, and turned and jogged off with Jimmie huffing to keep up as we left the courthouse.

As Jimmie prattled beside me on the short, but hot and trafficky walk back to my office, in the humidity my hair felt like a thick, dark blanket on my head and shoulders. Stifling a pant, I scooped it up into a temporary ponytail, anchored by my hand, and let a hint of the Gulf breeze cool my neck. Then I wondered how many people got sued in Florida for defaming fruit. Was there a trend there I might capitalize on? I mean, how hard could it be to defend a lawsuit against an orange?

Jimmie grabbed my hand as we ran across Ringling Boulevard, dodging the cars that never stop, and we landed safely on the other

side. But before I convinced him to go home, I saw Angus John milling around outside the front of the Smith, O'Leary, and Stanley law
office. Off slightly to one side stood a tall, thin man with long, wavy
black hair and just about the most beautiful face I'd ever seen on a
man. It looked like he was preaching to Angus, with his arms raised
and his hands open.

I stopped walking and inhaled so deeply that Jimmie took my
hand again and said, "Lady, are you all right?"

All right? My fingertips tingled. My lips began to part. The rub of
my panty hose on my thighs was electrocuting me. Suddenly I could
smell my own pheromones.

All that from one look at a black-haired stranger ten feet away
from me.

And I was, more or less, or at least in the eyes of Philip Cohen,
my ardently persistent lover, an engaged woman.

"Oh, my lord," Jimmie said, turning to follow my stare. "Don't he
look like a Mexican Jesus fixing to feed the poor ones."

I licked my lips and tried to breathe.

Chapter Three

Olivia was crouched over Bonita's desk, where they appeared to be hatching some plot, and they both looked up at me with practiced expressions of neutrality when I pranced into Bonita's cubbyhole on the way to my own office.

"Lilly," Olivia said, "my goodness, Bonita was just telling me about M. David. Why does that deputy sheriff think you had something to do with killing him?"

"I'm not a suspect," I said.

"Are you sure? I mean, everybody knows you hated the man. I can't say I cared much for M. David myself, his politics being what they were, though he danced divinely with me every year at the United Way ball, but what a terrible way to go. How did . . ." Olivia paused when she noticed the parade of men I had been leading, the short Angus, the slightly smelly Jimmie, and the most-beautiful-man-alive. "Oh, good," she said, standing up and pushing an oddly cut clump of hair behind her ear, and smiling. "I see you and Miguel have met." She offered her hand to Miguel, who took it, held it, and sighed.

"Olivia, Olivia, my sweet Olivia," he said.

I imagined for a moment what "Lilly, oh Lilly" would sound like coming from his lips, especially if his mouth was on his head on a pillow in my bed. Then I stood back to study the scenario. Olivia was actually blushing. I didn't think I had ever seen that before. She pushed that clump of hair back again with her free hand, and then shoved her glasses up her nose. Okay, she was flustered. So was I. Miguel had that effect. Then he leaned into Olivia and whispered something into her pink ear, and let go of her hand.

A strange little kick of jealousy hit me in my gut. Olivia was married, okay, married well, in fact, and she was a good deal older than Miguel, and she had some grooming issues. On the other hand, she was smart and strong and hardworking. Back home in Bugfest, we'd have called her a handsome woman, which is small-town south for a plain woman you like a lot.

But all in all, not the kind of woman Miguel should be flirting with.

No, I was the kind of woman Miguel should be flirting with.

I stepped up to the plate so he'd notice that too. "Yes," I said, and put my hand on Miguel's arm, "Angus introduced us in the parking lot."

"You will be able to help them, Lilly, won't you? Angus and Miguel? From that stupid orange lawsuit. It's nothing more than a SLAPP suit," Olivia said, regaining her usual den-mother composure.

"What's a SLAPP suit?" Jimmie asked, angling through the pack to get closer to Bonita.

"Harassment, but legal," I said, and softly slid my hand off Miguel's arm, making sure my fingers traced his skin before I let go. "Stands for 'strategic litigation against public participation.' Say an environmentalist goes after a polluter using standard practices like getting petitions signed, letters to the editor, speaking at public hearings, instigating others to write letters to regulatory agencies. Then the targeted polluter, who almost always has big corporate bucks and an army of attorneys, sues the environmentalist, usually for bogus claims, but the idea is that the lawsuit will break the activist either through the financial costs of the defense, or the lost time. Defending against a lawsuit, even a stupid one, is expensive, very expensive, and very unpleasant." I stopped when I realized I was using my lecture voice and no one was listening to me.

"Huh," Jimmie said, and then turned his attentions to Bonita. "Hey, sweet lady, got anything needing fixing, cutting, or cleaning at your place? I'd do it for free. Sure like to see them five little children of yours again."

Just like a man, I thought, to ignore the serious stuff when a good-looking woman was nearby.

Jimmie leaned even closer to Bonita, who surely got a whiff of him, but she had the good grace not to jerk back.

Grooming school, I thought. If this lawyer thing doesn't work out, I was going to open a good-grooming academy. Jimmie, take a bath; Olivia, get a decent haircut and a pair of pants made in this decade; Angus, come on, cowboy boots in Florida in late spring? And Miguel—perfect.

Well, he could, now that I looked at them, use a pair of pants made in this decade too.

Then everybody started talking at once, interrupting my daydream of alternative career number 412, Lilly's Grooming Academy.

"Listen," I said, feeling the press of too many bodies in one small space, "Miguel and Angus and I are going in my office to discuss the terms of my representing them. If you will excuse us. Jimmie, sorry about the hearing, but we'll get your case settled quickly now, you'll see. I'll be in touch."

With that I backed into my office, hoping Miguel would follow and Angus would stay behind, but both dutifully followed me.

"Sit," I said, and waved my arms in a general sweep of my office. "Let's get acquainted first. Please, tell me about yourself."

I looked right at Miguel, but Angus started talking.

"I wash sailboats for a living, but mostly I fight phosphate. I was born in Mulberry, near Bartow, and I've seen what those phosphate mines do to a community, to the land, the water."

"You wash sailboats for a living?" I said, roughly translating that into the fact that he'd never be able to pay my hourly rate.

"Not much money in it, but the work's steady, and nobody asks my politics."

Yeah, okay, you can't pay me and I don't want to date you. "So," I said, and turned my face and whole body toward Miguel, beaming my best smile at him. "And you?"

"My mother is Cuban, my father is a Seminole Indian, and I've lived all my life in Florida. We lived in the Everglades until the sugar people drove us out. Now my folks live in Chokoloskee and I move around, setting up shop where I'm needed."

"Uh-huh." It's hard to be articulate when you're resisting the urge to pounce on somebody.

"Tell her what you do for a living," Angus the ignored said.

"Yes, oh, yes," I said and hoped it would be something that didn't involve a lot of women but did actually earn money.

"I'm a certified Rolfer."

"A what?"

"He's like a fancy masseuse."

"It's a bit more complex than that, but I'd be glad to explain it to you. In detail. But another time." Miguel smiled at me and my heart leaped up.

"Date," I said. "I mean, deal."

"Let's talk about this lawsuit," Angus the not to be ignored said. "The media wouldn't give us the time of day. I mean, they were dumping enough toxic gyp waste on those groves to turn it into a Superfund site, and then thinking it was all right for folks to eat those oranges. And you think the newspapers would run a story? Hell no."

Yeah, yeah, yeah.

"And another thing, all this was a year and a half, almost two years ago. So far as we could tell, they weren't dumping the gyp out there this year."

Nodding, I scribbled a note to check the statute of limitations for fruit-libel lawsuits. "We'll need to schedule an appointment to discuss the merits of your case next week. This is just our introductory meeting, to make sure we want to formally enter an attorney-client relationship."

"So, okay, why would we want to hire you?" Angus asked.

Thus queried, I went through my standard introduction to litigation and what a lawyer does and why I was a great lawyer and why they should hire me to defend them. I figured the fact that neither could pay my standard hourly fee pretty much balanced out the fact that I didn't know jack about defending First Amendment, fruit-defamation cases, and so I didn't mention my lack of expertise on the subject matter of their particular lawsuit. When I was done with my spiel, they both nodded.

"Olivia recommended you, and that's good enough for me," Miguel said.

Angus grunted.

"Fine, I'll have Bonita draft a retainer agreement, and I'll file a notice of appearance for both of you first thing Monday, and we'll spend some time going over the facts early next week, then I'll file an answer on your behalf."

"So, you are officially our attorney now, right?" Miguel asked.

"Yes. You can tell me all your secrets now and I'm ethically bound to keep them." I held my breath so I wouldn't pant.

"Cool," Angus said.

"We'll be in touch," Miguel said, and stood up.

The word *touch* hung in the air until I saw little flames around it, and I nodded, and watched them walk out of my office, concentrating on the way Miguel's butt muscles moved in his worn jeans.

Oh, boy, I thought.

But before I could work myself up too much further, Bonita and Olivia bounded into my office.

"You will take their case, right," Olivia said, and I registered the fact that she hadn't said it as a question. Besides being my friend, Olivia's status as the wife of Fred O'Leary, as in Smith, O'Leary, and Stanley, pretty much guaranteed I'd take on anyone she wanted me to defend. A barely mid-tier partner like me knows to jump when a Smith or an O'Leary says to, and wives counted the same as the actual partner. Stanley, as in Ashton Stanley the maniac, partner number three, was still in California, where I'd last heard from him when he called from a hot tub he was sharing with a starlet, and the power vacuum created by his extended leave had pretty much been filled by Smith and O'Leary themselves.

"So, yes, of course," I said.

Olivia gave me a little hug, and said to come and visit anytime, and she left.

Bonita gave me that what-have-you-done-now look, and I beamed. "Olivia the rainmaker," I said, though I generally prefer clients with large trust funds or liability policies that will pay my standard fees. "You know the drill. Let's do the notices of appearances for Monday filing."

"He's not your type," Bonita said. She has a tendency to mother me, this, no doubt, is an overflow of her maternal instincts not fully exhausted by her five kids.

"Part Cuban, part Seminole, and totally gorgeous," I said. "Why is he not my type?"

Bonita sighed, and went back to her computer.

Okay, okay, as it turned out, she was totally right about that, but a man like Miguel makes one look past common sense.

Chapter Four

Oh, great, now what?

Jimmie Rodgers was parked in a dilapidated Oldsmobile, waiting for me, in my driveway, in front of my own house, blocking my way inside my own carport.

Being that it was now officially late, i.e., past quitting time at Smith, O'Leary, and Stanley, I wanted to go inside my home and be quiet. Not that I had earned that right, per se, given the lagging last hours I'd put in after Miguel and Angus left. No, I'd spent what was left of the afternoon doing billable work that didn't require me to actually think—laypeople would be amazed by how much of lawyers' work meets this definition.

By dark, I'd charted enough hours on my time sheet to rival the firm's average daily billings, and so I had sprinted out the door after a good-bye-good-weekend-call-me-if-any-of-your-kids-do-anything-that-needs-a-lawyer to Bonita, and driven home to my modest little Florida ranch in Southgate.

Where Jimmie was waiting for me.

I parked behind Jimmie's ratty vehicle, and got out of my own just as he pushed himself out of his front seat and into open air. Before Jimmie or I could speak, my neighbor, the Hall Monitor of the Universe, opened her front door and came out, with Bearess, my former rottweiler, beside her.

"I was about to call the police on that car," Dolly shouted. "Do you know this man?"

"I do. Thank you. We're fine," I said, and waved, hoping to head her off.

But no, of course not. Dolly was not to be headed off. Now that Dolly was officially my grandmother-by-proxy, we spent way more time than necessary chatting about my shortcomings, and having an old car with a strange man in it in my driveway would count as a transgression against good neighborliness. This from a woman who had stolen the affections of my own dog. She and Bearess ambled over toward us. Bearess woofed, jumped on me, and licked my chin, like she was saying, you know, no hard feelings, and then dashed back to sit beside her new momma.

Dolly squinted at Jimmie. "You sure you know him?"

"Yes, Dolly, I'm sure. I know him."

"Jimmie Rodgers," Jimmie said, and stuck out his hand. Bearess, never known for her guard-dog talents, licked his hand as it passed under her nose. Dolly squinted at him again.

"Yes, that's right, I remember you. You spent a summer fixing her porch after that storm. You left trash on the front lawn."

"Dolly Gorman, this is Jimmie Rodgers, Jimmie, this is Dolly."

Now, I wanted everybody to go home and leave me alone, but I stood a moment waiting to see who would leave first.

Dolly shot a last hostile glare at Jimmie and his car, and said, "Well, dear, call me if you need me. Oh, and Bearess is about out of that food from that health food store that you feed her."

Despite the fact that Bearess had moved in with Dolly, I still had to buy her food, take her to the vet, and pay for her expenses. All this because Dolly's official stance was that she just baby-sat for Bearess while I was gone, and I was gone most of the time, so Bearess was still officially my dog, she just didn't live with me anymore, and I was lucky Dolly didn't charge me for dog-sitting. Bearess woofed good-bye at me and bounced off with Dolly.

When they were gone, Jimmie looked at me and grinned. "I's wondering if I might borrow your second bath and take me a shower?"

"Why can't you shower at your place?"

"Ah, I got me some plumbing problems. Serious plumbing problems. Gonna take me a while to get it all fixed up."

Okay, that explained his less than daisy freshness earlier. "So, you're the home handyman, aren't you?"

"Yeah, and I'm fixing to fix it, but right now I needs a shower. Can I use yours or not?"

"Of course. Come on in. You can shower," I said, though I wanted Jimmie in my guest bathroom about as much as I wanted him to bring me another used poetry book full of gosh-knows-what germs and viruses. But it didn't seem nice to send him out smelly in the world on a weekend. In other words, I didn't see any other option—other than coldheartedness—and no way could I be coldhearted to Jimmie. But after his shower, I was going to run him off as fast as I could.

Which I did, but not before he promised to return first thing in the morning and cut my grass.

But the next morning, when Jimmie banged on my front door and wanted to know if I had any bacon, coldheartedness didn't look so bad. Especially since my own beloved, Philip Cohen, the criminal-defense-attorney genius who had once rendered me nearly mute by touching the inside of my arm while talking in his Dean Martin voice, was sitting across the table from me when Jimmie barged into the kitchen. Philip, who had arrived before Jimmie had, came bearing gifts of organic, stone-ground, whole wheat muffins, organic fresh-squeezed orange juice, and a dozen red roses, lust on his agenda. He had been just about to remind me of why I was considering marrying him when Jimmie rang the doorbell.

Having barged into my kitchen, Jimmie glared at Philip, then grinned and stuck out his hand. "I knows you. You got me out a the jail that time I's in for driving drunk. The second time. Jimmie, Jimmie Rodgers. Good to see you."

Like this was his house, like Philip was his guest.

"Lady, I'll cook it myself, if you got any bacon," Jimmie said, turning his attentions back to me. "Them plumbing problems done spread to my kitchen, and I can't cook nothing right now."

"I'm a vegetarian," I said, eyeing Philip, who, being Mr. Manners, had naturally stood up and taken Jimmie's hand, and was waiting for Jimmie and me to shut up so he could speak.

"Philip Cohen," he said, and gestured toward a chair. "Join us?"

"Thank you, thank you. I jes' might at that," Jimmie said, edging toward a chair, then veering off toward my French press. "That coffee?"

"Help yourself," I said, but Jimmie was already getting a cup from my cupboard.

Jimmie poured, sipped, made a loud, "Ahh," and then turned back to me. "You loan me the money and I'll go and get us some bacon. It'd be real nice with those muffins."

"I'm a vegetarian. Vegetarians don't eat bacon. Bacon is a dead pig with carcinogenic chemicals added for flavorings and I don't eat dead pigs."

"And I'm Jewish and we don't consume pork either," Philip added.

"Well, okay, but if you ask me, bacon don't offend God. Why you think they's about forty different kind a it for sale over to the Publix?" Jimmie sat down and took a muffin, slathered enough butter on it for an entire pound cake, and ate it—without a plate and dribbling crumbs everywhere.

To my relief, Philip let the theological debate pass and sat back down, cast me a quizzical but not totally unfriendly look, and picked up another muffin.

"At least get a plate," I said to Jimmie as he splattered another round of crumbs on the table.

"Two different drunk drivings, and I ain't spent but six days in jail on any of 'em. But I durn learnt my lesson. Ain't been driving while drinking in ages. Don't want to hurt nobody," Jimmie said as he helped himself to a plate from my cupboard, and returned to his muffin. "Maybe some ham? I gotta have meat with my breakfast."

"I'll give you the money to go to a drive-through, and you can get some breakfast." Normally I wouldn't contribute to the delinquency of dead-pig eating, but I wanted Jimmie to be gone so Philip could continue with his post-breakfast seduction.

"Aw, I reckon this is awright. Good company, anyways. Did I tell you, Lady, that this here man got me out of jail on my second driving while drunk?"

Yeah, coldheartedness was looking better and better.

"I finished a trial late yesterday evening," Philip said. "Too late and too tired to entertain Lilly last night, but I was hoping to spend some quality time with her this morning. Before we both have to go into the office." Philip looked at me with his bedroom eyes, and then he and I both looked at Jimmie with our "get out of here" eyes.

"Y'all got to go to the office today? It's Saturday." Jimmie buttered still another muffin. For a skinny man, he sure could eat.

I sighed. If I'd only had enough sense not to have let Jimmie inside the door this morning, Philip would be just about to make me forget the good-looking Cuban who had caught my fancy yesterday. Instead, I found myself daydreaming about Miguel while Jimmie prattled on.

After the coffee, the juice, and all but two of the muffins were gone, Jimmie said to me, "I'd offer to clean up the kitchen, but I knows how you get about that. So, I'll get started on cutting the grass."

I bowed to the inevitable, but not before scrubbing down the kitchen—nobody, not even the meticulous Philip, cleans a kitchen good enough for me. But letting Jimmie cut the grass for me was okay. I'd tried that once and couldn't get the lawn mower to start and figured that was a cosmic message that I needed to always make enough money to hire a lawn man. And since Benicio, Bonita's sixteen-year-old son and my official yardman and unofficial godson, had gotten a driver's license and discovered girls, he didn't have much interest in cutting my grass. So, Jimmie was it, I figured, for my new yardman.

Once Jimmie was straight on money for gas, and had a key to my house, I made him promise not to cut his foot off, or not to sue me if he did. Then, as the early morning and the romantic moment had passed, Philip walked me to my car.

With what I took for a bemused smile, Philip asked, "Why is your yardman so personal with you?"

"Sorry about that," I said. "I mean Jimmie and the interruption. I've known him for ages. He can talk the ears off a mule, but he's a nice man, and my client, and he reminds me of my granddad. His bathroom is busted and he showered here last night, and, I guess he figured breakfast came with the hot water."

Philip leaned over and gave me a casual kiss on the cheek. "You are so sweet."

I jerked back my head from his lips. "I am not." You can't be sweet and be a tough-minded, tough-hearted Big-time Trial Lawyer at the same time.

"Lillian, it's not an insult."

I hated it when he called me Lillian. I hated that look on his face—the one that bordered on patronizing.

"We'll make up for it later," Philip said, in that sensual, silky voice that used to literally make me weak in the knees. He ran a finger down my arm. But instead of the tingle that trailing touch used to give me, I suddenly wondered how Miguel would have acted if Jimmie had interrupted his planned breakfast-and-bed routine. I bet I would have been happily bedded despite Jimmie. By the time I came out of that fantasy, I realized that Philip had moved on to new topics.

"Why don't you spend tonight with me? I'll come over around six, we can go out for dinner, and then retire to my house."

I made a noncommittal noise.

"We should definitely start planning the wedding tonight. I think we should consider a neutral spot to avoid any religious issues," Philip said. "Perhaps Selby Gardens."

The word *wedding* made the muffins in my stomach pitch and swirl like I was on the downhill swing of a really high roller coaster. If that wasn't bad enough, something like PMS times ten came over me. "You think maybe we should wait to plan the wedding until I've actually said yes?"

"Lilly, we've talked about this." Philip stopped using his sexy voice. He was using his Philip-in-charge voice. Which, I might add, did nothing to alleviate that PMS-times-ten feeling that was now reverberating behind my eyes in a sickening pulse.

All the man had to do was say *wedding* and a baby migraine started.

Not a good sign.

When I didn't speak, Philip said, "It's time to stop being coy."

"I'm not being coy, I'm being indecisive."

"Lillian, you've just got bridal jitters. You'll get over it." With that, Philip opened my car door for me.

But instead of getting in the car and driving away, I said, "Bud, don't patronize me."

"Then, please, make up your mind and tell me tonight. And do not call me 'bud.' I'm not one of your good old boys. Shall I call for you at six?" This in a tone of pure patronizing. I mean, did this man even know me?

"Don't you dare come over here at six. I'm not going to be here, and if I am, I'm not going out with you." With that I got into my car, slammed the door, and started the engine. Through my tinted window, I could see him standing there, looking a tad dazed and definitely befuddled, as I gunned my ancient Honda and sped away.

If I'd known then that I would nearly get blown up later that night, I would have made nice and gone to dinner with Philip instead.

Chapter Five

Not sure whether I had just broken off my alleged engagement or not, I jolted down Shade Avenue over the five hundred speed bumps the city had installed to keep commuters like me from using the road— I mean, okay, why put a road there in the first place if people aren't supposed to actually use it? After that less than soothing commute to my office, I pulled into my named parking spot, right next to Jackson Smith's car, right as Jackson, the firm's founding partner and the living, breathing reincarnation of Stonewall Jackson, was getting out.

Jackson slammed his car door, then opened mine for me, stepping back like a perfect gentleman, but drawing the line at offering me his hand. I eased out of my car and flashed him a grin—if I'd been in a dress, I'd have flashed him some leg too, but pants have that drawback.

"Heard you're a suspect in the M. David Moody murder," Jackson thundered. He didn't sound so loud outside.

"I'm not a suspect," I said. "Hello. How are you?"

"Didn't think you'd wait that long to kill him."

"I'm not a suspect and I didn't kill him." I noticed Jackson was wearing his golfing clothes, and made a mental note to add to my grooming school curriculum a list of things men over fifty and under a hundred should not wear, i.e., bright green golf pants. "Golfing with the judges this afternoon?" I asked.

"Why did the homicide detective want to question you if you're not a suspect?"

"Just general stuff. Nice day for a golf game. Why don't you take me with you sometime?"

"Uh-huh. So, the detective just randomly chose you from a phone book to interview about why M. David ended up facedown in a gyp stack?" As he said this, Jackson took giant Jackson steps toward the back door, punched in the code on the lock with his big, long finger, and opened the door, standing back so I could ease in by him.

"He had my firm bio and had told his secretary to make an appointment with me, so naturally, the detective wanted to find out what that was about." So saying, I walked past Jackson to the inside of our law firm, where the overly air-conditioned frigid atmosphere engulfed me.

"What was that about?"

"Beats me." I shivered from the cold and cursed our office-manager jackal for locking up the air-conditioning controls so that only she could adjust them.

"You sure?" Jackson's voice reverberated down the hallway and bounced back to me.

"I'm sure I don't have any idea why he wanted to see me." And I was equally sure the real Stonewall Jackson would never have worn green pants, I thought, but was wise enough not to say so.

"You get questioned any more, doll, you let me know, you hear?"

"Yes, sir."

"I wouldn't hold it against you if you had killed that son of a bitch. Crossed my mind a time or two to kill him myself." With that, Jackson stormed away and left me to my own counsel.

So people were thinking I was a suspect in M. David's murder, eh? I wondered if a reputation for having killed someone would balance out the parrot-and-bikini and orange-defamation cases in terms of restoring my image as a tough litigator among the community's lawyers.

Once inside my own office, I reread the Florida Food Disparagement Act, hoping, I guess, that I'd failed to find the tiny print yesterday that said, "April Fools', just kidding." So, okay, where were the free-speech lobbyists when that bill was passed?

I sighed, made more coffee, and then studied the two separate orange-defamation complaints against Angus and Miguel. Both lawsuits pled the same allegations against the two men, both were brought by the same plaintiff—Delilah Groves, Inc.—and both were signed by the same lawyer. Both complaints claimed that Miguel and Angus had economically damaged the groves by claiming the oranges grown by Delilah were fertilized with a radioactive waste by-product of phosphate processing—phosphogypsum, or gyp, in phosphate-speak—and that as a result, the oranges were toxic. The lawsuit sought a monetary judgment because of past, lost profits, as well as an injunction that would forbid Angus and Miguel from speaking out in the future about the groves' agricultural practices.

I got out my phone book and looked up Delilah Groves. On a whim, I called the number in the book and asked to speak to the owner. A moment later, a gruff voice came over the line and said, "Yeah."

Oh, management from the suave school of MBAs, I thought, and said, "Yes, I'm interested in buying some oranges to ship and—"

"Season's over, lady."

"Oh. Could you tell me your name, please?"

"Why?"

"So I can be sure to ask for you next winter when I order some oranges. I'm talking a big buy. I'd like to talk discounts for volume. We can start talking now if you'd like."

"Big volume?"

"Yes, very big. I represent a new food cooperative that's franchising in New England and—"

"I'd need payment in advance. A down payment now to guarantee the availability."

Yeah, right, I thought. "Please, sir, tell me your name?"

"Rayford Clothier. And who are you?"

"Sunny McDemis. Now, sir, do you own Delilah Groves?"

"Yeah. You want to come by the groves today, leave me a deposit, and we can do the paperwork on next winter's crop. Take the State Road 72 exit off I-75 and turn north on Sugar Bowl Road, can't miss it."

"Oh lovely. Now my buyers are fussy. They don't require organic, but I'll need a list of the chemicals you use on the oranges before I contract."

"And I'll need a down payment on the order. After all, we ship most of our oranges up north, and we have standing contracts already. If you want to reserve a portion of the crop, you need to act quickly."

"Fine, you get that list of chemicals and I'll bring my checkbook."

With that exchange of lies and fraud-in-the-making, we hung up the phone. I debated the wisdom of sweet-talking Olivia into running out to Sugar Bowl Road and leaving a bad check in exchange for a list of chemicals, but a list obtained that way wouldn't be admissible into evidence at the trial, and, anyway, already I could tell Rayford Clothier was the sort who'd lie. So for half a second, I wondered how long he'd wait for me and my checkbook, then I went back to work.

Being the List Queen of the law firm, I listed the things I wanted to know: all about Delilah Groves, Rayford the suave owner, phosphogypsum as fertilizer, and other such things, and then I listed the legal issues, which all pretty much turned out to be First Amendment questions. Because I hadn't been a star student in constitutional law in law school, I was going to need help—especially since this was either a reduced-fee or a pro bono case. One of the unwritten rules of the successful maintenance of a partnership in a law firm is this: delegate any project that doesn't earn big bucks. That meant law clerks. And law clerks, those entry-level peons who toiled in the library hoping to be noticed and promoted, meant a chance for error.

To cut that distinct possibility for mistakes, I decided I'd put two of them on the case, and pit them against each other.

With that plan in mind, I marched into the library, where, despite the bright, sunny Saturday, all the law clerks at Smith, O'Leary, and Stanley, were shoulder deep in fine print.

Everybody looked up when I came into the library.

"Anybody in here make an A in constitutional law?"

Everybody looked down.

Okay, next round. "Anybody make a B in constitutional law?"

Two heads popped up, the rest looked farther down. One of the heads belonged to a young woman, who quickly asked, "Do you mean both semesters? Or would one B do?"

The popped-up head that belonged to a young man retorted, "I got a B one semester also."

Oh, good, competition already.

"Fine. If you two would come with me to my office."

They both hopped up, and I stood back and gestured that they should go in front of me. As they walked past me, I studied them for telltale hints of character traits that might suggest some competency.

The woman, who was elegant to the point of irritation, looked like a young Whitney Houston. The man, with his sharp, pointed face and manic gestures, reminded me of a Jack Russell terrier.

Once seated in my office, they introduced themselves and then both listened as I explained my basic queries—whether I could successfully defend Miguel and Angus against orange-defamation charges by claiming they had a First Amendment right to speak on what was surely considered a public issue? Would the *New York Times v. Sullivan* standard of willful malice apply? Was the veggie-defamation statute unconstitutional on the face of it, et cetera, et cetera.

Okay, the real query was, could I win quickly (read: cheaply) with a motion to dismiss on First Amendment grounds, but I had to throw out a lot of big words in the process of asking that question to indicate that I might know what I was talking about. I shoved a copy of the complaint at Jack Russell and a copy of my list of legal issues at Whitney Houston and told them to make copies, return the originals, and get cracking.

"You want us both working on the same issues?" Jack asked, a hint of a yippy quality to his voice.

"Yes, this is very important, very important, big clients, and we need to know absolutely everything we can—state law and federal law. Very big project. The kind of project that can make or break you, show whether you are associate material or not." Tantalize a law clerk with the promise of a promotion to associate and he or she will do just about anything.

They looked a little unsure, but I shooed them out of my office anyway. I was counting on their natural competitive streaks to guarantee an adequate job.

Alone in my office, I looked at my remaining active cases. Piddling. All of them. And while it's true an attorney can make a nice living on piddling cases if the cases are milked hard enough, what I wanted was a big-ass, page-one, above-the-fold medical malpractice case to defend. I punched in Henry Platt's number, though I knew he wouldn't be in the office today because he was busy courting Bonita and her five children. Henry is the claims adjuster at a Big Medical Malpractice Liability Insurance Company and his main job is to assign cases to me so that I can defend doctors, bill heavily, and make good press in the local newspaper.

Well, okay, he'd probably describe his job differently.

When his answering machine came on, I said, "Henry, Lilly here. I need a med-mal case. A big case. The biggest case you've got. Now."

Having accomplished little thus far, and nothing I could bill for, I attacked my piddling files with all the determination of a small terrier and churned my paperwork till lunch.

By noon my coffeepot was empty, Jack Russell had popped his head in my office five times to ask irritating First Amendment questions of the sort I thought he understood he was supposed to be answering, and I'd billed enough time to take a break. I stretched and stood and went out the back door, where I got into my little Honda and drove home.

My couscous was steaming in the pot while I cut up some beet greens and toasted some walnuts to make a hot salad, and, damn, Jimmie popped in. Opened the door, and shouted out, "Hey, Lady, you home?" and came right into the kitchen before I could say boo. He held up a greasy sack. "Want some?"

"No, thank you. I'm a vegetarian."

"Well, suit yourself." With that, Jimmie sat down at my kitchen table, opened his sack, and started eating. "Bacon cheeseburger," he said. "Sure you don't want some? I'll cut you off half."

Apparently there wasn't much point in explaining the vegetarian thing to Jimmie, and, after all, he must be close to eighty and he looked pretty healthy, and then, like my grandmother was overly fond of explaining, you just can't teach a pig to sing or a cow to waltz. So instead of proselytizing about the moral and health benefits of being a vegetarian, I simply asked, "Get much grass cut?"

"Oh, yeah, the back half."

I tossed my greens, nuts, and grains together, dribbled toasted sesame seed oil over my dish of healthy goodies, put it on the table next to Jimmie, and then pointedly walked into the den and looked out at the backyard. "Doesn't look cut to me."

"Well, I only got to the half of it. Behind the oak tree. You can't see it good from in here."

Oh, in other words, he hadn't done anything.

"Listen to this, I done got more of this here poem memorized." With that, he put down his hamburger, stood up, spread his arms, and recited: "'We were, er, er, a ménage à trois of lightning bugs in a jar with no air holes. Busted, William crashed. I danced through the shards with no visible wound.'"

While he recited, I peeked into my trash can under the sink and, sure enough, saw an empty bottle of wine. Mine. The expensive organic stuff. I pulled the bottle out, and said, "Recycle glass, okay?"

So, I didn't need to wonder what he'd been up to all morning instead of cutting the grass.

"It's some more of that poem I told you 'bout yesterday. I done been studying them poems in that book between cutting your grass."

"But you gave me that book," I said, even though I'd promptly tossed it in the trash.

"Oh, Bonita done give it back to me. Says you was too busy hep'ing them wild boys to read poetry right now. I'll get it back to you, but after I got it all in my memory."

"No hurry." I washed my hands and sat down to eat.

As we ate, Jimmie prattled about stuff around my house that needed his special handyman touch, soffits and eaves and trims and door hinges and such, and I calculated that at his current speed, he'd managed to find about two years' worth of work. Before I could dodge his pitch, the doorbell rang.

"Might could be that Dolly woman agin. She done been over bitchin' 'bout my car, twiced now. Says I can't leave it out in the open like that."

"We do have neighborhood covenants," I said, hoping to imply that Dolly was correct. But when Jimmie didn't respond, I went to answer the door.

Miguel and Angus stood there, Miguel with a come-home-with-me grin and Angus with a scowl. I matched Miguel's grin and hoped I didn't have beet greens stuck in my teeth.

"How'd you find out where I lived?" I asked.

"Olivia," Miguel said.

If it had been just Angus, I'd have sent him on his way and fussed later at Olivia. But Miguel made it a different matter, and I stepped back and invited them in, curious as to what they might want.

"We're going for a hike on the Antheus property, thought you might want to come with us. So you can see what it is we do," Miguel said.

"It's a pretty warm afternoon for hiking," Angus said. "I'd understand, you didn't want to go."

Jimmie came out of the kitchen with a handful of French fries. "What you boys doing here?" he asked, sounding a little fatherly for my tastes.

"Where's Antheus?" I asked.

"It's out in the Four Corners area of east Manatee County, where Manatee, Hillsborough, Desoto, and Hardee Counties all touch. Acres of prime woodlands, wetlands, and Florida hammocks," Miguel said.

"What is it, a new park?" I asked, innocently enough, not knowing what a can of worms that was going to be.

"Don't you read the newspaper?" Angus asked.

"It's the proposed site for a new phosphate mine, first phase of mining is planned for Hardee County. Eventually, if the company gets its way, it will mine in Manatee."

"Oh, that. Yes, Olivia has"—ranted, cursed, and yelled were the appropriate words, but I was in sociable mode and wordsmithed this a bit—"mentioned that to me. By Horse Creek. And, yes, Angus, I do read the newspaper."

Headlines count as reading, right? "So, y'all are going hiking on the Antheus property?" I flipped my hair, widened my eyes, and smiled at Miguel so he would pay attention to me, not my lack of radical environmental politics. "Hiking? By invitation?"

Angus and Miguel both laughed.

Oh, okay, a trespassing hike was at hand. Oddly enough that made it more enticing. Not as enticing as Miguel made it, of course, but there's nothing like a little breaking of the law in the courtship ritual to get my blood going. Someday I might pay a psychiatrist to explain that, but for now I was just going to go with it.

I aimed a slow, sensual smile at Miguel, bypassing entirely both Angus and Jimmie. Then I thought about all the bugs, plus my piddling but still necessary work back at the office, and I started an internal debate.

"If you're gonna go, I reckon I'll go too," Jimmie said. "You needs somebody to look out fer you."

"Oh, we'll look out for her," Miguel said, matching my smile and making my sap rise.

"Besides, Jimmie, you promised to cut the grass. Remember?" I added.

"Maybe you best not run off with these two," Jimmie said. "I don't reckon you should go."

Okay, that settled it. When a man tells me to do something, I usually don't—obedience to the male voice not being one of my character traits—oh, except for Jackson. Everyone obeys him. I bet he could tell God what to do.

"So, this will be fun," I said, and winked at Miguel. "Five minutes to get ready, and I'll be right with you."

While Jimmie sputtered, I dashed into the bathroom to brush my teeth and wash up, dabbed tinted sunscreen on my face, fluffed my hair, dotted citronella, a natural bug-repellent alternative to DEET that usually works, at my pulse points, reddened my lips with something from the health food store that used berry juice and beeswax instead of chemicals, and then dashed into the bedroom. Hiking, let's see, I thought, aiming for practical, yet alluring. Skip the shorts and sandals, as hiking in wild Florida involves a lot of things that bite, cut, snarl, snag, and itch. Even though it was a warm spring, I went for jeans, a man's long-sleeved, white cotton shirt, hiking boots, swept my hair back in a ponytail, and squinted into the mirror. Okay, a good look for a sixteen-year-old, but I wasn't sure about me. But my five minutes were over and I still had to clean up from lunch, and I sprinted out to the kitchen.

Jimmie and Miguel were busily putting up food and wiping counters and Angus was stuffing dishes into the dishwasher. Okay, I'd have to redo all that, using some serious cleaning stuff. As I shooed them all out of the kitchen, Jimmie said, "Didn't I tell you boys she'd go and do it over? Didn't I?"

"Can't you just leave it till later?" Angus said, who was not staying shooed and was peering back into the kitchen.

"Son, you don't know this gal, do you?" Jimmie said.

"Shoo," I said, and waved my hands at Angus until he left again. Like a whirling-dervish imitator of the all-natural version of Mr. Clean, I sprayed, wiped, cleaned, mopped, cleared, and disinfected, as fast as I could using borax and something natural from the Granary that contained orange-peel oil and claimed it killed germs as good as the high-tech chemical stuff. Still, breaking my Clorox habit was hard. I left the kitchen, smiled at Miguel, and then, as if invisible hooks were pulling me, I scampered back into the kitchen for a quick spray-and-wipe with Clorox while I held my breath. When I was done, definitely so were any germs, but now my kitchen smelled like Clorox and not oranges, so I had to do the orange-peel spray again.

"Damnation, you're not cleaning up after slaughtered hogs in here," Angus said, again hovering in the doorway.

"I sure was hoping you'd gotten over this," Jimmie said from beside Angus. "Reckon you ought to see that doctor again?"

"All ready," I said, ignoring them both, and detouring toward the laundry room and tossing the cleaning cloths in the hamper on the way toward Miguel.

Now I was primed for a hike in the hammocks with Miguel.

Oh, and, drat, with Angus too. He reminded me he was going to be there by saying, "Aren't you gonna be hot in that?" Oh, and this from a man in cowboy boots.

"Better hot than sunburned and bug bit," I said. "Besides, I am pretty heat tolerant." Yeah, all those folks who migrate down from Michigan complain about how hot the Gulf Coast is, but they don't know what hot is. Hot is the dog days of late summer in Bugfest, Georgia, my hometown, where 105 degrees with 90 percent humidity, coupled with a generous facial coating of gnats, was the norm.

"Yeah, me too," Angus said, "heat tolerant, I mean." He smiled at me, and I had the odd feeling I was winning him over, though I wasn't trying to do so. I glanced at Miguel to gauge my approval rating in his eyes, but he was looking out my front window.

As we darted out the door, Jimmie gave me a stern, disapproving look, and I mentally dared him to say anything.

"You don't mind riding in the middle, do you? Might be a bit tight," Miguel asked as I took in his small, red pickup. No, tight was good, I thought, and hoped he liked the scent of citronella.

We crowded into the truck and roared away. When we were well into Manatee County, Miguel pulled off the interstate at Moccasin Wallow Road, dropped down to Duette Road, and then turned onto an unnamed road with pavement apparently left over from the FDR era. We crossed a bridge, over a tea brown river framed by water and live oaks, and Miguel said, "That's the east fork of the Manatee River."

After bumping along, Miguel finally stopped the truck by a gate across a little driveway, but kept the engine running. Behind the gate and fence, a dense hammock of slash and loblolly pines, saw palmettos, cabbage palms, and live oaks stretched before us, dappled with shades of green and yellow in the afternoon sunlight.

"This is one of the last remaining big wildernesses in the area, outside of the park system," Miguel said. "The mining company owns about ten thousand acres all together, three thousand of it in Manatee County, in this tract. Wetlands from forks off the Manatee River and Horse Creek run through it. Isn't it beautiful?"

It was. We all made little noises of appreciation.

"You know what it'll look like if they get to mine it?" Angus asked.

Yes, thank you, I'd manage to get outside of the Sarasota city limits in my lifetime, and I'd driven through the nearby moonscaped phosphate-mined areas in other counties. Reclamation claims aside, this pretty little subtropical forest would never be the same once the phosphate miners were done digging the ore from beneath the surface. I sighed, sadly, and said, "It'll be ruined."

"Well, it ain't over yet," Angus said. "They don't have their permits. You wait and see." And he grinned, lifting the moroseness that crept into the truck cab as we thought about the potential destruction of the land in front of us.

"Let's hide the truck and take a walk," Miguel said, and drove the pickup off the road until a clump of trees more or less hid it, that is, if you weren't looking right at it. He grabbed a sack from the back of the truck, and I thought, Oh, good, a picnic.

As we walked along the fence, I counted nine "No Trespassing/ Violators Will Be Prosecuted" signs before Miguel held the barbed wire apart for me and I scampered through the opening in the fence, with Angus on my tail.

Though a perfectly good trail presented itself to us, Miguel led us away from it, and some thrashing was involved as we stumbled through the thick undergrowth. A wild blackberry bush, with its clinging thorns, attacked me, and I was glad I'd worn the long jeans, though I wished I'd been a little more liberal with the citronella. We went through a sandy patch of scrub before we passed into a low-lying area, with ancient-looking cypress trees guarding a wetland scattered with the white petals of wild lilies and sedge.

Angus brought us to an abrupt stop to point out a jack-in-the-pulpit, a green and maroon flower, saying, "You can eat the corm, a bit pungent raw, but good boiled."

None of us seemed inclined to pluck it for a snack, so Miguel took the lead, and had us traipsing back toward a drier wooded area. As small, flying things lit and bit, I watched Miguel's butt to keep my mind off Lyme disease and West Nile.

In short order, but not before I'd begun to sweat in a totally non-sexy way, we came to a creek with a slow current of brown water. "The famous Horse Creek, I presume," I said.

"Yep, but it's the west fork of it. Most of the existing mining on Horse Creek is on the main branch in Hardee County. Now they want to start mining on this part of it."

Miguel opened the sack and pulled out a stick thing with something round and oddly shaped at the end of it, and then still another stick thing with the same thing on the end, and then a Baggie of what looked and smelled like big-cat poop.

It suddenly occurred to me that Jimmie's fatherly advice might have been well offered. I mean, come on, I was miles from other people, I had no weapons, I was with two men I hadn't known before yesterday, and they had poop in a bag and weird stick things.

It did not seem to bode well for me. I started backing up, aiming for at least a head start.

"Cat paws," Miguel said, and dangled the stick thing near me. "Take it," he offered.

I snatched it, thinking, Weapon.

Oh, yeah, like I was Wonder Woman and could fend off two men in their prime with a stick that had a cat paw on the end of it. For good measure, I kept backing up.

"Where're you going?" Angus asked.

To hell, eventually, if you believe the preacher in my brother Delvon's Pentecostal church. But my plan was to postpone the trip for a few more decades, and I was certainly in no mood today to be cast in that direction by loco boys with evil plans. I was contemplating running backward when I saw Miguel pull two more stick things out of the sack.

"All four paws. Anatomically correct. Made from plaster casts of real tracks." Miguel grinned like a little kid with new Christmas toys.

The grin reassured me for a moment. But then he held up the Baggie. "Panther poop. Fresh. Totally authentic."

I jumped when Angus touched my arm. "Look at the end of that. Look at that paw. Ain't that a beauty?" he said.

"What the hell are you two up to?" I said, hoping I didn't sound as spooked as I felt.

"Panther tracks by the creek. Panther scat in just the right places. A phone call to the U.S. Fish and Wildlife folks, and you know what you've got?" Angus asked.

Yeah, crazy people with poop fetishes thrashing in the woods, I thought, but then, I actually thought about it. And stopped backing up.

"Evidence of a protected species," I said. And, a popular endangered species at that. The rare and elusive Florida panther, the darling of the armchair environmentalists, the poster child of the nearly extinct. A Florida panther needed a wide territorial range to hunt, breed, and survive, and to protect the drastically dwindling number of panthers, that range was protected under state and federal law. That much even I knew. What my loco boys were doing was setting up a rallying point for those who were trying to save the panther by saving its habitat.

"You've got a way to stop the mine," I said. Between the state and fed regs that would protect the habitat and the influx of the save-the-panther crowd, those mining permits were, if not doomed, then at least on hold for a long time. And Olivia had managed, despite my inattention, to teach me this much: In the fight to save habitat, a long delay of the inevitable destruction was usually your only victory.

"Yep," Angus said and grinned at me like he was the proud father and I was the mentally handicapped two-year-old who finally said my first word. "Once we show there's an endangered Florida panther on this property, feds and other folks will come out of the woodwork to stop those permits."

I looked at the end of the stick I held. It did indeed look like a model of a big cat's paw. Cool, I thought, wait until I tell my brother Delvon, who had once lived in the woods and had run an unadvertised U-pick marijuana and opium farm until the Georgia Bureau of Investigations put him out of business. Delvon loved wild things, being one himself, and he loved the big cats. Also, he especially loved screwing with Official Big Boys.

"You remember, another panther was sighted here, a few months ago. When the fish and wildlife people confirmed it, those mining permits the Antheus people were pushing for came to a halt," Miguel said. "For a while, anyway."

I heard the sadness in his voice, and tried to remember. There'd been something I'd read in the newspaper about a panther and a mine site, but I only vaguely recalled it. Seems like I'd been in trial that week. When I'm in trial, nothing except that case sticks in my brain. But I didn't think the story had a happy ending.

"Sons of bitches killed it," Angus said, his voice low and angry.

"They killed it?" I said, in disbelief. Who kills a Florida panther? They are almost all gone anyway. "Who would kill it?"

"Think about it," Miguel said. "Who had the most to gain?"

"Antheus? Somebody from the mining company killed it?"

"Left the body by that gate, where we stopped. Right outside the gate, on the public easement. A female panther. Gut shot, and left to die. Fish and Wildlife investigated, but never could prove who killed it."

Suddenly I hated people.

"Fish and Wildlife folks still coming out here, looking around, thinking they might find a mate," Angus said. "But nobody's found any evidence of a second panther. Yet."

"So, that's why we're here. We're going to introduce the world to this new panther." Miguel held up the Baggie of cat poop. "Little panther scat, plus a set of tracks down to the creek, should leave a convincing trail."

"Let's do it," I said, and grinned like I meant it.

While Angus showed off how much he knew about Florida panthers by telling us how far to space the tracks, and all such stuff as that, Miguel and I walked side by side, me with the left paws, and him with the right, and we made a clear track of the panther along the edge of Horse Creek, then down into the water, as if the big cat was drinking, then back to the high grasses, where Miguel left the scat, I scratched sand over most of it, and then Angus neatly followed our trail, brushing out all our footprints with a palmetto frond.

We hooped and hollered a bit, danced in the thick undergrowth where we wouldn't leave prints, and Miguel pulled a camera out of the sack, snapped a couple shots of the scat and a long view of the panther's tracks, and then we boogied out of there, happy as kids who'd put a scarlet king snake in the teacher's desk.

Back in the truck, I took both Miguel's and Angus's hand for a second, and said, "Thank you for including me."

They nodded and we crawled into the cab of the pickup and started back toward pavement.

Okay, I was glad to have been along on this Screw the Big Boys trip, and I couldn't wait to tell Delvon what we'd done, but I got to puzzling. "Why'd you take me?" I asked.

"We wanted to test your dedication to the Cause," Miguel said.

What cause? I thought, but then Miguel took a curve a bit too fast and I slid into him, thigh to thigh, and my brain just stopped working.

Yeah, okay, I was kind of engaged to Philip, even if I wasn't talking to him right now, and I needed to get a grip on this lusting-after-Miguel thing. Pushing my leg away from physically touching Miguel, I promised myself not to act upon that lust until I resolved things with Philip, one way or the other.

Philip the steady, Philip the smart, Philip who brings wine and roses—I started listing his positive traits. For starters, he'd never have led me across a barbed-wire fence, through the no trespassing signs, on a cat-track-and-scat spree.

But that was as much a negative as a plus for Philip, I realized, and leaned down to scratch a bug bite.

Angus scratched at something on his leg at the same time and pushed against me, and when I pulled away, I bumped back up against Miguel. Yeah, okay, it wasn't my fault the front seat was so small, so I went with the flow and let my thigh sit there bouncing against Miguel's and setting off electrical charges as the little red truck lurched down the road.

Angus broke my reverie. "Hey, Mike, let's go by and check on Lenora. We're in the neighborhood."

"I was just thinking the same thing," Miguel said, then smiled at me. "It'll be another education for Lilly."

Not sure I wanted to learn anything else today from my fake-the-panther clients, I glanced at my watch. I wondered when my next chance at getting some bottled water was going to be. A Save the Forest trail mix bar wouldn't hurt either.

Apparently catching me looking at my watch, Miguel the considerate asked, "Lilly, is it all right with you if we take a side trip?"

"Does she have a refrigerator with bottled water?"

"Yep," Angus said.

Miguel turned on a dirt road, then bumped along until he cut left on a branch that I would have considered a primitive trail not meant for motorized vehicles. Bump, lurch, rub went my thigh against Miguel. Definitely foreplay potential.

"You ought to see these roads after a good rain, hardly passable at all. The Manatee River is just right over there, behind those water oaks," Angus said, pointing to a stand of oaks to the left of the truck, and once more breaking my sexual reverie.

Okay, the cosmic forces had assigned Angus the role of keeping me from getting in too over my head with Miguel. I should be grateful. No, Philip the almost forgotten should be grateful.

On that disrupted note, Miguel drove through a tunnel of loblolly pines and live oaks, and turned left toward the hidden river, into a wide opening. When he stopped the truck, I looked about. I couldn't see the river, but I could smell its wet-moss and primordial scent. In front of me, I saw a collection of Florida-cracker outbuildings, a barn with a rusted tin roof, and a dog-trot house, well past its prime. By, say, like a lifetime. A boxy Volvo was parked under a tree, and, given its dings and bangs, I figured it for an old one.

Lots of plastic animal cages, a pump, a metal watering trough, piles of stuff, and more piles of stuff. My can't-stand-piles-of-stuff inner alarm went off—big time. On the other hand, I felt like I had just been transported back to Marjorie Kinnan Rawlings's time and place. The dog-trot house with its central hallway and tin roof had a certain charm.

As Miguel and Angus jumped out of their respective sides of the truck, I followed, watching closely where my feet landed. When I looked up, a woman was standing in the doorway of the old house.

She was wearing a blue scarf around her head, turban style, and had the taut yellow skin of someone seriously ill. Then I realized there was no hair showing beneath the turban. Her lips were drawn and narrow, deep lines and purple shadows surrounded her eyes, and her thinness had passed fashionable about ten pounds back.

"Angus, Miguel, you boys are a sight for sore eyes. Come on in and help me feed the baby birds." Her voice was light, chipper.

"Lenora, we'd like to introduce you to our friend Lilly. She's our lawyer." Miguel offered a hand to Lenora and she took it, squeezed it, and smiled.

But Angus barreled past me, straight into Lenora, and he hugged her until I worried he would crack a rib.

"Lilly, delighted," she said, when Angus finally let her go. "If you are *their* lawyer, you must be smart and dedicated. Do you like birds?"

Nodding, I held my ground and didn't move toward her. I was still nervous about all the piles of stuff, and, okay, a little nervous about her. I don't always know how to act around sick people; crazy people, yes, but there I've had plenty of experience.

Nervous or not, the next thing I knew I was inside the dog-trot cabin, listening to a raucous chorus of feed-me-feed-me chirps and shoving dampened chunks of puppy chow mix down the throats of baby birds, while Lenora coached me. "Easy, easy. Just a little bit at a time. They've got tiny throats."

Well, okay, at least I didn't have to regurgitate worms.

Out of the corner of my eye, I saw that Miguel and Angus were working a row of cages, feeding the baby birds with a rhythm that suggested knowledge and comfort with the routine.

Once assured that I wasn't going to strangle a bird, Lenora turned to her own brood, feeding, sweet-talking, and making a kind of a humming noise about it all.

"What are they? I mean, what kind?" I asked.

"Mockingbirds, a lot of them, wrens, cardinals, red-wing black-birds, chickadees, jays." She ran the names of the birds past me in a quiet voice until even their names sounded like humming.

"Where do they all come from?"

"From everywhere. Domestic cats get their momma, or they fall out of the nest, the trees get cut down, you name it. Bad boys shoot the momma bird; I hate a BB gun. There's a hundred different ways the average person kills a bird, usually without even knowing it. You know how many thousands of birds die every day just smashing into cell-phone towers?"

No, and I didn't especially want to learn that fact. Thank you, but I had enough trouble getting to sleep as it was.

"So you run, like, a bird-and-wild-animal rescue?" I asked, dodging the dead-bird lecture and shooting for the obvious.

"And some farm animals. I got three goats, all of them lame. Some sicko had them cuffed around a foot, each of them, so tight that the skin rotted. Sheriff's detective rescued them after a call, but the infections were so bad they all went lame. I've been holding them for the court that's going to prosecute the owner for abuse. I reckon those goats are mine, though. When the case is over, who's going to want a small herd of limping goats?"

Assuming this was a rhetorical question, I didn't jump on it. Besides, if I came home with even one disabled goat, my neighbor Dolly the Hall Monitor of the Universe would have the zoning police on me in half a minute.

Ducking possible goat adoptions, I reached into the next cage, where something that looked like a cartoon version of a blue jay was hoping up and down and shrilling at me—as if this were my fault! When I tried to catch it, it pecked at my hand and jumped back.

"Don't be shy. That one's got an attitude," Lenora said.

I grabbed for the little miscreant and nabbed him. After I lifted him out of his cage so that I could do my Mother-Teresa-with-birds thing, it pecked me again so hard I nearly flung it down.

But Lenora and Angus burst out laughing.

"Here," Angus said. "Let me take him."

I passed off the jay to Angus, and turned back to Lenora. "Aren't jays the bad guys of the bird world?"

"A little bit, but that's mostly exaggerated. Besides, it's the bad boys we love the most, isn't it?" she said, and looked right into Angus's eyes and smiled. As if on cue, I looked soulfully into Miguel's eyes, and wondered why he was being so quiet.

When Miguel more or less ignored me, I eased off to the next cage and the next bird. Furtively, I eyed Lenora and Angus, trying to make up my mind whether they were lovers, friends, or what.

Finally we finished feeding the birds, and Lenora said, "I'd show you around, but I'm pretty tired. There's a lot of small animals in cages and fences outside. I've got some gopher tortoises with busted shells in a fence out back. You know, you can fix 'em when they get hit—if the body's okay, that is—by using duct tape on the cracked shells."

As I nodded, not sure how useful that tidbit would prove to be in my litigation practice, Angus took her arm. "Let's go sit down," he said. "We'll give Lilly the grand tour another day."

At Lenora's invitation, the four of us went into a primitive kitchen, where we took turns washing our hands. The tap water smelled of sulfur, but I splashed my face anyway. Miguel asked for water for me and Lenora pulled a bottle of Zephyr Hills, the local spring water, out of an ancient and rusting refrigerator. I all but snatched it from her.

"Sit," she said, but she kept standing, so we did too.

"We can't stay long," Angus said. "We've got that phosphate meeting in Bradenton. Sure you don't want to come? Help stop Antheus Mines?"

"I hate those bastards so much. Especially that M. David Moody, what he was trying to do to this place. But I have a few more animals to tend. I can't go."

At the mention of M. David's name, I stopped gurgling water and listened closer, hoping for some enlightenment on the subject of his recent death.

"What about Adam? Can't he help?" Angus asked.

Oh, okay, no enlightenment.

"He's got Samantha and they're off touring until next weekend. But I'll be all right. My creatures can be left long enough for me to go home and get some sleep. Nobody stays here all night anyway unless there's an animal in active crisis. But as long as there's daylight, I want to be here, so, forgive me, I need to pass on your meeting."

I wanted to jump in and ask a bunch of questions, but something in the look I saw pass between Angus and Lenora stopped me. Theirs was a private conversation.

"I'll skip the meeting and stay with you," Angus said.

"Don't be silly. That phosphate meeting is your thing, these birds and creatures are mine."

"All right. But I'll come back after the meeting."

"You don't need to come back. I'm fine. You can't treat me like an invalid. Besides, I've got Bob to keep me company."

"Bob?" Angus asked

"Sure. Hang on, let me go get him."

Lenora left for a minute and when she came back in, she had a baby squirrel cupped against her chest. Something was wrong with its head, but her hand held it in place and I couldn't get a good look.

"Bob," she said, by way of introduction. "Go on, y'all, sit down."

We all sat, and Lenora cooed at the baby squirrel and curled down into the kitchen chair nearest Angus's. "Got his skull cracked. They were clearing out some woods on Antheus's property last week, to put up some kind of office building or something, and one of the crew cut down a tree with a squirrel's nest in it. Mom and the rest of the babies got run over by a Bush-hog, but one of the men saved this one, hurt as he was. He brought it to me."

No one spoke.

"With a baby squirrel, they grow so fast. So incredibly fast. His brain will grow too big before the skull heals."

Angus leaned toward her from his chair, but none of us spoke.

"He won't make it," she said, her voice almost a whisper, but she rubbed the soft skin under Bob's chin and smiled at the little animal.

I realized I was holding my breath.

"But he eats, he's not in any pain. I call him Bob because of the way his head bobs around if I don't hold it."

"Is there any hope for him?" I asked, finally breaking the silence and forcing myself to inhale.

"He's okay for now. That's enough, isn't it?"

I looked down at my hands, still holding the bottle of water, and I was embarrassed by my question, though I wasn't sure why.

When I looked up, I saw that Angus was crying. Not deep, loud sobbing, but a definite sniffling, with tears streaming down his face.

"Oh, baby," Lenora said, and stood up. In a quick, but gentle move, she handed Bob to me, and I cuddled the small animal, trying to hold its head like I'd seen Lenora do, and the little guy crawled up my shirt until he could rub his head against the skin on my neck. I looked down at it, just a tiny, little animal trying to live, with big, dark eyes, a little nose and mouth, brownish-gray fur, and a wound on his scalp.

Bob the doomed squirrel chirped a little and then curled under my chin as if to sleep. I looked up and saw Lenora take Angus's hand and pull him up and into her. "It's all right," she whispered.

"Excuse us, please." Lenora led Angus out of the kitchen and I didn't trust myself to speak, so I rubbed Bob's shoulders, and looked down.

A few moments later, Angus came back into the kitchen, alone, red-eyed, and took Bob in his big hands. "Let me take him back to Lenora. Then we better get on to the meeting," he said, gruffly.

We left soon after that. There were about a hundred questions I wanted to ask. But I had enough sense not to ask any of them. Not just then, anyway.

Chapter Six

Nobody bothered to tell me they were not taking me home.

We rode in a strangled silence toward a main highway, and then Miguel turned the truck toward Bradenton, the county seat of Manatee, and not south, toward my house and Sarasota.

"Whoa, wrong direction. Aren't you going to take me home?" I said, waking up out of my sadness.

"Can't. Don't have time to get you there and us back here. Meeting starts at five-thirty."

I glanced at my watch. "Where's the meeting?"

"Got a room at MCC reserved," Angus said. "You ought to come to the meeting, anyway. If you're going to represent me and Miguel, you need to know about this."

"What's this?"

"Public meeting of all the Manatee County people who oppose the Antheus mine permits. We're trying to stop them. By turning public opinion against them," Miguel said.

Uh-huh, and you'll get another SLAPP suit filed against you for your efforts, and you're not going to be able to afford to pay me for defending the first one, the stupid orange-defamation case, I thought, but graciously didn't say.

Then I thought, well, okay, a radical meeting with Miguel and Angus was probably a better topper for a day of saving fake panthers and feeding baby birds than arguing with Philip over where to have our alleged wedding. "Shoot, let's go, then," I said.

"Good. Let me get you some literature," Angus said, and reached into the glove compartment and pulled out a ream of folded papers, forcibly stuffing other papers back into the compartment. "This is the list of the Antheus shareholders, you might recognize some of the names from Boogie Bog."

No, Boogie Bog and its real name, Bougainvillea Bayou, were about the only names on that topic I was apt to recognize, but I took the list.

"Here's a list of the names and addresses of people and government agencies you should write to and protest." He shoved another sheet of paper at me. "And here's a sample letter. All that information is correct. But put it in your own words. Handwritten letters are supposed to carry more weight," he said.

Yeah, a primer in public participation—a handwritten note? Like, without, say, a donation of thousands? How naive was this guy?

But I was soon distracted from my cynical appraisal of Angus's activities. "Well, I'll be damned," I said, looking at the short list of Antheus shareholders, all four of them. And M. David Moody's name, big as Bob's baby squirrel eyes, was first on the list. Someone had redlined through his name. "What did M. David have to do with Antheus?"

"M. David pretty much *was* Antheus. He owned sixty percent of the stock. A lot of that land was his initially, acreage he bought in the seventies and eighties when it was relatively cheap. So he put his land into the company, and kept the controlling interest," Miguel said, and pulled the truck into the Manatee Community College parking lot.

I folded up the various sheets of paper and stuffed them into my purse.

"M. David had valuable contacts with international phosphate companies. I always figured that Antheus, once they got their per-

mits, would either sell out completely to one of those phosphate gi-
ants at a huge profit, or he'd at least bring one of those companies in
as a partner," Miguel said.

As I tumbled out of the truck, I thought, so M. David had been
the mover and shaker on Antheus. Okay, this had just gotten a whole
lot more interesting.

Trudging after Miguel and Angus as they made their way inside a
conference room, I wished I'd had a chance to change clothes, wash up,
and maybe grab a trail mix bar, but people were already milling about.
Serious-looking people started shaking hands with Miguel and Angus.

"There are snacks and drinks over there, if you want any," Miguel
said.

Hungry, I walked over to the table, quickly deduced there was
nothing I could eat, but snagged another Zephyr Hills water. By the
time I had it opened, Miguel and Angus had already walked up to the
front of the room and Angus was calling the meeting to order.

Apparently, antiphosphate meetings were run by the same set of
rules by which my brother Delvon's church was run, that is, anybody can say anything at anytime, and the louder the better. In other
words, a good deal of free-form crowd rant ensued about the destruction and environmental disaster that a phosphate mine by the east
fork of the Manatee River would create. I got the point in thirty seconds—the mines would suck up millions of gallons of precious water
and leave behind slime ponds of toxic waste—and ducked out to find
a bathroom.

When I came back in, a serious-looking man behind the microphone was droning in way too much detail about how phosphate run-
off was killing our streams, bays, and Gulf, destroying marine life,
and otherwise becoming the chemical agent of Armageddon. Then
he cursed our luck for living on the outer edge of the so-called bone
valley region, named after the ancient bones of bygone creatures that

time and nature had turned into one of the world's richest deposits
of phosphate ore.

Truth is, I'm just not much for scientific discourse unless it per-
tains to one of my own cases. Besides, I already had the big picture—
phosphate mining, processing, and use were all bad; green trees and
clean streams were all good.

Edgy now, I bit back a yawn and scanned the crowd, looking for
entertainment or information. Naturally I started with the most beautiful person there, that being Miguel, but he was not playing eye contact with me anymore, so I branched out my visual reconnaissance.

Not halfway through my study of the various people crowded into
the meeting room, damned if I didn't see Mrs. M. David Moody, aka
Sherilyn the beauty queen, standing in the back corner. An older man
with a strong build was standing nearby, but his head was turned away
from me. I couldn't make out whether he was with Mrs. Moody or
not. After a quick glance at his bulked-up body and his thin, gray hair,
I dismissed him as a grandpa-weight-lifter-on-steroids, and turned
back to Mrs. Moody.

Something was wrong with her face. Even from across the room,
I could see that her complexion looked wounded, like a bad sunburn
that had peeled into different layers of skin and colors, but not healed.
What in the world had happened to her? Mrs. Moody was known for
her beauty and her splendid parties—parties I was never invited to
attend but which I read all about in Marjorie North's column in the
Sarasota Herald-Tribune. Okay, I wasn't necessarily a Sherilyn fan,
but, still, to see her looking so unattractive seemed so—so what? Sad
wasn't the right word, not after meeting Bob the doomed baby squirrel and Lenora the saint with a serious disease. Still, I felt myself feeling a little sorry for the woman.

But before I could think further on Mrs. Moody's ruined complexion, Detective Josey Something Farmer came into the room, right

through the door I was guarding, and she spotted me and stopped to shake hands.

"Interesting, meeting you here," she said.

"I'm here as a citizen with a vital, but routine, interest in learning more about phosphate mining. Why are you here?"

"Yeah. Me too."

"Anything new on M. David?"

"Yeah. It'll all be in tomorrow's newspaper. Sunday paper recap and follow-up story. Lots of pressure on the department on this one, high-profile victim and all, so the sheriff gave an in-depth interview."

"Tomorrow, huh? I'm not real good at waiting," I said, and flashed what I hoped was an endearing girl-bonding grin.

Josey grinned back. "Yeah, I hate to wait too."

"So tell me." She hesitated, and I said, "Hey, you said it would be in the paper. Not like you're selling government secrets."

"Yeah, right. Autopsy's not complete yet, but the obvious physical evidence indicates he had been held down in the phosphogypsum pond until he drowned. Bruises on the back of his neck."

"Phosphogypsum pond? I thought he drowned in a gyp stack."

"Same thing. They take all the processing waste and store it in gyp stacks, or ponds, behind earthen dams. The dams are around seventy feet high, and you can drive or walk around on top of them. If you are on the top of the dam, it looks like a big pond. So some folks call them gyp ponds because it looks like a pond from the top. Other folks call them gyp stacks because the stuff is stacked behind those dirt dams."

Okay, so there's a whole vocabulary to this phosphate stuff. But at the moment I was more interested in the mechanics of M. David's death. "So somebody forced M. David to the top of the dam, and drowned him in the . . . gyp stuff?"

"About that."

As much as I disliked M. David—and that was a lot and for good reason—I couldn't help but shudder at the image. Bad karma is ugly.

"Any leads?" I asked.

"The high sheriff's official position is that we have a number of leads, all of which we are vigorously pursuing."

Okay, that was the public relations speech. What was the truth, I wondered.

"Prints, tire tracks, motives, what do you have?" I asked.

"It's all in the paper. Sheriff's not so good with 'no comment' when the media sticks their collective thumb in his eyes," Josey said. "Somebody drove a Jeep to the top of the dam and left some tracks. Looks like it might be the DEP Jeep left on-site."

"DEP Jeep?"

"The Florida Department of Environmental Protection. Their engineers watch the gyp stacks regularly, so they leave a Jeep at the plant so they can drive up on the stacks and check on things. Saves wear and tear and muck on their own cars."

"Think somebody from the DEP did it?"

"No." Josey gave me a look like I'd just accused Mother Teresa of being a serial killer.

"But if the killer drove a DEP Jeep—"

"Anybody who could hot-wire that Jeep could drive it."

"But anybody with a DEP key could drive it too."

Josey gave me that look again. All right, all right, I thought. Nobody from the DEP is a suspect, but that left a whole lot of other people to fill out the list.

Eager to hear more, I leaned into Josey's personal space, but she was eyeing the crowd and ignoring me. "Hey, that's Mrs. Moody. Wonder what the missus is doing here?" she said, and marched over to her.

I watched them from my spot by the door. Their body language didn't suggest dinner and drinks were in the offing. A moment later Josey sauntered back toward me.

"So, what'd she have to say?" I asked, like Josey and I were first-class buds, or partners. I liked it that she was unusually chatty for a cop.

"Blah, blah, blah, loosely translated, she's with that guy with the big arms."

"She's on a date? With Mr. Big? What, two days after her husband is murdered?" Plus, I thought, who goes on a date to an antiphosphate rally?

"Yeah, well, the rich are different, you know."

I eyed the good widow for a long moment, assessing both her facial damage and the clinging Capri pants she was wearing very successfully. "Is Mrs. Moody a suspect? I take it she'll inherit M. David's vast holdings."

Josey ignored my question, and instead pointed toward the muscle guy. "The man with her, that's Galleon Theibuet."

"He's one of the Antheus shareholders, isn't he?"

"How'd you know that?"

I patted my pocket where I'd stuffed the papers Angus had given me outside the meeting. But what I said was, "Oh, we lawyers have our tricks."

"Yeah, well, Theibuet's part of the Antheus phosphate group. Reckon he's here casing the opposition."

I glanced back at grandpa-on-steroids. He still had his back to me as he bent toward Mrs. Moody, apparently listening to her.

"Yeah," Josey said. "I'd say he spent some time lifting and punching the bag. Check those biceps."

Before Josey and I could complete our girl bonding by discussing Galleon's well-maintained body further, Angus John took the podium, and we stopped talking to listen to him.

Angus jumped over the requisite intro joke and right into denouncing the proposed Antheus Mines. Before long, Angus had the crowd stamping their feet and shouting, "No more phosphate! No more phosphate!"

Go, Angus, go, I thought, latent cheerleader instincts surfacing in me. Then I looked over at Mrs. Moody, who stood tall and held her formerly fine face straight ahead. I don't know, but if I were her, bodyguard or not, I'd slip out the door and go home.

And just in case the crowd was not already riled up, Angus rallied it by his retelling of the Boogie Bog debacle. As a result of the company's bankruptcy, huge phosphogypsum stacks—such as the one in which M. David was forcibly and against his will drowned—were left at the Boogie Bog site for the state to clean up. These gyp ponds contained millions of gallons of toxic sludge retained behind those earthen dams, which were at high risk of breaking or overflowing.

I leaned over to Josey. "Is that all true?"

"You *don't* read the newspaper much, do you?"

"Okay, I'm real busy. I'm a lawyer. I have to read tons for my clients. Sometimes I miss stuff in the papers."

"Yes," Josey said. "It's true. It'll cost the state of Florida millions to clean up the site, that is, if the DEP can even figure out how to do it. Early estimate is around a hundred and sixty million. Right now, they're talking about transporting the sludge by way of barges and dumping it out in the Gulf of Mexico."

"That's totally insane," I said.

"Yeah. Isn't it, though? The DEP will treat the sludge as best they can before they dump it, but it'll still be a risk to the entire Gulf of Mexico and the marine life and the coral reefs. The fishermen are up in arms about the plan. But if the state leaves the gyp stacks like they are, they pose a worse threat. If the stacks overflow during our summer rains, the path of least resistance will be to take that poisonous sludge, *untreated*, straight into Bishop Harbor and then into Tampa Bay. Where we know for certain it will kill off the sea grasses and marine life, destroying the bay. God help us if a hurricane hits one of those gyp stacks."

Appalled by the catch-22, I nodded.

"It's like nuclear waste," Josey said. "There's nothing you can do with that gyp waste that won't hurt something."

Okay, Josey knew her stuff. I needed to introduce her to Olivia, let them preach to each other's choir. Maybe I ought to listen more closely too. After all, Florida was my adopted home state. Okay, Lilly Belle, memo to internal file: Learn more about Boogie Bog, Antheus, and, actually, you know, start listening to Olivia. Oh, and actually read the whole newspaper once in a while.

Having thus chastised myself for my ignorance, I nodded thoughtfully at Josey, but then the angry increase in volume from Angus at the podium made me turn back to him.

"Let those Antheus people think long and hard about what M. David's body in that gyp pond means," he said. "There's a message there to those who would wreak similar havoc in this county."

Oh, not good, not good at all, I thought. Championing violence is not a desirable trait in a client I was defending, even if his case was just stupid orange libel. I waved my hands frantically at Angus. But before he saw me, Josey pulled out her steno pad and started jabbing down little notes.

Angus kept talking in a threatening way. Desperate to shut him up, I kicked over a folding metal chair in front of me, and the clatter drew everybody's attention. In the ensuing break, I saw Miguel grab Angus and physically pull him away.

After wrenching Angus's arm and whispering something in his face, Miguel took the stage, introduced himself, and apologized for the disorder. Angus stomped off out of my line of vision.

Miguel, in all his regal male beauty, talked peace and love and patience and petition signing, no doubt as an attempted antidote to Angus's tirade. He did one of those love your enemy, but teach them the error of their ways with letters to the editor speeches. Sweet, I thought, but naively ineffective in today's world; at least Josey didn't jot down notes during his little pep talk. What she did was smile,

smile bigger, and start swaying to the rhythm of Miguel's speech. So, yeah, right before my eyes, Miguel worked his magic on Josey too. But before I could contemplate what that might mean in either her quest for a murderer, or mine for Miguel, the object of our mutual admiration stepped down from the stage. After that the meeting ran down, and I was glad of it.

When we spilled outside in the dusky, early dark, Miguel and Angus shook a lot of hands, while Josey watched, her eyes seemingly taking notes. Finally, people drifted off, but not before some over-weight woman with a flowered dress told Miguel to take the remaining drinks and snacks. "I don't need them," she said, and laughed. Then she patted his flat stomach and giggled. "Anything else I can do for you, honey?" she asked.

"You've already done more than your share," Miguel said, and leaned over and kissed the woman on the cheek. She turned red, giggled again, and left us.

Dutifully, Miguel went back inside and gathered up a box of the leftover snacks and loaded them in the back of his red pickup, while I said good night to Josey.

As Josey walked off, Miguel walked back to me and took my hand. "Nice try with the chair. Damn, I don't know why that boy can't learn when to shut up." Then he smiled his slow, Jesus-Feeds-the-Poor smile, the one that seemed soul deep and real. I leaned into his space, his hand still holding mine, and I started to melt.

"Join us for supper? On my sailboat?" Miguel asked.

Oh, sure, I'd join him for supper, that night, the next couple of weeks. Just let me take a shower first, I thought. But what I said was a conventional, "Yes. That would be nice."

"Okay, we'll have to stop at Publix and grab something from the deli."

Uh-oh. Food phobias kicked in. I wanted a nice, big, organic salad. "Where's the closest health food store?"

"There's a health food store on the way to the island, west of town, on Manatee Avenue. They have a deli, but it's a long drive," Miguel said. "Publix has a good deli."

"Why'd you knock that chair over?" Angus said, joining us and scowling at me.

"To shut you up. Advocating violence when you're a defendant in an orange-defamation case isn't a good idea," I said.

"Or when a deputy sheriff is listening," Miguel added.

Oh, yeah, that too.

"I'm not a suspect," Angus said.

"Well, you probably are now," I added, and then turned to Miguel. "Publix is a great store. I buy stuff there all the time, but let's go to the health food store, and get some organics."

"They have organics at Publix, and it's not ten miles out of the way," Angus said. "We'll go to Publix."

"Oh, yeah, who put you in charge?" I said, my ire rising.

Miguel stepped physically between us, all peace and love, and said, "It's not that far out of the way."

Angus glowered and muttered all the way to the health food store, which, as it turned out, was a hell of a long way out of the way.

Once there, to continue his protest, Angus waited in the car. Miguel and I flirted our way through the produce and the deli, and practically licked each other in front of the frozen-dessert freezer, and finally sauntered back to a sullen Angus, simmering in the pickup.

On the long drive back to his sailboat, Miguel put one hand on my neck and rubbed, while he steered with the other. "You need to let me Rolf you. It'll help you relax and breathe better."

"I breathe just fine. I'm alive, aren't I?" I didn't mean to be so snappy, but Angus was poking the sack of groceries into my thigh and I thought he was doing it deliberately. I pushed the sack back toward Angus.

"I can get rid of that sore neck," Miguel promised.

"I don't have a sore neck." Oh, yeah, that was a whopper. Every trial attorney I've ever known has a sore neck. Tension, stress, bending over desks and reading small print—it would be freakish not to have a sore neck in my business.

"Yes, you do. I can tell by the way you hold yourself."

Before I could respond, Angus dumped the grocery sack in my lap with some force. Something popped, then squished, and I felt cold and damp soak through my jeans. I didn't want Miguel thinking I was a quarrelsome person, so I took the sack from Angus.

"So what do you do, sail from port to port and Rolf the needy of neck?" I asked, trying to get my Flirty Girl voice back.

"Basically," Miguel said, "but I've been in Manatee County long enough to buy a truck and develop a steady client base. Getting Rolfed on a sailboat adds a certain allure that helps me attract clients."

Jealousy kicked me in the gut, just about where the deli package Angus had squished was leaking junk on me. I'd just bet those clients were all women.

"Yeah, and Rolfing on a sailboat lets him charge more, you know," Angus the still-pissed-off said.

"So what exactly is Rolfing?" I asked.

"Sometime real soon, I'll show you," Miguel said, and my heart thumped so loud I was sure they could both hear it. Miguel chattered on, but my ears had disconnected from my brain. I was in fantasy overload.

By the time we finally got to the Bradenton Pier, where his boat was docked near the neck of the Manatee River and Tampa Bay, I was hungry enough to eat the paper sack, but this was all but overridden by the thought of Miguel Rolfing me—I mean, wasn't Rolfing like a massage? Didn't that mean I got to get naked and he would rub his hands all over me?

We scrambled out of the truck, me all eager to wash stuff, eat, see the sailboat, and then get naked.

"I live here on the boat too," Angus said, as if he were reading my mind and wanted to thwart me.

Well, damn, he *was* the chaperone from hell.

"Just temporary, till I get a new house," Angus added, as if I cared unless he was moving out by midnight.

Thus, brought back from my fantasies, I looked around me. The lights on the pier gave off a ghostly glow in the heavy mist from the river and the humidity of a subtropical night. Boats of different kinds and sizes lined the pier. Here and there, some murmurs of voices floated out toward us, but I didn't see anybody else on the pier or on the boats. Under the pier, the water slapped at the pilings in its rhythmic ebb and flow.

While I listened to the water, Angus snatched the groceries from the front seat where I'd left the sack, and, grunting like it was too heavy, glared at me. Miguel took my hand as Angus stomped past us and headed down the pier, toward the end.

"Come on, I'll show you my boat," Miguel said. We walked hand in hand, saying nothing. The inside of his palms felt rough, almost calloused, like a man who had done a lot of hard work. They would feel wonderful on my skin.

For a moment, walking side by side through the river's mist with Miguel, I wondered if what I felt was more than just primitive, animal lust. Miguel was a man of great passion, I thought, admiring in retrospect the care with which he'd faked a second panther on the Antheus property and how he seemed to believe he could save the world by curing sore necks and having people sign petitions.

"This is it," Miguel said, and pointed to a sailboat.

Boats I don't know, having grown up landlocked in Bugfest, Georgia, where a Jon boat or a bass boat was about as fancy as anyone got. But this sailboat looked small. Maybe a tad junky. While I was trying to wordsmith my reaction into something pleasant, Angus started to climb onboard.

"Hey, Lilly," Miguel said, "I forgot the snacks and drinks in the back of the truck. Come back with me and help me bring them in?" He smiled in a way that seemed to suggest we might stop on the way to make love.

More walking in the mist hand in hand, who was I to refuse? Though it did seem to me that he was perfectly capable of carrying the junk food by himself. We walked off, leaving Angus struggling with a bag of health food and a latch on the boat.

We were almost back to the pickup when I heard a big boom. A very big boom. Before my brain could process it, Miguel threw himself on top of me, knocked me down on the ground, and covered me up with his body.

The wooden pier seemed to vibrate beneath me, and the lights popped and crackled, and then went black.

I had a sexy man lying on top of me in the dark, but all I felt was fear.

Chapter Seven

Something close by had just blown up in megadecibels that would be the envy of any punk-metal rock band; a man was lying on top of me; buzzy, indistinct sounds ricocheted about my ringing ears, and I was beyond dazed and confused, and hungry to boot.

Little sprinkles of hot, flighty things rained down on me, burning tiny spots on my hands, which were splayed out beside me, the only skin not covered by Miguel's spread-eagled bodily protection.

The night wasn't turning out well.

But as Miguel climbed off me, and I shook my head and struggled to stand up, it still hadn't hit me what had happened.

Until I heard Miguel scream.

A long, inarticulate sound that crashed against my already wounded ears.

Then I looked at the space where Angus and the sailboat had been, and I saw smoke and fire and black things floating up and down in the strange air currents of river mist and destruction.

Miguel grabbed my shoulders. "Get out of here. Now."

With that Miguel jammed his keys into my hands. Though the streetlights on the pier had blown out, the fire and the background city lights illuminated the area in a netherworld sort of gloom.

I stood there stupidly, trying not to vomit.

"Go!" he yelled at me. "Get out while you can." With that, and a small shove, Miguel turned and ran toward the fiery debris.

Then my head melted. That's exactly what it felt like, something warm and wet oozing down inside my skull. I stumbled back against a bench on the pier and almost lost my footing. Something wet trickled down my chin and I realized my nose was bleeding, and I rubbed my hand across my face, smearing it. My purse lay on the pier, and when I stooped to pick it up, I threw up, missing my purse by mere inches.

When I righted myself and looked around, I saw that people were coming out on the decks of the other boats.

Clutching my purse in one hand and Miguel's keys in the other, I wondered: Why should I run? Dizzy, I leaned back against the bench. What *had* Miguel said?

"Get out while you can." That's what he'd said, and Miguel's command was clear. Maybe he knew something I didn't. Could I be in trouble? I mean, more trouble than ringing ears, bleeding nose, and the banging-head contemplation of the great hereafter that nearly being blown up had just wrenched up from my gut? Trouble from the police? From the bomber?

Then I thought of Angus. Could he possibly still be alive?

People began to dash past me in the poor light. Against the glow of the fire, I saw Miguel dive into the smoke and water where his boat had recently been.

Please, God, let Angus be alive, I said. There didn't seem to be anything else useful I could do.

No one was paying attention to me—yet. For reasons wholly unclear to me, I started sprinting like a track star on meth and yanked open the door to Miguel's red pickup and squealed the wheels backing up and spinning out of there. Nobody tried to stop me, and before I could inhale, I was several blocks down the road, heading for the relative safety and open spaces of the Tamiami Trail.

In the evening traffic, I slowed down, and I cried.

By the time I was nearly back at my little concrete-block great-starter-home in Southgate, my ears were still ringing, but my head was clearing—a little, anyway. Enough that I didn't think parking Miguel's red pickup in front of my own house was a good idea. I still wasn't sure why Miguel had commanded me to run and thrust his keys at me, but now that I had, I didn't think I wanted to advertise the fact that I had fled the scene of a felony, if not a murder.

Running away doesn't look good to Official People.

It didn't feel so good to me either.

Nonetheless, I rubbed at my nose again with my sleeve, not having anything else, and I parked the truck in the lot at the Southgate Community Center. Full felon-in-flight mode took over—I don't quite get this part of me, like I was a major criminal in a past life, oh, yeah, well, and that minor criminal phase in the youthful part of this life—but I was usually good at things like breaking and entering and remembering to wipe off my prints.

Which is what I did—I practically scrubbed the keys on my shirt. Then, holding them by my shirttail, I eased the keys under the front seat. After that, I carefully wiped off the steering wheel, the inside of the cab, and the outside doors with the same shirttail. I backed off from the truck, wondered if I was missing something, checked for nearby witnesses watching me, and, seeing none, I anchored my purse around my shoulder, ran a few feet, and stopped.

I went back to the truck. After yanking open the passenger-side door, I banged open the glove compartment. Looking for what, I didn't know—maybe a gun, a handkerchief, a spare Handi Wipe, or some more of the paper that Angus had pulled out earlier with phosphate data on it. As a trial attorney, I'd learned never to underestimate the potential value of scrap pieces with odd bits of information written on them.

Papers jumped out at me. So Miguel was a slob, I thought, itching to organize and label the jumble, which at a quick glance appeared to be mostly shopping receipts. Then a modicum of reason sputtered through me, and I grabbed up the random sheets and stuffed them in my purse to study later. I rewiped down the inside and outside of the truck, and made my escape, jogging down the side road toward the humble haven of my own home.

If a cop drove by, I was dead. I mean, my shirt was bloody, my face was bloody, I was running, and without a real clue as to why I was running.

But no one stopped me. I got home, and there, I swear, was Jimmie's car in my driveway. Actually, the thought of Jimmie was reassuring, like the thought of my granddad waiting up to hear my adventures. I burst inside my own house, and hyperventilated. Jimmie came staggering into the living room, clutching a bottle of wine, and before I could say anything like "I almost got killed," damned if he didn't start complaining about Dolly.

"That there neighbor lady done been over a couple times about my car. So I reckon I got to go move it, now you're home. Anyways, I done promised her I'd get it out of here."

Then I watched Jimmie actually look at me, and watched him processing what he saw. "Lady, sweet Lord, what in tarnation happened to you? You awright?"

"No. I'm not. I nearly got killed and I threw up in public." Okay, so that might have missed the more important part of the evening, but throwing up in public is not only pretty disgusting, it is also clearly a mark of someone not on their way up the social or professional ladder.

Jimmie inched forward toward me like I might explode.

Which is, more or less, what I did—I burst into tears, not the dainty sniffling I'd done on the Tamiami Trail, but great, gulping, end-of-the-world-horror sobs. Angus was surely dead. That was finally sinking in.

Angus, oh, poor, volatile little man, I thought, and cried harder.
Then I thought of Lenora, and that whatever Angus had been to her
was gone now, and I sobbed so convulsively I couldn't get enough air
to breathe. Frankly, if I had cried any harder, I would have passed
out.

Jimmie grabbed me into his skinny arms, holding on, and hug-
ging me, and he even smelled like my granddad—which is to say, he
smelled like liquor and sweat.

"Nobody's gonna hurt you now I got you," he said, and for a moment, I believed him.

I calmed down, but got the hiccups. With Jimmie's encouragement, I managed to tell him what had happened on the pier, in little
bits and pieces of information between hiccups and sniffles and wiping my nose on the same damn sleeve.

"Reckon I otta call Philip?" Jimmie asked.

"No. Not Philip." I needed to think, and Philip would want me to
call the police or do something that he, Philip, in his usual alpha-male
manner, would decide I should do. Also, I looked gross, and the last I
could remember, I was mad at Philip.

No, instead of letting Philip tell me what to do, I was going to
decide what to do myself.

What I decided to do was take a shower and pop a Xanax.

I stayed in the shower until I drained the hot-water tank and I
could feel the little peaceful chemical fingers of Xanax soothing out
the bunched muscles in my neck and easing my brain back into a
state that didn't call for fight, flight, or hysterical tears.

With the last of the hot water gone, I toweled off, slipped into a
T-shirt and shorts, and went in search of the rest of the bottle of my
wine that Jimmie was obviously taking for his own.

And there sat Philip, in my kitchen, with Jimmie blabbing an ear-
ful at him.

"I done called him anyways," Jimmie said, and ducked his head.

When Philip saw me, he eased out of his chair and moved slowly toward me, keeping eye contact and searching my face. For what I didn't know.

"Are you all right?" he asked.

Physically, yes, but I wouldn't know about the rest until the Xanax wore off. "Fine," I said. And I waited for him to hug me. But he didn't.

Instead, Philip asked me for an exact accounting, and I understood this was his client-in-trouble approach, not his the-woman-I-love approach.

I walked past him, got a glass, and poured a trickle of wine from the nearly empty bottle on the table.

Jimmie hopped up and said, "Ah, Lady, let me open you another one. I, er, 'bout drunk that 'un, well, you was gone a long time."

"I don't think wine is a good idea. Not until you tell me exactly what happened," Philip the substance-abuse counselor said. "You should be clearheaded."

No, clearheaded was the last thing I wanted to be. So I said, and perfectly nicely too, "Yes, Jimmie, that would be good of you to open another bottle. A glass of wine would be good." Xanax kept my voice calm, my vision of the explosion soft and fuzzy in the memory box, and it kept me from snapping at Philip, who, after all, was only trying to help, and, might just possibly, I now realized, also have been mad at me. After all, not only does mad beget mad, but I'd snapped at him this morning, stood him up for a date so I could eat supper on a boat with another man, and entangled myself in a felony, if not a murder.

Jimmie, guided no doubt by some granddadlike radar, stopped to hug me on his way to open the bottle of wine.

Maybe I'd marry him instead of Philip, I thought.

As soon as I had half a glass of wine floating through my system, which punched up the Xanax nicely, thank you, I eased my way into explaining the explosion to Philip.

"Why were you going to have dinner on the boat with them? We had a date for tonight."

I sighed. Yeah, definitely mad. I sipped more wine. "I canceled that date, don't you remember?"

Philip eyed me curiously. I couldn't read his expression. Possibly because I couldn't read anything by then.

"How come you run off like that?" Jimmie asked, and then poured himself another glass of wine. "From that pier, I mean. You hadn't done nothing bad."

"A very good question," Philip said, "that is, why you ran. And one I would like to explore in greater detail. But first, tell me, where was the explosion? Was it within the jurisdiction of the city police?"

I nodded. "The pier was right off downtown Bradenton. You know the one, it's not all that far from your Bradenton office."

"All right, then. I have a source in the Bradenton Police Department. Let me call him and see if he can tell me anything." Philip rose from his chair at the kitchen table, neglected to kiss me, and moved toward my den and my phone, leaving Jimmie and me alone so we could do what we so clearly had decided was the most sensible option open to us under the circumstances: We refilled our wineglasses.

A few gulps later, Philip came back into the kitchen, picked up the bottle, corked it, and shoved it in the refrigerator, and then gave Jimmie and me the same look my grandmother gave my grandfather the day he drank a fifth of Black Jack and drove his riding lawn mower over her petunia bed and straight through the plate-glass window. "He does not know anything yet. The police are at the scene, investigating," Philip said.

"What about Angus? Any word on whether he . . . survived?"

"We don't know, Lilly. I just told you, my informant doesn't know anything yet."

I sat back and closed my eyes, trying to visualize some version of what I remembered where Angus might have survived the explosion.

"You being a criminal-defense lawyer what gets the bad guys out of jail, how come you got somebody at the PD that'll tell you stuff?" Jimmie asked.

Philip shrugged. "Money will buy you information any day of the week."

Yeah, sure. I was long used to paying large hourly fees to expert witnesses who would tell a jury anything I wanted them to say. Idly, and wholly off the main point, I wondered if paid police-insider informants were more reliable. "Money will buy you words, but truth is a whole other issue," I said.

Disregarding this wine-induced philosophical quip, Philip said there wasn't anything to do now but wait and see what his man could find out. "Thank you, Jimmie, for your help tonight," he said, in clear tones of dismissal.

"I reckon I better stay the night, 'case something more happens."

"I believe I can handle things," Philip said.

"Jimmie, there are clean sheets for the futon in the hall closet," I said, and rose from my chair, suddenly feeling all too sober. I couldn't for the life of me get shed of the idea that not only was Angus surely dead, but that he had died while I was mad at him, and he at me.

Not that it probably made any difference in the great hereafter.

But in the here and now, it might have been easier to bear if my last words to him had been something nice.

Chapter Eight

My head hurt like a son of a bitch, and then some. I tried not to make noise as I crawled out of my own bed and looked back at the still-sleeping Philip.

I tiptoed to the guest bathroom, hoping to delay waking Philip up by moving the noise down the hallway. Washing my face helped. Seeing that Jimmie had spread his man-thing toiletries about in the second bath didn't.

Still, morning is an optimistic time, and I wondered: Could Angus still be alive? I had hope. Perhaps he had jumped clear somehow. I said a quick prayer—for his life, or his soul—and left it to God to apply whichever fit the best. Then I slipped quietly into my own kitchen and put on filtered water to heat for the French press and the copious amounts of coffee I knew we'd all want, and I popped three Advil for my head, two capsules of ginger to settle my stomach, and a couple of multivitamins on general principle. While I waited for the water to boil, the anxiety kept at bay last night via better-living-through-chemistry came rolling back over me.

Where was Miguel?

Where was Angus?

And what in the hell was going on?

That line of worry led me to fetch my purse, where I had stuffed the papers and receipts from Miguel's glove compartment. After riffling through the loose collection of paper, I learned such things as: Miguel bought most of his groceries at Publix on a credit card, but that he'd recently bought some motor oil, a couple of plastic five-gallon fuel cans, a car battery, wire, wood screws, and, of all things, clothespins from Wal-Mart, and for those things he'd paid cash. He had also bought something called potassium sulfate, and, for a man who lived yardless on a sailboat, he had purchased an awful lot of fertilizer from a home-and-garden supply.

The fertilizer receipt definitely caught my eye.

Fertilizer, as Timothy McVeigh had taught us all, made bombs.

If you knew what you were doing.

I looked at the rest of the receipts, not much liking what was beginning to twirl around in my gray matter. Diesel fuel and fertilizer. Okay, okay, maybe he needed some diesel fuel for the auxiliary motor in his sailboat. Maybe he had a large number of houseplants on board.

But he wouldn't need that much fertilizer.

No, this was fertilizer in amounts for small forests, or at least very large yards.

A nice spike in my anxiety level hit both my head and gut, and, no closer to understanding anything, I smoothed out the receipts and slipped them into my desk drawer to be organized, memorized, copied, and filed later. Then I eased back to my kitchen.

Just as I scooped out my shade-grown, fair-trade, ten-dollars-a-pound coffee into the French press, Jimmie came tiptoeing into the kitchen and gave me a big bear hug. I felt tears start up until I noticed he had helped himself to a pair of Philip's pajamas, which were about twice too big on him. He looked like a goofy old clown, and I ended up smiling. I hugged him back.

A toilet flushed, I heard the sound of running water, and sighed. Philip was awake. By the time I poured the hot water over the ground coffee in the French press, Philip was in the kitchen, eyeing me, I thought, just a bit tentatively.

"Thought we'd be quiet, let you sleep in," I said.

He nodded, quietly and possibly guardedly.

The doorbell rang. A bit early for company, I thought. Jimmie and I were still in pajamas. Philip, of course, was dressed, and nattily at that for a Sunday morning after an explosion. "Would you please get that for me?" I asked, keeping my voice carefully neutral.

While he went to the door, I went to get dressed, leaving Jimmie with cursory instructions on the French press. "Push that plunger thing down in another minute."

By the time I got back to the kitchen, Dolly and Bearess were milling around, with Dolly making herself right at home, and rather pointedly ignoring Jimmie, who was drinking coffee, still wearing too-big pajamas.

"This isn't a good morning for company," I said, looking at Dolly. "We had an . . . an . . . accident last night."

"Are you all right, dearie?" Dolly asked as she opened my cabinet, fetched out a china bowl, and poured a smidge of coffee in it, ladled milk into it, and put it on the floor for Bearess, who slurped it up in one bold tongue stroke and wagged for more.

I started to point out that that was my grandmother's china bowl, but Jimmie was faster on the draw than I was.

"She near got blowed up," Jimmie said, and poured his second cup of coffee.

"I don't think we should be discussing this," Philip said, and poured a cup of coffee.

"The correct statement would be, she was nearly blown up," Dolly said, and poured herself a cup of coffee and topped off Bearess's china bowl.

By the time I got to the French press, there was no coffee left and my dull Xanax-and-wine hangover had swelled with the crowd in my kitchen.

"You know, I could pressure-clean that house of yours for you,"

Jimmie said to Dolly. "That is, if you was to cook me a homemade meal sometime. Chicken is what I likes the best. Lilly don't fry chicken."

Dolly was studying on Jimmie, while I heated water for a second pot of coffee, and then the phone rang. I ducked out of the kitchen to the bedroom, Philip close behind me, and I answered it and somebody I didn't know asked for Philip. I shoved the phone at him and went back to the kitchen. Right then my primary goal was to consume a large cup of coffee and as soon as possible.

A few minutes later, as finally the caffeine began to seep into my system, Philip beckoned me back to the bedroom.

"I am very sorry to report that Angus John Cartright perished in the explosion last night," Philip said. "That was, as you no doubt suspected, my informant in the Bradenton Police Department."

Still clutching my coffee cup, I more or less collapsed on the bed, mourning Angus for real and in earnest now that his death was confirmed.

Philip sat beside me. He took my hand, and held it in both of his own big hands. The pressure was light, the touch reassuring. Perhaps he was done with being mad at me over our broken date. "I'm sorry," he said. "Really, very sorry."

"Me too." I leaned my head against his shoulder. Perhaps I was done being mad at him too.

Then I thought about the living. My head popped off Philip's shoulder. "What about Miguel?" I asked, wondering where he was and if he was safe.

"There was only the one body. No one has been arrested. No one named Miguel was mentioned by my informant."

"But . . ." So, what exactly did that mean? Had Miguel run off too?

"Angus died around eight-fifteen P.M. People from the other boats told the investigators that two men—both tall and dark haired and thin—were seen running from the area of the explosion and escaping in a red pickup." Philip paused, but I didn't speak. "Lilly, did you and Miguel run off together? That appears to be what the witnesses are saying."

"No, I told you. He shoved the keys at me and told me to save myself, and then he dove into the water, looking, I guess, for Angus."

"Are you sure?"

"Of course I'm sure. You don't think I'd've noticed if Miguel had hopped into the truck with me?" I didn't care for Philip's tone or his question, either one. Maybe we weren't 100 percent over being mad at each other.

"They said *two* men ran away in a red pickup. Who would those two men be? Or, in the unlikely event that you were mistakenly identified as a man, who would that second man be?"

"I ran away in his red pickup. There was no second man. I was wearing jeans and a man's shirt, and my hair was in a ponytail. The streetlights on the pier had blown out. Maybe I looked like a man. Maybe I looked like two men. I don't know. Nobody was looking at me, anyway," I said. But I wondered: Did I look like a man in jeans? Whoa, no more ponytails and men's shirts for me.

"Where did you leave the truck?"

"I told you. At the Southgate Community Center."

"What are you hiding from me?" Philip asked.

"Nothing." That is, nothing other than the fact that I had been entertaining serious sexual fantasies about another man. Oh, and there was that fake-panther trespassing thing I hadn't bothered to mention.

"Did you wipe down that truck? If any of your prints—"

"I wiped down the pickup. I told you." I heard that shrill tone I don't much care for kicking into my voice, and I stopped, closed my eyes, and visualized my calming waterfall.

Apparently Philip didn't know I was trying to visualize inner calm, and he said, "If that truck is linked to Miguel and the explosion, you don't want your fingerprints on it."

"I know that," I snapped. Yep, that shrill tone was definitely there. "I know enough to wipe off my prints in a getaway vehicle after fleeing a homicide, okay? I wasn't raised in Disneyland by Pollyanna."

But then I thought—oh, damnation. What difference would wiping off my prints really make? Now in the caffeinated clarity of post-panic, I remembered that Officer Detective Josey knew I had been with Angus and Miguel before the explosion. With Angus dead, the police would surely look for Miguel, as the sailboat's owner, and Josey would no doubt confer with the city police, putting me smack-dab in the middle of the picture quick enough.

"Now what?" Philip said, apparently reading my expression correctly.

"A homicide detective from the sheriff's office, Josey Something Farmer, saw me hanging out with Angus and Miguel after the phosphate meeting. She might have seen me leave with them."

"Why would she know you?"

"Because she was asking me questions about M. David Moody's murder."

"Damn it!" he shouted. "How in the hell do you get into these kinds of messes? Are you a suspect?"

This was the first time Philip had raised his voice to me. I decided to ponder the meaning of this later and to defend my honor in the present. "No. I'm not a suspect." I hoped that was still true.

"Please, Lilly, back up. And this time tell me everything."

But Philip's cross-examination was cut off by Bearess's early-warning barking, and then, sure enough, the doorbell rang.

Before either of us could react, I heard Jimmie open the door and invite someone in. A woman's voice, general chatter, dog barking, the sound of something breaking, scramble noises, more female voices.

Listening so hard it made my head hurt worse, I finished drinking my coffee. Mostly I wanted to go back to bed very badly, wake up on the previous Friday morning, and tell Olivia, "No thank you, I can't meet Angus." He might still be dead, but at least I wouldn't have pissed him off right before he began his journey in a fiery explosion toward his new incarnation.

Instead, what I said was, "Well, speak of the devil. That's Josey. The detective. I recognize her voice."

"Hey, Lilly Belle, you might wanta get yourself out here," Jimmie shouted in my general direction.

"Please, do not give that woman any information. Not until we have thoroughly discussed all of this," Philip said.

Though I bristled at his directive, I had to admit that not only was Philip a criminal-defense attorney, but also he was not suffering from the lagging half-life of Xanax, and he hadn't recently fled the scene of a murder for no apparent reason. Also, early in my life I'd developed the habit of not telling law-enforcement officials much more than good morning.

Given all that, I just nodded and we eased out into the kitchen.

"Guess we're having a neighborhood brunch," Dolly said, and helped herself once more to my kitchen and handed Josey a cup of coffee.

"I kinda stepped on that dog bowl," Jimmie said. "I sure hope you didn't set great store by it."

"You really shouldn't use your good china for the dog," Dolly said, as if she hadn't been the one who put it on the floor in the first place.

Bearess was busy waggling and licking Josey as if they had been Timmy and Lassie in a former life together.

Stepping over the busted china, I pushed aside my phobias of crowds and junk and aimed myself at a second cup of coffee, only to discover that Dolly had poured the last of it for Josey. As much as I wanted to do so, snatching the cup from a homicide detective's hands didn't seem like the smart thing to do.

Not that doing smart things had lately been my specialty.

I put more water on to heat for the third pot of coffee, then sat down. My new theory was that if I sat still long enough, everyone else would settle themselves into some kind of workable pattern. Or leave.

Acting the host, Jimmie introduced himself to Josey, and then introduced Dolly to Josey, and while everybody was drinking my coffee and shaking hands, he said, "I reckon you know them two lovebirds, over there. That Philip and Lilly, they ain't been out a the bedroom since they jumped in it last night. I had to turn me up that Garrison Keillor guy loud on the radio, give 'em some privacy. Ain't love grand?"

I was astonished by how quickly Jimmie had just alibied me. Or had he? I double-checked Jimmie's math, which is painful without a sufficient level of caffeine—Angus, Miguel, and I had left the phosphate meeting a little after seven. Then we'd gone out of our way, at my insistence, to get organic food, sparking the snit between Angus and me. Philip had said his mole told him the explosion was at eight-fifteen P.M. So if I had really gone straight home from the phosphate meeting, I could have made it to my house before eight. Garrison Keillor's radio show was over at eight. Therefore, Jimmie had me home and in bed with Philip before the explosion.

Damn, Jimmie was not only sweet, he was handy.

Or, was he just digging the hole deeper?

I kind of thought that fleeing the scene of a felony is itself a felony—or is that a car wreck you cause?—but I couldn't ask Philip about that in front of Josey without raising questions in her mind I didn't currently wish to raise, so I tried to look embarrassed by Jimmie's story. Saying nothing, I took Philip's hand. He squeezed it and I assumed that meant "Play along," so I did.

"Shall I make us some eggs and toast?" Dolly asked.

"She ain't got no bacon," Jimmie said. "And don't dare ask her how come, neither, not lests you wants a lecture."

"Unless you want a lecture," Dolly corrected.

"Well, I don't wants no lecture on bacon. I already done got one. From both of them, yesterday. But you wants one, go on and ask her how come she don't got bacon."

"Doesn't have bacon," Dolly said.

"I jes' told you, she ain't got no bacon."

Oh hell. Screw that second cup of coffee, what I really wanted was the rest of that wine. I stood up and peeked in the refrigerator, but the bottle was gone. I peered into my trash, and found the bottle, presumably empty, in with the nonrecyclables.

"Recycle glass," I said, glaring at Jimmie.

"Reckon them pieces of the china bowl what got busted are recyclable?" he asked back at me.

"Lilly, if you do not mind, could I have a word with you? Alone?" Josey asked.

"You go on, dearie, and gossip with your friend. I'll cook us some breakfast and Jimmie will clean up the broken bowl," Dolly said.

Ignoring them all, I put the wine bottle in the glass-recycling bin, washed my hands, finished brewing my coffee, poured a cup, got a plate and put one of yesterday's leftover muffins on it and didn't offer anyone anything except the back of my head as I walked out of the kitchen and into the dining room.

I sat down at the dining room table, bowed my head as if in prayer, then reluctantly looked up. Josey and Philip had both followed me.

"Alone," Josey said, and looked at Philip.

"Quite a good idea," Philip said. "No one could think in that circus in the kitchen."

To Josey's credit, she didn't push the point of "alone" any further. With Philip still hovering, she asked me if I had left the phosphate meeting with Miguel and Angus last night.

I crammed my day-old muffin in my mouth to buy time to think. Had Josey seen me get into the red truck with the two of them? And what business was it of Josey's, anyway, since Angus John's murder was outside her jurisdiction?

"May I ask you, what is the reason for this inquiry?" Philip asked in his smooth seduce-the-jury voice and pulled off his glasses and smiled at Josey as if to distract her with his deep, black eyes. Still further to her credit, Josey was having nothing to do with that, and looked back at me and repeated the question.

Thinking of the safest lie I could on short notice, I swallowed and said, "Miguel drove me back to my car at Philip's office on Manatee Avenue." Thank goodness, I thought, that Philip had a satellite office in Bradenton and, that late on a Saturday, he alone would have manned it. So long as he backed me up, this seemed like a pretty good lie.

Josey looked like she was buying that story, so I sipped more coffee, and then asked, in my best innocent voice, "What's going on?"

In terse and unhappy detail, Josey explained about the explosion. Philip and I both acted surprised and distraught.

After what seemed like the appropriate interval of gasping and dismaying, I asked, "What about Miguel?"

"Don't know. Can't find him or his red truck. Any ideas?" Josey peered into my eyes in a way I didn't much like.

"They just dropped me off and didn't talk about any plans."

"Y'all want to come and get it," Jimmie shouted from the kitchen. "Dolly done got a regular breakfast feast started in here."

Taking the distraction for what it was—a gift of time to think—I smiled at Josey. "Please, join us for breakfast?"

"I could eat," she said, which turned out to be something of an understatement.

Fortunately, Dolly had scrambled all of my eggs from free-range, organic-fed chickens—eggs, which, by the way, cost about four dollars a dozen—but I didn't begrudge the food going down anybody's throat because while Josey was eating, she wasn't asking me questions I didn't want to answer. But Jimmie was flitting around Dolly and saw the price tag on the egg carton. "Why you reckon those free-range eggs cost so much? Seems like if you jes' let the chickens run around in the yard and fend for theyrself, it'd cost less. Don't it?"

I nursed my coffee, declined toast because I wasn't sure if Dolly had properly washed her hands before handling it, but ate the eggs because, after all, they were cooked and I couldn't imagine why Dolly would stick her fingers, clean or unclean, in the cooked eggs, and I had to eat something more than a bite of a stale muffin because my supper last night had been wine and Xanax. Which, incidentally, produced a far better night's sleep than I would have expected given the heart-to-heart discussion Philip had tried to instigate while I was passing out. While we ate, Bearess made soft, growly begging noises until she was stuffed from under-the-table handouts.

Finally, after more postbreakfast questions and dodges, Josey left, but not before she'd given me her business card and jotted down her home number and her cell phone number. Dolly and Bearess followed her out.

Jimmie, once prodded by my freely expressed anxiety, volunteered to hightail it down to the community center and move Miguel's red truck, lest Josey discover it and think it interesting that it was so close to my own house.

"I left the keys in it under the seat," I said, and Jimmie took off in an old-man jog toward the community center, leaving me alone, finally, with Philip.

"Did it ever occur to you to call 911, stay on the pier until law-enforcement officers appeared, and then tell the truth about what had happened?" Philip asked. "See, that way you would not have engaged Jimmie and me in a third-class felony, along with yourself."

"Discretion being the better part of valor," I said. "Besides, it wasn't like I saw anything helpful."

"We need to have a serious discussion about the nature of our relationship," he said.

Yeah, he'd mentioned that last night.

"But first, I need to make sure neither of us is placed in further jeopardy with the law by any oversight on our part in our recent fabrications."

That must have been Philip's way of conceding it was now officially too late to just tell the truth. So we spent the next half hour making sure we hadn't overlooked something, or contradicted ourselves.

We were on the arrogant brink of thinking we'd pulled one over on Josey when Jimmie returned to announce that the truck was already gone. "That's what leaving the keys in it'll do now days," he said. "Tell you what, 'n my day, weren't nothing to leaving keys in the truck, leaving your house doors unlocked." He shook his head. Then he spread his arms out wide in what I'd come to recognize as the poetry-recital prelude.

"Like that girl says," Jimmie said, "'every time I go back, the island is smaller. Even the iron hills of Alabama slip out beneath me in red circles that end in the Gulf.'"

What's erosion got to do with rising crime rates? I wondered. As for the red truck, I just figured some free-range teenagers had found it and were in Coconut Grove by now.

"What girl?" Philip asked.

"This girl that wrote herself a book of poems. She's always losing stuff and feeling real bad. I'm learning all the verses 'fore I gives the book back to Lilly."

Philip looked at me oddly. "Back to you? A book of poetry? You like poetry?"

"Oh, she jes' loves it," Jimmie said.

Then I stopped listening to them. I was thinking about Lenora.

Someone with some sensitivity needed to drive out and tell her about Angus.

Okay, so, yeah, maybe sensitivity wasn't my strong suit, but I'd give it a whirl. Also, I wanted to see if she knew where Miguel was—perhaps he was even with her. After all, I had some serious questions for that good-looking boy who took me on a date to trespass and nearly got me blown up.

Chapter Nine

Even with my sharp sense of direction, I had a hell of a time finding Lenora's backwoods wildlife rescue. But after a few scenic tours of the wrong dirt roads, I bumped my way into her front yard. The same beat-up Volvo I'd noticed on my first visit was parked under a tree.

Lenora was sitting on the front steps of the porch of the worn-out cracker house, her head bent down, and when I sat beside her and she finally looked up, I figured from her expression she already knew about Angus.

"I'm very sorry," I said.

"Thank you."

"I know Angus was a big loss for you."

Lenora didn't speak, but put her head down again. There was such weariness and despair in that gesture that I knew any sensitivity on my part meant waiting before I asked about Miguel.

We sat there for a long moment. From inside the house, I could hear the baby birds chirping for food. A cool breeze flew over my face, and I caught a whiff of honeysuckle. I took a long stare around the place, at first searching for any hint of Miguel's presence, past or present. Then I was just looking.

Everywhere I gazed, I saw something that needed fixing, cleaning, moving, or feeding.

Lenora needed help.

I pulled out my cell phone thinking I'd call Jimmie and pay him to do whatever needed doing, but then I took stock again. Lenora needed more than an old man could do, even as spry a one as Jimmie. I punched in the number for my brother Delvon, a born-again, dope-smoking, Jesus-loving man in his prime with a strong back and a good heart, even if he was apt to dress like John the Baptist and speak in tongues at inappropriate times. Delvon was the caretaker of my apple orchard in north Georgia, the haven to which I hoped to retire, sooner being better than later.

After a long series of rings, my brother said "Praise the Lord" over the phone so loud that Lenora lifted her head and looked over at me, and then, as if that required too much effort, she put her head down again.

"You need to get somebody to drive you to Atlanta and get on a plane as soon as you can. Fly into Tampa or Sarasota, whichever is quicker. I'll pay you back for the ticket."

"I know Jesus said suffer the little chirren, but he didn't say nothing 'bout suffering broke-heart fools and I don't care if Farmer Dave is my best friend on the face of this earth, he's about drove me nuts. He brought him back a burro over from the Grand Canyon."

This was the first I'd heard that Dave, an old boyfriend from my outlaw adolescence who last year had almost gotten me arrested or killed, or both, was back in Georgia, where he often hid out between adventures, tending my apple orchard with Delvon. I took it as good news that he'd returned to the orchard. "How'd he get the donkey to Georgia?"

"He hitchhiked with it."

I wondered for a moment who in the world would pick up a fifty-year-old man with pigtails and a donkey, especially nowadays when everyone is afraid of everyone else.

"And don't you be calling it a donkey in front of Dave," Delvon said. "It's a burro. He'll sure tell you that. From the Grand Canyon. Apparently, they're shooting 'em out there 'cause there's too many of 'em, and he rescued this one. I know that man is nursing heartache, but, praise Jesus for this lesson in patience, that man is driving me crazy."

Passing over the technical point that if one was already crazy, one couldn't be driven there, I started thinking about Delvon actually getting on a plane. "How long's your hair?" I asked.

"Don't know."

"You don't know how long your hair is?" So, I guess that answered any unspoken question about his current drug consumption. "Well, look at it."

There was a clank, and I imagined the phone at the other end hitting something.

"My brother," I said to the top of Lenora's head. "He and his friend Farmer Dave run an apple orchard in north Georgia for me. He's due for a visit. He likes animals. He's real handy. I think he could help you out here."

Lenora made a grunt that I took for a positive response.

"Sixteen and a third inches," Delvon said over the phone.

"What?"

"My hair. You forget? You asked me how long it was."

I sighed. In addition to being long, Delvon's hair was red. And, he was tall. There was no overlooking him in a crowd. He'd have to get to the airport a good three hours ahead to clear security. "Do you have a driver's license?"

"Yeah. Got one Dave and me bought last time we went to Atlanta. You can just about buy anything there these days. Name's Frank Straight on mine. His is Earnest Straight."

Again, I sighed. Yeah, security at the airport would be touch and go. At least he wasn't conspicuously Middle Eastern, so maybe they'd let him on a plane.

Over the phone, I heard slamming noises in the background, and then a braying noise, followed in short order by a Willie Nelson song about lost love. "Are you letting him bring the donkey in the house?" I asked.

"Can't stop him. It's not near as messy as you'd think. And another thing, he plays that same damn song over and over again. I mean, I like Willie, but—"

"Delvon, listen to me. You need to get to Atlanta, get on a plane, and come here as quick as you can. There's a woman here who needs your help."

"Okay, why didn't you jes' say so? Takes about two hours to get to the airport from here. I'll get the first plane out I can get."

"You got a credit card?"

"Got about thirty of them."

"Thirty?"

"Yeah. All in different names. Case I need to flee the country."

"Any in the name of Frank Straight?"

"One."

"Good. Be sure to use that one to buy the ticket. You'll need a picture ID to get through security. Try to look"—what? normal would be beyond the ability of a six-foot, two-inch man with sixteen inches of red hair—"like, you know, you're not going to hijack the plane. Call me from the airport when you get to Tampa."

We said our good-byes, and I put up my cell and asked Lenora, "What can I do?"

"Help me into the kitchen, would you?"

Together we stood up, she staggered a bit and I held on to her, and then she made little dry-heave noises, but pulled herself together and we struggled up the steps, across the porch, rested in the doorway, and then eased into the kitchen, where she sat down.

"Chemo," she said, and that effort seemed to exhaust her.

"You got any ginger ale? I'll fix you a glass."

"Could you roll me a joint instead?"

"Yes."

"Freezer," she whispered.

Delvon would have been proud of the speed at which I found the pot, rolled a joint, and lit it for her. I had to hold the joint for her at first, but then, as it soothed her, she took it and finished it.

"Thank you," she said. "It stops the throwing up better than any drugs they've given me."

"Let me go feed the birds. You just rest."

"I will be fine," she said.

"Sure. I know you will, but I've got the time to help out today." A bit of a whopper, as I had a full day of worry and agitation planned, but I wasn't about to leave her alone with all that raucous bird-hunger noise. I stood up and moved into the racket, grabbing the puppy food blend and a bowl of water.

As I was stuffing food into the beaks of baby birds, I calculated how long it would take Delvon to get here, and whether I should ask Lenora today what she could tell me about Angus and Miguel, or wait until she was stronger. Maybe Miguel was the one who told her about Angus being blown up? But how would he get out here without his truck? And, if he'd come to see Lenora, how could he possibly have left her here, sick and alone?

Such questions distracted me from the ick factor as I fed the baby birds. But then I stopped in front of the baby blue jay and contemplated skipping it since the same bird had previously bitten me. While studying on that, I heard a car drive up, and peeked out the window. Damn, a sheriff's department vehicle.

I grabbed the jay out of its cage for my cover story.

Officer Detective First Class Josey Something Farmer came right up the steps and into the room, and took a long, hard look at me, hard enough I must have squeezed the baby jay, because it squawked something terrible and then pecked repetitively at my hand.

"Interesting," Josey said.

"What? Blue jays?"

"You."

"Me?" I smiled at Josey. "I'm just a volunteer, feeding the baby birds." I all but chirped myself.

"You. Just popping up at the phosphate meeting. Now here. What with M. David having your bio in his pocket when he died, and Ang . . . er, is Lenora here?"

"Kitchen." Then I thought about the pot, the papers, and the roach, all on the kitchen table. "But she's pretty tired. You wait here, right here, and I'll go check on her." Trying to block Josey, I ran into the kitchen, still clutching the pecking little bird monster, but Josey followed right behind me.

Still hoping to block the pot from Josey's vision, I stood between her and Lenora. "Lenora, I'd like for you to meet Officer Detective Josey, er . . . Farmer and—"

Josey pushed past me in half a heartbeat, glanced at the marijuana roach, and said, "I'm homicide, not vice." She looked right at me. "And Lenora and I have met. I brought her some wounded goats once and she nursed them."

Josey turned away from me and put her hand on Lenora's back. "How are you?"

"Fine. I will be fine. Lilly is helping me feed the birds."

"Why don't you let me take you home?" Josey asked.

"Tell me what to do," I said, "about the others, I mean the animals. I'll feed 'em, or whatever, and you can go home, rest."

"Thank you. But by the time I explained it, I could have done it. I'm feeling better." Lenora slid back her chair and made a motion like she was going to get up. Then she saw the jay in my hand. "Strong little fellow. Didn't have a feather on him when we got him, he was so young. He's almost a brancher now, past infancy. Why don't you take him home with you?"

Why on earth would I want to do that? I thought, but held my tongue.

"Take some of the puppy food mix, but you'll need to wean him off the wet chow pretty soon. Right now, you'll need to feed him four or five times a day—you can't be leaving him alone and unfed all day. You're lucky; when they are real little, you have to feed them every twenty minutes during the day, but nature lets the mother birds rest at night. He's ready for seeds and bugs now."

Josey reached over to help Lenora while I contemplated mothering an ill-tempered blue jay.

"He's pretty close to being ready to leave the nest. You need to get him ready for that. Hang his cage near a window, or on a porch," Lenora said. "Get him used to your backyard. Then in a week or so, move the cage outside. Feed him only seeds and bugs. When he starts flying around in the cage, leave the door open. When he's ready, he'll go. But keep putting food in the cage until he stops coming back. You have to keep feeding them until they learn to get it themselves."

I'd pretty much stopped absorbing the information at the feed-him-bugs part. How, exactly, was I to get said bugs?

While I was still pondering the bug-food issue, I heard the peep of my cell phone from inside my purse on the table. The irate jay continued to squawk and peck in my other hand as I answered.

"Midnight, coming into Tampa," Delvon said. "Delta."

"Put your hair in a ponytail, and wear normal clothes," I said, and glanced at Josey. "No contraband, you hear?"

"Praise the Lord," he said, and the line went dead.

"I'll go put him back in his cage and finish feeding the rest of them," I said, hoping that when I was done with that, Josey would have left and I could ask Lenora about Miguel. But shoving mush down tiny throats wasn't something I could hurry too much, not unless I wanted a casualty rate, and it was pushing late afternoon when I got done and went back into the kitchen.

Of course, Josey was still there. That ruled out any questions about Miguel because I didn't want to redline my connection to the man who owned the boat that blew up, killing Angus, in light of the fact that I had lied to Josey, an Official Person, about my presence on the dock.

Besides that, the two of them had their heads bent together and they weren't paying me any attention. I heard Josey say, "Angus," and saw Lenora nodding. Leaving seemed to be a good thing for me to do, and I eased out silently.

But not silently enough.

"Thank you, Lilly. And don't forget to take the juvenile jay," Lenora said.

On the way out, I snatched up the cage and glared at my new charge. He screamed so insanely on the car ride home, I named him Rasputin.

By ten-thirty that night, having fulfilled my evening agenda of fretting, I threw myself behind the steering wheel of my ancient Honda and headed north, toward the Tampa airport. The traffic was heavy, but a nice break from listening to Rasputin share his shrilly critical view of his new home.

Naturally, Delvon didn't get off the Atlanta Delta flight at midnight.

I went to the official Delta counter where a frazzled young woman took a superior tone with me, but finally agreed that a Frank Straight was booked as a passenger on the flight, but had not boarded the plane.

No, he wasn't booked on any other flights according to her computer, she said, after I had asked. Type, type, type on her little Delta computer, then she looked up at me with an even less friendly look. "What exactly is your connection to Frank Straight?" she asked.

Suddenly I decided to leave the counter, and did so without answering.

Once safely out of sight of the Delta counter, I punched in the north Georgia apple farm number on my cell and let it ring until even the donkey must have been beside herself from the noise.

Frigging great.

A mean, bad man had drowned; an angry, good man had exploded; a tenderhearted, sick woman had too many hungry mouths to feed; I had custody of an irate juvenile jay; and now my brother was missing.

Chapter Ten

Competing law clerks Jack Russell and Whitney Houston were perched in Bonita's cubbyhole, waiting to pounce on me with tales of constitutional woes in the wayward world of fruit libel.

Barely awake, I was not ready for dialogue, constitutional or otherwise. What with the pointless trip to the Tampa airport that returned me home at two in the morning and Rasputin the Jay's insistent and piercing early-morning call for breakfast, sleep wasn't something I had enjoyed.

Then, during my breakfast, I had listened to the morning news and heard a quick report about an incident at the Atlanta airport involving an apparent religious zealot who had refused to take his shoes off and physically resisted the security police's suggestion of a further body search. The reporter quoted unnamed sources as saying the man had exclaimed loudly that he expected to stand naked before his maker on Judgment Day, but damned if he was doing it in the Atlanta airport for some glorified SS sorts, and then he had run, triggering a manhunt, a bomb scare, and a security-alert shutdown. All flights were delayed for hours. The man escaped and information regarding his identify was pending, the reporter said, before moving on to other topics.

Well, I guessed that Frank Straight driver's license was useless now.

Finally fully dressed, hair-fluffed and made up, off to work I had gone, raucous jay and all. I mean, okay, Lenora had been clear on the feeding schedule. I couldn't just leave it at home to starve all day.

Thus, my initial not-happy mood upon waking up from the sleep I hadn't had enough of had substantially deteriorated by the time I got to the law office, and Jack and Whitney pointed at me with their bright, young faces.

Bonita immediately rose, as if to formalize her statement. "I am very sorry about Angus John."

"Thank you. We can talk about it later," I said, not wanting to discuss it in front of the two law clerks. Bonita sat back down, and before I could say anything else, Terrier Clerk leaped.

"We've worked all weekend, and we've got lots of law to tell you about," he said. At first I thought he was literally jumping up and down, but when I looked at his feet, they stayed on the ground.

"Yes, I've got some significant law to discuss with you," Whitney said, still looking too elegant for normal society.

"Well, good morning, er—" While I struggled with the name-remembering part of my brain, Rasputin squawked dementedly and we all turned to stare at the jay.

"New pet?" Bonita asked.

"Long story," I said. I held the birdcage up and looked at the three of them, mentally gauging which one would be the easiest to badger into feeding Rasputin on an hourly schedule.

"Jack, you look like a bird lover. How would you like to take over caring for Rasputin?"

"Er, er . . . hum, George, I'm George. Eh, no, thank you. On the bird. See, I'm . . . allergic."

Allergic? To birds? Come on, I thought, he was going to need to master the quick excuse better than that to succeed in the world of tort litigation. Then I leaned back a moment and waited, wondering how long it would take before he fully comprehended that I was a partner and he was a law clerk, and that if he ever wanted to be any-thing more at Smith, O'Leary, and Stanley than a lowly law clerk, he had to do whatever I, the partner, asked him to do.

Rachel caught on pretty darn quick. Before George spoke again, she reached out and took the cage from me. "I like birds," she said, though her face didn't beam with glee. "I'm not allergic to anything. I'll take care of him."

George finished processing his full situation and reached for the cage. "No, I . . . I'll do it. I can wear . . . gloves . . . or something."

For a moment, the two of them jerked the birdcage back and forth between them, in a brewing tug-of-war. Then Bonita, as the mother of five headstrong children and therefore, no doubt, well versed in settling sibling rivalries, stood up and reached for the cage. "Let me, please." She sounded so sweet. "My daughter, Carmen, loves birds, and she needs a science project. This would be perfect."

George and Rachel both let go of the cage.

Crisis solved. Lord, I loved Bonita.

After some instructions on the care and feeding of Rasputin, I slipped into my office, with the eager George and the elegant Rachel in tow, all ready to educate me, no doubt, on the veggie-libel statute and how I could save my clients—though one was dead and the other miss-ing—from the dreaded orange-defamation suit filed against them.

"So, shoot," I said. "What'd you find?"

"You know, at least twelve other states besides Florida have such veggie libel laws. They came about after the alar apple scare and where, when CBS exposed the dangers of alar, the apple industry lost a great deal of money, so they sued CBS for telling people about the dangers of pesticides on the apples, but lost the suit," George said.

Well, if I were writing a term paper, that might be helpful.

"Thank you. Put all that in your memo. Rachel?"

"The constitutional issues involved in these veggie libel statutes are complex," Rachel said. "First, no court has actually ruled upon whether these veggie libel laws are an unconstitutional violation of the First Amendment's rights to freedom of speech. But a good many law professors have written articles which argue that these statutes are unconstitutional."

Yeah, okay, that and three bucks would buy me a cup of Starbucks, I thought.

"Most of these so-called veggie libel statutes punish clearly protected First Amendment expression—that is, speech on a matter of public interest, in this case the safety of our food. And the statutes make it far easier for the plaintiff to win against a food-safety advocate."

"Uh-huh," I added to show I was still listening.

"Certainly such laws lend themselves to abusive litigation practices," Rachel said.

Oh, yeah, like lawyers need help on that score.

"So, what happens, basically, is that these veggie libel laws create a whole new tort, hand-designed to help big agribusiness win. It's almost ludicrous. These laws endanger our safe food supply by shutting up people who would tell us about pesticides, bovine growth hormones, Frankenstein foods, and unsafe levels of who-knows-what."

When Rachel stopped to inhale, I sensed a kindred spirit. "Good," I said, and nodded in what I hoped was a judicious manner.

Simultaneous with a light knock on my door, Bonita stepped into my office.

"Don't forget you've got to talk with Ms. McDemis, the insurance adjuster in Jimmie Rogers's case," Bonita said.

Ah, yes, Jimmie's case, the parrot-drops-a-lizard-in-a-bikini-top car-wreck case, the stupidest lawsuit of my career thus far. Ah, yes, the glorious life of a busy lawyer, I thought, and nodded at Bonita.

"Okay, write it all up in a memo for me," I said, after turning back to Rachel. "And let me call this insurance adjuster on another case."

After they shut the door behind them, I cradled my phone for a moment, then mentally summoned up dear Ms. McDemis's phone number, dialed it, waded through the usual phone-recorded crap nonsense stuff before actually getting the woman, who was inappropriately nicknamed Sunny. Hello and hello, and all that.

"That stupid cracker has only the minimum auto insurance required by Florida law," Sunny said, setting a negative tone.

"Pretty good for an unemployed man driving a clunker," I said, thinking the fact that Jimmie bothered with any car insurance was a point in his favor.

"If you think this insurance company is going to waste its resources defending him in that stupid lawsuit, you need to go back to law school."

Blah blah blah, the usual just-because-we-took-your-premiums-doesn't-mean-we're-going-to-pay-anything insurance company guff.

After Sunny shut up, I asked her to hire a private detective for video surveillance on the plaintiff, as I was sure he was faking injuries from the minor rear-ender.

"Of course he's faking it. Idiot. Wasting everybody's time. Fool doesn't get it that there is only ten thousand dollars available under Rodgers's policy and that the old man's private resources don't add up to squat. His car's not worth more than five hundred. I told you to settle this thing for five thousand. You want to waste money on video surveillance, you pay for it out of your fee," Sunny said, and hung up.

Reluctantly, I called the green attorney, Jason Quartermire, the young man representing the man, the plaintiff, the stupid faker, who was suing Jimmie. Without the usual lawyer protestations and affectations, Jason agreed to see me that morning. Amazed that he didn't yet know the game of playing hard to get to show how busy he was, I gathered my mental resources so that I might convince him to take the $5,000 on behalf of his client, the faker plaintiff, and go home. Then I could return in earnest to worrying about when, or if, Miguel, my client on the lam, and my errant brother, Delvon the religious terrorist who had shut down the Atlanta airport, would show up.

Not only did Jason not play "too busy," he actually came to the office building of Smith, O'Leary, and Stanley to let me badger him into taking a mere $5,000 on a worthless claim.

Bonita led the young man into my office, and then mouthed the words *Have mercy* behind his head.

Nobody offered him coffee.

I worked my way through the standard settlement spiel, with special emphasis on the fact that Jimmie didn't have any money and if Jason had to try this sucker in front of a jury, I'd personally guarantee he would lose big.

"My client won't take less than a quarter of a million," Jason the imbecile said to my impeccable presentation.

"Don't be greedy," I said.

"It's not up to me. My client won't take less than a quarter of a million."

This time I laughed.

When I stopped laughing, I reiterated, as if greed had made big, dumb Jason deaf, "Look, it was only a slow-speed rear-ender with modest property damage. No way anyone was really hurt by tapping fenders. And, even if you had a case you could win at trial, there's no pot of money to be had anywhere. Back home, we have this saying: 'You can't get blood from a turnip.'"

"My client won't take less than a quarter of a million."

So, okay, this was boring, I thought, and stood up as a prelude to dismissing Jason. "Thank you for your time," I said.

"You keep saying Mr. Rodgers is broke, but my law firm's investigator reported Jimmie has approximately two hundred and fifty thousand dollars' worth of Exxon-Mobile stock," Jason sputtered.

This time I laughed so loud, Bonita actually stuck her head in the door, with a quizzical look.

"Jason thinks Jimmie is worth a quarter of a million," I said.

Bonita laughed too, and closed the door behind her.

"You need to get a better investigator. When you do, you'll find out Jimmie is broke, old, and unemployed. His Social Security is minimal, and the law doesn't allow garnishment of Social Security anyway." Actually, I wasn't at all sure that was true, so I said it with extra conviction in my voice. "Now go away until you come to your senses."

"I'll bring you my investigator's report."

"Do that," I said. "Now, good-bye."

Jason the fool left. I ranted at Bonita for a few minutes over how stupid this case was, how stupid Jason was, how stupid Sunny the claims adjuster was, and how stupid the practice of law was. Bonita smiled and nodded, probably not listening to a word. Eventually I ran down in my rant, went back to my office, and presumably Bonita returned to her work while I pecked away at my piddling files.

When Rasputin started squawking at unignorable levels, Bonita stuck her head in my door and said, "I think I will take my lunch break now and feed *your* bird."

"Yeah, me too. I'm going home for lunch."

We parted company and I sped home to Tulip Street, eager to wash my hands and face, and eat something cool and clean and organic, and be alone, in the clear, open spaces of my own house.

All the way home, I chewed my lip and fretted over Angus and Miguel. I was so deep in my worry that I almost clipped Jimmie's car, parked as it was on the street, but blocking about half of my own driveway. Good, I thought, I can send him out to Lenora's to help her. Then I realized I'd have to lead him out to the sanctuary since I couldn't begin to describe how to get there, plus Lenora wouldn't know Jimmie from Adam's house cat, and he wasn't the sort who universally made good first impressions. But at least I knew where Jimmie was, and that was momentarily reassuring.

Inside my house, at my kitchen table, Jimmie the delinquent grass cutter was sitting with Dolly. They were drinking coffee. Mine. Bearess was snuffling across the kitchen floor, alternately rolling and eating a leftover muffin from Saturday and leaving a trail of crumbs. When she bumped into me, she gave me a doggy snort and a lick, then went back to distributing muffin crumbs around my kitchen.

Seeing as how I needed Jimmie to help Lenora, I didn't yell at him. Instead, I greeted my uninvited guests as if they were welcome and asked Jimmie if he could help a friend of mine for the next few days.

"Sure," he said, but he smiled at Dolly, not at me.

"I'll have to lead you out there, it's way out in northeast Manatee County."

"Sure," Jimmie said.

Bearess lost interest in actually eating the muffin, and smashed it with her big paw into a greasy pile of mush right in front of the sink. After I cleaned that up, I politely declined Dolly's offer to fix me a sandwich, and fixed my own salad while Jimmie and Dolly flirted with each other. When I couldn't stand listening to them anymore, I asked Jimmie if he knew anything about video cameras.

"Sure, I can work one of them." He smiled at Dolly big time, as if knowledge of the on-and-off buttons on a camcorder qualified him for a sleepover.

"I used to work some for a woman who filmed weddings. I was real good with a video camera. Man, that was a great job," he said.

"So, why'd you quit?" I asked.

"Didn't quit. Got fired. They's this open bar at my last wedding. I hep'd myself plenty and then clumb up on the table and recited some Sylvia Plath—you know that one about her daddy?"

Dolly corrected his pronunciation and grammar and said she much preferred the romantic poets over the moderns, and I ignored her, instead explaining to Jimmie that he needed to follow the man suing him until he could get a video of him doing something like playing golf, lifting weights, or building a brick patio.

"Got'cha," Jimmie said. "Prove him the faker he is."

"Exactly."

"Maybe Dolly'd like to go with me."

"Only if she signs a waiver of liability. You too. Can't have y'all getting hurt and suing me or the law firm. I'll bring home the firm's video camera and some film tonight. But meantime, as soon as I'm finished here, I'd like for you to follow me out to a wildlife sanctuary and help the woman who runs it. Just do anything she asks you to do, all right? I'll pay you. Don't let her pay you."

"Sure," Jimmie said. "Dolly, would you care to join me?"

As it turned out, the idea of cleaning out cages filled with soggy newspapers full of bird poop didn't much appeal to Dolly, and she said a polite, but firm, no thank you to Jimmie's kind invitation.

Naturally, when we got out to Lenora's, after only two misturns down identical-looking dirt roads and Jimmie, following in his ancient car, honking at me on every turn, there was no sign of Lenora's old Volvo. Instead there was a trendy-looking little SUV. The front door of the old cracker house that served as a bird-and-animal rescue center was open, so we walked right in. Instead of Lenora, we found a wide, squat man, with the big arms and thick neck of a former football player, or a wrestler.

"Adam, U.S. Fish and Wildlife," he said, after I introduced myself and Jimmie. "Lenora and I have been working on this place for years."

As Adam wasn't wearing a uniform, I assumed this was a day-off venture, and I was glad to know Lenora had someone else to count on.

"I'm Lenora's friend, and I've brought my . . . er, gardener, Jimmie Rodgers, to help out. He will do whatever you tell him to."

"Is he bonded?" Adam asked, staring first at me, then at Jimmie, then back at me, with the suspicious eyes of someone with law-enforcement experience.

"Yes," I lied.

After a few more exchanges, Adam seemed to accept Jimmie and gave him a preliminary order. As Jimmie trotted out to gather cleaning supplies, I asked Adam, "Do you expect Lenora today?"

"No."

"Could you tell me where she is?"

"She's not here."

"Then, please tell me her last name."

"I thought you said you were her friend."

I sighed. "Fine," I said. "I was out here both Saturday and Sunday. I took a jay home with me. But we were working too hard to discuss personal details like last names. I just want to know if she's all right."

"She'll be fine."

Jimmie came back into the room, whistling and carrying a jug of bleach and a handful of rags. "You gonna stay and help out?" he asked, looking at me.

Yeah, like I was going to handle bleach in my gray Brooks Brothers suit. "Busy day at the office, sorry, got to run."

I left, but not before I gave Lenora's guardian my business card and a request that he ask Lenora to call me.

By the time I drove back to Smith, O'Leary, and Stanley, it was nearly three and I slammed my way back inside my own office. I pulled out some depositions in an active legal-malpractice case and started churning away.

Depos are boring as a rule, and I lost interest fifteen seconds into the project. I jumped up and stuck my head out the door. "You file my notice of appearances for Angus's estate and Miguel in that stupid orange-defamation case?"

"Yes. And I've done a notice of death in Angus's case. I've asked Rachel to research whether the cause of action dies with him, and to prepare a rough draft of a motion to dismiss if it does, and I will have a draft of an answer to the two complaints ready for you to review by tomorrow."

"You're drafting the answer?"

"Yes. I've admitted the defendants' names and addresses, and I have said 'without knowledge' in response to the other allegations in the complaint. That's how you always draft answers to the complaints, isn't it?"

Well, yes, but I had a degree from a state university's law school that gave me the technical right to deny knowledge. I wasn't sure what I thought about my secretary practicing law. Besides, all of this strongly suggested that nobody needed me. "You know I'll have to add the affirmative defenses, don't you?"

"Yes." Bonita said, her face resting in her neutral, but attractive, expression.

"Well, I'll certainly look it over," I said, then remembered to say, "Thank you."

"If you would like to talk about Angus—"

"Later," I said, not entirely trusting myself to talk about that, even to Bonita, who often acts as my therapist, and I shut myself back in my office. I picked up the stupid, boring depos, highlighted some stuff to better absorb later, and then put them down again. I jotted fifteen minutes on my time sheet, and booted up my computer. I couldn't get my mind off Angus and Miguel. So I was going to go with that flow.

The last meaningful things Angus had said in my presence concerned M. David Moody. M. David Moody had some interest in me right before he learned whether there was a special circle in hell for Big-time Mine CEOs who gouge the earth and leave ponds of radioactive crap behind. M. David had wanted Antheus Mines to dig up east Manatee County by the west fork of Horse Creek. Angus had wanted to stop M. David and Antheus. Both of them had been murdered.

My client and my anti-client.

Linked by phosphate.

That felt like a circle I needed to figure out.

Starting with M. David the devious.

Within seconds, I'd typed Angus's client number into the LEXIS computerized legal-research system, and gone to the major news database, and punched in M. David's name, limiting my search to the last two weeks.

In quick order, I read through the standard newspaper stories about his murder—facedown in a phosphogypsum pond had actually made for some modest national attention. It seems the weirder the murder, the broader the publicity. But none of the stories had anything to add to what I already knew.

So, I went further back, and concentrated on business news.

In no time at all, I read enough to be horrified by the mess the Boogie Bog corporation had left. Angus had told it right at the meeting—billions of gallons of toxic sludge, the by-product of processing the phosphate ore into fertilizer, was stored on-site behind what the company and the press euphemistically called earthen dams. In other words, all that kept that radioactive semiliquid waste from pouring out and over all in its path was a pile of dirt around it.

I didn't feel too secure.

But I was damn glad I didn't live down the hill from Boogie Bog.

Up until now, I'd thought Manatee County was a pretty neat place, a county that had all Sarasota had to offer, but with lower real estate prices and less pretentiousness.

But billions of gallons of poison sitting behind piles of dirt sort of made me rethink that one.

As for Boogie Bog, again, Angus had it right. The corporation had just cashed in its chips and left all that toxic sludge for the state of Florida to clean up.

Only, there was no way to clean it up.

I remembered what Josey had said. It was like nuclear waste—there's nothing safe anyone can do with it.

From that research, I segued into the corporation business stuff on Boogie Bog. One news story in a Florida business magazine indicated that a year before the Boogie Bog Corporation declared bankruptcy, M. David had resigned as its CEO and sold all his stock back to the corporation. Because the stock was privately held, its value at the time of sale was set by a CPA's independent accounting at a high price, based on the corporation's land, physical plant, and equipment holdings as well as its balance sheets, which, of course, had been inflated to improve the company's credit worthiness. However, because the corporation had insignificant ready liquid assets, it had to borrow the money to buy back M. David's shares. Taking on the additional loan had proved to be the debt that broke the already fragile back of the camel, so to speak.

In other words, M. David had gutted the corporation.

Some of his colleagues in Boogie Bog had not been as financially lucky as M. David had been. When Boogie Bog's corporate finances hit bottom, so did much of their individual fortunes.

Perfect motive, I thought. Any of the damaged Boogie Bog corporation players could have killed M. David for revenge.

But for the life of me, I couldn't figure out how Angus fit into that picture.

Outside my window, I heard the sound of various cars starting up, and glanced up. Yep, after five. The worker bees were going home. I should do likewise since I was clearly not accomplishing anything. But, not wanting to be caught in the five o'clock traffic, or worse, have Jackson see me leaving at five, which was way too early for an attorney to leave this office, I settled back in my red leather chair and concentrated.

On M. David.

He didn't just take the money before the ship went down, he took the money that made the ship go down. Just like him. He'd increased his fortune, skated clear of the coming bankruptcy, and probably slept soundly at night, proud, I rather imagined, that his actions effectively dumped Boogie Bog's toxic waste on the good taxpayers to deal with.

Yeah, okay, that made his manipulative coup de grace in trying to ruin my life before I was twenty-five seem pretty minor. But I was still mad.

And M. David would know that. I mean, the man wasn't stupid, and I hadn't been shy in expressing my attitude toward him. Given our history, I couldn't even imagine why M. David had a file on me, and had apparently been planning to make an appointment with me.

While I was cogitating, Bonita stuck her head in the doorway. "Anything else you need before I leave?" She was holding Rasputin's cage, and the jay punctuated her question with loud, insistent squawks.

"No, thank you," I said.

Good nights all around, and I was alone.

Alone in my office, I did what I do. I started to make a list of things I knew and the things I needed to learn. The first thing I wrote down was: "Find Miguel."

And that took me right back to the explosion. A wave of nausea passed through me as I remembered. This time, instead of blocking the memories, I pressed through them, mentally examining the details of what I had seen and done that night. And what Miguel had done that night.

One detail surfaced insistently. Miguel had been so emphatic that I should flee. Why, I wondered, had Miguel insisted I run away?

And why, really, had I?

Yeah, like most Americans, I had some basic, ingrained instinct to avoid the police, honed perhaps in my case beyond the norm by an adolescence spent living with Delvon and Farmer Dave growing marijuana and avoiding truancy, social workers, juvie hall, and high school expulsion by good timing and luck.

Then, like the bad fairy of negative thoughts had just sprinkled me with paranoia dust, I suddenly realized how convenient it was for Miguel that he had stepped back from the boat even as Angus stepped onto it.

Like that actor who puts his irritating wife in a car and then suddenly remembers he left something inside the restaurant and is, thus, conveniently out of the way when someone shoots his wife to death.

Stepping aside from death at the right moment is suspicious.

While that suspicion licked at me, I couldn't figure out any reason Miguel would want to kill Angus. Or blow up his own sailboat.

But if he had, then he surely would not want me hanging around to say to the police: "Oh, hey, wasn't that good timing that Miguel stepped back from the boat just before it blew?" Like he, Miguel, knew exactly what was coming.

Was Miguel a killer?

I chewed unhappily on that anxiety until it was time for me to go home. On my way out, I stopped in the equipment room and picked up a video camera and some blank tapes for Jimmie, and headed toward my house.

My house. Home, my sweet haven and harbor.

Yeah, okay, so wrong again.

Chapter Eleven

At my front-door stoop, Dolly and a man with long, red hair were jumping around, throwing air punches at each other while a small contingent of my neighbors watched.

Delvon—with his usual grand entrance.

Bearess ran over to me in a doggy frantic way, barking at me as if I were supposed to do something.

After studying the situation for a second, I could tell Delvon wasn't really trying to hit Dolly, he was just self-defensively dodging and feinting. Dolly, however, appeared ready to smash his face if he'd just hold still and let her land a punch.

One of my neighbors said, "We've called the police. He was trying to break into your house, only Dolly stopped him."

"Oh, *mierda*," I shouted. "That's my brother." Apparently it had never occurred to Delvon that long, red hair and a torn T-shirt worn over cutoffs that also had big holes in them, and black chukka boots on pale, skinny legs, wouldn't, like, you know, raise an eyebrow in a sedate, suburban, Sarasota neighborhood.

I pushed my way between Delvon and Dolly, who finally landed a punch, but on me, because I made the mistake of standing still in front of her. Fortunately, being as she's about eighty, it didn't hurt that much. I yelled a lot at everybody to stop it, I told Dolly to tell the police that it was all a mistake, and then I dragged Delvon back to my Honda and we sped away.

No way I wanted the local police to have a look at Delvon.

"How'd you get here?" I asked.

"Traded a bag of crip for an old car."

"Crip?"

"Man, you're out of touch. It's a superpot. I grow it by—"

"You traded a bag of pot for a car?"

"Yep."

"Get a title?"

"What I need a title for?"

I sighed. "So you can get auto insurance."

"What I need car insurance for?"

"It's the law. Under Florida law, you need a title and car insurance."

"Want to show me where it says that in the Ten Commandments?"

I sighed again, longer and slower. "Where's the car?"

"Oh, I traded it to a guy on I-75 for a ride to your house and a six-pack. He dropped me off at your place and I was just minding my own business when that crazy lady came over and started beating on me."

There was probably a chapter missing in the story of the frequently traded car. But I didn't care to know it any more than I wanted to know how he'd gotten out of the airport with a band of highly trained federal security personnel chasing him.

Instead, I explained about Lenora, and the birds, and the chemo, and the big piles of messes, and the cages of hungry creatures, and how she needed more help than Jimmie alone could provide.

"Cool," Delvon said. "I can help. Lift and tote. Get a prayer circle going for her."

"She might need some medicinal marijuana. It helps with the side effects."

"Cool. I got some. Organic. Not the crip, I had to trade that for the car, outside the Atlanta terminal. Man, that place sucks."

"Where is it?"

"In Atlanta. Man, where else would the Atlanta airport be?"

"I mean the pot."

"Oh, I stashed it in your carport, behind the potting soil, in that little storage room."

Frigging great. With my luck, Dolly had seen Delvon stash it, assumed it was a bomb, and would lead the police right to it.

"You still got that ferret?" Delvon asked.

"No."

"Too bad, that was a cool little dude."

We drove the rest of the way to Lenora's exchanging non sequiturs. Once we pulled up to the house, I was relieved to see that Jimmie's car, and therefore presumably Jimmie himself, was still there. Delvon and I piled out, and Jimmie, reeking of bleach, tumbled out the front door, his fatigue apparent.

"Damnation, that fish and wildlife guy like to wear me out," he said. Then he looked at Delvon.

"Praise Jesus," Delvon said. "The FBI is out after me 'cause—"

"Delvon," I said, "shut up."

"Oh, this here's your brother, the religious 'un. Pleased to meet you. I'm Jimmie."

"Delvon, can you stay here and help Jimmie as long as y'all can this evening? There's at least an hour of daylight left. Maybe there's a place here where Delvon can shower and sleep? Or maybe he can stay with you, Jimmie?" I asked, thinking a wanted airport terrorist staying with me so soon after Dolly the helpful neighbor had alerted the police to strange doings at my house might not be a totally great notion.

"Not much of a spot to sleep and the shower don't work and it's full of stuff, anyways."

"I guess there's an epidemic of that," I said.

"Huh?"

"You know, your shower doesn't work."

"Huh? . . . Oh, yeah, that. Like I's saying, they's a hose out back hung up in a tree that I done used for a shower, you don't mind cold water and getting naked in the great outdoors. Sure plenty to do. And they's some real cute critters out here."

While Jimmie and I chattered, Delvon had been looking around. Then he beamed and said, "Cool."

"Well, come on, then," Jimmie said to Delvon, "and let me show what that bossy old wildlife man said I should be doing. I reckon we can both sleep in my car."

I watched the two of them wander off. No doubt by the time I got home, they'd be drinking and smoking and trading arrest stories. I wrote a note of explanation, folded it, addressed it to Lenora, and put it under a magnet on the refrigerator, emptied my wallet of cash for Delvon and Jimmie, with a note that they should run to the nearest store for supplies and food, and then I prepared to flee the scene.

Then it hit me: Why would Jimmie sleep in his car?

I caught up with them in the backyard, where Jimmie was explaining about feeding the raccoons, and I interrupted. "Lenora doesn't stay here at night. Why are you?"

"Why am I what?" Jimmie asked.

"Sleeping in your car? If there's no place to sleep, I don't think you need to stay here at night. I just thought it'd be a good place for Delvon to sleep—temporarily, that's all. So why are *you* going to sleep here in your car?"

"Oh, I . . ." Jimmie stopped talking and looked down at the raccoon. "You know them things can carry rabies virus without being sick, so less'n you've had the shots, you ain't suppose to play with them."

"Jimmie, why are you sleeping in your car?"

"'Cause that's where I been living. See, 'cause I kinda got kicked out a my apartment."

"What do you mean, you got kicked out?"

"I got kicked out."

Okay, that articulated the problem better. "What'd you do?"

"I didn't pay any rent for a couple a months."

Well, that'd pretty much do it for an eviction, I thought. Plus, that explained why he was hanging around my house. The poor man was homeless.

I sighed. Deeply. Confronted with a desire to help and a desire not to have Jimmie and Delvon both living with me, coldheartedness sounded pretty good at the moment.

"We'll be jes' fine, don't you worry," Jimmie said.

"Jesus slept outside," Delvon said.

"Just come to my house when you're done here," I said, knowing full well I'd regret this. "We'll work out something more permanent tomorrow. One of you can have the futon and one of you can have the couch."

"Cool," Delvon said.

"You always was a good-hearted woman," Jimmie said.

Internally, I cursed the thought of funding a new apartment for Jimmie in the land of high rents and wondered what Delvon's cash reserves were, as he was certainly going to need to buy some clothes, normal ones at that, and I think I said my good-byes, but, anyway, I got in my car and drove off.

No doubt the police and possession charges awaited me at my house, but I went home anyway. Instead, I was actually rather pleased to see Bonita, her daughter, Carmen, and Armando, the more squat of her mismatched twin boys, all waiting for me inside the carport, by my side door. Dolly was entertaining them with a story that involved a lot of hand waving, and the rest of the neighbors had left. Johnny Winter, the albino ferret that once saved my life, was wrapped around Armando's neck, and neither of them seemed happy to see me.

"I need to return the bird," Bonita said, and held up the cage in my general direction.

"Why?" I asked, pointedly not reaching for the cage.

"Johnny the ferret was most determined to eat it," she said.

"You could take Armando and Johnny and leave me the bird," Carmen said, in her happy, hopeful, seven-year-old voice.

I glanced at Armando and Johnny. They glared back at me.

I reached for the birdcage. "Thank you for trying," I said.

"Henry is bringing pizza if you would like to join us for supper," Bonita said, no doubt prompted by guilt at returning the bird to invite me to join her faithful suitor and her five children for supper.

"Thank you, but I have plans," I said.

"I'm not taking that bird," Dolly said. "It's bad enough I have to take care of your dog."

This from the woman who had alienated the affections of my own dog and then, in effect, stolen Bearess from right under my nose, was too much, and I opened my mouth to say rude things, but Carmen tugged at my arm.

I looked down at her perfect, sweet face. "What, Carmen?"

"I bet if you gave him a nicer name, he'd be nicer," she said.

"What?"

"The bird," Bonita said. "Carmen thinks Rasputin is a bad name." So explaining, Bonita gathered up her two children and the ferret and they left.

As Bonita drove off, Dolly managed to squeeze out enough information between her complaints that I gathered she had told the police it was all a big mistake and they'd left. Neither of us mentioned the organic marijuana now stored in the little room off my carport, and I decided not to say rude things to my neighbor after all, but went conventional: "Thank you."

After Dolly left, I took the stupid jay into the house, where I realized I was about half starved, and I put the birdcage on the patio table on the screened-in back porch and walked back to the kitchen, where I triple-washed my hands and grabbed a sack of sunflower seeds and a box of Save the Forest trail mix bars. Seeds for the jay, trail mix bars for me—just to tide me over until I could shower and fix a decent meal.

Rasputin raised hell and refused to eat the sunflower seeds.

After I explained to him in careful detail exactly why it was in his best interests to shut up and, no, I wasn't going to fetch him any bugs, I bit into my trail mix bar. Organic, free of high-fructose syrup, but sweetened with rice-bran syrup and honey.

As I chewed, Rasputin danced and pranced and screamed.

I looked at the bird. Then I looked at the trail mix bar. What the heck, it's mostly oatmeal, seeds, and tasty, healthy dried fruit, I thought, and broke off a piece and shoved it in the cage.

Rasputin pecked at it, then he ate it. Then he looked at me with a look that, I swear, said, "More please." I gave him the rest of the bar and watched him eat it.

For the first time since I'd known the bird, it curled up, calm and quiet, and just sat there, looking rather serene in a fluffy juvenile-bird sort of way.

Well, I'll be damned. All the poor thing needed was something sweet.

I could relate. I ate another trail mix bar and headed toward my shower.

A half hour later, dressed in an old camp shirt and a pair of threadbare yard-work shorts, minus bra and panties, I was contentedly washing and chopping produce for a big salad when the doorbell rang. Figuring it for Delvon and Jimmie, I didn't bother to fluff my shower-damp hair or worry that I was dressed like riffraff.

But when I opened the door, Miguel jumped into my living room and into my arms.

Who grabbed who first I couldn't say. But we were hot and full of hands and hugs and tongues even before I got the door shut.

He kissed me like the scene in the movie right before the soldier boy goes off to war, and I kissed him like I knew he'd never come home to me.

I could not get enough of this man. I pressed so hard against him he almost stumbled backward. His hands slipped up under my shirt and I was glad I hadn't bothered with a bra. His trained Rolfer's fingers flicked at my nipples, and, as if it had a mind entirely of its own, my right leg rose and curled about his, and I thanked my yoga teacher for all those cursed hours of flexibility training.

Just about the time I was going to rip his shirt off him, I remembered something: Who knew my brain could work at that stage of excitement, but this man, my mind reminded my body, was the man who had suspiciously stepped aside from an explosion with almost premeditated precision.

I pulled out of his embrace and demanded to know what was going on.

"Don't worry. I parked my truck at the community center. In case anyone is watching your house," Miguel said, slightly panting, as I unwound my leg from his.

"Why would anybody be watching my house? Are *you* watching my house? What the hell is going on?" I asked, rather shrilly given my ardor seconds before. "And how'd you get your truck back?"

His hands crept out from under my shirt, and wrapped themselves around my neck, and I tensed, realizing I was alone with a suspicious man who had just put his hands around my neck in the classic TV setup for strangulation.

Then he began to massage my neck and the tops of my shoulders. "You need to relax," he said, his voice hypnotic. "Let me help you relax."

"How'd you get your truck back?" I asked, leaning into the massage.

"Easy enough. We think alike, you and me. That's a good sign, isn't it?"

"How'd you get your truck back?" I repeated, pulling out of the massage in my frustration. I wanted to know what was going on more than I wanted his hands all over me.

"After I knew Angus was dead . . ." Miguel said, and then paused, his fingers still, his face sad.

"I'm sorry," I said.

He dropped his hands and walked toward the couch in the living room, where he more or less collapsed.

"Once I knew he was dead, there wasn't any point in hanging around. The cops were coming, I heard the sirens. People were shouting and diving into the water, looking for survivors, I guess. So I ran."

"Why'd you run?"

Miguel studied me for a moment after that question, then shrugged. "Seemed the thing to do. I hid out until I dried off, then I hitchhiked to your house. My truck wasn't in your driveway, but there was this old car I think was your yardman's. And another car, looked like a fancy lawyer car."

Yeah, I thought, Jimmie's wreck and Philip's Lexus.

"So, I just cased the neighborhood, and then started thinking where I would have put my truck if I'd been you. The community center seemed a good spot, and, there it was. Like you radioed me a mental message."

"I didn't leave it there for you, I left it there so the cops wouldn't find it at my place and ask me a lot of hard questions."

"Good thinking," he said.

"Why did you tell me to run away?"

"Oh, Lilly, sweet Lilly, I didn't want you in the middle. I didn't want you hurt." Miguel smiled at me, a slow, sensual smile. "Sit," he said, and patted the couch.

I collapsed on the couch next to him. But I didn't smile back. I didn't smile back, sensually or otherwise, because I kept thinking how terribly convenient his stepping away from the boat had been. But if he knew the boat was going to blow up, why invite me to be a witness?

While I tried to make this make sense, Miguel pulled me into another ardent embrace as if I *had* smiled sensually back at him.

While I struggled hard enough to be emphatic, he resisted my resistance until his fingers and his tongue changed my mind. My pulse was so loud in my ears I could hardly hear, and I had definitely stopped thinking.

This time I had my hands under his shirt, and I rubbed my thumbs over his nipples until they hardened. We tumbled farther down into my couch, and before my mind could proffer any more reasons not to—like, say, Philip or the possibility that Miguel was a really bad person—we had our shirts off.

His mouth was making me glad my breasts were free and clear of cloth, and my hands wandered below his beltway and were playfully fingering his zipper. Miguel did something delicious with his tongue and my nipple, and my fingers slipped that zipper down just a tad before my shower-fetish-obsession-thing kicked in, and I wondered if I needed to shower again before we consummated our obvious passion. I mean, before I'd showered for sleeping, not for sex.

And then, there was the possibility Miguel would shower with me.

Obsessing, or fantasizing, or whatever about another shower made me realize that for an apparent fugitive on the run, Miguel smelled—well, not just clean, but powdered and pampered and perfumed in his cleanness. I pulled away from him, not without considerable effort, both mental and physical, and I asked, "Where have you been staying since your boat blew up?"

"Around," he said.

Oh, yeah, I heard that soft tone of his voice and I took one more sniff—sandalwood, and a fine product at that—and deduced that "around" was a woman, and one with good taste in toiletries, and this chilled my ardor enough for me to regain my good sense and my blouse.

"What just happened?" Miguel asked as I buttoned the last button on my shirt.

"There is too much I need to know—"

My front door burst open and Delvon and Jimmie tumbled in, still reeking of bleach, but with an overtone of marijuana and wine. Delvon carried a box of pizza with the lid opened, and tomato sauce ran down his chin.

Thank goodness I had had time to put my shirt back on, even if Miguel hadn't.

"Uh-oh," Delvon said. "Bad timing."

"Perfect timing," I said, knowing full well Miguel would have had me fully naked in another half hour, tops, if he and Jimmie hadn't burst back into my house.

Miguel, perfectly lovely in his shirtless state, stood up and offered his hand to Delvon. "Miguel," he said.

"Delvon," my brother answered, and shook his hand.

"I knows you for the devil you are," Jimmie said, a bit too loud, and poked a rude finger in Miguel's chest.

"I'm just leaving," Miguel said.

"Then put your clothes back on," Jimmie said. "You wants the neighbors talking?"

That ship had pretty much sailed, I figured, what with the earlier scene with Dolly and Delvon duking it out in front of my house.

But Miguel slipped his shirt back on and buttoned it in haste, but not before all three of us took a good look at his chest. Though his build was slender, his stomach was flat and muscled, and his chest was sprinkled with a light fluff of jet black hair. I mean, was this man perfect or what?

Despite Jimmie's hovering and sputtering, I followed Miguel outside. "I need to know how to get in touch with you. And we need to talk. I want to know about Lenora and Angus, and that night your boat blew up—"

"Lilly, I'm a running target. But I'll catch up with you." Then he took off, jogging away down Tulip Street.

A little dazed, I wandered back into my own house, and my own kitchen, where Delvon was eating frozen peas straight from the freezer bag. "Tasty, but a bit chewy," he said.

"I done told you we'd need a second pizza," Jimmie said to Delvon.

"It was an extra large," Delvon said. "You want to call out for another one?"

Jimmie turned back to me. "What you doing with that crazy boy when you got a nice fella like Philip?"

Well, exactly. What was I doing with Miguel?

Or, not doing, as the case seemed to be.

Chapter Twelve

Sherilyn Moody, the good widow of the man who had ended his life facedown in a pond of toxic waste he himself had created, had called me.

Had, in fact, called me twice. And early. And without leaving any message except her private phone number.

This I learned as Bonita gave me the early-morning report and then shifted her gaze to the clock on the wall.

Okay, so, of course I was late to work, what with having to stumble around a stoned airport outlaw, a hungover homeless handyman, and a chirpy juvenile jay on a trail-mix-bar high.

Late though I was, two calls from the former beauty Sherilyn raised my curiosity level a notch. I mean, I doubted she was extending a personal invitation to the funeral of her late husband.

"You sure she didn't leave any message? No hint what this is about?"

"Yes. None."

Of course, calling her back would probably have solved the mystery, but I didn't want to appear unbusy, or eager. In fact, I wanted to make her wait. I wanted her to leave a message that explained why I was supposed to call her back so I could be perfectly prepared. I wanted to deal with her when I was in a better mood—say, five or six higher evolutionary lifetimes from now.

"When she calls back, don't put her through to me until you get a reason," I said, and then fled into my private office, closing the door behind me.

I was desperate to be alone.

But before I could turn around twice, Olivia poked her head in without knocking. "Are you all right?" she asked.

"Sure. And you?"

"I'm all right. I'm very sorry about Angus."

"Me too. He was your friend also."

"Not a friend, not really, he kept to himself. But an admirable environmental soldier."

Being as how Olivia stayed in tune with the local environmental soldiers, maybe I could pry some useful information from her before I ran her off. "So, what was with Angus and Lenora?" I asked the easy question first.

"I'm not really sure. Funny, but I never saw them together."

I nodded.

"Funeral arrangements are up in the air, apparently," Olivia said, "but my conservation group is planning a memorial. I hope you will come."

"Of course." I paused, waiting to see if Olivia would volunteer anything. When she didn't seem likely to do so, I asked her, "Do you know anything about Angus and the explosion?" I trusted Olivia, of course, but decided to keep it just between me and Jimmie, oh, and Philip, that I'd been on the pier the night Miguel's boat blew up, never volunteer anything you might have to deny later having been an early lesson in my career.

"No. Just what I read in the paper," Olivia said. "But it seems strange, maybe suspicious, that he got killed so soon after M. David's murder. Both of them being, you know, involved in that Antheus mine project. Think there's a connection?"

"Yeah. But I can't imagine what, since they were on such diametrically opposed sides of the mine project. Still, it does seem too coincidental," I said. "Detective Josey Somebody apparently thinks that M. David was killed by an enraged former business cohort." Actually, come to think of it, that was my theory; Josey had not offered me any insider theories of her own to amount to much.

"Well, frankly, I'm more concerned with who killed Angus John," Olivia said.

"Maybe," I speculated, "the mine owners blew up the sailboat, hoping to take out both Angus and Miguel and end the local opposition to the permitting process."

"No, I doubt that. Phosphate companies hire lawyers, not killers, to stop environmentalists."

"Yeah, I'm surprised that Antheus hadn't slapped a SLAPP suit on Angus and Miguel. Seems like Antheus had more at risk from Angus's and Miguel's activities than the orange groves. I mean, those protests at the orange groves were last year and old news."

"Well, I wondered about that. But it'd be such bad publicity for Antheus to sue people like Angus and Miguel when part of what the company is doing now is just public relations. You know, 'Trust us, we'll bring jobs and taxes. Phosphate feeds the world.' All that," Olivia said.

"Yeah. I guess." I let the sound of someone, i.e., me, who didn't necessarily want to pursue conversation, hang there, silent in the air.

But as I did, the little gray and white swirls of my cerebrum hummed and twirled to connect the random dots into a straight line.

Antheus didn't want the editorial pages of the newspapers calling them bad sports if they sued people like Angus and Miguel. Also, as a practical matter, Antheus couldn't very well sue anybody under the veggie libel statute because phosphate wasn't a Florida agricultural product like the oranges.

Angus had told me others had been sued by Delilah Groves, and now I wondered about them. "Olivia, the other folks sued for protesting about the gyp waste on the oranges, were they also involved in protesting Antheus?"

"Oh, sure. Same group. For the most part. Well, not a hundred percent, I guess."

"The people who protested the groves, but didn't protest the mine, did they get sued?"

"Er . . . a couple named Susie and Rick, big on food safety. Real nice couple. They didn't get sued. But they aren't involved in fighting Antheus. Why . . ." Olivia redistributed her facial muscles thoughtfully for a moment, and I watched the way her mental processes played across her expressions.

Beating her to what now felt like the obvious punch, I said, "I bet that's what those orange-defamation lawsuits against them were *really* about."

"You mean, like a SLAPP suit, but to shut them up over Antheus and not the oranges?"

"Yeah," I said, nodding in rhythm to my ping-ponging mental functions. "A suit designed to tie up their time and their limited finances so they couldn't keep agitating over the proposed mine. Maybe it didn't really have anything to do with the oranges."

"Why didn't I get sued?"

"Olivia, maybe because your husband is a partner in Sarasota's biggest and best law firm?" Yeah, that made sense. Bullies generally prefer to pick on people who cannot effectively fight back. And Olivia, bless her well-connected heart, could have hurled all of Smith, O'Leary, and Stanley back at Delilah Groves.

"Let me check the corporation papers," I said, "and see who really owns Delilah, if there's a link between it and Antheus, then we can—"

"Oh, let me do that for you. Just point me to a computer and I'll dust off those old paralegal research skills. I can look up the corporation info on LEXIS or Westlaw."

Good deal, I thought, and led Olivia to the central computer in the library, in the process brushing off a law clerk dawdling over the keys. Then I practically skipped back to my office, not entirely sure what effect this potential new discovery had on anything, but sure somehow that it did.

Bonita had my French press full of fresh coffee by the time I got back to my office. And as the coffee further percolated in my brain, I sat down at my desk with firm instructions to myself: Do some actual, billable work for paying clients.

But as I piddled around with my piddling files, my mind kept ricocheting back to the notion that maybe the orange-defamation suit had something to do with Antheus Mines and the big-picture notion at play in the field of the SLAPP suit was to shut Angus and Miguel up about the phosphate mine. And not the oranges. After all, hadn't that man who claimed he owned Delilah Groves said that they shipped most of their oranges up north? Presumably, a handful of Floridians marching with banners and slogans about glow-in-the-dark fruit wouldn't have made the morning paper or the evening network news "up north."

And what in the world was taking Olivia so long to find out who actually owned Delilah Groves? While she was practicing her computer skills, I figured I'd polish my people skills, and I had Rayford Clothier, alleged owner of Delilah, on the phone before Bonita could ask me what I was doing.

"Yeah," Rayford the charmer said, by way of initial greeting.

"Hi. My name is Bunny LeCroy, and I'm with the Better Business Bureau, and I just need a smidge of your valuable time." With just so much perky charm that I almost choked myself, I explained I needed some answers to some very basic questions for the bureau.

Like, hey, are you just a cover for Antheus?

"What do I get out of this?" Rayford said, not at all like an eager businessman seeking goodwill and an expanded local market.

"Oh, I promise your orange groves a prominent mention in our annual citrus publication, which is county-wide publicity. *Free* publicity."

"It'll be sold by then, and full of big, pink houses."

Sold? For more development? Then Rayford the silver-tongued devil really had been trying to defraud me during our first conversation when he wanted a check as a deposit on next year's crop of oranges. Okay, so that made me feel a lot better about my serial lying to the man.

"Well, please, sir, all this is public record. But you'd really be helping me out by answering my questions, saving me the time of digging in those old records."

"You don't listen. The groves are being sold."

"Well, sure, but my boss says to find this out, and as long as you are an operating grove right now, I need to list you in our publication. You don't want to get me in trouble, do you?" I pitched my voice up a tad, trying hard to project over the phone the picture of a young, pretty woman in need of Rayford's kind assistance.

"Yeah. Okay. Sorry. Just having a bad day. What do you need?"

Okay, so he wasn't a total jerk. "First, could you tell me who owns Delilah Groves?"

"Me. I own half. And Plantation, Inc., owns the other half."

"And who owns Plantation, Inc.?"

"That, little darling, I don't know. I just have to deal with their lawyer."

"Oh, and who might that be?" Oh, yeah, like the Better Business Bureau would need that info for its alleged citrus publication. Rayford's long silence told me I'd pushed it too far.

About the time the silence got really awkward, Rayford said, "Listen, my other phone is ringing." And then the line went dead. And I was glad that Smith, O'Leary, and Stanley had invested in that high-techie stuff that blocks others from using caller ID on us.

So, what had I learned? Delilah was being sold, and Rayford was a semijerk, but not all together stupid enough to tell me who his real partner was.

I didn't necessarily feel any closer to answering any of the pressing questions.

Then Olivia burst back into my office, with not even a knock. "Wow," she said. "I can trace an ownership interest in Delilah Groves back to M. David, who also owned fifty-five percent of Antheus. The corporation that owns Delilah has two shareholders, one corporation that owns fifty-five percent of Delilah and an individual. But M. David was the sole shareholder in the corporation that owned over half of the groves."

Oh, huh? I thought, but nodded as if what she had said also appeared in black ink on a chart in front of me and made perfect sense.

"See, M. David owned the controlling interest in the orange grove with just one other guy, but M. David's ownership was cloaked by that privately held corporation, something called Plantation, Inc. A corporation that owns fifty-five percent of another corporation," Olivia said, making it clearer.

"M. David must have made his attorneys very happy, all this incorporation work," I said.

"You're missing the point," Olivia said. "I really do worry that you might have that attention deficit disorder, you know, ADD."

No, I wasn't missing the point, I thought, I was making a joke, forgetting momentarily that Olivia could be as humorless as most lawyers.

"Like you suspected," she said, "the orange-defamation suits were just harassment against Angus John and Miguel. Because Antheus wanted to shut them up about the mine, M. David decided to use Delilah Groves, Inc., as a plaintiff and grind Angus and Miguel up in litigation. That made sense since Angus and Miguel were the ringleaders in the fight against the Antheus Mines. If all their money and time was sucked up in depositions and hearings, Angus and Miguel wouldn't have the energy or the money to keep fighting Antheus. Any litigation pursued hard enough would pretty much do the trick, it wouldn't have to be Antheus that sued them. Plus, if the groves actually got a judgment against them, it could hound them mercilessly, trying to collect it, and basically put those two out of the protest business."

I nodded, thinking it was pretty gracious of me to listen to Olivia as if she were the attorney and I was not. Also I thought that was a pretty clever idea on the Antheus people's part. No doubt M. David's idea.

"A SLAPP suit by proxy. Get the benefits without public outrage. Strategically sound from Antheus's point of view. But probably all for naught," I said. "Angus is dead, and Miguel on the lam. And, Delilah Groves is being sold for big, pink houses."

"It's already being sold?" Olivia asked. "This soon?"

"Yeah. I guess the late M. David's good widow and her new orange-grove partner didn't waste any time on that."

"How do you know it's being sold?"

"I just had a delightful chat with the other owner, Rayford Clothier. Just then."

"Oh. Yeah, that was the other name." Olivia squinted behind her glasses, in deep thought. "I'm still not sure we really know anything that helps."

Well, yeah, that was often typical of lawyerly activities.

"Let's just cogitate on it some more," I said.

"Let me get in touch with the right offices in Tallahassee and see if I can't get a copy of the Delilah corporate bylaws. Don't they have to file those by law?"

I nodded yes, though being a malpractice-defense attorney, the truth was that I was clueless. But the bylaws would be interesting, and who knows?

In the ensuing silence, I began to be acutely aware of the fact that I hadn't really billed anything to a paying client all day. I tapped a pen on my empty time sheet, and Olivia watched the motion.

"I need to let you get back to work," Olivia said.

In short order Olivia said good-bye, and left me to my cold coffee and cogitation.

Naturally, then, the cosmic forces at play in the field of the lawyer had to fling another raw egg at me.

Philip tapped on my window.

"There's a front door, why doesn't anybody use the front door?" I shouted to the empty air. Yelling calmed me down somewhat, so I went through Bonita's office and let Philip inside.

Peeved as I was by these interruptions, I suddenly felt guilty when I looked into Philip's deep black eyes. He was a good man, he loved me, and I had gleefully, albeit briefly, made out shirtlessly on my couch with another man.

While I pushed my shame at bay, Philip said all the nice, normal things one says in greeting. After I returned the favor, Philip got to the point. "The Bradenton police have officially narrowed their investigation into Angus's murder to Miguel as the prime suspect. He's wanted for questioning."

"What? *What?*" Okay, but "what, what?" is better than "ohshitoh-shit." I mean, it was one thing for *me* to wonder about Miguel, my client and make-out buddy, but wholly another to have Officialdom after him.

"My informant in the police department tells me it looks like the explosion that killed Angus on the boat was a primitive, homemade bomb. Forensic evidence at the explosion showed significant traces of ammonium, which naturally led the investigators to believe it was a fertilizer bomb, fresh from terrorism 101 class," Philip said.

Nearly simultaneously, I flashed on Miguel looking more like a potential client for Philip than a future lover for me and those damn receipts I'd taken out of his pickup. The ones showing the purchase of way more fertilizer than a man on a boat had any logical need to buy. Rather than confess to Philip that I was hoarding evidence in a pending murder case, I asked, "How was this bomb ignited?"

"Maybe dynamite, which can be had fairly easily from criminal sources, or plain vanilla gunpowder. Because the bomb apparently went off as Angus was opening the hatch, they suspect some type of a motion-activated device was used to trigger it. Probably something as simple as a clothespin with two wires separated by an insulator attached to a cord on the hatch."

Damn, damn, damn, this was getting worse by the minute. Miguel had receipts for clothespins too.

Philip, oblivious to my mounting distress, explained that the police were zeroing in on Miguel because of an old arrest of his. "He and a relative, an uncle, I believe, used a fertilizer bomb, a smaller one, to blow up an equipment warehouse in the Everglades. Nobody was hurt, but he destroyed an earth-digging machine of some sort. He did some time for it."

"Miguel blew up . . . stuff? When?"

"Nearly twenty years ago. He was young, with no prior record, and that shortened his sentence."

"So, okay, exactly how easy is it to make a fertilizer bomb?" I asked, thinking all of this put the home-and-garden center on the corner block in a new light.

"It's not that easy."

Well, thank goodness for that, I thought.

"It's the ammonium nitrate in the fertilizer that makes the bomb," Philip said. "But bomb-grade ammonium nitrate is regulated by the government and you cannot just walk into a store and buy it like you can fertilizer. Ordinary fertilizer is much denser than bomb-grade ammonium nitrate, so the would-be bomber must first add aluminum, zinc, or potassium sulfate to lower the temperature threshold above which the fertilizer will explode."

In that entire illustrative lesson, one phrase danced in bright red before my eyes: potassium sulfate. Uh-oh. Didn't I have a receipt for that too, taken from Miguel's own truck?

By now, Philip had entered his college-professor zone, and continued with the introductory bomb-building 101 lecture. "Fortunately, not just anybody can get the mixture correct; there's some expertise involved. Add, say, too much zinc or potassium sulfate, and the material is apt to blow up while the would-be bomber is moving it around."

"So, it could be . . . an accident? I mean, Angus. Maybe he . . . just accidentally knocked some over?"

"Maybe, but I doubt it because the sailboat moves with the waves, so it couldn't have been too sensitive. And even if it was an accident, it had to be there on the boat and it had to be treated—your ordinary, untreated fertilizer will not explode, you understand? So regardless, Miguel was up to something, having ammonium nitrate–based fertilizer treated to explode aboard his sailboard. The experts are still trying to reconstruct exactly how it happened. There wasn't much left of the boat."

Or, apparently, of Angus, I thought, feeling sick again.

"Well, what in the world do they think is Miguel's motive? I mean, Angus was his friend and his shipmate. Besides, if you're going to kill somebody, wouldn't you do it without destroying your own place of abode and transportation? I mean, that sailboat didn't come cheap."

Two seconds too late I realized I was being a tad shrill in my sudden defense of Miguel and that Philip was studying me very closely.

"I do not know yet what the suspected motive might be. Why does it matter so much to you that the police consider Miguel the prime suspect?" Philip sounded suspicious.

"He's a client."

A client who had had me half naked on my own couch.

We went back and forth a bit more without actually putting anything new in play until finally Philip said he would come over tonight, and he'd bring a nice wine and some deli food from the Granary. "That is," he added, "if your yardman is not joining you for dinner."

"Actually, Jimmie is staying with me, and so is Delvon, on a temporary basis. It's just until I find them a place of their own."

Philip gave me half of a smile, which I read as some version of "I told you so." After all, this was the man who had accused me of being sweet.

"Then, for the sake of our peace and privacy, I'll pick you up at seven and we will retire to my house," Philip said, so chivalrously out-of-date he forgot I was perfectly capable of driving myself to his house. If I had wanted to go there. But since I did not, I made the excuse of too much work to be romantic, and shoved Philip out of my office.

Once Philip was truly gone, I stood and stared out the window, as if some rhyme or reason might be found by studying the back parking lot of my law building.

But all I came up with was that it certainly was convenient for Angus's killer that Miguel had purchased the raw materials for the bomb. In my heart of hearts, I didn't believe Miguel was a killer. But that was primarily based upon the fact that he was awfully cute and I had the hots for him. And he seemed to be the poster child for love and peace and changing the world via letter writing.

Oh, well, there was that conviction with Uncle Bomb Guy for blowing up Bush-hogs in the Glades. That was definitely a little left of letter writing.

And, I had to remember Miguel handing Angus the sack of groceries and then stepping away from the ship and leading me from the explosion. Awfully, awfully convenient for Miguel.

And that was way too much convenience for coincidence.

Chapter Thirteen

The number one suspect in the murder of Angus John lobbed the ball so firmly into my court that I suspected karmic forces were at play, destined to rob me of any sense of peace and quiet.

That is, Miguel was lurking in the bougainvillea near my car when I left my office in the cool Florida evening. Before I could properly express my surprise, Miguel pulled me into the lush bushes where he was hidden and, grabbing me in earnest, kissed me like we *had* made love the evening before.

"How are you?" he asked, his voice all lovey-dovey tender.

"We need to talk. I've got a lot of questions."

Instead of answering, Miguel kissed me again, slipping his hands inside my blouse. Prime suspect or not, Miguel's fingers made reason leave my head wholly as I pressed into his touch.

Just as I felt like I might rip our clothes off, right there in the shrubbery of my own law office—I mean, how wild would that be?—Miguel pulled away from me, leaving me with tiny trickles of sweat gathering between my legs and a hint of a pant in my breath.

"Meet me at the Peace River Canoe Outpost tomorrow and I'll take you canoeing," he said, as if he'd picked up the wrong page of the script.

Canoeing? In this conflict and chaos? What was he, a Boy Scout on an escape-reality trip?

"That's totally crazy," I said, giving voice to the obvious.

Miguel grinned a toe-curling grin. "I'm an unpredictable type of guy. Come on, let's go canoeing."

But the power of reason had returned to my brain. I didn't lean into him, instead, I snapped, "This isn't summer camp. The police are looking for you. They think you made a fertilizer bomb and killed Angus. We definitely need to have a long chat."

"On the river. Tomorrow."

"No, right now. And, hey, in case you didn't notice, I work for a living. See, that's my office. What I need from you is an explanation. Not canoe lessons."

"Lilly, I want to show you that river, up close and personal. If Antheus puts that mine in, all kinds of toxic crap will drain into Horse Creek and the Peace. That river is a bull's-eye for phosphate waste. I want us to enjoy it, now, so you'll understand what I'm fighting for—that's why I want to take you canoeing."

Suddenly an alternative Miguel motive popped into my brain, trained as it was toward paranoia by too many trials in the free-for-all world of Florida tort litigation.

Maybe Miguel wanted to take me canoeing to kill me and dump me in the river. After all, not only was he was the prime suspect in Angus's murder, but I could testify that he had conveniently turned away from the boat just as Angus went aboard.

But more important, I had the receipts showing Miguel had purchased the raw materials for the bomb that probably killed Angus. I'd been smart enough—or distracted enough—not to have mentioned this to him before. But by now, he'd surely have looked for those receipts to destroy them, and once he noticed they were missing from his glove compartment, he had to figure I was the most logical thief. I mean, I'd had temporary custody of his truck Saturday night.

So, yeah, I might be a kink in Miguel's plans to avoid the death penalty.

"No, I can't get away," I said, hoping I sounded coy and not suspicious. But even as I said that, I knew Bonita could reschedule my paltry little appointments, and that the greatest test of Miguel the Suspect would be to go with him.

I mean, if he tried to kill me, obviously he was a killer.

And if he didn't try to kill me, then maybe he'd give me some answers, and we could figure this out and get him out of trouble.

While I weighed just how much I wanted to know this man's true character versus just how much I did not want to be the cheese in the trap, Miguel kissed me again. But I could tell his mind was already elsewhere. Mine certainly was. Instead of the kiss, my mind was curling more thickly around the notion that if Miguel got me out on the river without any witnesses who could identify him, killing me and dumping me overboard left a lot fewer suspicions directed at him than if he'd choked me in my own house yesterday, where my neighbors routinely watch me like I'm reality TV.

The kicker was, I just had to test this new theory, and in the only way I could think of. So I let him think the kiss convinced me. But what won out was my need to know if he was really a killer. "Okay, let's canoe and talk."

"See you at the Peace, at eight. We should get an early start," he said.

After Miguel left—fled would be a good word, actually—I stood in the bushes for a moment and wondered at the inherent lack of wisdom in becoming bait in my quest to learn if Miguel wanted to kill me to cover up his other murder. Or murders. I mean, M. David was still out there as an unsolved murder.

Clearly, I needed backup.

Chapter Fourteen

If I had my childhood to do over, I'd make my brothers teach me more about the fine art of warfare, gang or military. I mean, yeah, bless their wild country-boy hearts, those guys had taught me to kick and punch and throw a knife and shoot a gun, and run like hell, plus all the other rudimentary basics of a red-dirt childhood. I mean, we could do things with a slingshot and chinaberries that to this day I don't know why we aren't blind in at least one eye. But I didn't learn much about the tactics of war. Troop movements, strategy, keeping a unit in reserve, backup safety plans, and all that sneaky stuff of the cover-your-ass variety.

That is, I was clueless as to the potential stratagems of this backup thing.

It was tricky, this balance between how to provide for my own personal safety but not tip my hand. Okay, I mean I couldn't cradle a .12 gauge or bring a bodyguard and still expect Miguel to either spill his guts or physically confess by shoving me underwater. Nor, given the logistics, could I just have someone hide in the bushes.

So, yeah, backup was a problem.

My first thought was Jackson, I mean, he was the reincarnation of Stonewall Jackson, and he stood tall and wide and knew his weapons. But quickly I realized Jackson would be a tad too obvious. And hard to hide.

Finally, I came to the reluctant conclusion that I had to be my own backup. That is, I'd take my gun. I mean, I had that perfectly usable Glock I'd bought off-the-record when I was in danger from that hippie-woman vintner who'd broken Farmer Dave's heart and driven him to hitchhiking with a burro from the Grand Canyon. Having paid good money, and cash at that, for the gun, I figured I might as well tote it along. Not only did I know how to use it, but Miguel would not expect me to be armed.

But just in case I was miscalculating this whole thing, I wanted somebody to know what I was up to, and so I called Olivia.

After all, if Olivia hadn't brought Angus John into my office as a client, I would never have become involved in any of this. As I spilled my plan to Olivia, I did a bit of heavy editing on my motive. That is, I didn't say my primary goal was to determine if Miguel was a killer by seeing if he tried to kill me. Rather, I emphasized to Olivia that I hoped to convince Miguel to tell me everything he knew about Angus and the explosion.

"I don't think you should go with him, canoeing, I mean," Olivia said.

"What? Why?"

"He's got a temper."

Yeah, but, hey, so what? I had a temper and I didn't blow up my friends or dump people in the Peace River. And I said as much, suddenly eager to defend not only Miguel but the wisdom of my plan.

"Do you remember what happened to the first panther out at the Antheus site?" Olivia asked, in the weary tone of someone starting a long, unhappy story.

"Sure, some son of a bitch shot it."

"Yes. What the newspapers didn't tell, you know how they never follow up on stories, was that it was a female. With kittens."

My stomach did a nosedive at the sudden images leaping up in my imagination. "No. Please don't tell me those kittens were shot too."

"Worse," Olivia said. "They were left to starve."

"Don't tell me any more."

"But you need to know this. It tells you something about Miguel. He found the dead panther, and saw she had been nursing before she was killed. After that, Miguel went about half mad and scaled the wall at M. David's house to raise holy hell with him, accused him of killing it. He did a pretty good job of beating the tar out of him before M. David's bodyguard heard the noise and came in the room and pulled Miguel off him."

"They call the police?"

"Yes, but then after the police hauled Miguel off, M. David declined to press charges. PR problems, probably. Miguel went back into the wilderness and didn't leave until he found the two kittens. He was out there for three days. One kitten was already dead, but he kept the second one alive, and he and Lenora nursed it back to health."

"Where is it now?" I asked, not remembering any baby panthers at Lenora's.

"At Big Cat Rescue in Tampa. Lenora already had a panther, one she and Adam rescued a few years back. There's a lot of government red tape in having a Florida panther, plus the cost and time, and, what with her being sick, she couldn't keep the kitten."

"Adam? The U.S. Fish and Wildlife guy?"

"Oh, yeah. You met him?"

"Barely. He was out at Lenora's when I took Jimmie out there to help her."

"Cool guy. Does a lot of work with Lenora. He takes the panther around to schools, and stuff like that, trying to educate people about them."

While Olivia talked, I realized that I'd never told her about meeting Lenora, or going out there. I didn't even know Olivia knew Lenora, and, yet, Olivia's conversation, like our last one, assumed that we both knew her and we both knew we both knew her. But she didn't learn it from me that I'd met Lenora. That made me wonder if Miguel had told her about me and Lenora. Plus, Olivia clearly knew an awful lot more about Miguel than I did. All of this conspired to make me a tad curious, if not suspicious.

"When was the last time you talked to Miguel?" I asked.

Olivia breathed over the phone for a few minutes. Then she said, "You know, that day in your office."

Somehow, that didn't seem likely. But I let it slide. For now.

"Well, just because he beat up M. David doesn't mean he'll hurt me," I said, paradoxically, I suppose, given that I envisioned the canoe ride as a test of that very theory. "So I'm going to go with him, but, in case I'm wrong, if you don't hear from me by noon, call the sheriff's department," I said, moving my agenda along.

"I'll bring my kayak, paddle nearby, keeping you in my line of vision at all times," she said.

Nice of her to offer, but, see, that was the problem with the backup thing again. If she was there, then Miguel wouldn't have the chance to try and kill me, and I wouldn't gain any insight into his true character. But I had to wordsmith my objections.

"But paddling in tandem would seem too obvious," I said. "I don't want him to know I'm suspicious about him. If you're there, he probably won't open up and talk to me, and I need to know what is going on."

After a modicum of weakening protests, Olivia finally agreed that she would do no more than alert the law if I didn't give her a call by noon. But I knew she wasn't happy about it.

Next, I made a quick call to Bonita to tell her I was taking the day off to go canoeing with Miguel, and that she needed to clear my schedule. After processing her loud sigh as disapproval, I hung up. I mean, I didn't need Bonita to mother me. I was a grown-up professional woman with a closetful of gray and blue business suits and I could skip work and play hooky with a suspected murderer if I wanted to.

Having thus planned my canoe trip, a half hour later I was gleefully washing food in the kitchen when Jimmie bounded in, dangling my spare key in his hand. "I done found that fake-injury plaintiff, that one who is suing me, and I got him on video, jes' sitting on his patio drinking beer. I got me some good film of it."

"That doesn't help," I said. "A man with spinal damage can still drink beer."

Jimmie recited a line of poetry that sounded like something I remembered from high school, about those who sit and wait also serve, and then he assured me he would spend tomorrow and the next days tracking the beer-drinking, faker plaintiff until the man did get something on film showing he didn't have any real injury.

"That would be nice," I said. "Now where's Delvon? Were you at Lenora's preserve today? How's Lenora?"

"Oh, I done forgot," he said, and pulled out a scrap of paper. "This here's a note Lenora done wrote you. She's thanking you, and giving you her home number and telling you where she lives."

"So, I guess you read the note."

"Sure did, that's how come I know what it says. You think I done took up mind reading?"

No, not mind reading, why bother to mind-read when you snooped as well as Jimmie did? I took the note, read it, and pocketed it. Lenora had been profuse in her praise of Delvon and Jimmie. "Seems like you and Delvon are getting a lot of work done out at the bird place."

"Oh, she got more'n birds. And it ain't just work. We done had some fun out there with her and all them critters. She's a great lady. Why, I tell you what, Delvon done fallen in love with that sick woman. I might've falled in love with her myself if'n I hadn't met up with Dolly first."

"You're in love with Dolly?"

"I might be."

"And Delvon's in love with Lenora?"

"He sure is."

"In one day?"

"Sometimes it'll sure hit you like that. Didn't you tell me yourself when you done met Philip the first time, you couldn't say nothing. And I ain't never knowed you not to have something to say. Philip is a real fine man."

"Yes, he is a fine man." And on that point, I wanted to change the subject once again before Jimmie segued back to accusing me of being mean to Philip. "A glass of wine before supper?"

Jimmie's scowl lifted. "I could sure use me some of that good wine." Then he eyed my pile of lettuce, endive, and arugula. "I'm plum saladed out. Could we have cooked-something? Maybe some meat?"

"I've got some sausage I can fix you. Italian sausage."

"I don't care what nationality they is, so long as they ain't salad."

"Sausage it is, then." I bagged my produce for later, and didn't tell Jimmie our sausages were Boca Italian, made out of soy, and if he wondered why I, the vegetarian, was eating them, he didn't ask. He never said another word about Philip, or Miguel, as we ate our soy sausages with some whole wheat spaghetti smothered in a nice, bottled organic tomato sauce from the Granary.

After Jimmie ate every bite, he said, "I know it won't do no good to offer to help you with the dishes, so I'm gonna go over and check up on Dolly."

And he did. Leaving me to disinfect the kitchen and plan my canoe trip with a man who might want to be either my murderer or my lover.

Chapter Fifteen

Where to hide my gun and what to wear took equal top billing the next morning.

This was tricky. The gun had to be out of sight, but handy. And clotheswise, I had to find a balance between what was sexy and what revealed too much skin for too much sun exposure. I settled on a tight blue tank top, with a see-through lacy white blouse worn loose and tied at my waist over the tank, and a pair of short cotton shorts. Yeah, that left a lot of skin out for the gamma-beta-UVH-whatever-devil rays of sun to fry, but after all, that's why I'd twice coated myself in sunscreen.

Clothing settled, I moved on to gun control—I decided a cooler made more sense than a backpack, and who takes a purse canoeing? In nothing flat, I'd packed a small cooler with Save the Forest trail mix bars, Handi Wipes, bottled water, my still-unused Glock, extra sunscreen, and big chunks of that fake, blue ice stuff.

Then in a fit of something or other, I changed my clothes to a nice, thin-knit white shirt with three-quarter sleeves and a pair of loose cotton Capri pants with a Hollywood waist that would leave me freer to paddle. Not as sexy, but more practical.

When I heard Jimmie in the shower in the guest bath, I wrote him a note reminding him to feed Rasputin and cut the grass, and left.

Miguel was already at the canoe outpost, and I parked a discreet distance from him, and fairly trotted up to him, toting the cooler with the gun I hoped I didn't need. We hugged, but his hug was like I was his second cousin at a reunion, not like I was the soon-to-be new lover. When I sniffed him, I caught that lovely touch of sandalwood. "You smell good," I said, and hugged him again. I let my hands play around a little, not too naughty-girl, but enough to check for a reaction. He pressed against me, and his hands got to playing a little. When he slipped his hands down inside the loose waist of my Capri pants and cupped my lower buttocks at the same time he pressed his own chest against mine, the part of my brain that did risk-benefit analysis simply shut down. I forgot the whole murder-test motive, and wondered instead if we could skip the canoe thing and find a hotel. I'd have to shower off all the damn sunscreen first, though.

But then he pulled away.

Jeez, but that boy was a tease.

"Why don't I wait out here while you go in and rent a canoe. Here, I'll give you the money." Miguel pulled out his wallet and handed me some bills. Half panting, I took the cash and composed myself back down from heat and lust to business casual. Then, I wondered briefly about Miguel's ready-cash supply. I mean, that billfold looked pretty stuffed—like, maybe, someone who had planned in advance for not going home the night he blew up his boat and also his best friend. But, I didn't want to alert him to my suspicions, so instead of interrogating him about his money, I asked, "Why can't you go rent a canoe? Or come with me?"

"I don't want to give an ID. Like I told you yesterday, I'm a running target. Harder to hit."

Okay, a tad melodramatic, and I couldn't imagine why on earth one would have to provide a picture ID to rent a canoe even in this post–9/11 security-hysterical world, but on the off chance Miguel was right, and since the police were looking for him, I could see his point about not flashing a driver's license.

I also thought, nice touch if he doesn't want anyone seeing him with me. You know, eliminate witnesses.

My lust and my paranoia brawled with each other a bit in my head, but finally my need to know won out over both. I felt supremely confident in my ability to defend myself, especially with that Glock in the cooler.

And, at the moment, with my own skin still on low sizzle from his recent fondling of it, I really did not think he was a killer.

But I had to find out.

So, okay, I agreed to go inside and rent the canoe, walking away in what I hoped was an enticing saunter.

It did cross my mind that the last time I'd agreed to get on a boat with this man, I'd nearly gotten blown up.

Chapter Sixteen

As it turns out, you do need a picture ID to rent a canoe and I was gearing up to make a Big Deal out of this, I mean, come on, looking every bit the terrorist that I was, I was going to what? Crash into Bubba Joe's fence in a rented canoe and single-handedly end civilization as we knew it? But the man behind the counter gave me one of those "Hey, lady, you want to make an issue of this, we don't have to rent the canoe to you" responses, so I caved because I had a bigger mullet to fry than some counter jockey.

Just as I was walking out of the canoe-rental place, I spotted Jimmie coming in. Jimmie was no doubt trying to be inconspicuous, but he was lugging the video camera with him and panting as if the camera weighed a hundred thousand pounds, and he was wearing one of Delvon's hand-painted, red-poppy T-shirts and stood out like Michael Moore at a thousand-dollar-a-plate Republican dinner.

Of course I wondered what in the hell he was doing at the canoe outpost, but after a moment of pondering my possible reactions, I decided it was easiest to pretend not to see him, just as Jimmie apparently pretended he hadn't seen me see him.

After all, having him around might not be a bad idea, so long as Miguel didn't know it.

On that note, I practically sprinted back to my car to get my cooler and headed toward the stacks of canoes, while Miguel hovered off to the side, no doubt trying not to draw attention to himself.

"Picnic," I said, when he nodded toward the cooler with a quizzical look. I put it in the center of the canoe we selected, and eyed the paddles. I wouldn't mind having a few germ-killing Handi Wipe moments with them, but was afraid if I opened the cooler, Miguel would spot the Glock.

I decided it was better to risk the unclean handles, and we pushed the canoe off into the river and set down the Peace to paddle. Hopefully, I would find out exactly what Miguel might know about Angus being blown up, what sandalwood-soaked sweetie he was staying with, and, of course, the key question of the morning: Was Miguel a killer?

"So, okay. Where are you staying? What do you know about Angus and the explosion? Why did you—"

"We can talk later," Miguel said. "For now, enjoy the river."

We went another round before I grumped internally a bit to myself. I didn't want to wait for answers, and I couldn't even watch Miguel's beautiful body as he paddled because I was sitting in the front of the canoe.

So there I was, testing the warranty on my sunscreen, a few miles down the river, when I inhaled and looked around. And looked around again. The water was tea colored, rich with the tannic acids from the leaves of the live oaks that shaded the banks, their gray roots pushing out into the river and hiding small zoos of live things. Silently, we canoed into the center of the river, clear of the trees, out where we were open to the sun and the morning breeze. Overhead, two red-shouldered hawks circled. A moment later, I spotted an anhinga perched on a cypress tree, its wings spread out to the sun to dry, and lifted my paddle to point it out, as if somehow Miguel had gone blind.

Miguel was right. This was worth saving.

The current had us now, and we let the river take us. Lulled as we were by the morning and the river, we drifted until we spotted another canoe ahead of us, with a red-faced man and a preteen kid type. They were yelling stuff and laughing, over the sounds of a portable radio.

Instinctively I reached for my paddle and matched Miguel's increased paddling to try to get past them and all the ruckus they were creating on the quiet river.

At that point the Peace River ran through a cow pasture and a Brahman bull was watering at the edge of the river. Miguel and I paused for a moment to admire the creature. The bull was large, and regal, with a big hump on its back, and serious horns. While we studied it, the bull eased himself into the river and began swimming, as if to cross over to the other side. As the animal approached the loud people's canoe, the kid threw a pop can at it. Then the man chunked something at it that hit its broadside with a clear thunk.

"Damn fools," Miguel said, and stopped paddling. I turned around to stare at him as he started taking his shoes off.

"What are you doing?"

"That bull is going to dump that canoe. I'm going after them."

And just as if the bull had understood perfectly what Miguel had said, it tipped the canoe with the tops of its horns while I watched. The loud people weren't laughing anymore. I didn't feel so good myself.

Miguel dove into the Peace, and quickly grabbed the boy as he floundered in the river. As I watched Miguel struggling in the water with the now-frantic youngster, I looked for the red-faced man, and saw him swimming awkwardly, but steadily, with one hand up in the air, holding something. Since he clearly wasn't drowning, I turned back to watch the Brahman bull. It continued to cross the river, having, I suppose, made its point and lost interest.

Miguel, apparently gauging the distance to our canoe as shorter than to the drifting flipped canoe, or the shore, swam, dragging the screaming and struggling kid—hey, didn't he get it? Miguel was rescuing him?—toward me.

In a swift and jarring throw, Miguel pitched the kid in the canoe behind me. "Having fun yet?" he asked me.

But Rescued Kid, the one who was not going to get his Canoe Scout ribbon out of this trip, took one look at us and started flailing about as if Miguel and I were recruiters for Hannibal Lector, and the next thing I knew, splash. Damn, the kid and I were in the river.

Miguel came up from the water cussing me, as if somehow this was entirely my fault. "Damn it, Lilly, don't you even know how to canoe? Why didn't you—"

Why didn't I what? Throw the kid out of the canoe? Alter the nature of gravity? But before I could retort, Miguel grabbed the kid with one hand, and one-handedly swam back to the bank of the river, where the red-faced man had finally gotten to shore.

Abandoned by the man who seemed less and less like my next lover, I tried to grab my now-capsized, though carefully packed cooler—I mean, it had all that bottled water, our snacks, and my gun. But the cooler was too heavy and it sank with great speed and gusto and I didn't feel like diving to the bottom of the Peace River to rescue it. Yeah, I mean, sure, I'd spent a lot of money on that Glock, but God knows what was at the bottom of that river, and I didn't want to inhale it, taste it, or feel it. I let the cooler stay sunk. Besides, our paddles were floating out to sea, and it seemed the better part of valor to snag them instead of the bottled water and weaponry, so I did.

So, yeah, spank me, but I was just a little pissed off that Miguel had yelled at me, then forsaken me and the capsized canoe. But this was also an opportunity to show him just how clever and independent I was. In no time at all, I had the canoe right side up, the paddles tossed into the boat, and I climbed in, not, perhaps, too gracefully, but I didn't think anybody was scoring this, and I paddled the canoe toward Miguel and the loud, wet people on the shore. Just as proud as if I were Catwoman, I beached the canoe and climbed out into the pasture.

Everybody on the narrow river beach stopped screaming long enough to turn and stare at me. At first I thought it was because I so clearly deserved a merit badge, not chastisement by Miguel for the canoe spilling. But then, I watched where Red Face's eyes landed, and it occurred to me that my thin white blouse, now soaking wet, was essentially see-through. I knew the boy-child was all right when I noticed that his little pervert, preteen eyes had noticed this too. Good thing I'd worn a bra, though not much of one.

The mutual male fascination with my thin bra didn't last long. I guess it's more fun to yell at each other than stare at a wet woman in a white shirt.

Red Face waved a cell phone at us like a weapon—I guess that was what he had decided to rescue from his canoe instead of the boy or the radio—and started punching in numbers, shouting, "The law needs to put that bull down. Shoot that animal. Kill it. It's a dangerous beast."

Before the man completed his dialing, Miguel snatched the phone from him and threw it into the river. Red Face then screamed at Miguel, who tried to explain to him, though he was clearly in no mood to listen to anyone, that the bull was right where it was supposed to be, doing what it was supposed to be doing, and that it was them throwing things at the animal that had caused the problem.

"I'm gonna call the law out on you too," Red Face said. "Throwing away my cell, why that thing cost sixty dollars. You got no right."

So, yeah, obviously Red Face lacked any semblance of sense or class, what with threatening Miguel with the police for throwing away his cell phone, and this despite the fact that Miguel had gone to considerable effort to help his kid and to educate the man about the root cause of the trouble, that being, them.

Hmm? Threatened with legal action for trying to save people from their own foolish, destructive behavior. This was a perfect analogy to the plight of the environmentalists, and, despite the fact that the tannins in the river had surely eaten away my sunscreen and I was standing totally exposed to the deadly rays of Florida sun, I started to pontificate on this observation. "You know, having Miguel arrested when what he did was to save your kid and explain to you about the abuse of large animals, that's kind of like when Green Peace was prosecuted for trying to save the rain forest—I mean, it's punishing the do-gooders. And—"

Miguel turned, glared at me, and said, "Shut up."

"The hell I will," I shouted back. Nobody tells me to shut up. I mean, except a judge during Official Courtroom Proceedings. So despite the fact that I was standing on the shore of a river many wet miles from my car with a red-faced angry man, my red-faced angry date, and a recently hysterical kid, and that the Brahman bull was out there somewhere, I added to the bedlam by yelling back. "I can talk as much and as loud as I damn well please," I tossed out there for the general benefit of no one.

By then, everybody, including Miguel, was shouting at everybody. Yelling begets yelling, after all. For an unpleasant and uninvited moment, scenes exploded in my head from my childhood, where everybody shouting at everybody was as common as nobody taking the garbage out. While I shook off my flashback, Miguel stopped verbalizing his displeasure and stomped toward our beached canoe. Then Miguel hopped into our canoe and started pushing it off the sand with one of the paddles I had carefully thought to rescue.

Thinking better the devil I already knew than the stranded loud people, I jumped in after Miguel, just as he steered the canoe into the water. I was relieved when he turned the canoe around and began paddling back to the outpost. Especially since my backup, that is, my Glock, was at the bottom of the river.

Okay, okay, so Miguel was not as peace and love as I had first supposed. But as my brother Delvon had once told me when we were teenagers busily busting out all of the football coach's windows because he'd punched a fat kid in gym, even Jesus had trashed a temple and yelled at his mother.

Since we were both paddling like we were in an Olympic event, it didn't take us long to get back to the canoe outpost. We jumped out on the sandy bank by the canoe-rental building and dragged the canoe back toward the drop-off rack before I said, "I'm going to say a few things, important things, now. I don't think it will spoil the moment."

Miguel ignored me.

"You're in a lot of trouble, as far as I can see," I said. "Tell me what's going on and maybe I can help."

"I don't see how," he said. "You seem pretty useless to me."

"Screw you, you can piss up a green rope," I shouted loud enough to draw stares, forgetting all those years Bonita and Jackson had spent making me into a well-mannered sophisticate. I turned my back on him and stomped and squished in my wet shoes up the landing and into the outpost and up to the front desk and reported that a kid and his dad were stranded upstream after their canoe capsized. I did my best to describe the location.

"What's your name?" the desk man asked, and stared at my wet white shirt and what was beneath it before he finally started writing down notes. Fortunately, it was a different man from the one who had earlier demanded my photo ID.

Thinking of the potential liability, or criminal charges—what? Willful destruction of cell phone? Canoeing with wanted police suspect? Or at the very least some extremely unpleasant encounters generated by the red-faced man—I said, "Sunny McDemis," and I recited Sunny's office number from memory, thinking that that would at least ruin one day in the life of Jimmie's snide insurance adjuster. Then I stomped out toward my car.

While I was leaning against my Honda taking off my wet shoes, Miguel came up to me, still carrying his canoe paddle.

"Aren't you supposed to turn that in?" I said, eyeing the paddle and speaking in a definitely snippy tone.

"Don't you get it?" he yelled at me, and shook the paddle near my face. "Don't you fucking get it at all?"

"Get what?" I yelled back, not one to be easily outshouted thanks to my early childhood training.

"It's all dying, going to hell, and I can't save any of it. Nothing I do, *nothing,* I can't save any of it. Not a damn piece of it, not the Glades, not the Peace. Hell, they're even fucking up the Suwannee River, mining the water for Miami. Between the doughfaces and the greedy motherfuckers, it's all but all gone."

It?

Florida? I wondered, studying Miguel's face closely.

"The Everglades aren't even there anymore, just some dried-up little park with boardwalks and airboat rides for tourists," he yelled, but a notch lower on the shouting index. "Gone. Dead. And they're going to dump that gyp shit in the Gulf and finish it off. The coral reefs are dying, the whole fucking Gulf is dying. Do you know what it takes to kill an eco system that big?"

Then he gulped air, and, holding the canoe paddle like a baseball bat, he raised it like a weapon.

I flinched, and jerked backward, thinking my head was the target.

But Miguel spun away from me and smashed the oar into the concrete edge of a nearby picnic table with a splintering whack that definitely commanded my attention.

Yeah, and maybe some attention from the folks loitering about.

Miguel flung the piece of the oar he still held at the table, and I saw something like a shudder pass through his shoulders.

I did not want to face his hard-core rage. What I wanted was to leave. But I stood my ground and waited.

The thing was, for once, I totally got him. Like Olivia, in love with her sweet, little, blue birds, the scrub jays, Miguel loved something that was doomed. The whole damn natural state of Florida. And I thought of my grandfather, for once sober as a Methodist minister, out in the backyard, firing off every gun he owned, and being a red-dirt Georgia farmer, that was a goodly number, blamming at the stars and the sky and the dark clouds and the half-moon the night the cancer finally finished eating up my grandmother. He kept shooting and raging until finally Delvon and I tackled him and threw him in Delvon's truck and got him away from there, not five minutes ahead of the deputy sheriff the neighbors had called on him.

Later, I asked my grandfather what he was shooting at, and he said, "I was trying to kill God. Stupid, huh?"

Yeah, stupid. Like blowing up Bush-hogs, trying to save the Glades.

But waste and destruction and dying can make us angry.

And anger can damn sure make us stupid.

Finally, Miguel turned back around toward me. Over his shoulder I could see a few stragglers watching him. Luckily, nobody official was running up, and nobody appeared to be punching in 911 on their cells.

He glared at me, and his expression scared me.

"Look, they think I blew Angus up."

"Why would you possibly want to kill Angus? He was your friend." I tried to sound calm, even soft, as if I were soothing a distraught child, which maybe I was.

"I didn't kill him, my God, Lilly, I loved that man like a brother. He was a pissed-off little genius when it came to fighting the phosphate mines."

I thought about the fake cat paws, and nodded. Yeah, he had been a pissed-off little genius.

"But I, ah, blew up some . . . some sugar grower's machinery in the Glades. I destroyed their bulldozer and a Bush-hog. We were careful not to blow up anything where people or animals could get hurt."

"How'd you blow them up?" Though, of course, thanks to Philip's resourcefulness in having a high-quality snitch in the Bradenton PD, I knew the basic answer, I thought I'd fish around in Miguel's confession and compare what he'd tell me with what I already knew.

"Fertilizer that we did stuff to so it would be more explosive. My uncle, my mom's brother, taught me how to do it. He was . . . ah, a low-bid demolition guy. Did a lot of . . . building . . . work in Miami."

Uh-huh. He was an arsonist and outlaw bomb guy, I translated.

Then I began thinking like a lawyer, which is, after all, what I am, and I wondered how I could exclude evidence of Miguel's past incarceration during the orange-defamation trial—if we ever had a trial—because, to a trial attorney, something isn't necessarily a fact unless you can prove it in court. Then I realized the more immediate need was to keep Miguel out of jail right now.

"You need help. If I can't help you, Phillip Cohen can. He is an excellent criminal-defense attorney." Sidestepping mentally the fact that having my lover defending a guy I'd made out half naked with on my couch might not be the best idea I'd ever had, I said, "Miguel, please. Follow me home. We'll call Philip Cohen. He's the greatest criminal-defense attorney in the whole state. He'll represent you. I'll see to that. And I'll tear up those receipts."

Miguel grabbed me by both of my arms. "What are you talking about?"

Oops.

I hadn't meant to say that. Though I thought Miguel had surely already figured out I had taken the receipts from his truck, on the off chance he was stupid or something, I hadn't seen any point in highlighting the fact that I possessed evidence he might be a bomb murderer.

Sometimes my mouth just works faster than my brain.

With a tight grip on my arm, Miguel shook me. "What receipts?"

Suddenly I was glad there were other people milling around.

"Take your hands off of me," I said, deliberately lowering my voice and pacing the words.

He dropped his hands. "Sorry, Lilly, I'm sorry. But, what receipts?"

"The, er, the . . ." Where was my famous ability to conjure up alt-realities out of small factual details when I needed them?

But then I decided to tell him the truth, and check for reactions. After all, he would hardly choke me in plain view of people who looked like good potential witnesses. "The receipts for fertilizer and stuff. Diesel and clothespin and potassium something."

"Where'd you get them?" Miguel's face was a perfect blank screen.

"In your truck. In the glove compartment."

"They aren't mine," he said, and I took careful note of his eyes, which were angry, and I simply could not tell if he was lying or not.

"Look, this is over my head," I said. "You really need to speak with Philip."

"I've got to go." Miguel turned and started jogging away from me.

"Wait," I said, and ran after him. "How do I get in touch with you? Where are you staying? You're still my client, you know. About those receipts, I can't testify against you. Wait."

Miguel stopped and faced me, giving me that look again, the one that scared me. "I'll catch up with you somewhere down the road."

Funny, it sounded just a tad like a threat.

But threat or no, with that, Miguel left me standing at high noon in a parking lot with a questionable coat of sunscreen melting into my burning eyeballs and some potentially damning receipts in my desk drawer.

And a whole new peek at Miguel's soul.

"Damnation to hell," I said, using my grandfather's favorite curse. Then, ducking the failure of the whole stupid canoe trip and the burning UV rays, I crawled into my little Honda, squishing river water in the seat. From inside my car, I did the only thing left that made any sense at the moment. I called Olivia on my cell phone and reported to her that I was safe and that Miguel had driven off. Then I turned and drove home.

When I got to my house, there was no sign of Jimmie or Delvon, and so I took a shower, dressed, fed Rasputin a trail mix bar and a handful of sunflower seeds, ate some yogurt and blueberries, and headed to the law office.

I'd hardly gotten inside the back door before Bonita was telling me that Sherilyn Moody had called again. I sighed. Bonita sighed.

"What did she want?"

"She will not say. You really need to call her back."

"You really need to get her to tell you why she wants to talk to me," I said, a little snappy at the edges what with my futile but still taxing morning.

"The most efficient way to do that would be for you to call her. She will not tell me why she is calling. I've tried."

Bonita smiled softly, patiently, not at all mad at me for my bad manners, which, of course, immediately made me ashamed of my snappishness.

After making nice, I retreated into my office.

Officially, so far my day sucked. While I was sitting behind my desk contemplating the details of that assessment, and fuming over the lost cooler, the lost Glock, the lost opportunity to learn something from, or about, Miguel, I heard the soft voice of Henry Platt, the insurance adjuster who was courting Bonita, drifting through my closed door. I have uncannily sharp hearing, and I stood up and tiptoed closer to eavesdrop on Henry as he attempted to woo Bonita in her little cubbyhole office. At the first reasonably polite moment, I planned to lure Henry into my office on business. My business.

After all, although Henry's current obsession was convincing Bonita to marry him, he was still my friend and a steady hand at referring medical-malpractice cases for me to defend. He'd obviously come by to see Bonita, so I would give them a few minutes alone before I went out to greet him and renew my request for an Official Big Case. I needed a med-mal case, and he was just the man to give it to me.

Judging that he'd had enough courting time, I sprang out of my office and watched him flinch. "Good afternoon, Henry," I said, my face beaming.

"Er, um . . . hello. I, er . . . got your message. About getting . . . giving . . . assigning you a med-mal case."

"Good. So you've got one coming down the pike for me?"

After his usual start-and-stop conversational style, Henry said that his office had had two incident notices from their doctor clients filed in the last few months that he was watching closely, but so far no new suits had been filed.

"One of the incident reports mentioned a badly blotched face-laser procedure. I believe . . . think . . . that is, my professional opinion is"—he smiled at Bonita as if he was particularly proud of coming up with that last phrase—"is that one will surely . . . maybe . . . more than likely . . . end up in litigation."

A blotched face laser? Yeah, that'd be worth a couple years of discovery and pretrial billings and high stepping, but blessedly without the emotional drama of anybody actually dead. "What happened?" I asked, my interest definitely piqued.

"The plastic surgeon was using lasers to, er, erase . . . er, smooth out . . . this woman's wrinkles and he says . . . er, claims, the woman didn't follow postop orders."

"I'm sure her attorney will have a different story if she sues. How bad does she look?"

"The doc admits, er, doesn't admit, er, but, er, says, er, reports . . . She looks pretty bad."

"Like a really bad sunburn that peeled and left the skin three or four different shades of red, pink, and blistered?" I asked, remembering Ms. Moody's face at the antiphosphate rally.

"Yes, something like that."

"What's the woman's name?" I mean, really, how interesting would it be if I ended up defending a doctor Mrs. Moody ended up suing? There was a karmic circle in there someplace.

Naturally, Henry couldn't remember the client's name, though he did remember it was a woman.

But come on, how often could that happen? Well, in Sarasota, where plastic surgery ads in the newspaper far outnumber actual news stories, maybe it happened more than once. Still, I thought it had to be Mrs. Moody. "Go, scoot, look it up and call me," I said to Henry, prompting him to promise to call me as soon as he had that information.

Bonita walked Henry to the back door, and returned.

"So, what's with you and Henry?" I asked.

"So, what is with you and Philip?" Bonita asked.

"Same old, same old," I said.

"There is a story in the newspaper you might want to read," she said, effectively ending our gossip as she handed me the *Sarasota Herald-Tribune*.

Back inside my own office, I laughed out loud when I read the lead story in the B section announcing to the readership at large that a second panther at the Antheus proposed phosphate-mine site had been confirmed by Fish and Wildlife federal agents. This, the story proclaimed, though without any attribution, had apparently put a stop to the forward progress of the proposed mining permits for Antheus. Protected species, protected habitat, et cetera, et cetera. Then the article superficially reviewed the endangered-species regulations and habitat protection and such things as I'd learned from Miguel and Angus about the Florida panther, and the efforts to save it from extinction. But I wondered why the article didn't mention the first panther, the one someone had gut-shot and pitched out by the public road next to the locked gate to the Antheus property.

Still, the important thing was that the findings by Official People had at least temporarily put a stop to the mining-permit process. And rallied the animal lovers to the cause.

And, I thought, this time nobody can kill the panther, because it wasn't real.

While I was basking in the glory of thinking I had done something that was useful in a cosmic sense, Henry called me.

"Er, that woman, the one with . . . the blotched . . . the face—"

"Henry, just tell me her name."

"Er, it's, her name is, she's . . . Sherilyn Moody."

Aha.

I knew it. Mrs. M. David Moody, of all people. That's why the good widow had looked so bad at the phosphate meeting.

"Promise me, Henry," I said, trying to keep the eagerness in my voice under some control, "that you will refer that case to me. Promise me it's my case."

Henry chirped, "You're first on my list."

We made the usual nice, nice and then I transferred him to Bonita so they could finish their chat that I had interrupted when I sent him to his office to get Sherilyn's name, and I hung up my phone.

Oh, good. Plastic-surgery malpractice. I'd never had one of those before, and it would be exactly the kind of tricky, high-profile, and high-billing case I needed. So, yeah, call me a trial attorney, but I felt a surge of pure excitement.

But as I leaned back in my red leather chair with a sense of anticipation, an eerie feeling went thunk in my gut and my brain.

Mierda. I knew why Sherilyn Moody had been calling me.

And, no doubt, why M. David had my firm brochure and a note to make an appointment.

Not an appointment for him. But for her.

I stewed on it for a minute or two, hopped up, stuck my head out of my office and stared at Bonita until she put down the phone and gave me a worried look. "Don't, under any circumstances, none, let Sherilyn Moody into my office, or put her through on my phone."

Bonita nodded, and I ducked back into my office, swallowed the unpleasant sense of déjà vu narrowly averted, and made myself get back to work.

Before I knew it, Bonita came in to remind me that I had a hearing in Bradenton tomorrow morning, and to say good night. A few minutes later Jackson stuck his head in to say good night, and a few minutes after that I packed up the hearing file to rememorize in the comfort of my own sanctuary, and I went home.

Though Rasputin greeted me raucously, there was no sign that Jimmie had been in the house since he had left shortly after me that morning. Worrying about Jimmie, I fed Rasputin and fixed myself some salad.

By the time I had finished eating, there was still no Jimmie, and this increased my concern threefold. I chided myself for being anxious about him. After all, he was not my teenage son. He was a competent adult, one old enough to be my grandfather, and presumably able to take care of himself.

Thus, telling myself Jimmie was just off on an old-man frolic, I sat down with my hearing file, studied it until I could recite the important aspects backward, and glanced at the clock. Late. And still no Jimmie. So, I called Dolly. After she assured me that she had not seen or heard from him all day, I hung up and worried in overdrive. Finally I called the police department's nonemergency number, and an officer asked a few polite questions and then informed me that grown men frequently stayed out late by themselves, and I shouldn't worry, and I most assuredly shouldn't call him back.

Thinking Jimmie might be with Delvon, I found the scrap of paper with Lenora's phone number. When I called it, Delvon answered, said something that made no sense whatsoever, and then assured me that he had not seen Jimmie all day.

While I wondered where Jimmie was, Delvon said, "I'm gonna get my hair cut."

"Cut your hair?" I asked, not really completely listening to him.

"Yep. There's this organization in Tampa that takes donations of real human hair and makes wigs out of it."

"Why would you want somebody wearing your hair?"

"For Lenora. So that someone could use my hair to make a wig for Lenora. How do you think she would look as a redhead?" he asked.

"Fine, I guess. I don't know. What color was her hair before it"— okay, the truth is the truth—"all fell out?"

"Why, she was a redhead."

With Delvon, conversation is sometimes like that, and I decided just to let it go. But I was thinking that Jimmie was surely right, that Delvon must be deeply in love with Lenora. After all, Delvon had had long hair since he was eight years old. He had mostly grown it long because no one ever bothered to take him to the barbershop. But when the principal of Bugfest Elementary had called our home and made a ruckus about the fact that Delvon's hair was swinging below his shoulders, the long hair had become a conscious choice. Though our parents had not been concerned enough to defend Delvon against plans to expel him, or to cut his hair forcibly, my grandmother dragged my grandfather down to the principal's office to stick up for Delvon and his hair. Before they got to the principal's office, Grandmom had gone into the social studies room and yanked off the portrait of Jesus that hung there on a wall—separation of church and state had never played big in my little Georgia hometown—and

Grandmom toted the picture of Jesus into the principal. As if the principal was blind, Grandmom had pointed out to him that Jesus had long hair.

The upshot of that scene was basically that Delvon got to keep his long hair, and he'd had it long ever since, except once when it was forcibly cut while he was incarcerated in the county jail. That he was thinking about cutting his hair so that it might be made into a wig for Lenora, bald as she was from the chemotherapy, warmed my heart suddenly for not just Delvon, but for the potential of the whole human race. I don't usually feel warm and fuzzy about human potential. But there you had it, Delvon could do that.

Thus, perfectly comfortable with the idea that my brother Delvon and the new love of his life were doing about as well as they could under their particular set of circumstances, I hung up.

That night I was unable to sleep and kept listening for Jimmie.

After all, the world was a big and evil place for one old man to get lost in.

Chapter Seventeen

Still no Jimmie the next morning.

My anxiety was now a persistent kick in the gut, which I fueled with an extra cup or two of coffee, just in case I wasn't high-strung and heartburned enough.

Where coffee is concerned, I have no learning curve.

Ditto, worry.

But, regardless of the missing status of Jimmie, I had my hearing in Bradenton, the county seat of Manatee County, and had to be about my official, professional day. After promising Rasputin I'd come home at noon to feed him another trail mix bar, I had gathered up my purse, briefcase, and keys when the front door swung open.

"Hey, Lady," Jimmie said, as if he had not been out all night, leaving me to wonder in what ditch his dying body lay.

"Where have you been?"

"Out. Working. Busy." He held up the video camera. "I done been tracking that jerk who's suing me, jes' like you wanted me to."

If I didn't leave now, I'd be late for my hearing, and being late is something I never am at hearings. It puts you on the defensive from the get-go and pisses off most judges. "Jimmie, I have to go. *Right now.* I'll be home this evening. Can you feed Rasputin today?"

"Can do," he said. "I'll get that grass cut out back too."

"Good," I said, and slammed out my front door, glad that at least Jimmie was alive and well.

The hearing was one of those where basically all I had to do was show up and identify myself to win. My opposing counsel was an idiot who had failed to comply with the pretrial requirements for suing a physician, and all I had to do was establish that fact in black and white, recite the Florida statute on point, and listen to opposing counsel whine and babble in response, and rebut with a choice Florida Supreme Court case on point and in my favor.

After winning, I ducked out and got into my little Honda and sat for a moment with my bucketload of curiosity. Being in Bradenton and therefore already in Manatee County, I decided to find Josey at the Manatee County Sheriff's Office and see if I might convince her to provide me with some information.

Naturally, I arrived at the sheriff's office just as Josey was preparing to leave for lunch. Notwithstanding my coming in as she was going out timing, Josey seemed as interested in talking to me as I was to her, and invited me to join her for lunch. "But, I warn you, I have to go home and take care of all of my cats."

"How many cats do you have?" I asked, thinking she had overemphasized the plural a tad much.

"Only four," Josey said. "Though I'm cat-sitting for a fifth."

Oh great, cat-hair soup for lunch, I thought. Still, I wanted the chance to talk with Josey about M. David's murder, plus anything she might know about Angus John's murder. Yeah, okay, I really wanted to talk to her about Miguel. And after all, Josey might be more talkative in her own house than she would be at the sheriff's office, so I accepted her invitation to ride home with her.

After a ride with Josey in her official Manatee County car, we arrived at a small house in the old historic Wares Creek neighborhood. Small, but quaint, or maybe even funky, with a yard full of native plants, hibiscus, citrus, mango, and banana trees. A spray of fuchsia bougainvillea all but blocked the carport, built in the backyard in an old-timey fashion. A regular fruit salad growing in her yard, I thought rather enviously, as I ducked under an aggressive banana frond on my way up the front steps toward a bright red door, set against fading gray paint on what I bet, given the apparent age, that being old, of the house, was actually real cypress wood.

As soon as we went inside the house, we were assaulted by cats. It certainly seemed to me that there were more than five of them, but perhaps this was an illusion created by their constant movement and the free-floating swirls of cat hair they produced as they tromped through the house. Josey introduced each cat to me by its name, which I didn't even pretend to absorb, and showed me that the cats could actually do tricks.

"Roll over, Cleo," Josey said, and an orange tiger rolled over.

"Give me five, Bailey," Josey said, and a gray tabby stood on its back legs and patted the air with its right front paw.

That was actually pretty cute, I had to admit. "I didn't think you could teach a cat to do tricks."

"Of course you can," Josey said. "Cats are the smartest animals, next to pigs and dolphins. You just talk softly, look them in the eye, and tell them exactly what you want." Then she grinned. "Feeding them goodies helps," and she tossed each cat a kitty treat.

"Have a seat," Josey said, waving her hand with the big, beautiful sapphire ring toward a cane-bottom ladder-back chair that was either an antique or way, way past its prime. I sat, and the orange tabby immediately construed this as an invitation of some kind.

"Let me feed the boys and girls," Josey said, "then we can talk."

Nodding, I turned my attention to the big orange tabby that was pressing its butt in my face and commanded, under my breath, "Go away."

But the sound of the pop-top popping on the cat-food can made the orange tabby bounce out of my lap and up onto the top of the kitchen counter with the other four of her fellow felines.

"Say your prayers," Josey commanded, and all five cats sat down, and bowed their heads.

Okay. I was impressed, and maybe a bit puzzled, by Josey the domestic-cat trainer. While the cats ate, I scoped out the kitchen and what else I could see of the house, which was cluttered, though fundamentally clean, except for those little clouds of cat hair floating through the air.

"Bottled water?" Josey asked.

"Please."

"Grilled cheese?"

"Er, well"—I looked around at the floating cat hair again—"guess not. Watching my carbs."

"Why?" Josey asked. "You aren't skinny enough?"

Ignoring Josey's jab, I talked the kind of idle, flattering chitchat that one makes when you're trying to warm a person up so they'll spill their guts and tell you things they really weren't supposed to tell you. While I blabbered in my most charming way, Josey made her grilled cheese sandwich, and my mouth watered so badly I had to stop talking.

"Sure you don't want one?" she asked, making me wonder if I'd whimpered.

Tempted, I sniffed the air and checked out the countertop. Josey had used real cheese, real butter, and a grocery-store whole wheat bread. I knew the sandwich would taste really, really good. I knew it would add an inch where I didn't want an inch. Lord knows what was in the bread, probably high-fructose corn syrup and preservatives. "Thank you, but no."

"Okay, you don't eat meat, you don't eat carbs. What do you eat?"

Actually I ate carbs, I mean, trail mix bars were, at least lately, my mainstay in life. I just thought that "I don't eat carbs" would sound better than "No, thank you, I don't eat cat fur." What I answered was "Salads, fruit, brown rice, yogurt. But I'm fine, really. Not hungry." My mouth drooled as I lied.

"Okay, no fruit in the yard right now. Too late for citrus, too early for mangoes. Yogurt, I have."

My mouth watered again. "Full-fat, low-fat, no-fat, organic, or regular?"

Josey gave me the same look Philip often did at meals. "Banana," she said.

Okay, close enough. "That'd be great."

In no time at all, we were eating, as were the kitties.

I had stopped drooling, and was savoring, when Josey peered over her sandwich and asked, "Now, tell me, why did you want to talk to me?"

Okay, enough cat chatter and food talk. "Do you have anything new on the M. David murder case?"

"Not so you'd know."

"So, the widow's not a suspect?"

"Didn't say that," Josey said.

"What about the other shareholders in Boogie Bog? I understand they lost a bundle when M. David gutted the company and fled. I'd be pretty interested in the Boogie Bog gang. I mean, you know, revenge and all."

Josey kept eating.

"So, okay, who exactly were the shareholders in Boogie Bog?"

Josey stared at me for a moment, and then said, "You do know that you are not a law-enforcement officer, don't you?"

So, okay, apparently grilled cheese did not loosen Josey's tongue, like, say, maybe a bottle of wine would have. I didn't think she would drink on the job, though, so I didn't even try to induce her to open a bottle of wine. Instead I just nodded pleasantly and then tried to cajole some more information, but Josey pretty much took the position that she was going to pet her cats, eat her sandwich, and ignore the rest of my questions.

Just what I needed, a cajole-proof detective.

"So, that's M. David, then," I said, officially signaling that I was giving up that line of inquiry. "What have you learned about Angus John?"

"Nothing. Nothing except what I've read in the newspaper. You do remember, don't you, that his case is with the Bradenton police, out of my jurisdiction? Not my case," she said, with a deadpan expression.

Not her case, yeah, I remembered that. But I also remembered Josey questioning me, the Sunday after Angus died, like it was her case. So, okay, maybe being a lawyer made me cynical, but I suspected Josey knew more than she was admitting about Angus John.

But my bottle of water was empty, my banana yogurt was eaten, as was Josey's grilled cheese. It was time to go, so I stood up, thinking that was a pretty obvious hint.

But first, I asked, innocently enough, if I could use her bathroom. Josey pointed down a hallway that conveniently enough passed right by her second bedroom, which she had converted into a home office. I could hear Josey talking to her cats in the kitchen, so I cruised into the office, checked out her computer, her desk, her piles of stuff, and just sort of accidentally started reading exposed papers. What she had, sort of vaguely on top, if you shoved the other stuff out of the way, was a set of the Antheus corporation papers. I read as fast as I could, and learned in not too much longer than a real trip to the bathroom would have taken that the Antheus bylaws provided that M. David's private stock would go back into the corporation at his death, and not be inherited by his heirs. That's not so unusual, I knew, with privately held stock in a small company, where the shareholders want to control who is part of the business. My private shares in the Smith, O'Leary, and Smith stock have the same provision.

But what made this particularly interesting was that it meant the good widow, the very Mrs. Sherilyn Moody, would not get any share of Antheus. And even if the company couldn't mine it, that much pristine land was prime real estate gold. Rather than Sherilyn getting a cut, M. David's fellow Antheus shareholders' own cut would increase.

And that made for an interesting motive on the part of M. David's Antheus shareholders.

"Hey, you all right?" Josey called out.

Quickly, I put the papers back as neat as I had found them, dashed into the bath, flushed, washed my hands, and idled back into the kitchen. Josey gave me an odd look, and I smiled. "You have great light in your bathroom. I was checking my makeup. Think I need more blush?" Better she think me vapid and vain than a snoop who'd snooped in her own office.

Josey squinted her eyes and gave my face a serious look. "Naw, you look fine. Don't know why you'd fool with makeup anyway."

And with that, we got back into her car and left.

When Josey dropped me off in front of my Honda, she looked at me with cop eyes. "You be careful who you ask what to, you hear? There's something out there worth killing over. Sometimes when you turn over rocks, what's under there will bite you."

Chapter Eighteen

As the cosmic forces had obviously decreed that this was Field Trip Day, I thought, oh, what the heck, I might as well drive back to work via Delilah Groves in east Sarasota County and see if I could find out if it had already been sold, and to whom or what. I mean, it wasn't like I had a trial starting tomorrow morning. What had Rayford the antisuave said while he was trying to bilk me out of a deposit for a future crop that wouldn't be grown? Take State Road 72 to Sugar Bowl Road and turn north?

That meant bumper-cars-at-eighty till I hit Sugar Bowl Road, which was pretty far east, but a sweet little road through honest-to-gosh countryside.

The first thing I saw when I drove through the gates of the orange grove was a covey of surveyors working among the trees. I knew I'd have to see what that was all about, but at the moment, I filed it in the "later" box and continued to the office. Where I was rewarded by a "Closed" sign on the door and no one around.

I parked my car, tried the front door, and the back door, both of which were locked. Then I eyed the windows, but decided breaking into the headquarters of the plaintiff who was suing two of my clients, especially while surveyors were within shouting distance away, would not constitute a move that The Florida Bar's ethics division would in any possible way condone. Besides that, the lower windows had burglar bars on them, which immediately piqued my interest in what might be inside. I mean, who would want to steal a bunch of orange orders and shipping labels?

Curiosity thus raised, I found myself peeking in the windows, between the burglar bars, even jiggling things, testing for sturdiness. In fact, as fate would have it, I was doing my best to unfasten a loose screw on the attached bars when I heard a car drive up. Good thing I was in the back, and I inhaled myself back into lawyer, not burglar, mode and sallied around to the front to meet whoever was in the car.

A tubby blonde with Tammy-Faye-lite makeup jumped down from a tall SUV and said, "You looking for something?"

Mentally I added her to my list of prospects for my grooming school if I ever burned out on this lawyer thing, but said, "Oh, yes, thank you. I was looking for Rayford Clothier."

"You looking for him out back of the office?"

"Oh, just admiring the groves. Doesn't look like Rayford's here."

"Oh, he's here all right. Had me lock the doors while I was at lunch so nobody would bother him. What'cha need to see him 'bout?"

Well, it was none of her business, I thought, but I smiled, and introduced myself by name and trade and said I needed to speak with Rayford on business.

"I'm Odell," she said, and stuck out her hand, which I took as briefly as I could under the prevailing customs and conventions. Then she bent down, turned over a rock, got out a key, and clumped heavily on weirdly outdated platform shoes toward the door. "Rayford doesn't trust me to take the key with me."

My curiosity level hit a new high as Odell unlocked the door. What did Rayford have inside?

While I pondered Rayford's burglar bars and mistrust of Odell, she plunked the key back under the same rock.

So much for security, I thought, and made a careful mental note as to exactly which rock hid the door key. That information could come in pretty handy if my meeting wasn't quite as fruitful as I hoped.

"Rayford's not much for lawyers," Odell said as she went inside the orange-grove office. Assuming an implied invitation, I followed her.

Without saying anything further to me, Odell shouted out at a closed door, "Yo, Rayford."

Good professional manners, I thought, and waited. In another minute, a tall, dark-haired man, sporting a cowboy shirt, came out the door and glared at me. Then his glare softened.

"Well, little darling, no flies on you."

Okay, a western yahoo I needed to bend to do my bidding. How hard could that be? I smiled so big that my eyes squinted up, and fluffed up my half yard of perfect hair. "Hello, my name is Lilly Cleary, and I'm hoping to borrow you for just a few minutes."

Rayford stared at my chest for a second, and then took a good look at my legs.

When his eyes landed on my face, I said, "If we could just step into your office for a minute—"

"We know each other? You seem . . . familiar."

Uh-oh. Either a worn-out pickup line, which didn't seem necessary since I'd already come on to him, or he might have remembered my voice from my two alt-personality phone calls.

"Oh, no," I said, "I've never had the pleasure of meeting you until now." Which was, of course, technically true, though possibly misleading in the context, a well-used trick of trial lawyers.

"You sure?"

"Oh, quite. I'd remember *you*." Big movie-star smile.

"What do you want?" His tone sounded carefully neutral. But his grin was one inch off a salacious sneer.

"I'm an attorney and I was hoping to talk a little business."

The glare came back on Rayford Clothier's face. Okay, most

people lose the grin when they find out I'm an attorney. I'm used to that.

"What do you want with me?"

"I'm the attorney representing Angus John and Miguel."

"Who?"

"You know, the two men Delilah Groves is suing. The orange-defamation case."

"Look, I already told my attorney to get that lawsuit dropped. You don't need to waste my time any further. You can go now." But for good measure, Rayford stole another look at my legs.

"You told your attorney to dismiss it?"

"Yeah. You should get the paperwork today, tomorrow."

Well, that put a wholly new and interesting spin on things, didn't it? "Obviously I haven't yet received the notice of dismissal," I said, buying a few seconds to recompose my set of questions. "But . . . why?"

"Why's it matter to you, why? You afraid you won't get paid?" His salacious grin turned to a belligerent glare.

Pausing a moment to assimilate Rayford's mood change, and to figure out how to play the next round, I stared back at him. He was built solid, and almost handsome in that Marlborough man sort of way. I let him see I was looking at him. Tit for tat, so to speak.

"Well, good," I said, nodding and then aiming a playful sort of grin at him. "Thank you. For dismissing the suit. But I'd sure like to discuss this further with you. May we step inside your office?"

"Look, I told my lawyer to get rid of the suit. I'm sick and tired of all you lawyers, so I told him to get me out of it."

"That sounds like a fine plan," I said, gaining wind and composure. "Especially since there was never any money in the suit, and then there'd be all the bad publicity." I remembered what Angus had said, that the gyp waste would make the groves like a toxic-waste site, and I threw that in. "You surely didn't want your customers thinking you're growing oranges in a Superfund site." I was fishing around, hoping that if I came close enough to the *real* reason he'd dropped the suit, he'd own up to it.

He paused, and stared at me. At my face this time, not my body. As if he could read something from my carefully neutral expression. It felt like a whole minute ticked by before he spoke. "You're supposed to talk to my attorney, aren't you? I mean, you aren't allowed to talk directly to me, are you?"

Well, technically no. The Florida Bar ethics code prohibits an attorney on one side of the case from directly discussing a pending lawsuit with an opposing party like Rayford if he's represented by counsel. But I figured, hey, if he's already dropped the lawsuit, then he is not technically the opposing party anymore. Right? And that made talking directly to him a gray area in the law, and gray areas are to lawyers what coastal hurricanes are to rabid surfers.

Plus, I figured I could just say I came to place an early order on the honeybell tangelos if the ethics investigators were summoned and got huffy.

But what I said was, "Oh, I thought a direct conversation might benefit us both."

"I don't see how."

Change of tactics seemed appropriate, so I wandered to the window and looked out. "Such a lovely, lovely, grove. I saw surveyors out front? Are you . . . expanding the groves?"

"No." Rayford continued to stare at me. About this time I became keenly aware of the fact that Rayford had never invited me into his office and the overly eye-shadowed Odell was watching us as if we were the warm-up act for Toby Keith. "Perhaps we could discuss this whole situation in your office?"

"I'm fine where I am," Rayford said.

Okay, be that way, I thought. "Perhaps Mrs. Moody has some plans for the groves—surveyors laying out a plan for an office for her, perhaps?"

"How'd you know about her interest in the groves?" Belligerence brewed over to hostile.

"Plantation, Inc., was your partner in Delilah Groves. And M. David Moody was the sole shareholder in Plantation. See, I know how to look up incorporation papers. I'm a lawyer and we know how to do stuff like that." Actually, Olivia had looked up the Plantation, Inc., records, but Rayford didn't need to know that level of detail. "And, being a lawyer, I know that Mrs. Moody would inherit Mr. Moody's interest in the groves." A whopper of an assumption on my part since I'd never seen M. David's will, but Rayford's prior admission that Mrs. Moody had an interest in the groves indicated I'd guessed right.

Rayford didn't say anything. Odell wasn't even pretending to work. I didn't have the sense I was going to learn much more useful information from either. But it was too long a drive for me to just give up. So I smiled again, aiming for a sad, knowing smile, not a giddy one, and I said, "Poor woman. Maybe a new project at the groves would be just the thing to perk her up in her time of sorrow."

"Sorrow, my ass, that woman was calculating the inheritance tax before her old man was good and stiff. She was out here going through the books the same day they pulled him from the gyp stack."

Wow, okay, I'd finally hit a target Rayford wanted to chat about, and also I cattily remembered Mrs. Moody apparently being on a date with Galleon Theibuet two nights after her husband learned which circle in hell he was assigned to. So, let's gossip, I thought. Having worked up to a specific distrust and dislike of Sherilyn since her attempted phone calls to me wrenched open a Pandora's box of paranoia, I was more than willing to trash the woman. But before I said anything, Rayford Clothier walked back into his office and started to shut the door behind him.

"Wait," I practically screamed after him. Then I composed myself and asked in a sweeter tone, "Please, explain to me why you dropped the suit. I guess Mrs. Moody agreed too. Was it her idea?"

Rayford stopped retreating. He turned and glared at me. "Why?"

"I just thought the more I know, the better chance I have of convincing my client to let the whole matter drop. You know, not file a retaliatory lawsuit against Delilah for wrongful suit, abuse of process, or harassment, or trashing his First Amendment rights. That sort of thing. Also, perhaps if I fully understand what is going on, I can convince him not to protest the groves' fertilizer habits anymore."

"Look, I don't know you," Rayford snapped. "And I don't care if your lunatic client wants to sue the groves or march around it all day long. I'm tired of oranges and I'm tired of Florida. I'm selling out and going back west. I had a cattle ranch out there once and I'm going to get me another one. To hell with this state."

With that Rayford turned and walked into his office and picked up a drink that was sitting on his desk. He turned back to face me and took a sip. I saw that most of the glass was empty.

So, okay, that amber liquid explained the tart, if not completely loose tongue. No doubt Rayford had been sitting in his locked office, drinking, while Odell had been out. Well, all the better for me, I thought, and scooted right in after him. Sure, Rayford hadn't exactly invited me into his office, but I followed on the theory that it's pretty hard to shut the door in the face of someone who's already inside. I took a quick peek around, spotted a couple of intriguing filing cabinets, a door that was cracked just enough for me to see it was a bathroom, and wholly ordinary condo-art prints on the walls. Nothing of obvious, apparent value, like real art, to justify the burglar bars. I put my eyes right on Rayford.

"You seem like a very interesting man," I said, noting to myself that you should never overlook the obvious ploys because they usually work on men. "I did wonder about Mrs. Moody and that Theibuet fellow. Galleon Theibuet." Fishing, yeah, but the man had a drink, and apparently a grudge.

Rayford took another sip, and stared at me. Then he took a big swallow.

"Theibuet, Sherilyn?" I queried, prompting him.

"Yeah. I hear tell your grieving widow has been chasing Theibuet all over town for years. But then, she's come sniffing around me too. Funny thing was, old Theibuet and M. David were tight. Till M. David screwed him over royally."

And men complain that women gossip, I thought, but added, "Screwed, how?"

"You mean how old Sherilyn screwed Theibuet? I assume the traditional fashion. You need a drawing?"

"No, I mean what did you mean that M. David screwed over Theibuet?"

"Business. You wouldn't understand."

"Perhaps I might. I read the newspapers." Yeah, okay, okay, but I'm doing better now.

"Cutting to the chase," I added, "M. David was CEO at Boogie Bog. When it began having expensive problems disposing of the gypsum sludge, M. David, as its CEO, sold back his shares of company stock at an inflated value. The company had to borrow money to buy his stocks, and the additional debt killed it."

Clink, clink. Rayford took another swallow of his drink. "Yeah. Good for you," he said.

"So? What am I missing? You obviously know more of the story than the newspapers," I said, trying to appeal to his vanity.

As I waited for an answer, I watched Rayford's face. He took another sip, and swallowed loudly, and a furious little charade of emotions flickered across his cowboy features as I caught him, open-faced, apparently calculating how to play me. Maybe it was his version of a risk-benefit analysis. Or maybe it was just too much whiskey in the middle of the day. But finally he spoke.

"Yeah, before it gave up the ghost, Boogie Bog had all that gyp shit to get rid of. It looked at selling the gyp to road companies and building-supply companies to be mixed into pavement and concrete blocks and stuff, but the nuclear-waste folks had pretty much cornered that market. So the company decided, you know, what the fuck. Just leave it."

"Just leave it?"

Clink, clink, and another swallow. "There's a thousand different bugs and kinds of mold and fungus that kill citrus trees. I sweat like a pig all year round. One day you got a nice field, next day you got a damn swamp. I hate this state."

Smiling like he'd said something terribly clever, I wondered how much more info I could get out of him. My jaws were clinching from the fake smiling, but I gave him one more round. "Now tell me, how did the Boogie Bog company plan on getting away with just leaving the gyp stuff?"

"Just like it did. Like you said, M. David made Boogie Bog buy back his stock, and then he ditched the company. Made it go belly-up. The shareholders didn't have money for themselves, you think they're gonna borrow millions to clean up their messes? Left the gyp for the state to deal with. The rest of the company men, like Theibuet, were screwed. Their company stock became worthless."

"How'd Theibuet feel about that?" I asked.

"How did he feel about losing big money? How you think he felt?"

"And you, were you invested in Boogie Bog?"

"Look, I'm the man's . . . that is, I was the man's partner in these orange groves. You think he screws me on Boogie Bog, I go back in business with him? I sound stupid to you, or what?"

"Not at all. No, you sound like"—what, a bitter, gossipy drunk?— "a savvy businessman."

While I waited to see if that flirt had any benefit, I remembered that Josey had pointed out Theibuet as one of the four shareholders behind Antheus. So where'd he get the money to buy into Antheus? And why would he?

Rayford was looking at my legs again, and I was so glad I'd thought to wear a suit with the perfect little skirt, just a bare two inches above my knees. Pressing what I hoped was an advantage, I asked him, "But you're telling me Theibuet was in Boogie Bog, and now he's in Antheus. Doesn't that suggest a weak learning curve on his part? That's weird."

"That's the phosphate business."

"But, why would you go back in business with a man who had—"

"I'm tired of you, little lady, you aren't even close to my type, and I hate lawyers and I hate orange groves and when my check on the sale of this place clears, I'm out of here, you hear?"

"Yes, but just one more—"

"You don't listen good. I'm all out of answers."

After a few more smiles and queries, I decided Rayford was right—he was all out of answers. So I left.

Frustrated at all I hadn't learned, like why Rayford and Sherilyn had dropped the orange-defamation suits, I comforted myself with what I had learned: Where Odell hid the door key.

And that Rayford had a goodly number of filing cabinets I wouldn't mind carefully pursuing in the quiet of predawn.

I could read pretty good by the glow of a flashlight.

But one thing at a time, I reminded myself, then I got in my car and drove back to the law firm, stopping briefly to find out from one of the surveyors that a national housing-development corporation had a contract on the place, and the closing was next week.

Naturally, a grove this big would be a plum for a builder, I thought as I pushed the speed limit on my way back to my law firm. Though I was sorry to think that the last orange grove in Sarasota would soon be plowed asunder, I wanted to get back to my office and see if there really was a notice of dismissal in the stupid orange-defamation case in my as-yet-unread morning mail, and if not, get Bonita to call the circuit court and see if one had been filed. And then my plan was to churn and spin through the scant remaining day, and hurry home.

After all, I had a bird to feed, a delinquent handyman to grill, and two murders to figure out.

Chapter Nineteen

The amazing thing was that when I finally got home that evening, nobody else was there. Oh, except Rasputin.

Naturally, I went for one of the bottles of organic wine that I had hidden from Jimmie behind the laundry soap in the utility room, and headed straight back to my kitchen. While I was holding the bottle of wine in one hand and the corkscrew in the other, I heard the front door open and slam. Jimmie, as if guided by some homing device toward the good wine, came almost dancingly into the kitchen from the outside world, holding two videotapes in his hands.

"I done got her done," he said and beamed.

"What?" I asked, eyeing the tapes and twisting the corkscrew.

"This first one," Jimmie said, holding up a tape, "is of that spinal-injury-faker guy. I done got him carrying out garbage, lifting up what looks like at least a forty-pound sack of cow manure from his car trunk, and spreading the manure in his yard, then cutting the grass."

Pretty good, I thought, for a man who claims he needs daily chiropractic care for the rest of his life, plus a quarter of a million dollars.

"Reckon that'll 'bout do it on that," Jimmie said.

Nodding, I agreed that, effectively, the lawsuit against Jimmie was over. Technically, I still had to ambush Jason with the tape, then get him to dismiss the case, but how hard could that be?

"Good, then," he said, "I got me another project."

So saying, Jimmie took the other videotape, plus the video camera, and headed toward my guest room. He didn't ask for wine.

My something's-up antennae went on red alert. Curious, I followed.

"What are you up to? And where were you all night? And did you feed Rasputin today at all? Did you get the grass cut like you said you would?"

Oh great, didn't I sound like somebody's mother?

"I was busy," Jimmie said.

Well, after all, as the police and Dolly had both pointed out to me, he was a grown man, not a teenager. And he had made it home that morning, apparently safe, in time for breakfast, and that was a lot better than Delvon and I had managed on many occasions when we *were* teenagers.

"But I'm gonna need this video camera another few days," Jimmie said. "And I reckon maybe, Dolly might . . ."

Dolly? And the video camera? I tried to hide my amusement as I told Jimmie to keep the video camera for another few days. I almost giggled at my next thought, Jimmie videotaping him and Dolly fooling around in bed. Which was, despite Dolly's denials, exactly where I figured he'd been last night.

As I turned to leave my guest bedroom, which, of course, had now been wholly taken over and was Jimmie's room, I thought about what Jason the baby lawyer had said, that Jimmie owned a bucketload of Exxon stock. I turned back and asked Jimmie, "By the way, do you own about a quarter million dollars' worth of Exxon stock?"

I expected a denial, or even laughter. Instead, I saw Jimmie's cheeks turn pink.

"Yeah, I . . . not sure of their current value but, yeah, maybe. See, when I's a young man, I done bought me some shares back when I's working for Exxon. Course, this was all before I discovered the joys of wine and poetry and became a beatnik, and I's afraid I ain't never goin' to have a real job again, or earn me enough money to buy no more stock, see, so I ain't touchin' it for a while. I needs it for my old age."

"Jimmie," I said, "you're homeless. And you're . . . what? Closing in on eighty? Maybe you might want to consider breaking into your financial stash. I respect your saving your Exxon stock for your old age, but I think you're there now."

"I ain't homeless, I lives here with you," Jimmie said, and his voice sounded both indignant and hurt.

It occurred to me that now would be a very good time for me to gently point out to Jimmie that I didn't envision this as a permanent arrangement. But before I said anything, Jimmie said, "If you needs it, I can pay rent. I mean on top of all the work, you know, cutting your grass and fixin' your soffits and eaves and paintin' and feeding that bird, and, and . . . well, Lady, I thought . . ."

Uh-oh. Jimmie's feelings were hurt.

For some reason, I realized I didn't want to hurt Jimmie.

For some reason, I realized I liked having Jimmie around. Probably a grandfather thing.

"Listen, I'm sorry if I hurt you. Let's go have a glass of wine. We can talk finances and housing later."

"In a little bit. I got me some things I needs to do. I'll catch you later," he said, and I heard the sound of dismissal.

Thinking I must really have wounded his pride, and should let him sulk a bit, I nodded, and retreated to my kitchen, where I poured a glass of organic wine. Wine in hand, I went to my den and watched Jimmie's surveillance video, agreed it was of a professional quality that left no doubt that faker plaintiff was as strong and agile as any healthy young man, and I poured my second glass of wine and went in search of food in my own refrigerator.

After I'd picked at a salad, Jimmie staggered out into the kitchen and said, "I done plum forgot. Delvon wants us to come over tonight and join a prayer circle for Lenora. Maybe we can get some ice cream afterward."

"Of course. Let me clean up, and we can go. Call 'em for me, and tell Lenora we're on our way."

Naturally, I cleaned not only the kitchen, but myself. I fluffed, buffed, flossed, changed clothes, and flounced back into the living room, where Jimmie and Dolly were sitting. I hadn't realized Dolly was part of the evening's outing.

"We's waiting on you," Jimmie said, just in case I'd missed the impatience written big across his face.

"We are waiting on you," Dolly corrected.

"Dog-bite-it, woman. Why you gots to repeat ever thing I say's beyond me," Jimmie said.

Dolly puffed up a bit, but before she could retort, Jimmie turned to me. "All set?" Jimmie was wearing one of Philip's white-on-white, hand-pressed, tailor-made shirts. I guess Jimmie took an expansive view of using my guest room. Philip's shirt, of course, was several sizes too big on Jimmie, and the long sleeves dangled down Jimmie's skinny arms, the cuffs completely hiding his hands. He did not cut a dashing figure, but he was probably too set in his ways for tips from Lilly's Grooming School, so I applied my grandmom's can't-teach-a-pig-to-sing philosophy.

Dolly apparently didn't suffer from that same outlook, and said, "At least roll the sleeves up, especially if you plan to actually use your hands."

"No'm, you see how he done had these shirts pressed and starched and all? I ain't gonna mess that up by rolling up these sleeves."

Oh, please, I thought, like Philip's going to wear that shirt again without having it washed and pressed and starched all over. He kept clean, spare shirts at his office and changed after lunch. There's a whole village in Guatemala that could live off what Philip spends on his shirts alone, and don't even get me started on his *suits*. Tailor-made. Every single damn one of them—I'd gone through his closet once, when he was in the shower, and checked. I opened my mouth to give voice to this pet peeve I had against Philip—I mean, yes, I like to dress nice, but Philip was just way out there, but before I could get even the first peep of my rant out, the doorbell rang.

Since I was already standing up, I walked to the door and opened it, and there—speaking of the devil—was Philip. He was holding a package in his hand, elegantly wrapped in gold paper and a white satin ribbon.

"Hello, Lilly. This is for you," he said, and handed the present to me.

"It's not my birthday," I said.

"It's Edna St. Vincent Millay," Philip said. "A first edition. I didn't realize you were so enamored of poetry."

"Oh, she jes' loves the stuff, especially the gal ones."

I don't "jes' love" poetry. I mean, I don't have anything against it, except that I had to memorize a bunch of it in high school for some reason that has yet to become apparent. But it seemed the quickest way to get this outing over with, which was my new goal, was to get it started, and that called for getting us all out the door. "Thank you," I said, and put the book on the coffee table. "We're just on our way out to visit my brother Delvon and his friend Lenora." I left it up to Philip to decide if that was an invitation or a dismissal.

"I'd be glad to drive," Philip said.

"That's real nice of you," Jimmie said. "We all'll fit in Philip's nice, big car, and, 'sides, this time a night, they won't be no traffic much on the Trail."

"There won't be *any* traffic," Dolly said, and I felt the muscles at the back of my neck bunch into a tight, painful knot.

By the time we arrived at Lenora's, I was more than about halfway to full-blown batty, trapped as I was between Miss Grammar 1944 and Jimmie Don't Got None. Philip was mostly silent, though I'd noticed him noticing Jimmie in his own good shirt.

Lenora's house was small, a somewhat run-down Florida bungalow that backed up to Bowlees Creek, which is roughly the natural barrier between Manatee and Sarasota Counties.

While I was doing an instant property appraisal on Lenora's house, Delvon answered the door. He wore a hand-painted T-shirt that said "No More Bushit" over a pair of cutoffs. He was barefoot, and grinning fit to choke the Cheshire cat.

"Y'all come on in, come on in."

We paraded in, and the distinct, pungent order of marijuana hit me in the face. Not like Delvon was passing a bong, but like the stuff was baking. I sniffed, and turned and looked at Delvon.

"Just some skunk sativa I'm drying out in Lenora's convection oven. Won't be long. It got damp, what with the defrosting on my trip down and then sitting in your carport a couple of days like it did."

Dolly and Philip turned and stared at me as if I were dealing drugs out of my carport.

But when I shrugged, Philip turned back to my brother. "I don't believe we have formally met," Philip said. "I'm Philip Cohen, Lilly's fiancé." He offered his hand to Delvon.

Before Delvon processed the slight negative shake of my head, he pounced on Philip. "My brother-in-law, praise Jesus." And he proceeded to hug the stuffing out of Philip.

When Delvon stopped squeezing him, Philip breathlessly introduced Delvon to Dolly. She refused Delvon's hand, narrowed her eyes, and stepped back.

"Oh, they done met," Jimmie said.

I guessed one could call it that, remembering how I'd found them shadowboxing with each other after Dolly had called the police on Delvon. "Where's Lenora?" I asked.

"She's in the kitchen, go on in. Y'all got here just in time. We got two Episcopal nuns coming over to lay on hands and pray for her," Delvon said.

"Perhaps we are intruding and should leave," Philip said. I thought I caught a hopeful tone in his voice.

"Oh, no, the more prayer, the better," Delvon said.

Doubtlessly true, but I drifted away from the crowd anyway and ambled into the kitchen, where Lenora was sitting, listlessly holding a glass of ginger ale. Her face was a yellow-gray, with purple slashes under her eyes.

"How are you doing?" I asked, rather pointlessly given her appearance.

"Fine. I'll be fine." She put down her soda, rose from her chair, and gave me a weak hug. "Thank you for sharing your brother with me. He has so much . . . energy. Maybe this weekend, you can come out to the preserve and see what all he's managed to do." Her strength seemed to give way, and she sat back down.

Lenora rested for a moment, while I took in the kitchen. Classic Florida-in-the-Forties look to it, very charming, with a turquoise stove and pink tile.

"There'll be a memorial service for Angus John on Monday. Will you come?" Lenora asked me.

"Yes. Of course. Where?" I made myself stop staring at the pink tile and looked at Lenora.

"At the Manatee Garden Center, next to Lewis Park, down near the Manatee River. I'll get you the address later. Angus thought it was a pretty place."

"If you need any help, setting it up, or anything, let me know. I'll help."

"Thank you."

I couldn't help but ask, "Will Miguel be there, at the memorial? Do you know how to get in touch with him?"

"I think not, and no," she said. "Angus and I, we got married there, at the Manatee Garden Center. A long time ago."

"Really?" I said. I *had* wondered about them, and Olivia hadn't been any help on that score, and what with the press of other issues with Miguel, I'd never asked him about Angus and Lenora.

"Angus was my first love," Lenora said. Her voice was soft and wistful and I knew Lenora was not really here with me, but somewhere in the past with Angus.

"We grew up together, over near Mulberry and Bartow. But we screwed it up, got married too early. Right out of high school. My granddaddy gave me away there at that garden club. But Angus and me . . . we were just too young, and it didn't work. After we got divorced, I stayed here in Manatee County, and lived right here with my granddad. When he died, he left me this house, and that place by the river. He'd gotten 'em both dirt cheap back in the forties. So I had a house, free and clear, but I've had to mortgage it to pay my medical bills."

Like an involuntary muscle spasm, I went into lawyer mode. "You know, the house is judgment proof if you've homesteaded it, which I'm sure you have. Creditors like medical-care providers can't take your homesteaded house to pay bills. But the mortgage company can. If you were worried about paying the hospital bill, you should . . . er, could have . . . just owed them and not mortgaged your house."

Lenora took a deep breath. "I didn't have a choice. A pharmacy won't sell you chemo drugs without money. And the stuff costs thousands, *thousands.*"

Damn. I'd momentarily forgotten we lived in the one so-called civilized country in the world that routinely lets the uninsured or the un-moneyed die for lack of standard medical treatment.

"And the preserve," Lenora said. "The animal preserve by the river is not homesteaded, so the hospital can get that if I don't pay off the rest of my surgery bill. I had to sell some of the land when I first got sick and couldn't do any fund-raising or work my little jobs. I didn't know, but I ended up selling it to Antheus and M. David Moody." She gave a bitter half laugh, half snort. "Usually I'm not stupid," she said.

"No, I wouldn't think you are." But then seriously sick and uninsured means desperate. And desperate rarely improves the clarity of the choices one is forced to make.

"But M. David used this buyer for cover, sent out this real down-home guy, in cowboy boots and one of those little western string ties . . . what do you call those little string ties?"

"Um, I don't know. Little string ties?" I said, western attire being outside the range of my expertise.

"Yeah, well this guy came out and talked about how he wanted a quiet weekend getaway, and how he didn't believe in hunting. Snookered me right in. I needed money, and he seemed so . . . so nice. When I found out he was just a point man for Antheus, I was going to court to try and get out of the sale, claim fraud or something, but I didn't have the money for lawyers, or the energy by then."

Somebody needed to say something positive, so I gave it a whirl. "Well, just because M. David bought part of your place for his mining company doesn't mean he can get the rest. I mean, a private corporation doesn't have power of eminent domain. So, at least he can't get any more of your land."

"Well, *he* can't now, I don't guess, being dead and all. But Antheus Mines is still after me to sell out. I'm the only one of the original property owners in that swath of land out there who hasn't been tricked or forced to sell everything. Now the value of my land's plummeted because everybody just figures it will all be surrounded by this big ugly moonscape of strip mining inside a couple of years."

Ah, the catch-22. Even if she held on to her animal preserve, she'd be surrounded by a phosphate mine, and her land would be unmarketable and worthless—except to the phosphate company. With the threat of the mine, no one would buy her land now, except Antheus. And, knowing her land was essentially valueless, Antheus wouldn't even have to pay much for it. Hell, Antheus Mines could probably pick up her land dimes on the dollar after the hospital grabbed it for debt collection.

So to add to his list of sins, M. David had boxed in a seriously sick woman between a dragon and a whirlpool, and probably laughed all the way to the courthouse to record the deed to the part he and Antheus had managed to buy.

"How did M. David get away with so much for so long?" I asked.

"All I could figure was he was giving blow jobs to the devil."

A too-hearty laugh exploded out of my lips before I could stop it. Yes, that would explain the strange impunity with which M. David had plundered his way through southwest Florida.

Until, that is, somebody stopped him facedown in a gyp pond.

"Guess the devil got a new boyfriend," I said, thinking maybe M. David got what he deserved in the end after all.

It also occurred to me that if Antheus Mines was permanently denied any right to mine, then Lenora's property value would once more soar. Both her land, and the unmined Antheus land, would be ripe picking for still another housing development now that 90 percent of the retiring baby boomers from New Jersey, Ohio, and Michigan were moving to Manatee County.

I wondered how much of Angus's determination to stop M. David and Antheus had to do with Lenora's plight.

I wondered if it would have driven Angus to murder M. David.

For Lenora.

"Yeah, well, I was telling you about Angus," Lenora said, interrupting thoughts I didn't want to have.

"Yes, you were."

"After our divorce, we were mad at each other for a while. But Angus grew up and came looking for me. We were just getting back to where we could maybe make it work, talking about getting married again. I wouldn't let him live with me, though, and then I got sick, and now he's dead."

This story seemed to drain Lenora of whatever energy she'd had, and she slumped back in her chair. I was still standing, uneasily and uselessly, in the kitchen, near her chair. "I'm sorry," I said, and I was, though saying so didn't make anything any better.

"Everyone suffers in life," she said. "Mine is not special. I don't take it personally."

"Still," I said, "I'm sorry." The kitchen was hot, and I was sweating, the convection oven hummed and the smell of sativa was overwhelming. I deal with human tragedies for a living; that is, after all, what the tort litigation system was built upon. But with Lenora, there was no one to sue, or to defend, and no court of law that could make it better. I was at a loss.

"If you've got Episcopal nuns coming over, maybe I should turn off the oven and open the windows," I said, looking for some action to dispel the mood.

"Oh, I don't think they'll mind. If they work with many chemo patients, I rather imagine they're used to it. But the pot should be dry by now, so you could shut the oven off."

By the time I had done just that, everybody who had been in the living room was suddenly in Lenora's kitchen and a wave of claustrophobia hit me in the gut. I was giving serious thought to sneaking out the back door and calling a cab and going home to wrestle with my descending depression, but then the doorbell rang. Oh, good, more people to shove into a small room in a small house.

As I left the kitchen, everyone except Lenora pranced to the front door as if the pope was coming, and not just two nice church ladies. Delvon greeted them with a loud and hearty, "Praise Jesus," and then everyone apparently talked at once, with Delvon talking the loudest.

"Perhaps you would like to meet Lenora?" I asked, hoping to get this show on the road. Like I was shepherding wayward puppies, I redeployed the nuns to the kitchen. Philip, Delvon, Dolly, and Jimmie trudged along behind like the faithful. Introductions were made, and after much bumping into each other and stepping on everybody's toes, the faithful adjourned with Lenora and the nuns to her guest bedroom, where they would all pray over Lenora.

Not that I didn't believe in the healing power of prayer, but I needed to be in a room where there weren't already fifty other people breathing my air. And since I was here, I might as well check out Lenora's bathroom and see if she, by chance, used sandalwood soap. It would seem natural for her to hide Miguel, given their mutual bond through Angus.

Curious as to what I might learn while nobody was watching me, I eased down the hallway toward what I figured was another bedroom, and I went in, spotting the door to the bathroom, and checked it out. No sandalwood—not even close.

Quietly, I peeked in the medicine cabinet. No sandalwood there, either. I drifted back into her bedroom. Her double bed was crumpled, unmade, but the sheets were a delicate eggshell color and clean. Near the bed was a chaise lounge with a flannel sheet wadded up at the base of it and a pillow smushed at the head of it. No doubt Delvon had been sleeping on the lounge, keeping his watch over Lenora.

"Lilly," Philip said from the doorway. "Are you all right?"

"Fine, just hiding out. How 'bout you?"

"Wrong faith," he said, and inched toward me. "Are you really all right?"

His voice was so tender, so soft. He took my hand. He was solid. He was strong. He was sane. I sighed. I wondered why I liked Philip best when I was sad.

"Yes. I'm really all right." Inside my hand, his own felt warm.

"She'll be fine, you know. Lenora is very strong. Please don't worry so about her. And you gave her Delvon, and he is helping her get well. You'll see."

In the other room, I heard the sounds of "Amazing Grace," and I leaned against him.

We stood that way for a long time, long enough that I realized the hymn was over, and the house was silent. "Come on, let's go wait in the kitchen," I said, thinking maybe we shouldn't be hanging out in Lenora's bedroom.

Delvon burst in, praising the Lord for the healing power of His love, and then he encircled Philip and me into one big, captive hug, spinning us until we struggled free and regained our footing.

"How is Lenora? Now?" I asked.

"Oh, fine. The nuns did a real nice job. Lenora's resting for a moment. Then I think we're all going out."

"I done invited them all out for ice cream, my treat," Jimmie said, joining us in the bedroom, which apparently had become the new staging arena.

Wide-eyed Dolly joined us, but she was no longer clutching her purse. "I think I'll have those two pray over me for my arthritis," she said. "And it wouldn't hurt, Jimmie, for you to have a session too."

Oh, what, they could do a healing prayer for bad grammar? I thought, then started edging out of Lenora's bedroom, followed as I was by the faithful.

Eventually we did actually go out for ice cream, even the two nuns. The kid behind the counter took us all in without blinking more than once or twice, but a manager type sitting at a table and pushing paper around stood up and watched us, with alternating looks of puzzlement and concern on his face. We took our ice cream to a concrete table outside. Lenora had orange sherbet and we all held our breath to see if she could eat it.

She could.

After that, everybody else sucked up ice cream with goo on top. I had two modest scoops of vanilla, and no goo. But if I'd known this was almost going to be the last ice-cream parlor outing of my relatively young life, I would have had double chocolate with chocolate syrup.

Chapter Twenty

Well, damnation.

Odell must have been a tad more security conscious than I'd figured.

That is to say, the key was no longer under the big rock by the door. No matter how many times I flashed my flashlight at the damp dirt under the rock, no key appeared.

Well, that certainly put a kink in my plans for an easy B and E. But, hey, lawyers thrive on challenges. So, in a sort of optimistic jitter, I started rolling over rocks, hoping Odell had merely moved the key to another hiding place. The overhead security light beamed down enough brightness to aid my search, which is one thing I don't get about security lights—don't they just help the burglar see better while he breaks in?

Grateful for my gloved hands, I picked up enough rocks to count as an upper-body workout at the Y, and still didn't find a key. I checked over the door frame, under the mat, and in expanding circles outward, searched for pots or fake stones that might hide a key.

Nothing.

Being a lawyer, I'd come prepared with a backup plan of operation. I had the lock picks I'd sweet-talked out of Henry, along with his fifteen-minute lesson, which, as it turned out, proved to be woefully inadequate. Having Henry with me right now would have been much

better: Henry, the dutiful son of a locksmith who had worked sum-
mers with his dad until he had a B.A. and a real job, Henry the mal-
leable, Henry who wore a suit to our last B and E. Henry who might
have made the lock picks do what I couldn't seem to do—that is, open
the damn lock. But Bonita had made me promise not to take Henry
with me ever again on anything that was illegal. That was one sure
sign she was favorably inclined to his proposal—that is, not wanting
him arrested in case she did marry him. Given Bonita's morality and
strict religious outlook, in her mind a felon wouldn't have made a
good role model for her five kids.

 Yeah, I could have used Henry. But I had promised.

So there I was, dressed for B and E bear with my gloves and my
flashlight and my soft-soled shoes, in a deserted parking lot, outside
a deserted building, which possibly contained secrets that would en-
lighten me on any number of topics, including my dead client and my
live wanted-for-questioning client.

And I couldn't get in the damn building.

Cursing, I gave the lock picks one more whirl, until even I knew
they wouldn't work, and then I tucked them back into my pocket, and
glared at the building, thinking hard on my next option. The front
door had a decorative panel of glass, which I could break out and
maybe open the lock from within—but I didn't want to make the B
and E obvious, so I passed on that for the moment.

With my flashlight, I did a careful study of the front, then I walked
around the office building, studying the windows in the back. Low
windows with burglar bars and high windows with none.

I counted sixteen screws in the burglar bars on the window to
Rayford's office, and only the one I'd already played with was anything like loose. And wouldn't you know it, I didn't have a screwdriver
in my car.

I studied the high windows again. High windows with no bars,
high windows that might be unlocked.

So how hard could it be to reach those high windows?

I poked around in the dirt below them, testing for solid footing. Not for me, but for my car. My idea being that I could drive my Honda out back, climb up on its roof, slide open the window—if it wasn't locked—and crawl into the office that way.

The dirt seemed solid enough that I didn't need to worry about getting the Honda stuck, but I would definitely leave car tracks that would suggest to anyone who walked around the building that somebody had been up to something. All in all, I had hoped to come, see, conquer, photocopy, and leave without a trace.

Giving up my plan was out of the question, so I drove the car under the window, parked it, climbed up on the roof, figured I could take a page from Angus's book and wipe out the car tracks with a palm frond or something on my way out, and in short order became profoundly grateful I was both tall and persistent. I wrenched the unlocked window open.

So, if this lawyer thing and the grooming school didn't work out, maybe I had a calling for common burglary. Could I actually make a living at that? I wondered.

I punched out the screen, crawled through the window, gauged the likelihood of harm in jumping from the window to the floor, and, risk-benefit analysis finished, I lowered myself down and dangled from the windowsill by my fingers, inhaled, and let go. A little tough on the knees in the landing, but nothing a good oomph sound and a solid curse didn't cure.

Bingo! I was in Rayford's office. Rayford's office with all the file cabinets. Given that I was alone, it was three in the morning, and I was as close to the middle of nowhere as you can get in Sarasota County without taking an airplane to another country, I flipped on the lights.

Yeah, okay. Not my best move as it turned out.

I didn't really know what I was looking for, so I started with the obvious—his desk drawers. Bills, booze, crap, and copies of the orange-defamation lawsuits complaints, and a long letter from the attorney who had signed the complaint. I glanced at it, saw it was an analysis of the suit, but didn't readily appear to contain clues on the bigger issues, and I switched on the copy machine in the corner and put the letter on top. Worth copying to study later, I figured, but not worth memorizing on the spot.

While the copy machine hummed and droned to life, I plundered the first filing cabinet, which seemed to be all orange-grove stuff, well organized, but wholly useless to me. After checking the back and the undersides for hidden files, I slammed it shut.

The second filing cabinet was locked.

Oh, good. I mean, yeah, *oh good.* Rayford probably never in his whole life read the "Purloined Letter," a Poe classic, and didn't know the best place to hide something is in plain sight. No, he'd lock up his important stuff. Kinda like drawing a red arrow to it.

Hoping for a cheap lock, as opposed to the complex dead bolt on the front door, I dug out the lock picks and tinkered. Within about ten heartbeats, the lock unlocked. Way to go, Henry, I thought, pocketed the picks, and went to plundering.

Who would ever have thought the man was so impeccably organized? Suddenly, I had a warm and fuzzy feeling for Rayford. He had, get this, a file labeled "M. David/Groves" and one labeled "Groves" and two that made my heart go all a twitter, "Groves/Sales" and "M. David and Gyp." In a jiffy, I had those files out and was heading to the copy machine, when I heard in the not-too-distant distance something that made my heart jump into my throat and about choke me.

The sound of a car or a truck approaching.

I jumped for the light switch, hoped the place went dark before the driver saw a light on, and checked Rayford's door with my heavy-duty, hurricane-proof (read: expensive) flashlight, and discovered it was already locked. Secure for a few more moments, I grabbed up the lawyer's letter and my collection of M. David files. So much for leaving no trace behind. I headed back for the high window.

When it hit me: I didn't have a ladder. I couldn't drive my Honda inside, and I wasn't tall enough to leap up into the high window.

The burglar bars on the lower windows closed that escape route.

Nothing to do but shove Rayford's desk under the high window, which I started doing, briefly horrified by how heavy it was and how much noise dragging it made.

I paused to listen to the sound of the car outside. Closer, closer, close, engine off.

Someone was jiggling the door, and tapping at the burglar bars out front, while my chest pounded and my hands and forehead sweated.

While I wiped my hands on my jeans, I heard someone walking around outside, then footsteps near the burglar-barred windows of Rayford's office, and then someone banged on the window.

"Lilly, Lilly, let me in. It's Miguel. We need to talk."

Miguel?

Miguel breaking and entering into Rayford's office?

Or, Miguel following me and waiting for that perfect chance to snuff me? I mean, if his plan to drown me had been wrecked by the red-faced man and the kid-rescue, then surely this presented him with an even more ideal spot. Alone. Night. Deserted building. Hapless, unarmed victim, and nothing obvious to tie my dead body back to him.

"It's Miguel, let me in, Lilly. We need to talk. Now. Open the door."

Yeah, right.

"Lilly, I saw the light. I know your car. I need to talk to you."

So, the light hadn't been a good idea, and, of course, he would recognize my ancient Honda. I made a pledge then and there to get a gold sedan or an SUV like everybody else in the legal world so my car wouldn't keep giving me away, and then I fingered the heavy flashlight, and slapped it against my palm. Solid. Heavy. Police officers used flashlights as weapons, didn't they?

If Miguel got inside, I'd just have to hit him over the head and make my escape, carrying the files with me.

In no time at all, there was a crash of glass in the front of the office, and the front door scraped the floor as it opened.

I put the M. David files on the corner of Rayford's desk, which was now more or less under the window, but not quite close enough to use as a ladder, and I crouched in the corner behind the door, holding the heavy flashlight with both hands.

So how hard did you have to hit a man with a flashlight to knock him out? I wondered. Something, strangely enough, not covered in law school's criminal law 101.

Chapter Twenty-one

It might not sound like it's that hard to do, but let me tell you—running at top speed with armloads of M. David files wasn't easy.

Two of the files dropped and I was too scared to stop and pick them up. So I kept up my fifty-yard dash, made it to my car, which fortunately I'd left unlocked on the theory that it was three A.M. in the middle of an orange grove and there wouldn't be much transient traffic waiting to steal my purse and my Handi Wipes. Gasping now, I threw the files on the seat, got the key out of my purse and in the ignition in record time—if there isn't an Olympic event for this, there should be—and I hauled buggy out of there.

With Miguel and his red pickup too soon on my tail.

There being no traffic on Sugar Bowl Road, I couldn't weave and duck between other cars and had to count on speed alone to keep ahead of Miguel and his truck, and hope he couldn't run me off the road. I had the passing thought that I should have punctured his tire, though with exactly what I wasn't sure, and made a mental note to get something sharp and long to carry in my purse so I could puncture tires if this ever came up again. That should make passing security at the courthouse an interesting break in my routine.

Then I concentrated on driving as fast as an old Honda Civic can go.

Which turns out to be pretty fast. At least enough to keep me ahead of Miguel, who hung in there and kept honking his horn as if I somehow had managed not to notice he was following me.

By the time I hit State Road 72, where, despite the wee morning hour, there was traffic, and plenty of it, mostly trucks, I had enough of a lead to think.

And to conclude that perhaps I needed to consider giving up this B and E thing. It wasn't nearly as much fun as it used to be.

For one thing, Miguel had not only scared me, but ruined my attempts at sneaking away without leaving a trace. Now there was a busted window, a jimmied filing cabinet, a copy machine left running, and M. David files in the black loam behind the office. Not to mention car tracks.

But at least there wasn't a body—mine.

After he had tried to sweet-talk me into unlocking Rayford's office door, Miguel had simply hurled his thin but strong body against it. The sound and the fury of the first hurl suddenly and thoroughly convinced me that I wasn't really up to the task of rendering him unconscious with a flashlight, and inspired by the potential threat of imminent harm, I'd run into Rayford's private bath—seeking a second locked door or a weapon or just in a blind panic—but lo and behold, there was a small window over the toilet and it didn't have burglar bars.

So, okay, if Rayford had paid an expert to design his security, the man needed to seek a refund. Using the toilet as a ladder, I was up and out, not without some difficulty in juggling and grasping the M. David files, but I slipped through that window just about the same time Miguel busted through Rayford's outer office door, and shouted, "Lilly, Lilly, it's me. I won't hurt you." Or some such nonsense.

I decided his actions were louder than his reassurances—I mean, come on, you don't convince a girl you are harmless by smashing in not one, but two locked doors—and I sprinted for the Honda like the horsemen of Armageddon were on my tail.

So here I was, twenty minutes after my mad-dash escape, dodging giant trucks on 72, and, suddenly, going home didn't sound like a good idea.

I mean, Jimmie was spry, but old, and the Glock was at the bottom of the Peace River and Bearess was sleeping next door with Grandmom, and I wasn't at all sure just how sturdy my doors were.

Calling the sheriff's department was out of the question, given that my front passenger seat was covered in the spilled paperwork I had stolen after I'd climbed in a window in someone else's office without their consent, implied or otherwise.

As I whipped around a slow-moving and suspiciously weaving car, apparently scaring the probably drunk driver into spinning off onto the shoulder, I realized I had only one safe haven to go to.

Philip.

And so I went, spinning my Honda into his driveway at precisely 3:47 A.M. and banging on his door with rising levels of anxiety.

Philip was wearing a dark silk robe over his pajamas, nattily clothed in the wee hours of the morning, having taken the time to properly cover himself for company despite the shrill probability that it wasn't the Avon lady calling, but trouble.

He looked so calm and GQ that I wanted to slap him.

But then I wanted to hug him, and did so in great relief, and we tumbled back into the house and he locked the door, and flipped on a light and studied me.

"No blood," he said. "So what is going on that you need to—"

"Miguel is chasing me," I said, and grabbed him for a second hug, and with my face muffled in his silk robe, I gave Philip the sixty-second version of my second outing of the night.

"Did he hurt you? Are you all right, Lilly?"

"Yes, fine, fine, but Miguel is out there, maybe still chasing me, and—"

"Then let me move your car into the garage and out of sight,"

Philip said, like he'd had plenty of practice with this very type of thing.

Hell, he was a criminal-defense attorney in Florida. He probably *had* had practice with this sort of thing.

"And bring in the files in the front seat, would you?" I asked as I shut and locked the door behind him, my heart beginning to slow into its regular rhythm.

Chapter Twenty-two

Philip was sitting behind me on his king-size bed, his big, strong fingers massaging my sore neck. It felt delicious. So, okay, he wasn't a trained Rolfer, but then he hadn't busted down doors to try to kill me either. Besides, my skin still tingled from his recent devotions and our hot shower in the early morning. His legs straddled my hips and I could feel their pressure against me. I knew he wasn't eighteen, but I thought he might be good for another round, and I knew I was.

But as my fingers inched out to suggest just such a thing with just the right touch, Philip dropped his hands. "Maybe we should get some coffee and look at those files you salvaged."

My word, I really, really liked this man. I bang on his door before dawn, send him out into possible danger to hide my car and fetch some files I had stolen, and then he comes back inside, showers me, makes love to me, rubs my neck, and then comes up with a word like *salvaged*. Instead of stolen.

Maybe I loved him.

Maybe I could *marry* him.

But I didn't have to figure that out just right at this precise moment because the man had said "coffee" and suddenly that was the thing I needed more than anything else, even more than another round of great sex, and we untangled ourselves and went to the kitchen, where he put the twice-filtered water on to boil and ground the beans. While

Philip putzed with the coffee production, I dove into the salvaged files like a person looking for the lost winning lottery ticket.

Philip being the only other human besides me who fusses so over a cup of coffee, I had time to discover from these files that Rayford was not only organized, but ruthless in keeping paperwork.

A man after my own heart in some ways. Too bad he was otherwise such a yahoo.

What I learned from reading through the salvaged files was this: While M. David was the CEO of Boogie Bog, and the sole partner in the corporation that owned Delilah Groves, that is, before Rayford owned an interest in the groves, M. David had himself ordered the dumping of the waste phosphogypsum in his own groves. And detail-oriented cowboy Rayford had photocopied the documentation.

Why would M. David want to poison his own orange groves?

Philip handed me a steaming cup of coffee, topped off with just the right amount of organic soy milk, and kissed my ear. "I put in a half teaspoonful of sugar because you had such a hard night," he whispered.

I sipped, I let the caffeine enter my circulatory system, convinced, and not for the first time, that some evolutionary mistake had rid our own bodies of the ability to make our own caffeine—I mean, our bodies can manufacture vitamin D, why not caffeine?

While I pondered that, Philip read over my shoulder. "Why would he put that toxic waste in his own orange grove?"

Yes, hadn't I just asked myself the same thing?

But I remembered what Angus and Miguel had told me—there were millions of gallons of the stuff behind those earthen dams and no way to get rid of it.

"Rayford said Boogie Bog tried to sell it off to be mixed into concrete block or road materials, but the nuclear-waste folks had that market cornered. So, maybe, stupid as it sounds to us, M. David was experimenting to see if he could use the gyp as fertilizer."

"Actually," Philip said, slipping into college-professor mode once again, "I've read that phosphate companies are beginning to experiment with that. I think perhaps they've even sold some to third-world countries for fertilizer."

"Nice, real nice."

"This was two years ago, according to those documents, that M. David was dumping the gyp on his groves. That's strange timing for the lawsuit, isn't it?"

"Yep. That was the strange thing about the orange-defamation suits. All the protests took place a couple of seasons ago." Then I sipped and sipped and finally felt up to the long explanation about the SLAPP suit by proxy, and I told it, though Philip's expression suggested he would really rather nibble my ear again.

When I finished the tale, I gave Philip a serious look. He gave me a serious look back.

"What you are telling me is that M. David experiments with the gyp in his own groves, and when Miguel and Angus found out and started protesting, he stopped using the gyp at Delilah. Or maybe it was killing the trees. Who knows? But M. David quit using Boogie Bog's gyp in the groves and resigned as its CEO, and then nearly two years later, when Angus and Miguel start rallying the troops to stop his plans at Antheus, he files suit against them with the orange-defamation case."

"Yep, that's what I figured."

"How does that lead to M. David's murder? Or to Angus's murder?"

Well, there he had it—now that it no longer mattered, I'd proved my SLAPP suit by proxy theory, but still didn't have a solid clue as to who killed anybody.

"And how does that lead to Miguel chasing you last night?"

Oh, yeah, that. I'd started to explain to Philip after he had hidden my Honda and safely returned via his garage door, but then he'd looked at me with those Dean Martin eyes, and said soothing things in that Dean Martin voice, and the next thing I knew I was naked under a hot flow of water while he ran his soapy hands all over me, and then we were in bed, and then and then and then, and finally here we were, back to Miguel.

With a bit of careful editing, I explained to Philip about the receipts in the glove compartment that I had salvaged and how Miguel knew I had taken them, and that he might want to silence me in case I decided to turn over evidence of his crime to the police.

"Where are the receipts?" Philip asked, just as calmly as if I had told him I'd bought a new briefcase, not that I possessed evidence of a murder that I had myself stolen after fleeing the scene of that murder. So I answered the question like I was explaining where the new briefcase was.

"In my desk, at home."

A quick flicker of how-dumb-can-you-get passed over Philip's face before he restored his expression to a cross between Dean Martin sexy and criminal-defense attorney on guard. "You should—"

Then, in the middle of Philip's alpha-male order, and before I could bristle into my "don't boss me around" spiel, the man paused.

I watched his face as he reformulated his budding directive.

In a moment that challenged my grandmother's sage advice that a woman could never retrain a grown man and should therefore never expect to, Philip asked, "Lilly, would you like me to hide them for you? We could go get the receipts, and I could put them in my safe."

Suspiciously, I studied him for a minute. Suspicious, that is, that he seemed willing to let me make up my own mind about something important. But before I pondered too deeply on that, I thought about the risk of roping him into what was increasingly a big, frigging mess.

"Maybe we don't want them in your office. I don't want you implicated if this goes bad."

"My safe isn't in my office. It is at a secret and undisclosed location. My clients sometimes ask me to provide secure storage for them. Because of that, I have a location that is search-warrant proof because of its hidden location. If you will provide me with the receipts, I will take them there for proper safekeeping."

I noticed he didn't say I could go with him.

So the Golden Boy had a secret safe that he was going to keep secret even from me, and where he kept illegal things for his clients.

Yeah, okay, I was definitely warming to this guy. Especially since he gave me that Dean Martin look again.

"How about another shower?" I asked, not at all in the mood for a coy suggestion or an engaging game of sly hands on thighs.

So, we didn't end up solving any murders, but we were very, very clean and very, very satisfied when Philip followed me to my house, where I gave him the salvaged receipts. Before he left, Philip had to search my house for fugitives and unlocked windows, give me fifty kinds of instructions on staying safe, and make me promise all kinds of self-preservation things. Before Philip would leave me, I had to give him fifty kinds of reassurances that Miguel wouldn't gun me down in my own office in front of witnesses.

Thus reassured, but anxious, Philip left me to hide evidence that my client might well be a man whose passions had put him on a trail of murder. And who might have penciled me down on a list as "next."

Chapter Twenty-three

My brother Dan, the normal one, likes to say that if a door shuts, a window opens.

Me, I find that it isn't so much doors shutting and windows opening. Rather, I find that if you solve one crisis, another pops up.

Farmer Dave says it's all about attitude. Mine apparently sucks. But then he's the one living with a broken heart and an escaped burro from the Grand Canyon.

Opening and shutting things aside, I was fixing to solve one problem and gird the doors and windows in preparation for the next.

That is, I was going to finally get this stupid car case of Jimmie's settled. Then I could go back to solving M. David's and Angus's murders, armed as I now was with all but two of Rayford's M. David files. Since Josey didn't seem to be wrapping up M. David's case, and the police were focused on Miguel, and not even looking for anybody else in Angus's death, I had the deluded feeling that it was up to me to figure out those murders.

I owed that much to Angus.

I owed it to Miguel. Miguel might be off the list as potential lover, because with all that had happened in the last twenty-four hours, I didn't feel any remnant of lust for the boy, but he was still my client. And, as his attorney, I had a duty to either exonerate him from Angus's death or help collect information for his defense.

And I owed myself an answer too—had I really lusted after a killer while Philip paid court to me? If so, I might have to consider whether I'd dismissed that last psychologist too soon.

Thus with my mind in overload, zipping into my office in over-drive the next morning, I barely greeted Bonita before I phoned Jason the baby lawyer. The first thing I said was, "I officially withdraw the offer of settlement in the Jimmie Rodgers case."

"That's cool," he said, cluelessly. "I wasn't going to take it any-way."

"Fine, then," I said, and tried to put charm back in my voice. "Might you come over to my office this morning? There's something we need to discuss."

After a minimum of false pleasantries, Jason agreed to scamper right over.

How easy was this going to be? I thought, and, despite the fact that I had had no sleep to speak of, I actually hummed as I took the video of the faker plaintiff doing things proving that he was not remotely injured back to our audio room, where in no time at all I made a duplicate. Then, for good measure, I made another duplicate of the tape. I went back to my office and put one copy of the tape in the Jimmie Rodgers file, then went upstairs and locked the original in the firm's safe. By then our receptionist had buzzed me to tell me that Jason was waiting for me, and I flounced out front, greeted him as briefly as possible, and led him into one of our firm's conference rooms, where, without further ado, I popped a copy of the video into the player and turned on the TV.

Together Jason and I watched the faker plaintiff going through a morning's worth of yard chores that made my good back ache. Like an athletic and un-ailing young man, the faker plaintiff was lifting and toting and pulling and bending and scraping and mowing. Any judge or juror watching this tape could conclude only one thing: Nothing was wrong with this man's back.

"Jason, as soon as I play this videotape before the judge, your lawsuit against Jimmie Rodgers will be dismissed. Not only that, but I'll file a motion for sanctions for fraud upon the court. Under section 57.105, you'll have to pay my attorney's fees." And you can jolly well guess, I thought, without having to say, that I will document substantial attorney's fees on this case.

"Did you have a . . . I mean, a . . . a warrant?" Jason asked.

"I don't need a warrant to videotape someone who's doing something outside, in plain view."

Jason huffed and puffed and stammered and turned red and lost his cool and carried on and acted very much like the baby lawyer he was. When he finally began to recoup some of his dignity, he turned to me and said, "This isn't over yet. I'll, I'll . . . you'll see. You haven't won yet." And then he marched out.

Yes, yes, yes, yes, yes, I had won. It was all over but the paperwork. I danced all the way back to my office, where Bonita handed me five pink phone-message slips. "Philip. Worried. Call him." I did, not even bothering to tell him young Mr. Quartermine had been ever so vaguely threatening.

After all, possibly a trained Rolfer client who knew how to make bombs was trying to secretly do me in. So what was a kid lawyer on the scale of worry?

Chapter Twenty-four

A diamondback will rattle before it bites you.

A dog will growl before it bites you.

A cat will hiss before it bites you.

But Mrs. Sherilyn Moody, new widow and prospective murder suspect, determinedly thin and expensively dressed, followed Olivia right in through the back door and into the space outside my own office with a great pretense of graciousness, not a hint of a rattle, growl, or hiss about her. Despite the rain, she was neither damp nor fuzzy haired.

"Olivia," Sherilyn said, "thank you for escorting me inside."

"No, you can't—" I tried to say.

"Oh, it's all right, Lilly," Olivia said. "I ran into Sherilyn just a while ago and she wants to explain in person why she and that other guy decided to drop the orange-defamation cases."

Nope, sorry, but I didn't think that was the reason at all, and I sputtered, "I can't talk to you now."

I had the feeling I was standing naked in a snowstorm and fate had just dumped a bucket of ice cubes on me.

"Oh, Miss Cleary, I am sorry I invited myself here today. But this will only take a second. I want to discuss hiring you. As cocounsel in my—"

Part of my brain said to turn around and run from Sherilyn. But the part of my brain that controls my feet told me to stand pat and hold my ground. And the part of my brain that was heavily influenced by lawyer training told me I could talk my way out of this.

"No," I said, with great force and conviction in my voice. "I will not discuss anything with you."

Bonita and Olivia moved toward me, little worried looks on their faces at my apparent rudeness.

Sherilyn said something I couldn't hear over the sound of my own heartbeat hammering behind my eyeballs.

"Shut up and get out," I shouted.

The cute blond girl who worked in the mail room across the hallway from my office came out of her cubbyhole and peered around the wall at me.

"As I was saying, Miss Cleary, why I came here today is to discuss my malpractice case, and your role in it, that is, hiring you as cocounsel. My preliminary medical expert is quite certain that the plastic surgeon went too deep with his laser," Sherilyn said, with just as much force and conviction as I had shouted at her.

"Don't tell me anything—"

"Of course, Newly Moneta, my current attorney, I believe he is one of your ex-boyfriends, says—"

"Stop, no, NO."

"Oh, my dear, I didn't realize you still cared so about the man. Why, just wait until I tell him. If it's any comfort, he speaks well of you too. Anyway, Newly's theory is that I can—"

At that, I had flat out had enough of the Moody family, and I launched myself at the surviving Moody, my right fist formed and my arm raised. Only the combination of Bonita literally jumping in front of me and a quick back step on Sherilyn's part kept her from getting her face smashed in.

But Sherilyn didn't quit. "Newly's got an expert all lined up, a Dr.

Standfield Morgan, don't you just love how that name sounds, and here's a summary of Newly's trial strategy and his opening statement—"

I took another swing at Sherilyn, but my blow had only glanced off her helmet of hair when Bonita, who is quick on her feet, shoved me back a step even as I swung at Sherilyn. Out of the corner of my eye, I saw the cute blond mail-room girl make a run for it, presumably down the hall. Bonita grabbed my arm and held on, tugging on me to make me back up.

Sherilyn turned to Bonita and Olivia, and said, "I'm explaining to Lilly all the sordid details of what that horrid doctor did to me in ruining my face, and what my attorney has planned for trial, as you will surely note."

Bonita made shushing noises toward Sherilyn, but continued to hold my arms with her own strong hands. I struggled to get out of Bonita's grip, though I was reluctant to fight with my own secretary, and settled for shouting back at Sherilyn, the devil's own mistress, "I am not your attorney. I will never be your attorney. Shut up."

Sherilyn daintily dusted off her linen sheath as if I had thrown mud at her and said, "As I was telling you pursuant to hiring you as cocounsel in my case, what I did after the surgery was—"

I spun toward Sherilyn again, so fiercely that Bonita lost her hold on me, and my fist was ready and aimed when Jackson stepped between Sherilyn and me, and my punch bounced off his stomach, hurting my hand, but apparently not much bothering him.

As I struck the founding and controlling partner of the law firm in his iron gut, a chorus of gasps rose from the hallway.

But I didn't look at the rubberneckers. I looked at Jackson, standing as tall and strong and fierce as his namesake at First Bull Run, when General Bee's next-to-last words were, "There stands General Jackson, like a stone wall."

I dropped my fist. I inhaled. He had a stomach like a damn stone wall. I rubbed my sore hand against the soft cotton of my shirt, but that did nothing to take the sting out of it.

"You need to leave now, Mrs. Moody," Jackson said, in a voice that invited neither rebuttal nor refusal. So saying, he put both hands on her shoulders, forcibly turned her around, and pointed her at the exit. "Here, I'll let you out the back door. Much closer to the parking lot."

Mrs. Sherilyn Moody, plaintiff-designate from hell, gathered her poise around her and left.

The cute blond mail clerk hovered within touching distance of Jackson, and I saw her as an angel for fetching him, and made a mental note to see that she got a big Christmas bonus. Even if her interference had meant I'd hit my own mentor.

"I think everybody can leave now," Jackson said.

Only then did I peer out and see the faces in the small crowd of Smith, O'Leary, and Stanley regulars clustering in the hallway. But at Jackson's words, they quickly broke and scampered back to their offices.

Except for Olivia, who didn't actually work here anymore, but might as well have.

She slipped past Jackson in his commanding-general persona and put her hand on my other arm.

"All in all, doll, you shouldn't hit people in the office," Jackson said. "And you shouldn't ever try to punch a woman." Then he gave me a quizzical kind of grin, and added, "Even her." With that, he stomped off down the hallway.

Suddenly I could see the value of knowing voodoo and made a mental note to return to New Orleans soon and learn the basic curses, as much defensive as offensive, against the Moody virus. For the time being, I shook off both the protective hand of Bonita and the comforting hand of Olivia.

"That bitch was just about to do me out of defending a physician in what will probably be a very lucrative case," I said.

Bonita renewed her grip and pulled me back into my office. Olivia followed us inside and shut the door.

"Do you need a kava?" Olivia asked me.

No, I needed voodoo or Valium, or both, and quickly. Or an ice bag for my hand. So just how many crunches did Jackson do at the Y to make hitting his stomach like hitting stone?

Instead, I breathed. I closed my eyes. I visualized my peaceful waterfall. Then I opened my eyes and said, "Two, please."

Olivia riffled in her purse until she found the herbs, and Bonita poured me a glass of water from my triple-filtered water carafe, and I gulped the capsules.

And there, while I waited for Mother Nature's own weedy little roots to soothe me, I told them what had happened to Mrs. Moody's face. Then, I explained to Olivia that Henry had promised he would refer the defense of the plastic surgeon to me when Mrs. Moody filed her medical-malpractice suit.

If Sherilyn Moody had succeeded in telling me any of Newly's trial strategy or her own admissions in the guise of hiring me as her attorney, however fake her attempt to hire me really was, such information would have created a conflict of interest. No matter if I had tried to shout it out, had Sherilyn managed to tell me any of the "secrets" about her case, the rules of ethics would have precluded me from defending the surgeon she would sue. Because I could have used the private and privileged information that she had told me against her in her lawsuit.

"Even if it was a setup? Couldn't you just explain that to a judge, that it was a trap?" Bonita asked.

"It wouldn't matter," I said. "The point is, if Jackson and I hadn't stopped her and she had told me what they call client secrets, I'd never get to defend the case. If I'd entered an appearance on behalf of the plastic surgeon, Mrs. Moody would have filed a motion to have me disqualified, and any judge in this circuit would have granted it."

If it hadn't been my ox that had nearly been gored, I would have admired it—it could have been a perfectly executed setup if I hadn't seen it coming. Then, in a rising fit of pique at Newly, my twice-ex boyfriend, I called him. He came on his private line with his usual big, eager voice.

"Newly, you jerk," I said.

"Lilly? Is that you?"

"Why in hell's bells did you tell Sherilyn Moody I'd be defending that doctor who messed up her face?"

"Oh, that. I got the name of the doctor's liability insurer in a . . . er, a kind of, er . . . prediscovery. When I saw it was Henry's company, I knew Henry'd turn the case over to you. He always gives you the best cases. I warned Sherilyn that you'd be tough. You always have a trick up your sleeve."

"When was this? That you told Mrs. Moody I'd probably be the defense attorney?"

"Ah, let's see, a month, maybe, three weeks ago?"

"Well, she paid me a visit, tried to hire me as cocounsel and tell me all about your trial strategy."

"Whoo, hon. You know what that means?"

"She didn't tell me anything confidential. I stopped her in time. But I want to know this—when did you start, you know, actually preparing a case?"

"Hon, I hadn't done a thing on that case except get her to sign a contingency-fee contract."

"Well, get ready, '*hon*,' because I'm going to be on the other side, and dressed for bear, when that sucker hits the circuit-court docket," I shouted in his ear, and hung up.

When I issued forth with another round of cursing the dead and the living Moodys, Olivia and Bonita tried to quiet me. "You don't understand. M. David played the same trick on me to get Jackson out of a case," I said. "Only he pulled it off."

"Uh-oh," Olivia said, and I saw a glimmer of remembering. But it was before Bonita's time, and she frowned in puzzlement at me, while patting my arm and making those soft cooing sounds I'd heard her use on Carmen.

Maybe Bonita would stop making that noise if I just told her the story. Painfully, I explained that during my first year at Smith, O'Leary, and Stanley, Jackson Smith had been retained to defend a corporation in what was going to be a long, nasty lawsuit, the kind of lawsuit that defense firms love because, win or lose, it would not only bring the firm publicity, but net the law firm sizable legal fees. What we called the "money-tap" kind of lawsuit.

In his usual style, Jackson had proved to be a formidable foe for the plaintiff. At that stage of my career, i.e., right out of law school, I was floundering, stuck doing workers compensation and everyone's legal research. Overworked and underappreciated, I had not followed Jackson's case closely.

"That's when you met M. David," Olivia said. "I remember. I was there at one of those awful formal fund-raisers, and he zeroed right in on you. You were so pretty."

Letting the past tense in connection with *pretty* slide by for the moment, I nodded, remembering against my will how I'd been immediately smitten with M. David. I mean, okay, spank me for being that easily seduced, but M. David was a very handsome and rich man, he had sought me out, and he had courted me with a great deal of finesse that was wholly foreign to me at that point in my life—I mean, come on, my only prior lover had been Farmer Dave, a pot farmer and felon, the very same man now living with a Grand Canyon burro in my apple orchard in north Georgia. Farmer Dave had some sterling qualities, but finesse and elegance were not among them.

So, yeah, I was an easy target for M. David.

He'd romanced me with such grace I had managed to overlook

the fact that he had a wife. Certainly, as I later learned, he had a history of overlooking that fact.

"He promised he would love me forever," I said, hearing a catch in my voice and stopping it, right then. I'd spent too many years hating him to let that lost-love thing make my voice quiver like a teenage girl's.

"Then, one night he told me he wanted to hire me, since he thought he might be caught in some of the fallout from the lawsuit. I was thrilled. Stupid me, I thought Jackson and the firm would think I was this big rainmaker to bring in M. David as a client. So, yeah, I agreed on the spot to represent him."

I paused, collected myself, and said, "So, after he hired me, M. David told me a collection of 'insider information' about the corporation that was suing Jackson's client. All relative to Jackson's case, but I was too"—what? Brain-dead with young love was about the best description—"distracted to know how important the information was. I didn't even have a clue that M. David was a silent partner in the corporation suing Jackson's client. I thought he was an innocent bystander, at worst, a third party."

I looked up at Bonita in time to see the lightbulb of understanding flash across her face. To her credit, she quickly regained her neutral, calm expression, and didn't chastise me for having been stupid, or involved with a married man, which I guessed were redundancies, and she let me finish my story.

"See, like with what Sherilyn just tried to do, once M. David revealed the insider secrets to me, this disqualified Jackson from the case under the same conflict-of-interest ethics rules. Because what one lawyer in a firm knows is imputed to all members. So it was the same as if M. David had told client secrets straight to Jackson himself," I said. "Plus, M. David promised to spin it so that it looked like I had seduced him with the very intent of prying secrets out of him, and that Jackson had put me up to it."

Bonita gasped. "No one would believe that of Jackson. That he would . . . prostitute you like that."

It stung for a moment that she hadn't said, "No one would believe that of you."

Then I said, "But it wouldn't matter. Jackson and I would have had to testify, and, wholly aside from the damage to our reputations and the fact that the press would have had a field day, once we were called to testify, we would have had to withdraw as counsel because a lawyer cannot testify in a case where he or she is an attorney of record. You know that."

Bonita sighed, and nodded. I caught a small flicker of sympathy on her face.

There I had been, just a kid straight out of law school, and I thought this handsome, sophisticated man loved me. Not only had I thought M. David loved me, but I thought I loved him too. What a perfect mark I'd been. What a perfect, horrified fool I'd been when I found out that instead of a sudden infatuation with my charms, M. David had simply calculatedly and deliberately set me up for the sole reason of disqualifying Jackson.

"I remember the . . . fallout," Olivia said. I watched as Olivia shaped her words carefully, whether for my benefit, or Bonita's, I wasn't sure. "Jackson, once confronted by M. David, was forced to withdraw from representing his client, with a great financial burden for both the client and Jackson," she said, finally settling on a condensed version of the bare facts, and leaving out the fracas that had naturally followed the revelation that I'd been so easily duped at such a great cost to the law firm.

Still ashamed after all these years, I hung my head. "A lesser man would have ruined me, but Jackson took me under his wing," I murmured, my face still pointed at the floor, still grateful to Jackson after all these years.

Olivia stood up and walked toward me. "I never loved Fred so much in my life as I did then, or Jackson either. They stood down the rest of the partners who wanted to fire you." She put her hand under my chin and pulled my face up.

That sordid escapade would have destroyed my career if Jackson and Fred had not supported me. I would have ended up back in Bugfest, Georgia, eking out a meager and disgraced living in my father's old law office.

But Jackson had forgiven me, had told me not to make the same mistake again, and then had trained me in his own image to become a great trial attorney.

I lifted my head, and I smiled. After all, I hadn't made the same mistake twice. Jackson's faith was well placed. "Bonita, why don't you give Henry a call. After you're done chatting with him, put him on with me. I've already got some ideas on how to work that case against Sherilyn."

And I made a mental note to ask Jackson to be my coach at the punching bag at the Y. You wouldn't think a woman trial attorney would need to know how to land a solid blow to the head, but increasingly I was seeing the advantages of just that.

Little did I know.

Chapter Twenty-five

Rain, in a kind of pre-hurricane fierceness, stung my face when I left the office that evening, and water was pooling on Shade Avenue deep enough that I worried about my little Honda Civic sloshing through the high waters. But as my car did a car version of the dog paddle, I realized I had to make one stop on the way home, and I spun around and headed toward Bayshore Drive.

Much as I didn't really want to, I had to go to Sherilyn's McMansion on the bay and apologize to her. After all, I had tried not twice but three times to punch her, and I had most definitely yelled at her. Though she deserved both the hitting and the yelling at for trying to set me up, still, good professional manners, generally speaking, do not involve attorneys screaming or striking people in their office. We're supposed to file motions in court instead.

Oh, yeah, and then I still wanted to find out why she and Rayford had dropped the orange-defamation lawsuit, that is, if the post-apology moment should present itself to me to ask.

Given the rain, I whirled my little Honda right up in Sherilyn's big circle driveway as close as I could get to her gilded front door, and ran toward the house. After I banged on the door, it opened, and a woman in a black uniform answered with a suspicious and unfriendly look on her face.

"May I please speak with Mrs. Moody?" I asked.

"Name?"

"I'm Lilly Cleary."

She shut the door in my face. I heard a click, probably a lock. Given the events of the afternoon, I wasn't overly hopeful Sherilyn would send her maid back to admit me.

But moments later, Sherilyn herself appeared, snakelike and seductive, wearing clinging knit in a sea-wash soft blue-green that complimented her hazel eyes and chestnut hair, as well as her ardently trimmed body. There seemed to be an awful lot of cleavage showing for a stormy evening and a new widow.

"Hello," I said, hoping momentarily for at least an invite out of the rain.

Sherilyn nodded at me, and stood blocking the entrance to her house.

"I've come to apologize. For my behavior at the office today. I'm not usually so . . . aggressive."

Sherilyn glared at me.

Since her expression didn't suggest we'd be laughing over cocktails in the next half hour, I said, "Well, then, I'll be going."

"It was unexpectedly gracious of you to come by," Sherilyn said, surprising me. "I accept the apology."

We stared at each other for a strange moment.

"I told M.D. it wouldn't work, you know, that you could not possibly fall for the same trick twice."

This time I nodded, not quite trusting myself to speak.

"Really, it's better this way, don't you think?"

"How so?" I asked.

"Oh, now we'll be adversaries in court. You'll represent the doctor who did this to my face, and my attorney will have a splendid time, really, trouncing you and that fraud, that odious quack. I so look forward to it."

Yeah, me too. Actually, I realized, I really did look forward to it. Trounced, my ass, I thought. You just wait. But what I said, with a slight smile, was, "Until then, perhaps you would tell me why you and Rayford dropped the lawsuits against Angus and Miguel."

"You are just totally unbelievable," she said.

"So are you."

Sherilyn made a rude noise and shrugged. "If I tell you, will you go away?"

"Most assuredly."

"Rayford wanted to drop the suit, and I didn't care. There wasn't any money in it, it was just . . . Well, there wasn't any money in the suit for Rayford or me, and I didn't care what Rayford did. I was just as happy to be done with those groves."

"Rayford told me he owned a cattle ranch in Montana or something."

"That'd be Rayford," Sherilyn said, and snorted a short burst of gruff, most unladylike laughter. "He was a cowboy or something, but he didn't *own* any ranch. Rayford was M.D.'s bodyguard. You know, one of those guys who shows up from out west with a dollar inside in his shoe and big dreams."

"So how'd he get enough money to buy half of that orange grove? Bodyguarding pay that well?"

"I'm sure I don't know. On either question."

Thinking once again of how fortuitous M. David's death was for his good widow, I couldn't resist one last volley. "I see y'all didn't waste any time putting Delilah Groves up for sale."

"Don't be snide, dear."

"Snide," I half-shouted. "You tried to cheat me out of a big case."

"And you slept with my husband."

Oh, that, I thought. "But he didn't mean it. It was a setup."

"Yes, that's what he explained to me, years ago. And that's why he put me up to my little attempted coup d'état. M.D. thought it would be great fun, tricking you again. He thought it would take my mind off—well, you know, my face. Now, dear, the wind is blowing rain into my house, and I think you should say good-bye."

"Oh, I'm sorry. Just a couple more questions, please." I put a chipper, girlish sound in my voice that I didn't mean any more than I meant I was sorry the rain was blowing into her house. I hoped the wood peeled off her floors and the roof blew away.

Sherilyn laughed. "You *are* totally unreal."

But she didn't shut the door in my face.

"One more question—"

"Oh, probably not, but I'm bored with all this rain, and you are amusing in a certain backwoods sort of way. That's what M. David said about you—an exact quote, if you want to know."

No, thank you, I didn't want to know what M. David had said about me, whether exactly quoted or paraphrased, and I had to do that whole inhale, exhale, calm-down thing before jumping to my real point.

"So who do you think killed M. David?" I asked.

"I'll tell you the same thing I told that cop lady. I don't know. But if I ever find out, I'll kill them myself before I turn them over to the law."

Wow. That was great, I thought. She sounded like she meant it.

Then I thought, so, yeah, she *did* mean it.

"Good night," Sherilyn said, with a tone of finality.

With that, I figured we were done. But a large, dark man appeared behind Sherilyn in the shadows of her McMansion's vestibule. "Everything all right, Sherry?" he asked.

"Just fine, dear," she said, turning away from me long enough to give him a look.

Well, this warranted a moment's further study, I thought, and leaned in to see the man better. Quickly, my eyes focused on his body, I mean, you couldn't miss it. It was well developed, this body, and dressed in a tight black T-shirt with some designer squiggle over the chest pocket and tight black jeans.

Having digested the body, I looked at the face. Standard and aging. Gray hair. Dark eyes. Lines and wrinkles and thinning lips and hair.

Running from time, lifting weights at the gym.

This was Theibuet, I was sure of it, remembering back to the night of the antiphosphate rally, the last night of poor Angus John's life.

Great, this was like giving somebody rope and watching while they tied the noose themselves. Theibuet and Sherilyn, together, in her house, on a dark and stormy evening, with the endowed widow showing off nearly her entire bosom and the man dressed in tight black.

Yeah, these two had something going on.

"You need something?" Theibuet asked me, in a voice with a hint of menace in it.

Before I could answer, Sherilyn said, "Oh, her. She's just one of M. David's crazy ex-girlfriends. I think she's harmless enough. And, besides, she was just leaving."

"I was not M. David's girlfriend," I said, highly insulted by being categorized as "harmless." Her insults renewed my enthusiasm for taking boxing lessons from Jackson, and for taking her and her lawyer on in court. Wait till I subpoenaed all, as in *all*, of her medical records and read the juiciest parts—and there are always juicy parts—into evidence at trial, and hence, forevermore, into the public record. Instead of enlightening her on the various court-sanctioned, tried-and-true ways I could ruin her life during her lawsuit, I smiled like I meant it. "See you at the depositions," I said, turned and sprinted to my car, and slogged away home.

Home, where I found Jimmie, naturally enough, in my kitchen, drinking my grocery-store wine.

"It's not near as tasty as that other stuff you done hid from me, but it'll sure dog-knock your lights out."

"Pour me a glass, please, while I dry off."

"You better let me get you the good stuff. I done been feeding crickets to that durn bird of yours," Jimmie said. "He chases 'em around his cage till they jump out. I reckon you got a bunch of crickets jumping around on your porch, so don't leave the door 'ween the porch and the den open, you hear?"

"Why are you feeding Rasputin crickets?" I asked, and then wondered where he got the crickets, completely missing for the moment the real point of his confession, which was that my porch was teeming with little black hopping things.

"Lenora told me to get him on bugs when I told her you was feeding him candy bars."

"There're not candy bars, they are trail mix bars. They are organic, they are seeds and oats and perfectly healthy for a—"

"Bugs is better."

By then the real point was dawning on me, and I went into the den and peered out at the porch. Sure enough, black crickets in small-plague proportions were hopping around in the once-clear space of my screened-in porch.

"When it stops raining, I'll shoo 'em out into the backyard. It ain't no big deal," Jimmie said.

After I finished staring at the black bugs that now populated my porch, I stared at my backyard. The grass was somewhere between ankle and calf high in the spots where it actually grew. So far, I had to conclude that Jimmie as a live-in yardman was not working out especially well.

Jimmie spun around in a half circle, spread his arms wide, and said, "Browning says, 'the best yet is fixing to be.'"

Despite Jimmie's encouraging and goofy grin, I seriously doubted if that was the exact quote or was going to be the case. But before I protested, Jimmie winked and said, "Let's get that wine, you tell me where you got it hid. Then I got me a date next door."

In nothing flat, while I was still dripping water, Jimmie poured me some wine, then he ran out in the wet night, in search of love and fried meat.

Chapter Twenty-six

Two black crickets were sitting on top of my coffee table, and they appeared to be engaged in activities designed to produce more crickets.

Frigging great.

But watching the bugs reminded me about Sherilyn Moody and Gideon Theibuet.

First I'd seen him on an apparent date with the good widow at the antiphosphate rally, then I'd seen them together at Sherilyn's, and catty old Rayford had practically told me they were lovers. My mind quickly concocted a scenario in which the world-weary wife, tired of being left at home while M. David seduced the younger female population of Sarasota, convinced one Theibuet to off her husband, thereby relieving her of the burden of divorce court and a fifty-fifty split of the assets. I mean, why share if you can get it all?

Certainly from what I could remember, Theibuet would be strong enough to hold M. David down in the slime soup. Plus, with him dead, M. David's 60 percent of the Antheus shares would be divided between the remaining three shareholders, substantially increasing Theibuet's own holdings in the mining company.

And I remembered what Miguel had told me—that most of that land had been M. David's to begin with, which he'd put into the company in exchange for the controlling number of shares. Meaning the remaining three shareholders had acquired not only increased shares, but a huge chunk of valuable land at M. David's death.

Theibuet began to glow an even brighter shade of red in my mind's eye.

Shoot, maybe he even had a revenge angle, since Rayford said Theibuet had been involved in the Boogie Bog mess, and lost money.

If Rayford was right about that, Theibuet had revenge, economic gain, and the good widow all as inspiration for murdering M. David.

Hot damn. I'd done it again.

I hoped Josey wouldn't be mad at me for solving her case, and I pulled out her card, got her number, and rang her up.

"Detective Henry Farmer here," Josey said, answering on the second ring.

"Oh, good. You're home." Without further chitchat, I babbled forth my thoughtful theory about Theibuet and Mrs. Moody.

"You do know you are not an official law-enforcement agent?" Josey asked.

"Don't you think—"

"I think you need evidence."

"That's your job," I said.

"Raining cats and dogs, you stay high and dry."

The word *high* made me think of Delvon, which made me think of Lenora, which made me think of Angus, and that led naturally enough to my thinking of Miguel. "Hey, any word on where Miguel is? I mean, I heard that the police want him for questioning in Angus John's murder. He's my client and—"

"I told you, Angus John isn't my case."

"Yeah, but don't cops talk with each other? I mean, it's got to be related."

In the pause that followed, I listened to Josey breathe for longer than a polite moment. "Just be careful, okay? There's already dead people in this pile of rocks you keep kicking over." And she hung up.

Well, damn. Josey was hiding something from me.

Me, who had just basically solved the M. David murder case for her.

I picked up the phone and had dialed the first half of her number before it occurred to me that a more forthcoming source might be Philip's snitch.

Philip's snitch, who Philip was paying, without ever once hinting that I should contribute a dime. Philip, who was but a phone call away.

He answered on the third ring. "Hi, Philip, how are you?" I said, for lack of a better segue into finding out if he could find out something for me.

"Lilly? Are you all right? No further problems with Miguel? I can be there in ten minutes."

"Not unless your Lexus can swim. And, no, no further contact from Miguel. And these rains will probable keep Miguel off the streets. And Jimmie's with me. And I'm fine. How are you?"

"Lilly, I'm fine. Please tell me what you want."

"I, er . . . I just had this conversation with Josey, you know, the sheriff's detective?"

"I remember Josey."

"Oh, good. Anyway, I think there's been some kind of new development in the Angus murder, but she wouldn't tell me. Would you mind terribly calling your insider guy at the police department and seeing if he can find out anything? What's new, I mean."

"Actually, I have already spoken with my man. Under all the circumstances, it seemed the wisest course that I stay well informed."

"So, what?"

"This is thirdhand. It's actually from the sheriff's department's investigation into M. David's murder. My man got his information from—"

"What? *What?*" I didn't mean to interrupt, but at this precise moment in time I didn't give a rat's ass about the chain of custody or hearsay, I just wanted to know what Philip knew.

"The sheriff's department has evidence possibly linking Angus with M. David's murder."

"What?" I asked, suddenly anxious.

"At M. David's house, in his den, the crime-scene experts found three beer bottles, Dos Equis. One of them had M. David's fingerprints, and a can of honey-roasted peanuts had Angus's fingerprints on the lid. They can place the bottles in the den the night M. David was killed."

"So they had a drink. So what? I drink beer with people I don't kill."

"You don't think Angus and M. David make an odd couple?"

"Pretty much, yeah, but so what? They had a drink together at M. David's house. They can hardly arrest Angus for murder for that."

"They can hardly arrest Angus regardless," Philip said.

"You know what I mean," I said, trying to resist the urge to snap at him now that I thought I might love him. "What about Miguel? Any of his prints?"

"No, there were the two other bottles, but condensation had washed off the latents. The techies were luckier with M. David's bottle. And the peanut lid. They ran the prints through AFIS and got a match. You knew Angus had been arrested before?"

"Sure, yes," I said, though actually I had not.

"And there were a couple of Dos Equis bottles on top of the gyp stack when they found M. David, but, again, no latents. But same brand, so naturally the investigators are inclined to believe there is a connection. That is, in the absence of any other explanation."

"You got to wonder why anybody is stupid enough to kill somebody and toss out their beer bottles on the scene."

"There's more. Josey just got the phone records today, finally. Someone phoned M. David at his house from the pay phone at the pier where Miguel's sailboat was docked. A little after six P.M. the night he was killed. The maid left at five-thirty, and there were no beer bottles in the den then. When she came in the next morning, she spotted the bottles, but left them where they were because she had other chores, and, after all, neither Mr. nor Mrs. Moody was home."

"Where was Mrs. Moody?"

"At the Mayo Clinic in Jacksonville, on a consult. She has iron-clad witnesses. She wasn't anywhere around when M. David died."

"But she could have set it up," I said, wholly unwilling to let the woman who had nearly set me up off any retribution hook I might be able to bait.

"Angus could have set it up too," Philip said, sounding fatigued, and, maybe, a bit sad. "He calls from the pier, offers to set up a meeting, and presents himself at M. David's house for a drink. Perhaps he even implied he had some deal to propose about ceasing to protest the mine, or some similar plan or offer that would induce M. David to agree to meet him. Then he overpowers M. David, or pulls a gun. The third beer bottle suggests an accomplice."

That, I thought, would be Miguel. Damn. "Do you have anything that ties Miguel to this?"

"No."

But I imagined the sound of a hanging "yet" in Philip's words.

"If Angus was involved in killing M. David, it's a reasonable assumption Miguel was involved, or knew something about it. Those receipts you gave me suggest that Miguel was involved in making a bomb, even if he didn't mean to kill Angus. Given all that, and Miguel's recent aggressive behavior toward you, I think I should come and get you. You'll be safer here with me."

I was tempted. I looked out the window in case the rain had stopped in the last ten seconds. But it wasn't just rain, it was tropical-storm rain with attitude, and with thunder that would kill the living and raise the dead. "No, thank you. You are very kind to worry, but like I said, Jimmie is with me, and when it stops raining, I will go get Bearess. A hundred-pound rottweiler ought to slow Miguel down. And the door is locked."

Philip gave it another round of convincing me to spend the storm safely in his arms, but I resisted. It wasn't just the weather; I needed some time alone to consider my recent revelations. That I might love Philip. That Miguel was, after all, just lust that dissipated quickly enough after he tried to kill me.

So I put my best spin on turning down Philip's offer to come fetch me in a hurricane, I promised him I would be careful, and hung up.

And sat down to think.

What Philip told me suggested that Angus and a third man, who most surely was Miguel, had shared a beer with M. David the night he was killed. If I wasn't willing to leap to the next step—that is, that they had then killed M. David after sharing a drink with the man in his own den—that meant the beer bottles and the peanut lid with prints had to be a badly timed coincidence.

Or, a setup.

And a setup meant Sherilyn. I mean, hadn't she just proved she was damned clever at setting up setups?

My head swimming with unproven theories of conspiracies and setups, I checked the locks on all my doors, and poured another glass of the good organic wine.

And I wondered just how much protection an eighty-year-old man and a hundred-pound lapdog would actually be—especially since they were both next door.

Chapter Twenty-seven

A cricket landed on my face and chirped. As I woke up and swatted at it, I heard Rasputin issue a shrill morning whistle.

I rolled out of bed, looked out my window, and saw it was still raining a torrential tropical-storm gusher.

Great, a flood and a plague of locusts. Idly, I hoped no other biblical curses were in the offing, then stumbled to the kitchen and made my coffee. After feeding Rasputin his morning Save the Forest trail mix bar, I watched him jumping around on the porch after the many crickets. Though Rasputin seemed to be getting the basic idea, for the moment the crickets still had the upper hand. Well, let hopping birds hop, I thought, and ambled back to my coffee and my kitchen table.

I missed Philip. I missed Bearess my dog. I missed my grandmother. I was getting so mopey I wondered if I had a hormonal imbalance, and then I figured it was just the rain.

Remembering that I'd read caffeine is an antidepressant, I refilled my coffee mug, and looked out the kitchen window at the continuing storm. I hadn't missed a hurricane warning, had I? And weren't we months past the hurricane season, anyway? But as hurricane rules no longer seemed to apply, this because of global warming, according to Olivia, I coasted to the den and turned on the television to check the weather.

Blah, blah, blah. Rain. Thunder. Cold front hits warm Gulf something, something. More rain on the way, the Weather Channel reported, with worsening thunderstorms on the horizon. The explanation of the storm didn't interest me, but the predictions were beginning to catch my eye. Rapidly rising river levels in Sarasota and Manatee Counties, potential flooding.

Potential, my ass, had anybody seen Shade Avenue last night?

Then the TV offered me a big scene of a cute woman in a rain slicker standing in front of a big dam, talking into a microphone in one hand, clutching her hat to her head with the other hand, and smiling like Miss Bermuda Triangle in the semifinals. "Though the Manatee River is already nearing flood levels, officials explain that the dam on the river has a lock designed to open and divert the water when it hits flood stage, so east Manatee County is safe," she said. The camera crew cut away to a scene of hunched-over men in slickers frantically trying to turn a big wheel-like thing while truly huge amounts of water swirled around them and a series of concrete structures got pelted by more rain.

Okay, I had to say Miss Bermuda Triangle was more reassuring than the men, who seemed not to be succeeding in their attempts to turn the big wheel thing.

Then, shattering her previous reassurances, Bermuda T-girl returned to the TV screen and said, "However, the Myakka and the Peace Rivers in Sarasota County are nearing flood levels, and people living in the flood zones of those rivers are advised to stay tuned to their televisions and radios in case evacuation is ordered."

Well, that definitely ruled out driving to the office for another day of churning my in-coming mail and my deposition collection. I turned off the television, and started back to the kitchen, thinking maybe I'd make spice cookies for breakfast. I have a killer recipe for whole wheat spice cookies that uses canola oil instead of butter. But while I was pulling out my flour, something Sherilyn had said about Rayford, a bodyguard with nothing but "a dollar inside his shoe," slapped me in the face. So how did a cowboy with presumably zippo knowledge about growing oranges—I mean, okay, how many orange groves are there in Montana?—get that grove in the first place? Yeah, that was weird. Definitely weird.

My visions of spice cookies dancing in my head butted against the puzzle of a poor bodyguard who now owned a Florida millionaire-developer's dream of forty acres and a mule, or, that is, owned it until the sales contract was finalized. Then he owned 48 percent of a huge check. The *Sarasota Herald-Tribune* had run a story a couple months back on how farmland in the east part of the County was selling for up to $35,000 an acre, and the surveyor had told me there were a hundred acres in that grove. I had to get out a pencil to do the math, but I calculated Rayford's 48 percent as around $1,680,000. Okay, spare change to M. David, but megabucks for the rest of us.

That certainly invited further query.

Naturally I couldn't resist calling Rayford. Wondering if the rain would keep Rayford from the office, I looked in both the Sarasota and Manatee phone books for a private listing. Finding none for a Rayford Clothier, I dialed the number for Delilah Groves. Rayford answered on the fifth ring.

Picturing Lauren Bacall, I huskyed down my voice to low and sexy, and said, "Rayford, this is Lilly. Lilly Cleary. We met—"

"What do you want now?"

Okay, so we weren't going to be best friends. I switched to business mode, and said, "I wanted to let you know I received the notice of dismissal of the lawsuits against my clients."

"Goody. Thanks for letting me know. 'Bye now."

"Wait, wait . . . I'm wondering if you could tell me about the arrangements you and M. David had with the groves."

"You're the big, smart lawyer, you figure it out," Rayford said, and hung up.

When I called back, nobody answered. Doubly rebuffed made me more curious than ever.

If this were a trial, I'd collect every scrap of paper, evidence, information, and supposition, and analyze the dickens out of it. So that was what I was going to do on the multilayered riddles before me.

And the deed might be the place to start. So thinking, I booted up my computer. Within minutes, I was searching through the Sarasota County Property Appraisers Web site.

Oh, big, frigging surprise! I thought when, sure enough, I found that one of M. David's corporations had owned 100 percent of the orange grove, but had sold a 48 percent interest to Rayford just a few months ago. The property office's records listed the sale price as one dollar and "other considerations."

Weird. Definitely. In fact, fishy weird, not just weird weird.

I left the computer running while I leaned back in my chair and contemplated what I knew in the big-picture sense, and what it might mean. Taking the easy stuff first, I concluded that the note on M. David's body about making an appointment with me meant an appointment for Sherilyn. I made a mental note to try to exchange that information with Josey for something of value she might know.

Still cogitating, I wandered to the porch, where Rasputin hopped up on my arm and twittered up at me, beak parted, big bird eyes staring right into mine. I wondered if I could pet him, but then he hopped off and ran after a couple of chirping bugs.

After more fully taking in the disaster area that was formerly my porch, and having that sensation of my brain being squeezed to mush by collected debris throughout the house, I forgot baking cookies, gobbled a couple of trail mix bars, and fetched my buckets, mops, and herbal disinfecting all-natural spray cleaners, Borax, Clorox, and brushes. Jimmie saw me coming out of the laundry room armed with my cleaning tools, muttered a quick "Uh-oh," and disappeared back into his room.

I set to scrubbing the entire house with the ferocity of Catwoman on too much caffeine. I raged at the cracks and crevices where typhoid and TB and E. coli and bird flu viruses like to live, and Philip called four times before the sun went down to make sure I was all right and offered to come over, and I said no, and kept cleaning until my Borax, Clorox, and orange spray were all gone. I felt a smidgen saner.

Jimmie, apparently sensing it was safe to come out of his room, stuck his head in the kitchen and asked, "What you fixing to fix for supper?"

"Stuffed green peppers," I said. "I stuff the peppers with texturized vegetable protein, cheese, and a combo of onions and tomatoes, with sliced carrots on the side."

"Uh-huh. Maybe I bests go see how Dolly's doing in all this here mess."

"I think Dolly knows how to come in out of the rain."

"Yeah, and she also knows how to fry chicken," Jimmie said, and took my London Fog out of the hall closet without asking and ducked outside.

Seeing as I'd spent the day chasing dust and germs, I needed a shower before cooking, so I checked all the doors and windows, found them locked, and showered until the hot water was gone. After that, confident I was home by myself for a Saturday night, I threw on a pair of tight jeans a good decade out of style and a loose camp shirt with baggy front pockets. Because my feet were cold against the marbled-concrete terrazzo of my floors, I slipped on a pair of Keds that had thousands of miles on their soles. Thus, dressed appropriately for moping around the house alone on a Saturday night, I went into my kitchen and started sautéing some onions as a first step in preparing the stuffed peppers. The battering of the rain was driving me crazy, so I tried to drown it out by turning on the radio to listen to WMNF, the cool, alt-radio station out of Tampa.

As I started scraping carrots, it never once occurred to me that Henry and I weren't the only people in Sarasota who could open a locked door without a key or dynamite.

Chapter Twenty-eight

Someone threw a quilt over my head.

Needless to say, that got my attention and I started frantically flailing about, but the quilt thrower proved much stronger than me. Besides, dancing around blind inside a quilt didn't lend itself to effective self-defensive kicking. As I couldn't even raise my arms to punch, I tried the time-tested technique of screaming my brains out.

When my yelling didn't bring forth help, I tried to conquer panic by concentrating on the details, that is, until I could figure out what to do.

What I could tell so far was that someone had entered my house and thrown my own quilt—in the moments before darkness enveloped me, I had recognized the quilt as one that lived on the back of the couch in the den and was made of a blend of delicate blue organic cotton and wool and I had paid a small fortune for it and I didn't want it hurt, thank you—over my head. While I was assessing details, my assailant yanked tighter on what felt like a rope or a belt around my waist. Then he knocked me down and rolled me on the floor until I hit something, possibly the kitchen wall. In spite of it all, I was still clutching the carrot in one hand, and the small kitchen knife in the other.

Though the sound was muffled by the quilt over my ears, which was also doing a number on the breathable air quality in the immediate vicinity of my nose and mouth, I could hear my uninvited guest slamming drawers and other things around and figured Miguel had finally come after those fertilizer receipts. I profoundly wished that Bearess still lived with me, or that Jimmie would get his face out of Dolly's fried chicken and see or hear something amiss and call 911. I also realized this would not have happened if I had listened to Philip about going to his house. But now was hardly the time to rethink my past decisions, and I pushed against the wall with my body, trying to right myself, though for what purpose, I wasn't entirely sure.

After I gave up trying to stand, I rolled about on the floor trying to find the doorway on the off chance I could roll through it into a hiding place while Miguel looked for receipts.

But, proving my own adage that things can always go from bad to worse and one should never think otherwise, my assailant came stomping back into the kitchen and started banging on my head with his fist.

This didn't seem like very Miguel behavior.

But then I remembered the splintered canoe paddle, whacked to kindling in one hit against the picnic table.

"Where's the videotape?" a forced, whispery voice asked.

Muffled by the quilt, my fear, the rain, and the fakey stage whisper, I couldn't tell if this was Miguel.

But Miguel wouldn't want a videotape.

Miguel would want receipts.

Nope, I had an unknown assailant pummeling my head in my own house.

And, worse still, I could now smell the oil and the onions burning in my skillet. I tried to shout out to please turn the stove off before he burned down my house, but apparently people who break into your house, wrap you up in quilts, throw you on the floor, and then beat you about the head with their fists didn't care about such niceties as whether they accidentally burned your house down too.

That is to say, the person continued to hit me over the head and then punched at my face. Mercifully the quilt muffled the punches. But the hot oil sizzled hotter.

"Where's the damn tape, the videotape?" he repeated, as if somehow in my fear I had managed not to process the question the first time.

Not inclined at the moment to chat with this criminal about tapes, I tried to roll away from his fists. When he kicked me and ordered me to "stay put," I decided to stay put. All I could think now was that Jason the baby lawyer, or the now-exposed fake-spinal-injury plaintiff, was trying to find and destroy the tape of the faker working in his own yard. But the smell of the burning oil on the stove refocused me from trying to place the voice.

"Please, turn off the stove," I shouted through the quilt.

"Where's the damn tape?" Punch, punch, punch.

Okay, if that was the game, I guess I'd have to play it. "At the office, the tape is at my office," I cried out. "Right on top of my filing cabinet. Now turn off the stove." If my house burned up, not only would I lose, like, you know, my house, but poor Rasputin, my pet jay, frolicking on the porch with the wild crickets, would burn up too.

But obviously my attacker didn't care about adding arson or bird murder to his list of crimes, intent, apparently as he was, on kidnapping me. In other words, he was dragging me outside and I never heard the little popping sound the stove makes when turned off.

As he bounced me through my own house to the door, I was bound up so tight I couldn't fight back. In a minute, we were outside, and my door slammed shut behind us. Though the blanket protected me from the rain as the madman dragged me outside to a vehicle, I could hear the sound of the storm around me. Attack-kidnapper man unceremoniously dumped me in the back of a van, or an SUV, started the engine, and drove off.

Okay, I'm not too proud to admit this. I was scared. I was petrified. I'd been kidnapped and my house and my pet bird left to destruction by a hot-oil fire. On top of that, I seemed to be suffocating. I kept trying to roll inside my prison quilt, as if somehow that would improve my situation, but all that effort did was make me breathe heavier and use up air faster than it could filter through the cotton stuffing in the quilt.

In this haze and my ire, I slowly became conscious of being rocked against something hard, and realized it was the vehicle's door, and that we had slammed to a stop. Before I could get reoriented, I heard the man ask me what the combination to my law firm's back-door lock was, and too frightened not to, I told him.

The vehicle's door slammed, and then there was silence. I struggled to get a good breathful of air into my lungs before I passed out. Inhaling and exhaling, I forced myself into a deep, rhythmic pattern—air in, air out—until the panic passed. Oh, all right, I was still scared, but I made myself take stock. The knife. Yeah, the knife. It occurred to me that cutting my way out of the quilt and running into the night full tilt before my irate kidnapper came back might count as a good idea.

Struggling and groping, I discovered that the rope tied around my waist only trapped my arms above my elbows. Within the confines of my quilt prison, I could actually move my hands and lower my arms a little. Not, as an orthopedic surgeon would say, a full range of motion, but it was something. I still had the big carrot in one hand and the small kitchen knife in the other.

With some difficulty, I stuffed the carrot into the loose pocket of my camp shirt and started cutting my way out of the quilt with the knife. But then I heard the sound of a vehicle door opening.

"I got the tape," Maniac Man said, snarling in his hostile stage whisper.

"Jason Quartermine, you son of a bitch, you let me out of here right now or so help me, I'll see that The Florida Bar strips you of your license and the state attorney stomps you under the jail."

Instead of an abject apology, I heard laughter, muffled again by the quilt, and then I heard the door slam and the vehicle start off. Once more I took stock. The only tape I knew about was the one Jimmie had made of Jason's client clearly demonstrating to the world at large that he was not disabled, as he claimed in his lawsuit. Therefore, being a lawyer and an analytical sort, I had decided that Jason was trying to steal the tape so he could proceed with his stupid car-crash lawsuit. So it was all right that Jason—or the faker plaintiff if that's who my kidnapper was—took the tape because I, Lilly, Queen of the Duplicate, had the original locked up in the firm's safe upstairs, in addition to the copy my mad kidnapper must have readily found.

But obviously Jason, or the faker plaintiff, meant me harm or he'd have just rolled me out of the van and left me to either drown in the storm or be rescued. Of course, I realized, Jason had to shut me up now because I'd just told him I knew he was my assailant.

Chastising myself for doing a *really* stupid thing, I resolved earnestly not to do anything else stupid for the rest of my life, and to cut my way out of the quilt so that the rest of my life wouldn't be measured in minutes. Working within the limited range of motion I had with my hands, I began to cut, not without some regret at ruining my expensive quilt.

Okay, so, cut maybe was an overstatement. Saw, poke, jab, curse, breathe.

Breathing being the hardest part.

As I sawed at the quilt, I slid, bumped, and skittered about in the vehicle. My mad chauffeur was obviously taking a long and winding road to our destination. With nothing to do but worry and work at the quilt with my small kitchen knife, I sawed a little hole in the quilt, near my hands. Not without some struggling, I squeezed the knife and enough of my fingers out of this hole to get at the rope that bound the quilt around my body. My new plan was simple: Saw through the rope and be prepared to spring like a wild animal the first time the van stopped and the door opened. But naturally the rope was tough as all get out, and my little kitchen knife seemed hardly up to the task, and it was slow going, but it wasn't like I had anything else to do. My mind ping-ponged about in various degrees of fear and irritation, but I worked slowly, steadily, and kept sawing away at the rope. All of this was, I decided, a decent analogy to trial preparation—hard, dull work mixed with fear and loathing.

Still, it's amazing what one can do when highly motivated, and I was pretty highly motivated. At last, the threads shredded and the rope was cut and I hunkered down in the back of the vehicle and waited for a chance at escape.

While waiting and worrying, my feet went to sleep, and hunger bore down on me, and I felt a desperate need to both pee and take a shower. Suddenly the vehicle slowed, banging me against what I figured was a seat. I could feel the vehicle making a sharp turn onto what quickly appeared to be a very rough road, if in fact it was a road at all. Bump thunk bump thunk bump. The vehicle stopped again. Gears ground and tires whirled and my maniac captor cursed. After more wheel spinning and grinding, the vehicle started forward again, but more slowly. Bump—thunk—bump—thunk. Then the vehicle stopped, a door slammed open, and I could hear rain and thunder and a man's muffled cursing.

When the cursing faded, I surmised that this was my chance to break for new territory. After struggling out of the quilt, I found myself sitting inside an SUV. I slipped the knife into my jeans pocket, thinking I might need it again. Peering out the window, I saw nothing but dark and rain, but knew I was better off wet and lost than staying in the vehicle. I eased open the side door and climbed out.

The rain hit cold and hard against me, and I shivered, but kept moving as fast as one can move in tread-bare Keds in a slick, thick, mud bog. A bolt of lightning, followed almost immediately by a clap of thunder, startled me so badly I accidentally made a little screeching noise. I ran blindly, maybe another fifty yards, before I flat-ass slid down, butt first, in the slippery muck. Okay, these shoes failed the runs-well-in-mud consumer test. After making a quick mental note to henceforth always wear mud-worthy hiking boots while cooking dinner, on the off chance I was kidnapped from my kitchen in a storm a second time, I got up and started moving, a little more cautiously this time. Another bolt of lightning and clap of thunder made me screech again. Okay, so spank me, but I didn't have my usual self-control. Also, I didn't have a clue as to where my kidnapper was, but when the next bolt of lightning hit with its brief flash of light, I saw where I was—at Lenora's wildlife rescue.

Well, now what?

How would Jason know about this place?

So, hey, work it out later, I chided myself, and started running again in the general direction of where I thought the river was. In movies, those chased always flee to the river, and though no one with bloodhounds was on my tail, I figured it was as good a route as any. If I had a plan, I think it was to go to ground as soon as I was out of the compound.

But moments after my second bout of screeching, I was tackled by the madman and landed facedown in mud. I struggled, but was no match for the crazy man jumping on me and thrashing me about. As we wrestled, I realized I wasn't getting anywhere except worse off. Pummeled as I was by nature and a Ted Bundy reincarnate, I concentrated on keeping my nose out of the mud so I could breathe as the man lifted my head and smashed it down repeatedly into the soft, squishy ground under it.

Apparently I ceased to struggle. I mean, I wasn't totally paying attention to the details at this point, but I felt the man roll me over, slap me across my face, and begin to tie the rope around my waist, pulling my arms tight against my body. At least he didn't re-enshroud me in the quilt, and, except for some mud in my nose, I could at least breathe.

Grateful for the air that I was sucking into my lungs through my mouth in huge gasps, I made myself open my eyes and was rewarded by getting my face slapped at the same time that rain battered my eyeballs. Given the shortcomings of my situation, in the dark I got only the briefest, distorted glimpse of the man, and, in my renewed panic, I couldn't recognize him.

Maybe Jason. Maybe faker plaintiff. Maybe Jason had hired a tough guy to retrieve the videotape. By then I had forgotten to wonder who was mistreating me so, when the madman picked me up and carried me toward a shadowy building of some sort. One of Lenora's shacky outbuildings. After he opened a door, Maniac Man unceremoniously dropped me, then I heard the sound of a door slamming and I was alone.

Alone was good.

Alone was not having someone smashing my face into mud.

Alone was the reprieve I needed to get the damn knife out of my damn tight jeans, which, let me tell you, were destined for the Goodwill bag after this, and I slung my head trying to get the mud out of my eyes, and then I opened them. In the dank shed, I rolled and struggled to get to my feet, but I was unable to get any sense of balance. And then, to my horror, I heard the man return, laughing a laugh that I recognized as Big Trouble.

The building was dark, but I could make out an outline of black against black, and could tell the man was coming for me again.

Then he grabbed me and hauled me up to a sitting position.

When I opened my mouth to begin negotiating my freedom, or screaming—I wasn't sure which yet—Maniac Man began to smash raw hamburger all over me.

Here, I officially lost it.

And I screamed some more, for all the good it was doing me. I mean, under the best of circumstances, and these were not remotely in the running for even tolerable circumstances, let alone best, raw

dead cow scares me, but having a strong and apparently totally demented man smearing wet, raw meat all over me while I was muddy
and bound up in ropes plain scared me out of my wits.

Despite the lack of any obvious benefit, I gave screaming another round or two. While I aired my terror through my vocal cords,
my mad assailant pushed clumps of raw hamburger into my hair and
smashed small handfuls into my clothes, even smushing some inside
the pockets of my shirt. I imagined small, evil armies of E. coli bacteria crawling all over me and killing me slowly.

Maniac Man eventually seemed satisfied that he'd smushed
enough raw meat into me and he stopped. I stopped screaming. He
picked me up, threw me over his shoulders like I were no more than a
bedroll and we were on a *Texas Chainsaw* campout, and he carried me
out of the small building over rough and wet ground as the rain pelted
both of us. The next thing I knew, the man threw me on the ground,
which was pretty much a mud lagoon, and while I sank and sloshed,
Maniac Man pulled out a gun and shot something. The noise of the
firearm set me off shrieking again, plus it injured my eardrums.

Over my demented wailing, I thought I heard him say, "Gun'll
take a padlock any day."

Despite the kick to my ears and the mud and rain in my eyes,
I made myself pay attention. I heard the sound of metal on metal,
muffled as the sound was by my ringing ears and the pouring rain.
Before I could calculate what this sound might mean, my vile kidnapper picked me up from behind and rudely shoved me into something
that had a floor with straw on it. Without ever a clear look at the
madman's face, I rolled away from him until in the dark I hit a wall.

There was the sound of metal on metal again, then a clanking
noise. And I smelled cat.

Not house cat.

Big cat.

My lunatic captor said in his fake stage whisper, "In this rain, nobody'll come out here for a while. You'll be supper. Then they'll have to shoot the panther because it's a man killer."

Judging from the noise, my perverse kidnapper rammed a stick through the bars of the cage, taunting the big cat, which growled and thrashed.

It began to dawn on me that I was in more trouble than E. coli germs in my hair, more trouble than possibly I'd ever been in before.

"Bye-bye," the man whispered.

But in the dark, I couldn't see his face.

I heard the sounds of Maniac Man leaving, including the grinding sound his SUV made as it plowed through the mud on its path away from me.

With my eyes pried open by my own fear and my breathing more of a rasp than a breath, I sat still.

In the next flash of lightning, I could see the dark outline of the cat.

A big cat.

A big cat that was coming toward me.

Chapter Twenty-nine

Now that it seemed it was about to end, I had the wholly uninvited notion I might have wasted my life.

I mean, I hadn't saved the whales or even any starving children, I didn't have a child or a husband, I hadn't written *To Kill a Mockingbird,* and, frankly, I wasn't always truthful.

Not savoring the idea of the reckoning that might be coming toward me decades sooner than I'd calculated, I closed my eyes and started whispering the Lord's Prayer.

The Florida panther's growling closed in toward me. A new and profound panic gripped me. I forgot everything after "thy kingdom come." It's amazing how many degrees of fear there are; just when I thought I couldn't be any more scared, I was.

Frantically I tried to remember all the tips on wildlife survival I'd either read or been told in my short lifetime. "Grandmom," I whispered, but for the moment my grandmother was oddly silent. I guess being locked in a cage with a Florida panther was outside her range of experiences. But, come on, I mean, Grandmom was a ghost. Don't ghosts know everything?

So as the panther crept toward me, I had nothing to rely on except what few tips of wilderness survival I could recall without ancestral, spectral coaching. I remembered that you're never supposed to run, as that makes you seem like game and encourages the wild animal to chase you. Prey that draws attention to itself is often the first to be eaten. And as a practical matter, even if you're an Olympic sprinter, you can never outrun a gator, a bear, or a wild cat anyway. Besides, being in a cage muted that point. There was nowhere for me to run. I remembered the tip about raising your arms to look big, but I couldn't do that because I was still tied up. I inhaled, and gathered my inner resources. And cried for my grandmother.

Still, the cat hadn't attacked me, though I could hear it sniffing at me. Freeing my arms suddenly seemed like a good idea. I worked my hand into my pants pocket, and, not without great difficulty, I pulled out the knife and started sawing at the rope while praying the cat wasn't hungry, or easily irritated.

In an eerily elongated flash of lightning I got a better look at the panther, which was now standing about three feet away from me. Either I imagined it, or the panther had only one eye. In that flash of lightning, it looked like where one of the panther's eyes should have been was a narrow, closed slash. In the next burst of light, I thought one of the cat's ears was missing too.

Oh frigging great, I was in a cage with a one-eyed, one-eared panther. Assuming I lived through this, who in the whole world would ever believe me?

Then I got to thinking, a one-eyed, one-eared panther suggested veterinarian care, and that suggested the cat was used to people. Also, I remembered that wild cats, in fact, most animals, don't like to eat people because we don't taste good to them. One of the human being's baser survival gifts—a nasty flavor to other carnivores.

Not counting on tasting bad alone, I sawed and sawed at the ropes that bound me. I couldn't tell you how long it took me to finally break through the rope, but I did. And during all that time, as much as I could tell in the irregular illumination provided by the lightning, the cat had simply crouched there and was staring at me.

Once my hands were freed, I held the knife out in front of me, defensively. But as I stood there, fighting another round of panic, I realized the knife wouldn't do me any good against a panther. Come on, a kitchen knife against a Florida panther? I'd have to be Tarzan with a good scriptwriter for that to work.

Then I remembered what Josey had told me about training cats. "Look them in the eye and tell them what you want." I decided that making friends with the cat wouldn't hurt either, and how do you befriend an animal best?

With food, I thought. That's what Josey had said, feed them a treat.

A treat, of course, other than me. "I taste nasty," I whispered to the cat, which ignored me.

Moving as slowly and as fluidly as I could, I put the knife into my shirt pocket beside the carrot and then made myself stand up. That movement, unlike my unsolicited culinary comment, caused the panther to slink slowly toward me again.

"I'm not supper," I said, in as soft and soothing a voice as I could make myself use. "Bad taste." The cat paused, but then continued toward me after a second. I hoped the cat was more curious than anything else, and I created a new mantra, "Easy, easy, easy."

When the panther was within the reach of my hands, there was another flash of lightning and I could see that definitely the cat had only one eye and one ear. The roar of the thunder apparently spooked One-Eye as well as me. Over the sound of the storm and the rain, I could hear a low growl begin. Uh-oh, definitely not good. But over the sound of the growl, I heard my grandmother's voice. "Feed it. Now," she said.

Slowly, moving like I was in some Hitchcockian ballet, I raised my hand to my shirt and scraped off some raw hamburger. I offered my hand to the cat with the meat cupped in my palm. I held my breath. The cat licked the meat off my hand, and I came as close to peeing in my pants as I'd come since being fully potty trained. But slowly, I scraped some more meat out of my hair, and offered it to the cat, all the while talking softly. "Easy, easy, easy, easy."

I kept hand-feeding the one-eyed panther hamburger until the meat was gone. The panther moved so close to me that even in the dark I could see its face, and I tensed for an attack. But then the cat licked me, either cleaning me, or licking off the last of the hamburger. Its tongue was unbelievably large, and unbelievably rough.

When the cat finished licking me, it backed off a bit. Weak with fear, I sat down slowly. The cat sat down too. It made a guttural noise, which I hoped was the sound of a satisfied cat after a happy meal.

I listened to the cat and focused on not moving. I prayed. And doused as I was, despite the panther's licking, with residual raw hamburger juice, I worried about bacteria. But mostly I worried about my house burning down. Rasputin was not the right kind of bird to rise from the ashes.

Time passed. I couldn't tell you how much, except that I began to cramp from sitting still, so I slumped down a little and shifted my weight. Then off somewhere in the distance, I thought I heard the sound of a vehicle.

Oh, Lord, I prayed, don't let it be Maniac Man coming back.

Let it be, I prayed, a band of law-enforcement people with a lion tamer.

Chapter Thirty

I bunched my muscles for flight, pulled out my kitchen knife, and waited to learn if my would-be killer had come back to check on the panther's progress in eating me.

But it wasn't just one SUV, it was the sound of many vehicles.

Lights came driving into the area and vehicles and people were everywhere. Hallelujah, I was saved, I thought, figuring there weren't that many people who'd join my kidnapper in feeding me to a panther, so this crowd had to have a different mission in mind.

I opened my mouth to start screaming "Help, help, help," but feared hysterical yelling might upset the cat, possibly into attacking me. So I shut my mouth and stood up. Flashlights bobbed around and I heard the sound of slamming vehicle doors and excited voices. I wondered how they knew I was here. And then to my horror, I saw that they were moving away from me, dashing in different directions.

Shouting out a tentative "Hey," I watched for the cat's reaction. In the glow from the headlights, I could see that the cat had cocked its head, as if curious. However my "hey" had been so soft that no one heard me.

Eyeing the big panther in the trippy, strobe-light effect of bobbing flashlights and headlights, I shouted "Help" in a slightly louder tone. This time the panther omitted a low sort of growl.

Well, this was an interesting new catch-22, wasn't it?

Someone moved in my direction, or maybe a group of someones, and then clearly, like the voice of a guardian angel, a woman said, "Check on the panther."

Next thing I knew someone beamed a flashlight in the cage, first on the cat, and then at me. As soon as the man with the flashlight saw me, he shouted, "What the hell?" The cat was definitely growling now, though she was advancing on the man with the flashlight rather than on me. But the man with the flashlight was protected by cage bars. I wasn't. I didn't know how fickle an irritated cat could be, and did not want to learn. In more of a hiss than a voice, I said, "She doesn't like the flashlight."

Immediately the flashlight went dead. The man said to someone near him, "Get Adam. And that sheriff lady, tell them there's a woman in the cage."

The next sound I heard was Josey's voice, saying softly, "Stay still. I'll get some meat from the fridge to distract her."

"Wait. I've got to tranquilize her anyway, to move her into the trailer," a man said.

I heard the sound of running, a heavy thud, then more running, and people milling about, and, of course, the pounding rain. I heard the sound of my own heart beating. And over all of that noise, I could still hear the low, insistent growling of my companion in the cage, the one-eyed panther.

Then I heard clanking, and a man's voice telling me to get to the end of the cage, as far away from the cat as I could get—oh, like I needed encouragement on that angle—then pop, and thud. The man had raised what looked like a real gun and had apparently shot the panther with a tranquilizer dart.

Fleetingly, I wondered how they knew the drugs would waylay the cat rather than piss her off enough to eat me, but the cat growled, shook, staggered, and then collapsed.

Then Josey yanked open the cage door, grabbed me, and dragged me out. I stumbled onto the ground. And immediately started babbling.

But over the sound of my incoherent and panicked words, Josey asked, "Do you need to go to a hospital? Are you all right?"

Under the circumstances I had to agree that I was physically okay. But I sobbed out, "Shower. Bathroom. Cell phone. Police. Burning house."

As if I had merely amicably asked how she was doing, Josey looked at me and smiled. "Thank goodness, you're all right," she said. "Who put you in there?"

"Some big man who wanted a videotape. I've got to call my house, I think it burned down, see, there was this skillet of oil on the stove, and this man kidnapped me and left it on the stove, and I've got to see if my house burned down. Please, please, give me a cell phone."

"If it burned down, no one will answer," Josey said. "And if it didn't burn down, then it's okay. Now, if you're all right, you've got to help us. The Manatee River is rising, fast. The county dam personnel just put out the word to the sheriff's office and all emergency-rescue people about a half an hour ago that the lock on the dam is stuck and they can't open the gate to divert the water. It's going to flood, and flood bad. All spare officers are on evacuation duty right now, me, I'm volunteering. We've got to get these animals out of here before the road is too flooded to pass. This place will be underwater in a few more hours. If not sooner."

"Toilet. Shower. Phone. Police," I shouted at her again.

"You aren't hurt. You said so yourself," Josey said. "And you don't need a shower, you're standing in a downpour. Now get a grip."

"Bathroom. I need to pee."

"Go inside," Josey said. "And then get back out here and help us."

I scampered inside, skidding around in the hallway to the bathroom, and slammed the door shut. Frankly, I wanted to stay in the bathroom of Lenora's little cracker house. I wanted to keep washing my hands and my face. Although the sink was small and the water smelled like sulfur, I figured with a little luck I could stick my head in there and wash my hair, getting out the residual hamburger germs.

But then I thought about all of Lenora's little creatures, and all she had suffered to take care of them to this point.

"Go and be useful," my grandmother ordered me. It was her signature line. I left the shelter of the little house and went back outside. In the circle of car lights and bobbing flashlights, I saw frantic wildlife-rescue people, some in uniforms, some in slickers, some in the clothes they were wearing when they were called out. They were working at a frenzied pace to load an assortment of birds, squirrels, and other small game, plus some equipment. They must have organized quickly once the word went out about the failed lock on the dam. No one was paying the least attention to me.

"The cat's going to be a problem," a skinny man said.

"She's tranquilized, we can carry her into the smaller cage on the trailer. Then it's just a matter of hooking the trailer up to a truck and pulling it out," said another man in a hooded poncho. When I turned and studied him, I recognized Adam, the Fish and Wildlife man.

"You see that road? It's already underwater in spots. You think you can get that trailer out?" said the skinny man in an oddly hostile tone.

"I can get it out," Josey said. "I got four-wheel drive on my truck and it'll—"

"Then go last, after we've all driven out, so if you get stuck, you don't block all of us," the skinny man said.

"I'll go last," Josey said. "And I'll make sure everybody, including the cat, gets out."

"I won't leave the panther," Adam said. "You can hook her up to my SUV."

"No offense, Adam," Josey said, "but my truck is stronger than that little SUV."

While people scurried hither and yon, Josey and Adam engaged in a macho war of words, wheel bases, and horsepowers, and I lost interest. One of them would win, and one of them wouldn't.

As the rescue people moved about in earnest and in speed, I looked around me in dazed wonderment. The rain pelted me, pelted us all, as a small army of Lenora's people jostled in the wind and the lightning to save little wild things and unwanted domestic animals. Lenora must be pretty sick, I realized, not to be here herself.

But then Josey trumped Adam in the great cat-hauling vehicular contest, and turned to me. "Can you help the others? While Adam and I take care of the cat."

"Tell me what to do to help."

"Pick up those small cages and load them into the back of any truck that isn't already full."

Slip-sliding in mud, I joined the others in lifting cages and loading trucks with wet wildlife. Suddenly I wondered about Bob, the little squirrel Lenora had cuddled in her arms the first time I met her. After dumping a caged but playful raccoon into the back of a pickup, I dashed back into the cracker house to make sure no little squirrel named Bob, or any juvenile jays, had been left behind. No little Bob in the big room. When I peeked into the kitchen, I saw Olivia frantically throwing what looked like medicines into a cooler. I ran up to her and pulled her into a bear hug. Though she hugged me back, when she pulled her head away she looked at me with puzzlement. "Lilly, how'd you get here?"

How in the world had she missed all the excitement of my rescue?

Okay, yeah, she was single-minded, even to the point of rudeness, but, still, how had she not heard about the woman in the cage?

On a mission to remedy that oversight on Olivia's part, I started to babble forth my tale of horror, when instead, so relieved at seeing a good friend, I hugged her again. At the tail end of this hug, I smelled something that made me gasp. The spicy scent of sandalwood. I could smell it over Olivia's own smell of hard work, the rain, the mud, and the odor of my own fear.

Sandalwood?

Miguel and Olivia?

But before I could say anything about how interesting it was that Miguel and Olivia appeared to be using the same scented toiletries, a man stuck his head in the kitchen and shouted, "If it's not alive, leave it, come on. We gotta go. That road's bad, and getting worse."

Olivia, my more mysterious-than-before friend, grabbed one end of the cooler as I grabbed the other and we carried it out and slung it, none too gracefully, onto the back of the first pickup we came to.

"Everybody loaded?" Adam asked, yelling over the sounds of the rain.

Shouts of yes were muffled by weather, but then people started getting in their vehicles and turning the engines on and driving their trucks and SUVs out in a slow, muddy parade.

Olivia held on to my arm as if I needed guidance as we stood in the pouring rain, watching the strange procession, the two of us oddly companionable in the storm around us.

"Didn't you ride in with Lester?" Josey asked.

Olivia jumped a tad, and then said, "Yes. He picked me up 'cause he's got a truck."

"Well, his truck is about the second vehicle heading out. You can ride with me. You too, Lilly."

Olivia and I nodded.

"We'll go last, right behind Adam's SUV," Josey added. Then we followed her as she checked the trailer with the still-sleeping panther. "That man who put you in the cage, he shot off the padlock on the big cage, and I don't have another one. Don't suppose either of y'all got a lock on you?"

I still had a carrot and a knife, but I couldn't see how either could be fashioned into a lock, and I shook my head, sending an extra spray of water at Olivia.

"Might be a lock back in the house," Olivia said.

"Haven't got time to look," Josey said, definitely in officer-in-charge mode. She pulled off her thin cloth belt, threaded it through the hook where a padlock should go, twisted it into a knot, and pulled it tight.

Olivia, ever the den mother, glanced at the knot and said, "That's just a loose granny knot, you need something more secure. Let me—"

"We gotta go. It'll do for now. Come on, y'all get in the truck."

I lifted my face up to the rain in a celebration of the fact that I was still alive. Muddy, filthy, but alive. Fervently, I hoped it was still so for Rasputin.

But before I could wax sentimental, Josey poked me. "Get a move on," she said. Eyeing her truck, which was, I should note, truly a monster truck, I cast a last look at the panther. Good kitty, I thought as walked around the trailer to the passenger side of the Big Truck and I scrambled up into the cab. Olivia slid in next to me, muttering something about a loose knot while Josey jumped in behind the steering wheel.

Once Josey began the treacherous task of skidding out through the mud, under driving conditions considerably worsened by the passage of other vehicles churning up the muck pond that used to be a kind of road, stress and confusion made me need to talk. But I couldn't bring myself to ask Olivia about Miguel. Especially not in front of Josey, who, after all, was Official Law Enforcement. Rather, I started to talk out all that had happened to me, as well as my anxious request to summon diverse law-enforcement agencies to the scene to begin the search for the madman who had kidnapped me.

"Be quiet, please. I need to concentrate on driving," Josey said, not rudely, but firmly.

Olivia put her hand on my knee and squished it slightly, as if to cheer me up. Or maybe shut me up.

With a grimly determined Josey driving, we sloshed and slid our way out of the compound, grinding down and sticking a few times, and once spinning a half circle out of control and coming to rest against the slim trunk of a pine sapling. The cat trailer did a jackknife type of move, and then blammed into still another tree, but the trailer hitch held.

With four-wheel drive, a skilled driver, and perhaps an army of guardian angles corralled, no doubt, by Grandmom, we kept going. We finally arrived on a paved road, still in parade single file behind Adam's vehicle. Olivia had not said a single word the whole time.

Once relief at being on pavement began to seep into me, physical pain from my attack did also. I felt my swollen right eye tenderly with my fingers and wondered if the moment was right to demand anew a troop of police to track my assailant. But when I glanced at Josey, I saw such a look of forlorn focus on her face, I decided to follow Olivia's example and keep quiet.

When we finally got on Highway 64, in east Manatee County, Adam's baby SUV pulled off to the side and stopped. Josey pulled her truck in behind it, and jumped out. Olivia did too. Not wanting to miss a second of the story, I slid out after her. We watched as Josey and Adam checked on the panther.

"She looks okay, despite all the heavy bumping the trailer took," Adam said.

Josey only nodded.

Adam offered his hand, and Josey took it. "I just got a radio call from up north on the Little Manatee. Sorry to leave you. Take your friends home, or take them to the sheriff's office, get the cat high and dry, best you can. Don't worry," he said.

Josey nodded again, Adam patted my arm and said I'd "done good," and then drove off, leaving the three of us standing in the rain

on the side of the road for a moment, with a one-eyed panther teth-
ered to the back of the Big Truck.

"Come on, get in," Josey said.

Sitting for a moment on the side of the road in her truck, Josey
turned on the radio and listened as the announcer hyperventilated
about the rising flood and increasing dangers. "Twenty inches of rain
in the last thirty-six hours," he said, with the odd excitement that
media people get at a disaster. "A hundred-year flood."

"Shit," Josey shouted out at the rain. But she started the truck,
and, to my dismay, she turned north, driving away from downtown
Bradenton, away from the police station, away from the sheriff's office, and away even from her house.

"Where are we going?" I asked, aware of the demanding tone in
my voice, but not much caring.

"Boogie Bog," Josey said.

"Why in hell are we going there?" I asked. "Should you be dragging that cat around like this?"

"I've got to see if the gyp stacks will hold," Josey said.

"Oh my God," Olivia said. "The gyp stacks. All that toxic waste."

"What?" I asked, momentarily forgetting in my fatigue all the lessons about phosphogypsum that I had learned at the antiphosphate
meeting with Angus John and Miguel.

"Those two stacks at Boogie Bog," Josey said. "Two lakes filled
with toxic waste behind a seventy-foot dirt wall. They've been at risk
for a long time of breaking, leaking, or overflowing. This rain could
do it."

"You pour too much into any container and it'll spill over," Olivia
said. "Any fool should know that."

"If those gyp stacks don't hold," Josey said, "millions of gallons
of that shit will flow right down into Bishop Harbor, and then right
into Tampa Bay. The sea grasses and the marine life don't have a
chance."

"Can we help, with sandbags, or something?" I asked.

Like a Greek chorus, Olivia and Josey both shouted "Sandbags?" in much the same tone of voice they might have said "You idiot."

"You want to put up seventy feet of sandbags?" Josey asked.

Well, no, I personally didn't want to, but what else could we do? I mean, if we couldn't help out, why even go to Boogie Bog? Why weren't we going to the police station so I could report that I had been kidnapped by a madman and an arsonist?

In a low voice, Olivia said, "There'll be a massive fish kill if that gyp hits the bay waters."

Yeah, now I remembered Angus John's rant the night of the phosphate meeting, the night before he was blown up. And in the remembering, I understood why Josey and Olivia needed to go to the scene and see what was happening. Like rushing to the hospital, even after someone has called to say it's too late: You still have to go; you still have to see the wreckage and remains for yourself.

And I still had to fend for myself. "You got a cell phone? Or a police radio?" I asked Josey.

"Not in this truck. It's my own, not the SO's. That dinky SO's car wouldn't have made it through the muck back there, so I drove my big guy." She patted the truck with a look of satisfaction on her face.

"Do you have any Handi Wipes, especially some antibacterial ones?" I asked, reserving for a saner moment a complete analysis of Josey's relationship with her "big guy."

"Glove compartment," Josey said. "Now tell me again what happened to you."

Okay, finally, my turn. As I mentally began to organize my story for maximum dramatic effect, I leaned over Olivia and reached into Josey's glove compartment where I systematically used up her entire store of Handi Wipes. Then I told both of them everything I could remember, from the moment Jimmie had gone next door to eat Dolly's fried chicken, leaving me at the mercy of a crazed kidnapper with a raw-meat fetish who had demanded a videotape and then rewarded me by throwing me in the lion's den.

"Big fellow, you say?" Josey asked.

"I never really got a very good look at him," I said. "But yes, strong. Real strong. He kept picking me up and carrying me around like I was . . . well, like I was nothing." Okay, sure I'm thin, but I'm also tall. I didn't know many guys who could pick me up like I was a small puppy they were going to toss over a bridge into churning water. But I kept thinking about big guys, strong guys, which naturally led to me thinking about Theibuet.

"It could have been that Theibuet man," I said. "This would be like something Sherilyn Moody might have thought up, and made him do. But like I said, I didn't get a real good look at the face, I couldn't be sure if it was Theibuet."

"Why would Theibuet want a tape from you? What kind of tape?" Josey asked.

Oh, yeah, well, that would be the rub. I thought about it for a minute, and though I hated to let go of the Theibuet-Sherilyn conspiracy theory, I could not for the life of me imagine why either of them would want a tape of the man who was suing Jimmie doing manual labor. "He wouldn't." I had to admit it. Which led me straight back to my other theory. "Maybe that Jason Quartermine guy, or some thug he hired, came after that tape I had of his plaintiff—"

"Who is Jason Quartermine?" Josey asked.

"This lawyer guy, Jason is this lawyer guy, he represents this worm who sued Jimmie, Jimmie, who's like my friend and yardman, you know, you met him at my house at breakfast, and Jason's guy claimed that Jimmie hurt this guy's back by slamming into him at ten miles per hour. Jimmie got a videotape of the guy showing he wasn't even injured."

"That doesn't make any sense to me. Even if Jason stole the tape, why go through all the trouble to put you in a panther cage?" Olivia asked.

"Yeah, Jason wouldn't have thought of that. He's not really very imaginative," I said.

"By the way, you did real good with that cat, real good," Josey said. "You know how to keep your head."

"Yeah, you too," I said.

"The panther's name is Samantha," Olivia said. "She's a beauty, you need to see her in the sunlight. Very strong and graceful. Very smart."

As she talked, Josey eased up on the gas, much to my relief, since I'd noticed she was speeding on a wet road in a stormy night, and I'd already had enough brushes with death this past week that I didn't want to test the cosmic forces anymore. As she slowed down, Josey turned to me briefly, and said, "Samantha's been at the compound off and on for two years. With her permanent injuries, she wouldn't survive long back in the wild. Adam takes her away a lot, to show school kids, and civic clubs, trying to educate them on the beauty of the Florida panther. Some sick motherfucker shot Samantha up by where the new Wilderness Ridge Subdivision and Golf Course is now. Shot her in the head, and then cut off an ear, for a souvenir, I guess." Josey said. "Adam found her himself. She survived, but lost her eye during the head surgery."

"So, is she, like . . . tame?" I asked, thinking of her licking me in the cage.

"Not so you'd want to turn her loose in the kitchen," Josey said. "But she's a survivor, that's for sure. And another thing that's for sure, it's a whole lot easier to develop a wilderness if you kill off the endangered wildlife first."

As if working from the same script, Olivia added, "You got any idea how many bald eagles and ospreys and sand-hill cranes turn up dead just before a new subdivision or golf course or shopping center goes in?"

"No."

"You need to read more," Josey said.

"I read a lot," I said.

"Not the right stuff," Josey said.

Okay, enough about my reading habits. "What about the panther?"

"She's used to people, but I wouldn't want to get in a locked cage with her," Josey said. "Why'd he put you in the cage? Why not just shoot you?"

"He said . . . the man said they'd have to kill the cat after it ate me."

"Shit," Josey said.

"Shit," Olivia said.

"Why didn't he just shoot me *and* the cat? I mean, if he wanted us both dead." I thought this was a real good question. I mean, if I were going to kill somebody after stealing a videotape from them, I'd want to make sure they didn't live through the ordeal to testify against me.

Neither Josey nor Olivia said anything for a long time. Then, just as I had given up on either of them responding, and was getting ready to ask another question, say, like, was Olivia bathing with Miguel, Josey said, "Because he wanted one of the wildlife-rescue people to have to put Samantha down."

"Good Lord, do you know who grabbed me and put me in that cage?" I asked.

"Somebody who hates the big cats and wanted bad publicity for them, the panthers."

"Like a developer?" I asked. And then I thought, or a phosphate miner, someone who wanted unfettered control to ruin a healthy wilderness in east Manatee County, without having to deal with the protected habitat of the endangered Florida panther.

Somebody like Theibuet, one of the newly enriched surviving partners in Antheus.

"Folks like you and Olivia," Josey said, "forget there are a lot of people out there who hate the Florida panthers, or any big cat. Some cattle ranchers, for example, sheep ranchers, yeah, and developers. But right now, I'm thinking more like—"

"Phosphate miners," Olivia said, cutting off Josey.

"Yeah, but why put me in a cage with one?"

"To convince folks that the panthers and the mountain lions are dangerous and vile creatures, not worth saving. You scare people badly enough, and you can push them into anything. In all of our recorded history, there's no verified case of an unprovoked Florida panther attacking a human being. In fact, wild cats of any kind hardly ever attack people, but when a rabid one killed someone out west last year it unleashed a massive mountain-lion hunt. Before it was over, a bunch of cowboys had a cat roundup and killed four other mountain lions. And there weren't many more than that in the whole region. That knocked out a whole species in the area. When the population is as small as it is with wild cats, one cat dead is bad, but five is extinction. They put those cowboys on TV like they were heroes for killing those four mountain lions," she said, her voice bitter.

While I was mulling that over, Josey turned onto the service road into Boogie Bog. A tall security fence surrounded the site, but the gate itself was open, and Josey drove through it. I could see a lot of lights and activity up ahead.

"Did the dams hold?" Olivia asked the air around us.

I looked out at the night and the rain and the scurrying, and I could not help but wonder where in the storm Miguel was.

Chapter Thirty-one

Budding disaster.

That was the scene and the sense of it.

Josey pulled her truck up behind other cars and trucks, and at once we took in frantic movements. People were running around everywhere, shouting and waving their hands, dressed in official-looking bright yellow rain slickers with DEP written across the back, and, like the men trying to turn the wheel on the defective dam lock, they appeared not to be achieving their set goals. Out of the crowd running around, one man turned, and apparently recognized Josey, or perhaps Olivia, and began to walk toward us.

"Too late," he said.

"Dam break?" Josey asked.

"Nope, no break, but there's some crumbling at the top and they're overflowing. Both of them. Too much rain too fast. They were already full. We knew this would happen if it rained like this. We tried to drain them off into the collection ditches along Buckeye Road, but they're overflowing too."

"All that gypsum," Olivia said.

The DEP man turned and looked at her. "All that shit, rolling down the hill, to Bishop Harbor."

Josey took a step closer to the DEP guy, and then put her hand against his cheek. "I'm sorry. I know you tried."

The DEP guy took her hand, and kissed it. And smiled, a sad, little wet smile. "Glad you're still wearing the ring."

They looked at each other for a moment before he dropped her hand and she pulled back from him.

So, okay, now I knew a couple of new things—why Josey wore the big ring and why she was so adamant that no one from the DEP had driven the DEP truck up to the dam to drown M. David.

Yeah, and maybe why she knew so much about Boogie Bog and phosphate.

Another man, dressed in jeans and no rain gear, with his hair plastered against his anguished face, came up to us. "Go home," he said. "There's nothing any of you can do here now. Nothing any of us can do, until the rain stops."

But I watched Olivia turn and scan the crowd as if she were searching for someone. "Anybody see Miguel?" she asked.

"He was here, Olivia. But when the second pond began to overflow, he left," the rain-plastered man said.

At the familiarity between him and Olivia, I turned to study him, and recognized him as Mr. Science Guy from the antiphosphate rally the night Angus had died. That seemed so long ago, even though it had been only last week.

"I hope they all rot in hell for this," Josey said.

"We can only hope," Mr. Science Guy said.

When Josey didn't speak, I did. "Sheriff's office or police station. Phone. Please." I didn't even try to hide the sound of pleading in my voice. I needed to know if my house had burned, taking Rasputin up in the flames.

"Let me think," Josey snapped.

"Think about what? I need to call the police and my house. Don't any of you people have cell phones?"

The DEP man said, "I got a cell," and patted his slicker pocket.

"Don't know if it'll work out here in this rain. But let's get under the shed, out of this downpour, and give it a try."

Josey, Olivia, Mr. DEP, and I walked under the overhang of the shed. Science Guy drifted off into the crowd of other men, who were frantically doing things that apparently weren't going to do any good. DEP Guy pulled a cell out of the pocket in his rain slicker, and I snatched it. My hands shook as I dialed home.

Jimmie answered, saying, "I done told you, she ain't here."

"Jimmie, it's me, Lilly."

"My good God, Lady," he shouted out, "where're you at? I done looked and looked for you. Delvon 'bout done drove me crazy calling for you."

Instead of answering, I blurted out, "Did my house burn down?"

"Now would I be talkin' to you from the phone in your house if it had done burnt down? But the kitchen is . . . it is . . . kind of a mess. But, Lady, it ain't nothin' I can't fix, take a while. We can jes' eat at Dolly's tills I get it all fixed up. Don't you worry, Lady, but you got to tell me where're you at."

"What about Rasputin?"

"Oh, he's jes' fine. The fire didn't get to the porch. And, Lady, like I said, it ain't nothin' I can't fix. It'll jes' take a while."

Before I could absorb all that and respond, Jimmie started in on me. Where was I? Why had I run out in a storm? And why had I left an iron skillet of sizzling oil on the stove?

I interrupted him to give him a condensed version of the story— that is, a man broke in the house, wrapped me in a quilt, and de- manded a videotape, making me think that it was Jason Quartermine, or a thug he hired, trying to get the tape of the faker plaintiff back. But, now I wasn't so sure it was Jason's doing. I mean, why would Jason want people to hate panthers?

"Uh-oh," Jimmie said. "He wanted a tape? You mean, like, a tape? A videotape?"

"What do you know about a tape?" I asked, my voice suddenly snappish in the rain as little red bells of warning went off in my sore head.

"Was he a big guy?"

"I already told you that, strong anyway, if not big like tall big, but big like big big."

"Big guy that wanted a tape?"

"Jimmie, tell me what you know about a big guy and a tape." I motioned Josey in close so she could hear Jimmie over the phone. Something in the emphatic way he had said "Uh-oh" suggested to me that Official Law Enforcement was going to want to hear the answer. "Talk loud so Josey and Olivia can hear you," I said to Jimmie.

"How do, Olivia, Josey," he shouted out, his weedy old-man voice carrying with surprising volume. "I reckon he might've been after my videotape. One I done made with your camera."

"The one with the faker plaintiff doing yard chores, right?" I asked.

"No'm, the other one."

Oh, now what? Long ago, like a day or two in another lifetime, I had decided that Jimmie was hanging on to the firm's video camera so he could tape himself and Dolly, and I couldn't imagine why anyone would want to steal a video of two old people fooling around. Surely there couldn't be a porn market for that?

"Reckon I best tell you what's been going on," Jimmie said, still shouting fit to kill. "I got me a videotape of Miguel breaking into a shed in the backyard of a big man, and then he stolt him some stuff from the shed."

"How'd you know he was stealing it? Maybe it was his shed and his stuff?" Josey asked, shouting at the phone in my hand.

"Miguel done broke in. He done tried pryin' open a door, and when he couldn't get that to work, he jes' broke out the window, made him a good-size mess, and then he went on in."

"What'd he take?" Josey asked in a perfect, coplike way.

"Bags of fertilizer and some other stuff."

Uh-oh. But why would Miguel steal fertilizer after the bombing of his sailboat, and why steal what he had already purchased?

And this didn't seem to have anything to do with why a big guy had put me in a cage with a panther.

"What's this got to do with a big man?" I asked.

"It was some big man's shed."

"Where's the tape?" I asked.

"It's over at Dolly's house," Jimmie said.

"Why is it there?"

"I's workin' on it over there so that you wouldn't catch me at it. Watchin' it, her and me, tryin' to reads the labels of the other bags of stuff Miguel toted out a that shed. Looks like it says pot-ass-see-um something on it."

"Potassium sulfate?" I asked, and Josey swung around and stared at me like I'd just confessed to a felony.

"So what happened?" I asked, thinking I should divert Josey's stare from me.

"Miguel done stolt all them bags a stuff, and then he run out a there real quick, so I took off trying to follow him."

"Why were you following Miguel? Why'd you get that video in the first place?" I shouted over the phone. "I mean, I gave you that camera so you could catch the faker plaintiff being a fake, not to spy on Miguel and about get me killed. Why were you taping Miguel?"

"I didn't like how you was foolin' 'round with Miguel, so the day you was goin' canoein' with him, I done followed you out to the canoe outpost."

Remembering Jimmie skulking up, carrying the video camera that day, I nodded as if he could see me over the cell phone.

"After you and that Miguel fella paddled off, I stayed on at the canoe outpost for a bit, thinkin' maybe I'd ask about getting me a job there. Didn't seem like too much longer before you and that Miguel fella was coming back in. You didn't see me, but I saw y'all having like, maybe, a fight or something at your car. Then you done sped off in one direction and he done sped off in another."

"So you followed Miguel from the canoe outpost?" I asked. "Can you tell me where he went? Where this took place—I mean, where you videotaped him and the big guy's shed?"

"Sure 'nuff can. I got me the address and everything." Jimmie recited a house number on Morgan Johnson Road, in Manatee County.

"Say that over again," Josey shouted at the cell phone. When Jimmie did, Josey repeated the numbers back to herself a couple of times.

"Why didn't you tell me about this sooner?" I asked.

"I's tryin' to catch up with that Miguel fella again, follow him to where he's stayin'. I's gonna tell Miguel I got me this tape of him stealin' I'd take me to the law if'n he didn't leave off of you. See, the day I got this tape, afterward I tried to tail Miguel but he done lost me in all that damn traffic on the Trail. But I figured he'd've come back sooner or later to the big guy's house. So I's waitin' up on him. I waited plumb through a whole night outside that big guy's shed for him. That's how come I didn't show you the tape a him stealin' stuff. I knowed if you knowed what I was up to, you'd make me give you back the video camera."

"Damn straight," I shouted, in perhaps not a ladylike manner.

Josey put a hand on my back, and then took the phone from me. "Finish your story," she said over the cell to Jimmie. I shut up and squeezed into Josey so I could hear Jimmie.

"Like I said, I was hangin' 'round the big fella's house, hopin' to catch that Miguel fella again."

"Okay," I shouted at the cell, "but how did the big guy connect you and me?

"Reckon I shouldn't've mentioned you and the tape to that big fella," Jimmie said, a little less of the shout in his voice, but still audible.

I snatched the phone back from Josey. "You told the big guy about me?"

"Well, see, when Miguel didn't come back and I couldn't figure out how to find 'im, I done knocked on the front door of the house, and I told the big fella I's an investigator workin' for you, and I done got a tape of this here Miguel fellow stealin' his fertilizer and I's gonna turn it over to you, but first I gots to know how to find Miguel, if'n he knows. That big fella took it real bad, real bad, and was about to beat up on me when some real estate guy drove in. Anyhow, when the realty guy got out of the car and seen us, the big guy backed offa me and I lit outta there lickety-split."

"Jimmie, did you give that man my address too?" I asked.

"No, no, ma'am, I didn't. You shouldn't be thinkin' I'm that stupid. But . . . could be, yeah, that he followed me. He didn't spend no time with that real estate guy 'fore I seen him hop in his SUV. I seen this from my rearview mirror, and I sure thought I'd done lost him on the Trail, you know how the traffic gets, but maybe not."

Oh frigging great, my handyman-houseguest-client led a madman right to my own personal door.

Then I wondered why it would matter to the big guy that Jimmie had a video of Miguel stealing fertilizer from him. Big Guy must have been afraid that videotape would hurt him in some way, or he wouldn't have tied me up in a quilt, ransacked my house looking for the tape, and then forced me to tell him where it was in my office.

The only thing I could figure out, standing there in the rain at the scene of a disaster, was that the big guy was afraid the tape of Miguel stealing the fertilizer from his shed would implicate him in the fertilizer bomb that had killed Angus.

"Fertilizer bomb," I said, looking right at Josey.

"About that," she said.

"What?" Olivia asked.

"The big man must have been the one who made the fertilizer bomb that killed Angus. I mean, he had the fertilizer and the potassium sulfate. When he realized Miguel knew he had the stuff, and there was a tape showing Miguel taking it out of his shed, he must have panicked, and tried to get the tape back from me," I said. "He didn't want to be linked to the fertilizer and potassium, or to Miguel."

"Y'all still there?" Jimmie shouted over the cell phone.

Josey snatched the cell phone back from me. "You need to be real careful the man after that tape doesn't come back to Lilly's house, you hear?" she shouted. "Wouldn't be a bad idea for you to get out of there."

"Ain't hardly a fit night for travel."

I snatched the cell phone back. "Go to Dolly's. Lock the doors and give Bearess half a cup of coffee to make sure she stays awake. And don't lose that tape."

Josey grabbed the phone back, but then it went dead. She shook the cell, she banged on it, and she cursed at it, but the cell phone was still dead.

"Don't you think the rain finally got to it, maybe shorted it out?" Olivia asked.

"Well, frigging great," I said. "Let's find somebody else with a cell phone and call the Sarasota PD and get them out there to my house." I made a move in the general direction of the clot of men in yellow DEP rain slickers, but Josey beat me to it. She barreled her way into a crowd of wet men, and told them to find a phone that worked, or a radio, and call 911 and tell them an officer needed assistance and to get a team of armed deputies to the address on Morgan Johnson Road. And, then, to send a Sarasota police officer to Dolly's house on Tulip Street.

Josey squeezed my arm tight. "Come on. You two come with me."

With a sinking feeling, I realized my Big Night Out wasn't over yet. I also knew without being told that Josey, Olivia, and I were going to the address that Jimmie had given us.

Chapter Thirty-two

From Boogie Bog to Morgan Johnson Road in Manatee County was not a short trip, but Josey did her best to make it so by driving like a crazy woman. I was sorry I hadn't stayed at Boogie Bog. One of those nice DEP men would have eventually taken me someplace where I could have gotten a shower, a bottle of water, and a room full of sympathetic law-enforcement people.

Nonetheless there I was, and as we drove, I added up what I knew: a big man had tried to kill me and recover a tape of Miguel stealing fertilizer from his shed; Angus was killed by a homemade fertilizer bomb; Miguel had fertilizer receipts in his truck, but denied they were his; and Angus and M. David and a third man—be it Miguel or Big Guy or unknown third party—had hoisted a few cold ones right before M. David went to hell.

"So, the big guy who put me in the lion's den blew up Angus and tried to frame Miguel for it," I said, beginning to think out loud.

"How'd he try to frame him?" Josey asked.

I took a big breath and debated the wisdom of explaining about the receipts. Maybe, technically, I had broken the law in first stealing, then hiding, the receipts. Though Philip Cohen would defend me free of charge, I'd still rather avoid getting arrested. At that moment, it seemed prudent not to explain about the receipts.

Then I thought about the night of the explosion.

"That explosion was meant to kill both Miguel and Angus, I bet," I said. "Only Miguel stepped back from the boat just in time. The frame was . . . the killer must have known that Miguel had a record for using a similar bomb to blow up some Bush-hogs. Naturally he expected the police to figure Miguel was building a bomb on his boat, and, maybe it accidentally went off. Those fertilizer bombs are notorious for being overly sensitive to motion, and they were on a boat, which rocks, after all."

"Not bad," Josey said. "But how'd you know Miguel stepped back in the nick of time? And how do you know so much about fertilizer bombs."

Having lied about being on the pier the night of the explosion, I thought I'd sidestep the first question, and go for an honest answer on the second question. "Philip explained it all to me. You know, good criminal-defense attorneys like him know all that stuff."

"Then back it up a step—" Olivia started to say, then squealed as Josey lost control taking a curve too fast.

When we finished fishtailing and spun back into some kind of control, I said, "Taking it back a step, the big guy set up Miguel and Angus for killing M. David and then decided to kill Miguel and Angus, hoping the police would think it was accidental."

"That setup is easier to see," Josey said, as she drove over a downed limb and we bounced in the cab and I landed with a jolt along my spine that I knew I'd feel tomorrow. If the panther was awake, I'm sure she didn't enjoy that bump much either.

"Just concentrate on driving," I said. Besides, I wanted to show off. "Everybody knew Miguel and Angus hated M. David, not that that was an exclusive club. But, what with Boogie Bog and the Antheus Mines—"

"And the murdered panther and the orange-defamation lawsuit," Olivia tossed in.

"Yeah, we figured Angus and Miguel had fifty kinds of motive," Josey said.

"I never did think having those matching Dos Equis beer bottles at the gyp ponds made any kind of sense. I mean, who plans a murder, and then leaves their beer bottles behind in *two* places as evidence. So those bottles were planted," I said.

"Dos Equis," Josey said. "How'd you know about that?"

"Attorney work-product privilege," I said, and stumbled right on. "So, those bottles were probably supposed to have Miguel's and Angus's prints on them, both the ones in M. David's den and at the gyp ponds."

"Watch out," Olivia screamed as something large crashed down in the road in a gust of wind and Josey deftly skidded around it without crashing or stalling.

By now, the life-or-death driving in the storm wasn't nearly as scary as when we'd first started our journey to the killer's house on Morgan Johnson Road, and rather calmly, all things considered, I said, "And the phone call from the pier where Miguel had his sailboat, that could have been made by anybody, but the natural assumption would be either Miguel or Angus made it to set up a meeting that night with M. David. I mean, especially after y'all did get Angus's prints off the—"

"How'd you know about that?" Josey said.

"Attorney-client privilege," I said.

"Bull, no way Miguel knows all this," Josey said, a bit snappily.

"So the guy at Morgan Johnson Road is the killer," Olivia said, forestalling conflict in the cab. "And not Miguel."

Not Miguel.

I hoped we'd figured at least that much out correctly.

A little remorse at running from Miguel flicked me in the face, but I rubbed it aside. Okay, sure, now I knew Miguel wasn't trying to kill me, but probably just explain. If I hadn't been paranoid, I might have saved everybody, especially me, a whole lot of grief. Between us, Miguel and I probably knew enough to fit the pieces together. Certainly Miguel knew who the big guy was.

Okay, even without Miguel's input, and accepting that there were some loose ends here, I'd still figured out enough of the story to explain why we, and hopefully official backup, were driving to the big guy's house at dangerously high rates of speed.

"I'll lay down a big bet that Galleon Theibuet lives on Morgan Johnson Road, and that Sherilyn put him up to all this," I said, and leaned back against the bench seat of the cab in grim satisfaction.

But then Josey slammed into a big-ass lake of water on the road and lost control, spinning toward a stand of small oaks. As I squeezed my eyes in anticipation of a crash, I saw Lenora, plain as if she was sitting in the pickup with us. And heard her, just as clear as if she were repeating her story for Olivia and Josey, saying, "But M. David used this buyer for cover, sent out this real down-home guy, in cowboy boots and one of those little western string ties."

A cowboy who worked for M. David had cheated Lenora out of part of her land.

A cowboy who was M. David's bodyguard kept unusually detailed documentations of his bosses' unsavory activities.

A cowboy from Montana with a dollar in his shoe ended up a Florida real estate millionaire after M. David deeded over 48 percent of Delilah Groves to him.

Josey cursed as the truck careened into a resting place, slam-dunk against a tree.

Olivia took my hand and held it tightly, like we were teenage lovers. Or women fixing to die.

Chapter Thirty-three

If Olivia and I and Miguel and Josey had ever sat down and talked it out, we might all have made better choices.

If Miguel's red pickup hadn't been parked in front of the house on Morgan Johnson Road, we might all have made better choices.

But if wishes were wings, we could all fly, as Grandmom used to say.

As it was, after a cursory examination of the dent in the front of the truck, and a careful study of Samantha and her trailer, Josey had us back dashing through the storm to the address Jimmie had given us in nothing flat. And finally, finally, we turned on Morgan Johnson Road, and Olivia squinted through the weather and her glasses. "There it is, there it is," she said, and pointed.

"That's Miguel's pickup, isn't it?" Josey asked.

But before I could say anything about Miguel's pickup, or anything else, Josey skidded her own truck to a stop on the street.

"I can't wait for backup, not with Miguel in there." Then Josey jumped out of the truck. After a few running steps, she stopped, knelt down, and pulled a gun from a holster around her ankle. Olivia and I stumbled over each other getting out of the truck, and we hadn't landed firmly on the driveway before Josey turned and shouted back at us over the rain, "Get in the truck and stay there."

Oh, yeah, right, like we were going to miss this.

With no words spoken to confirm our mutual new plan, we let Josey run around to the back and get out of our sight because that presumably put us out of her sight too. Once Josey had disappeared, Olivia and I, as if we had one brain between us, advanced through the rain toward the house.

Because it seemed likely that Josey had gone through the back door, we did too. Scurrying inside, I saw that the door had been crudely pried open, no doubt by Miguel, as I didn't think Josey had had time. Dripping water, Olivia and I stopped and cocked our heads to listen. From the end of the hallway, I could hear the murmur of voices. I pointed in that direction, and Olivia nodded.

As Olivia and I started skulking down the long hallway, we both stopped, as if on cue, and stared around us at the dead animal heads hanging on the walls. Having grown up in Bugfest, Georgia, I was used to the occasional stuffed deer head or tarpon on a wall, but I didn't even recognize some of these animals. It was purely disgusting. I put a finger to my lips in the universal sign of silence, and stared at Olivia, whose face reflected that she was every bit as dismayed as I was.

Creeped out or not, we started walking again, following the hum of voices to just outside of what looked like a big den-type room. Like I was some TV cop who knew what I was doing, I motioned Olivia to one side of the door into the room, and I pressed myself against the hallway wall on the other side. Then we both peeked inside the den.

What I saw freaked me out far more than the stuffed dead animal heads hanging on the walls.

With his back more or less toward us, a big guy I assumed was Rayford had a gun pointed at Josey, who was kneeling on the floor near what looked like a body. After glancing at Olivia, I stared back at the crumpled body, and thought it might be Miguel's. Though face-down, the hair and the long, thin body fit Miguel. Plus, it didn't take a law degree to figure out that, what with his truck in the driveway, the man on the floor statistically stood a good chance of being Miguel.

To my relief, I didn't see any pooling blood and hoped that meant Miguel had not been shot.

Movement from Olivia caught my eye. She mimicked dialing a phone. When our eyes locked, she pointed down the hallway. I gathered she meant to go in search of a phone, and I motioned her first toward silence—oh, like I was 007 and she was an idiot who would thunk and bang—and then toward movement.

As Olivia slipped quietly down the hallway, I stared back into the den, my gaze first on the maybe-dead body, and then on Josey.

"Like I told you, you better put down the gun. I'm an investigator with the sheriff's department, and you don't want to shoot a cop," Josey said as she crawled up from the floor and stood.

I bit my tongue. I sweated. I listened for words of advice from Grandmom, and I shut up the part of my brain that was telling my mouth to scream. This was not the time to do something stupid, and I was already one in the hole on that. From my hiding place—that is, I was hidden if no one turned and looked at the space that I occupied— I basically froze in a panic of indecision.

Josey was no idiot, I reminded myself, she was a trained law-enforcement officer.

Too bad she didn't still have that gun. Too bad my Glock was at the bottom of the Peace River. Too bad I wasn't at home, sipping the good wine and listening to Nora Jones lull me into a moody sleep.

"You're not much of a cop," the man said, and laughed.

When he laughed, the space directly in front of my eyes went black for a moment and a piercing pain arched through my intestinal tract.

He'd laughed the same laugh when he put me in the panther cage.

Suddenly, I had less faith in Josey.

Trying to work past the pain in my gut and the black spots in front of my eyes, I took a moment to analyze the situation. Olivia had run on tiptoe to the left in the hallway in search of a phone; I should run on tiptoe to the right in search of a phone, and call 911.

But I didn't want to leave Josey, or Miguel.

Also, I realized that on a night like this, 911 would be overloaded, and there was no telling how long it would take to get a deputy sheriff out here, and I didn't think we had a generous leeway. Carefully, and quietly, I pulled out the only weapon I had, my carrot-scraping kitchen knife.

I don't have a superhero complex. But I had been pretty damn good at mumblety-peg as a kid.

"Not much of a cop at all," Rayford Clothier said, repeating himself, unnecessarily if you asked me. "Coming in here and bending over that loser while I knock you down and take your gun."

"I'm enough of a cop to have called backup. This place will be crazy with cops in a few minutes."

Thank goodness, I thought, and cocked my head like a dog listening for sirens. But then I wondered, had the DEP folks even found a cell phone that worked and gotten through to 911? But before I could calculate the reliability factor of the DEP cell phones in a hurricane-like hundred-year rainstorm, Rayford upped the ante.

"Yeah, then let's make this quick." Rayford raised the gun, and pointed it at Josey.

Rayford still stood with his back to me, and that broad back looked like a broad target. Besides, I had to do something, and quickly, if not sooner. Running on adrenaline, as I'd never gotten supper to properly fuel me, I spun into the doorway and raised my hand, poised to throw the knife at Rayford's back. Fervently, I prayed for the mercy of the gods and hoped that some vestige of my childhood tomboy talents remained in my throwing arm.

If not, I was hoping to at least distract the man, and then my well-thought-out-plan was to scream and run like hell, and I figured Josey would do the same.

Taking aim with my sore eyes, I threw my overextended kitchen knife at a big man who was about to shoot my new good friend.

Chapter Thirty-four

Jimmie likes to quote a poem by a woman who says she danced barefoot through shards of glass with no visible wound.

That rather summed up Rayford's and my experiment with knife throwing.

Instead of drawing blood, and at least stunning him, the knife merely ripped through Rayford's shirtsleeve.

When the knife tore through his shirt, Rayford spun around toward me, and pointed his gun smack-dab dead center at my head.

Uh-oh. I guessed the run-like-hell part should have started sooner, because now I was heavy, and leaden, and rooted, and tied in place by invisible cords and I couldn't make myself move.

Though, as a purely practical matter, I don't believe the human body can ordinarily outrun a bullet.

Considering that I was about to be seriously wounded, or killed, I felt a kind of strange calmness. Unable to do otherwise, I waited in place for a really, really mean man to shoot me.

But timing is everything in life. Just as I had begun to throw the knife, Josey had begun a head-down lunge toward him. And now, even as evil Rayford began to squeeze the trigger, Josey rammed him in the side, kidney level, with her head. Though this hardly seemed to hurt him, he did tilt, as if he was losing his balance.

No doubt thanks to the rammed-by-Josey impact, Rayford's shot went a bit to the left, but the sound of the bullet zipping by me released me from those strange ties that bound me to the floor, and I moved. I moved like an Olympic runner, a greyhound, a Derby winner at the wire, I moved as if all the forces of nature were compelling me forward. As if I were stealing home in a tied game, bottom of the ninth, game seven of the World Series.

I moved.

After a running jump start, I slid on the terrazzo floor toward the closest thing to another weapon I could see—a beer bottle on a low coffee table. Crashing into the table, I grabbed the bottle just as Josey kicked Rayford in the knee. Since I was conveniently crouched on the floor with a beer bottle in my hand, I started pummeling Rayford in the same knee with the bottle, and then I spun toplike away from him as he toppled.

Once he hit the floor, Josey started kicking him in the hand like some crazed kickboxer, tap dancer with just way, way too much cocaine in her system, and Rayford grunted, and lost his grip on the gun. Josey kicked the weapon and I watched with mixed feelings as the gun spun under the couch. Yeah, Rayford couldn't get it, but then, neither could I.

With the gun out of play, Rayford, down but not out, pounced for the upper hand. Before Josey could jump back, he grabbed her ankle and yanked her down on the floor with him.

If death hadn't been a seriously possible outcome, this might have been more fun. I dashed back into the fray, scurrying on my knees, and hit Rayford over the head with the beer bottle, which, amazingly enough, had not broken. Hitting Rayford with my puny weapon only seemed to irritate him further, but didn't make him stop banging Josey's head against the floor.

Works in the movies, I thought, and smacked him again with the beer bottle. I'd show him raw hamburger and getting locked in the lion's den. I'd show him banging Josey's head. I hit him again and again.

He stopped banging Josey's head.

A modest success, only briefly enjoyed, I noted, when he smashed his fist into my face. I stopped hitting him with the beer bottle.

Apparently, I went down easier than Josey, and I blacked out, or I think I blacked out, as there seemed to be this space of time in which I wasn't there at all. When I woke, out of a dizzyingly whirling and altered vision, I saw Rayford clobber Josey's face with his balled-up hand, and she flopped over, limp, apparently out of the game.

Hyperventilating against the fear and the pain in my face, I tried to tuck myself into a tight little ball and roll toward the couch that now protected the handgun. In the background, I heard the sound of a crash and breaking glass. Oh, Lord, I prayed, quickly as it were, let that be Olivia breaking into the gun cabinet. Let it be stocked with a loaded assault rifle.

And, please, dear Lord, let Olivia know how to shoot straight, I added. Okay, so yeah, maybe that's not a good Christian love-your-enemy type of prayer, but I needed somebody with a gun on my side, right now, because Rayford was much closer to me than I was to the handgun under the couch. And I had dropped the beer bottle somewhere in the melee.

When Olivia didn't sprint like John Wayne into the room, I spun out of my body ball, and tried to slide to the gun, but Rayford the maniac, now standing tall, grabbed me by my feet and dragged me back, where I landed, a wad of whimpering, wounded female flesh, right at his feet.

When I tried, for gosh knows what reason, to sit up, Rayford shoved me flat down again. My head hit the floor with a loud and painful thud, and Rayford, who I suddenly noticed had unusually large hands, starting using both of those unusually large hands to choke me about my tender neck. Even as I clawed at him with my free fingers, I felt the world going black.

"The carrot," Grandmom screamed into my ear.

The carrot? I'm dying and my grandmother wants to discuss vegetables?

Then I remembered the carrot in my shirt pocket and, moving amazingly fast for a near-dead woman with no air to breathe, I whipped it out. Rayford still had both his hands around my neck and his face hovered close enough over my own that I could see a small piece of something brown caught between two of his front teeth.

Air, glorious, wonderful air, I thought, and I jerked the carrot out of my shirt pocket and jabbed the man who was separating me from that wonderful air; I poked him as hard as I could in his right eye with the narrow end of the carrot. He screamed and banged my head on the floor, but he didn't let go of my neck. Tough guy, I thought, but without appreciation, and I jabbed him again in the same eye, which is actually a gross and definitely unladylike thing to be forced to do, but this time he let go of my neck to grab my hand with the carrot. Blood and mess and stuff were coming out of his right eye, but apparently Rayford was not about to let go of his immediate plan to kill me to seek medical attention. So, yeah, the bastard was tough, frighteningly tough.

Tough enough that with much less trouble than it should have been, Rayford wrenched the carrot from my hand. Then, to my increasing horror, he reached back the hand holding the carrot with the clear intention of jabbing the carrot in *my* eye.

I jerked my head sideways as quick as I could, and just before I became a blind woman, I saw Olivia running into the room.

Armed.

Armed, not with an assault rifle as in my prayers, but with a bottle of some kind of detergent. Dish detergent in a squirt bottle.

"It's got phosphate in it," Olivia screamed.

A minor point, I thought, at a time like this.

"Phosphate," she screeched, in the voice of an apocalyptic madwoman. And then, with perfect precision, she squirted that bottle of phosphated soap into both of Raymond's eyes.

Rayford uttered a series of inarticulate, anguished screams while grabbing at his face.

And then he rose off of me, and, blindly, he stumbled from the room.

I shook my head clear, gulped air, and sprang for the handgun, under the couch where Josey had kicked it.

Olivia ran for Josey, who was moaning, and struggling to move.

We could hear a trail of Rayford's screams as he ran down the hallway, then a door crashed open, and he must have run outside.

Maybe he thought the rain would wash the soap out of his eyes.

Maybe he was beyond thinking.

Maybe he was just regrouping for the next round.

I got the gun, and stood facing the den's door, the weapon held tightly in both hands, in case he came back. Behind my back, I heard Josey grunt.

"She's coming to," Olivia said.

"Did you call 911?" I said, still gasping for air.

"Yes. I broke into his gun cabinet, but none of them was loaded. I couldn't find the bullets," she said. "I'm so sorry. I'm so sorry."

"Olivia, you did good," I said, and turned for a moment to look at Josey, who seemed to be struggling to speak but not wholly succeeding, and then I looked at the still-prone body of Miguel.

"Is he—"

Before I could ask it, we heard a new scream, and the slamming sound of truck doors, and then gunfire.

"Rayford must have gotten a gun out of his truck," I said.

"Samantha," Olivia said, a new hysterical pitch to her voice. "My God, she's in the trailer."

"We better—" I started to say, then realized I didn't really want to leave this room until a small army of Official Law-Enforcement people were in it and another barrier of law-enforcement officers was between me and Rayford the killer.

"Save the panther," Olivia finished for me.

I looked at my friend. She had been cradling Josey's head in her lap, but she put it down gently on the floor, and jumped up. "Come on," she said.

"Don't go out there," Josey said, her voice faltering.

"We can't let Rayford shoot the cat," Olivia said, with no faltering at all.

No, instead, we'd let him shoot us, I thought. But I was the one with the gun, and Olivia was already out the den's door, so the only loyal thing I could do was follow her, so I did.

Down the hallway of the dead things, and out the same door we'd come in, and, around to the front of the house, and there we were, standing in the rain, again, and watching the cosmic forces set the stage for a tableau from hell.

Samantha, the one-eyed panther, was out of her cage, and seemingly stalking the madman with a gun and no clear vision.

"Told you that granny knot on the belt wasn't any good," Olivia said.

Hardly the time to play I-told-you-so, I thought, and waved the gun in my hand around, trying to figure out exactly what I was supposed to do now.

Even as I waved mine, Rayford positioned his gun in front of him with one hand and rubbed at his eyes with his other hand, all the while screaming out curses. The cat was circling him.

Then Samantha began to crouch. Even in the rain, I could see the tight bands of muscles in her chest and shoulders tighten.

"Give me the gun," Josey demanded. "Now."

I turned and looked at her. She was standing, but she was shaky.

"No," Olivia shouted, and Rayford turned in Olivia's direction and fired a couple of rounds. For a man half-blinded by phosphate soap and carrot jabs, he seemed to have a pretty good aim, I thought, as I fell prone to the ground, still clutching the gun.

"Give me the gun," Josey said, the distinct sound of an Official Order in her voice. I looked up. She was still standing. I glanced back at the crouched cat and the maniac, Rayford, the man who I now knew in some not fully detailed understanding had killed M. David and Angus and set up Miguel for both murders. All those animal heads on the wall—no doubt, he was the one who had killed that nursing panther back at Antheus.

A killer. No question. I stared at Rayford and Samantha. I had a clear shot at either of them. I turned the gun on Rayford.

Josey dropped down beside me and grabbed at the gun. "Give it to me," she shouted. For special emphasis, Rayford fired off another couple of shots toward us.

Hey, I'm a trial attorney, and not, as Josey had been apt to remind me, a member of the law-enforcement community. They don't pay me to carry *that* kind of kill-or-be-killed load, so I handed the gun to her. But I wished I'd gone ahead and shot Rayford instead when I saw Josey the Official Law-Enforcement person follow standard procedure and take aim in the rain at the crouched panther.

Chapter Thirty-five

Olivia and I watched Josey's grim face.

And we watched as she didn't fire, didn't shoot the panther, and finally dropped the gun to her side.

As Josey put down her official training that told her to kill the wild cat in order to save the man, Samantha leaped at Rayford in a single arch of power and grace, and he was down, and she was the wild beast she was designed by nature to be, and we knew he was dead before the 911 call could have brought anyone to the damned house on Morgan Johnson Road with the heads of dead animals on the wall.

"Get back inside," Josey said, rather calmly given the situation. "We don't want the cat coming after us."

Olivia and I scurried back inside the door, with Josey bringing up the rear. We huddled in the kitchen while Josey phoned Adam, told him Samantha had escaped from her trailer cage, and that he should bring the tranquilizer gun. After giving him the address, she said, in a bit of a classic understatement, "It's a long story. Get here as soon as you can."

As soon as she hung up the kitchen phone, we all ran to see about Miguel.

Olivia was the first of us to collapse beside Miguel and cradle his head. Then I fell down beside her.

"He's not shot, just knocked out," Josey said. "I was checking him when Rayford got the jump on me."

"I already called 911. For an ambulance and the law," Olivia said.

"Okay. Good job," Josey said. She was still holding the gun, and she was staring at Miguel with the eyes of someone snapping the last few pieces into the jigsaw.

Olivia stroked Miguel's face and made soft crooning noises.

So she was his lover, I thought, with a peculiar sense of betrayal. But then I looked again, with careful consideration and not like a cuckold. No, her acts were more like a mother than a lover. Olivia, the den mother for all of us. Naturally she would have let Miguel hide out with her, use her toiletries, and she could have hidden that from her husband if she had needed to.

"All right, let's see how badly hurt he is," Josey said, and knelt beside Miguel.

"I'll get a glass of water from the kitchen," I said, and I did, and I threw it on him.

"Works in the movies," I said when Miguel still didn't move.

"He needs an ambulance," Olivia said. "Where the hell are they?"

Josey checked Miguel's pulse. "It's steady and regular, like his breathing."

For want of something more productive to do, I got another glass of water and threw it in Miguel's face again. This time, Miguel moaned, slowly rolled his head, and gradually came awake.

"Olivia," he said, his voice so soft I could barely hear it. Then he saw me and reached a hand out. I took it; his skin felt cold, and a bit damp.

"Lilly, I wouldn't have hurt you," he said. "That night . . . no harm . . . meant."

If circumstances had been different, I might have pointed out that he could have conveyed that sentiment a tad better if he hadn't busted down two doors and then chased me first on foot, then in his truck. But he was shaky, weak, with the dazed look of a man recently unconscious. I squeezed his hand, and said, "Yeah, I know that. Now."

Josey went Official then and asked him questions about dates and names and who was president and how many fingers, then when he drooled out his answers, she pronounced him oriented as to time and place.

"I'll go get you some water," I said, "to drink."

"Make it whiskey," Miguel said.

I went into the kitchen in search of whiskey, and left Miguel with his head resting in Olivia's care.

In no time, I found the bottle, poured a jigger or so into a glass, and returned to the den, where Miguel was now sitting up, though Olivia braced him with her own body.

Miguel looked around as he sipped the whiskey. "Where's Rayford?"

"Outside. Dead," Josey said.

Miguel dropped his head and struggled with his breath before he looked up at Josey. "I'm sorry you had to kill him."

"No, the panther got him."

"Samantha?"

"Yeah."

"Man, talk about your poetic justice," Miguel said, and attempted a smile he could not quite make work.

Again, I thought about the trophy animal heads along the walls in Rayford's house.

Rayford. An evil man who could track and kill a panther to grease the path of the phosphate-mining permits. A bodyguard with a dollar in his shoe and dreams of Florida riches who suddenly owned 48 percent of an extremely valuable chunk of real estate, just days after a gut-shot panther died at the gate to Antheus, the would-be phosphate mine.

"Here's how I've got it figured," I said. "Jump in if any of y'all know anything more than I know."

Nobody spoke.

"Rayford Clothier was M. David's toady for years. Rayford killed that panther, the one with the kittens, back on the Antheus property. He's the tracker and hunter. Didn't y'all see the stuffed heads?"

"Yeah, I got that," Josey said.

"M. David gave Rayford forty-eight percent of that orange grove. *Gave* it to him. Property-office records show that M. David transferred the ownership right after the panther was shot," I said, fighting the urge to gloat over Josey the Official Law-Enforcement person.

"Why didn't you tell me about that deed?" Josey asked.

"I thought . . . I thought Miguel was involved. He was . . . is my client. I didn't, couldn't, make it worse for him."

"Well, there was that." Josey smiled at me then, not with an Official Law-Enforcement smile, but with a woman who has been in love smile.

"One thing I don't quite understand," Josey said, "was why Rayford killed M. David. Why didn't Rayford just sell his half? It wasn't like killing M. David meant he got the whole grove, right? Just his half."

"Forty-eight percent," the technical lawyer in me corrected her. "And with M. David having the controlling interest in the corporation, I figure Rayford couldn't sell."

"Lilly's right," Olivia said. "Under the Delilah Groves, Inc., by-laws, the groves were not divisible. And M. David wouldn't sell them because he needed the groves to hassle Angus and Miguel with that stupid orange-defamation lawsuit."

Josey and I both stared at her.

"Rayford had . . . kept files. It was all in there," Olivia said.

"Files? How'd you get his files?" Josey asked.

But I knew. I'd dropped them running from Miguel the night I'd broken into Rayford's office. No doubt Miguel had picked them up and presented them to Olivia.

"I gave them to her," Miguel the suddenly chivalrous said. "I stole them and gave them to her to take to Lilly, my lawyer. Only, Olivia didn't have time. She didn't know they were stolen."

"Ah, the break-in at the groves," Josey said. "Still, that much real estate seems a pretty high bounty for one panther."

"So maybe Rayford had some kind of blackmail thing going. No doubt Rayford'd been doing M. David's dirty work for years," I said. "But one thing's for certain. M. David didn't count on Rayford getting so pissed when he wouldn't agree to sell."

"Or Rayford just beat M. David to the punch. Could be M. David was planning to kill Rayford and recoup full ownership of the groves and get rid of whatever blackmail was involved," Josey said.

But then some silent synapses fired in my brain. I remembered what Angus had said, that M. David's dumping the toxic gyp in the orange grove was turning the land into a Superfund site.

Rayford didn't own any part of Antheus and wouldn't have given a rat's ass about M. David's using the Delilah lawsuit to stifle opposition to the mine. What he had was nearly half of an orange grove he wanted desperately to sell for top dollar. And M. David's SLAPP suit would have brought publicity about the gyp dumped there. Bad publicity about radioactive toxic waste sitting in the soil of the future Big Pink Expensive Homes subdivision where little children would play in the sunshine. Even in Florida, that would surely have brought down the selling price.

M. David had so much at stake in Antheus that he didn't mind devaluing the groves, but it sure looked like Rayford had minded.

Minded considerably, apparently.

"So, okay, Rayford wanted to turn the grove around fast, and he didn't want the publicity of the orange-defamation lawsuit as a taint on the property. No doubt he figured he could talk Sherilyn into dismissing the suit more easily than M. David. So, it was all greed, sell the grove at top dollar before the *Sarasota Herald-Tribune* exposed Boogie Bog's dumping toxic waste in the soil," I said.

"Yeah, okay, we get it," Josey said. "Why Rayford killed M. David. But—"

"Why'd he kill Angus?" Olivia interrupted.

"That explosion was meant to kill both you and Angus," I said, looking at a dazed and stunned Miguel. "You two were the natural suspects, but Rayford couldn't take the chance y'all could talk him into the picture."

Miguel perked up, and almost stopped looking like a man recently knocked out. "He had to kill us to cover up his setup. Keep the police from learning about how Rayford called us out to the groves, talking settlement. Offered us beer, and a can of peanuts, which we took, leaving our prints all over everything. Rayford said if we'd shut up about the groves, he'd drop the suit. We said—"

"Why didn't you tell me about that? I am your attorney, you're supposed to—"

"We'd've told you, only Angus got killed, and then it all spun out of control."

"You should've—" I started to say.

"Okay, I get it," Josey said, staring at Miguel. "Rayford carried those beer bottles and the can of peanuts to M. David's house, with a few bottles thrown out at Boogie Bog. Easy enough for Rayford to get a bottle with M. David's prints, being his bodyguard and all. Only, Rayford didn't know getting latent prints off beer bottles is tough. But even getting M. David's and Angus's prints was enough to point at Angus. And by association, you, Miguel."

"And, the phone call from the pier. Did you or Angus call M. David from the pier the night you met Rayford?" I asked.

"No. We never called M. David."

"So, Rayford figured the law would track the phone call and think you or Angus made it," Josey said. "Think you'd invited yourself over for beer and to kill him."

Remembering what Olivia had told me about the night Miguel attacked M. David, I said, "Rayford was there the night you threatened M. David over the panther killing. Maybe that planted the idea. Plus, Rayford probably learned about your Everglade's fertilizer-bomb episode from the police after that night."

"Yeah," Josey said, slapping me on the back. "You're pretty good at this, you know? You want a change of careers, I'll put in a word for you."

"Ah, so you weren't lying about those fertilizer receipts, were you?" I asked Miguel. "That was just something else Rayford planted in your truck."

"What receipts?" Josey said, and snapped her face around to stare at me, the congratulatory moment quickly having passed.

Uh-oh. While I did a risk calculation on telling Josey the truth, Miguel saved me the trouble.

"I found some receipts in my glove compartment, in my truck. Showing a big purchase of fertilize and potassium sulfate, some diesel. A cash sale. The receipts could've been anybody's, except they were in my glove compartment. I told Lilly about them," Miguel said, lying as smoothly as any veteran of the criminal-justice system, to protect me, just as he had already done for Olivia.

"You should have told me about them," Josey said to me, sounding a tad pissed off.

"Attorney-client privilege," I said, though I wasn't certain the doctrine applied when I had taken the receipts without my client's knowledge or permission. But Josey didn't need that level of detail, so I launched another distraction.

"So Rayford meant to kill you and Angus both, and hoped the

police would think you made the bomb, and then accidentally blew yourselves up by mixing too much potassium sulfate in with the fertilizer."

"Only Angus went aboard before I did."

"So after Angus was killed, you started your own . . . investigation. That's why you went snooping around at Rayford's and found the fertilizer in the shed," I said.

"Yeah, when I thought back on how he'd invited Angus and me over earlier in the same night M. David got drowned, I knew he'd been up to something. But how'd you know about me breaking into his shed?"

Oh, yeah, Miguel didn't know about Jimmie's tape, or my trip through the lion's den. With a somewhat curtailed dramatic flare, I explained that part of the story, and then summed up: "So naturally Rayford had to get the tape. Plus a break-in at his shed and his office had to make the man paranoid. And maybe, he was afraid you'd told me about the night he invited you over, being my client and all, and that I might connect those beer bottles with the ones at M. David's. So yeah, Rayford had to kill me and Jimmie because we could connect him with you, and you connected him with M. David's and Angus's murders. Only Jimmie was next door when he broke in, and the panther didn't eat me. And here we all are."

Off in the distance, faintly, I heard a siren, and stopped talking to listen.

Miguel struggled to stand up, and with a little shoving and holding from Olivia and me, finally did.

"Listen, I . . . you. I don't want anyone else getting hurt. So you might not want to let anybody go into Rayford's garage."

Mierda, so that was why Miguel had stolen all that fertilizer and potassium from Rayford's shed. "You made a bomb in Rayford's garage?" And then I thought like Philip would have. "Did you wear gloves when you put the bomb in the garage?"

"Nope. I figured the explosion would destroy my prints. Look, I knew Rayford would kill me if he ever found me. The cops weren't going to believe me. I figured it was self-defense."

"Perfect," Josey snapped. "Now we'll need the bomb squad."

I looked at my client, who had just confessed to an Official Law-Enforcement officer that he had planted a bomb with the intent to kill. Definitely I needed Philip to give me a primer course in criminal defense, but right now I had to wing it. "Miguel, shut up. Josey, you didn't read him his rights, so that . . . that statement is inadmissible."

Josey didn't even look at me.

"Get out of here. Now," Josey said, staring at Miguel. "You're not going to end up in jail for planning to blow up that cat-killer son of a bitch."

We all looked at Josey. The sirens were closer.

Miguel, showing no more indecisiveness than Josey had, gave me a quick kiss, whispered "Chokoloskee" in my ear, and jogged unsteadily out the door.

I hoped he had a full tank of gas, and that his wallet was still stuffed with bills.

And I thought, so, oh, okay, how are we going to explain all this?

"Josey, you do look stunned, all that beating you took," Olivia said, as if reading my mind. "We should just let Lilly figure out how to . . . to tell them what happened."

Why me? I thought. But I knew.

I was the lawyer.

And in any given crowd, the lawyer is usually the best storyteller.

As the sirens came closer and closer, I knew I needed to invent a good story.

A really good story that hid the fact that the three of us had just let a would-be murderer run off into a stormy night in a red pickup.

Because none of us had the heart to think of Miguel wasted and battered in jail. And, none of us thought trying to kill Rayford *really* counted as a crime.

And then, maybe, there was the fact that we were all at least a little bit in love with the man.

Epilogue

When the gyp sludge hit Tampa Bay and the big fish kill-off started and the bay stank and the fishermen and the tourists all fled and the economy took a hit and the citizens raised holy hell about the stink and the mess, Official Government did what it always does in a crisis. Its personnel pointed fingers and hired lawyers.

Everybody was suing everybody, while the DEP and the environmentalists and marine scientists went to work trying to salvage the life of the bay.

Olivia even tried to get some smidgen of justice and grab me a piece of the legal action by convincing her conservation group to hire me to sue somebody for the big, stinking mess on their behalf, but despite all the research that Rachel and I did, we couldn't find an angle. Angry citizens just don't have any standing in the law to sue the officials of a bankrupt corporation—or anyone else—for killing off an entire marine waterway.

However, failing on that project didn't stop me from trying to keep alive the goals of Angus and Miguel. That's why Olivia and I were out at the Antheus land at dawn with little Baggies of panther poop and the plaster casts of the cat's paws that Miguel had hidden at Olivia's. We intended to put the casts to good use.

I held the barbed wire down as Olivia crawled over it. Then she

did the same for me. We walked a bit in the thickets and the heat before I gave voice to something I'd been very curious about.

"So, okay, Olivia," I said, "why didn't you tell me you were hiding
Miguel?"

"Oh, Lilly, I thought he might have killed M. David, he and
Angus. I didn't want you to be in a position to have to lie to the
police, or to turn him in. I was the one who told Miguel and Angus
to hire you as their attorney, and I didn't want you getting hurt
because of it."

Noble, but fishy, all at the same time.

Pushing on the fishy part, I asked, "Why'd you send them to me
after M. David was killed?"

"Because when they told me M. David was dead, I was afraid
they'd done it, and so I brought Angus right to you—Miguel had to
go do something, but agreed to come by the law offices later. See, I
wanted them to hire you on the orange-defamation case, but also I
knew you'd know how to help them, no matter what they'd done."

Oh, frigging great. So it wasn't all some giant, stupid coincidence
that pulled me into the multiple orange-grove-sales-profits murders.
It was one of my best friends, in a misguided attempt to help her fellow environmental soldiers, and, perhaps, an overinflated belief in my
abilities.

Signaling a change of topic, Olivia asked, "You lonesome now
that Jimmie's living with Dolly?"

"No, Jimmie and Dolly come over all the time. But I've got to say,
first that woman steals the affections of my dog and then Jimmie."

"You'll survive." But Olivia smiled with sympathy.

"Sure. Hey, and I've still got Rasputin." Though the blue jay was
grown now, and eating bugs on his own, he'd sometimes fly onto my
patio table in the evenings, where I'd feed him a trail mix bar while I
drank my wine. Sometimes he'd even sit on my shoulder.

"And you and Miguel . . . you think you'll ever hear from him again?" Olivia's tone was soft, motherly.

"No," I said, though I still entertained fantasies. "Do you think you'll ever hear from him again?"

"No." But Olivia blushed. Though she had denied it when I finally point-blank asked if they had ever been lovers, if I were Fred the lawfully wedded husband, I'd keep my eyes open. Fred, who let his wife bring a fugitive into their house for hot meals, hot showers, and naps in the guest bedroom, seemed entirely too trusting for a grown-up, especially one who made his living in the practice of law.

But before I could pursue Miguel further with his blushing den mother, Olivia changed the subject. "So, what about you and Philip? Bonita tells me he sends you roses about once a week."

"I don't know. First I've got to—" I was going to say I had to get Miguel totally out of my system, but all that lust and the cursed lure of the promise of what might have been was all way, way too sappy and high school for me. So I finished by saying, "I just need some time and space." The classic cliché of the can't-commit crowd.

"I think the boy has potential," Olivia said.

I wasn't sure if she meant Philip or Miguel, but decided to go with the bird near the hand, and not the one on the lam. "Well, then, let's see if Philip will agree to take rotating weeks for putting out panther poop and faking the tracks."

"Now there's a test for a future husband—whether he'll break the law to perpetuate the myth of a panther at a proposed mine site."

We laughed, and made our way down to the western fork of Horse Creek. Then I laughed again, laughed at the beauty of how it had all turned out after Samantha the panther officially saved our lives.

That's what we told everybody.

Of course, no one in Official Law Enforcement believed our story for a minute. But being a trial lawyer, I had coached my witnesses well, and we stuck to the chronicle of the events of the great night when Samantha the one-eyed panther had become an official heroine.

What we rehearsed and told them wasn't too far off the truth, which in my experience is the best approach for a lie. We said, over and over again to various incredulous cop-type people, that the fight started outside, moved inside, moved outside again, and Samantha attacked Rayford, as he was clearly intent upon killing us all. As we told it, Josey and I had already been beat down by Rayford outside on the driveway, and Olivia, the only one without impressive wounds and cuts and bloody welts, had been tied up inside, and Rayford was cocking the trigger of the gun to send Josey and me into the netherworld, when, boom, like armed and dangerous karma, Samantha escaped from her cage and leaped upon Rayford, saving us all from certain death at the hands of a madman.

Of course, we also repeatedly explained that Rayford had killed M. David and Angus, and we were all just as fuzzy as one could get about what Miguel had to do with any of this. We never admitted for one moment that Miguel was in that house that night, and when the bomb squad dismantled Miguel's fertilizer bomb, and, yes, found Miguel's fingerprints, we just played dumb.

Of course, Officialdom would like to question Miguel about that bomb, except for a small hindrance, that being that they can't find him.

And, in the official story we had made up, just in case anyone thought that we all stood around with a gun in one of our hands and watched a panther kill a man, we made it clear we had no chance to save Rayford and that, in fact, the panther had *saved us.* After all, we had the bruises, we had the trail of conflict and busted things in the house, we had each backing the other up—the unassailable, proper wife of a prominent attorney; the equally if not more unassailable, honorable sheriff's department investigator; and me, perhaps assailable, what with being a trial lawyer and all, but equally firm in my convictions and consistent on the details.

So, it went down like we said: Samantha the panther saved our lives, Rayford killed M. David and Angus, and we didn't know squat about Miguel.

No, not a cop in sight bought that story. But nobody in copland could shake us from it, and they didn't have any witnesses or physical evidence to show otherwise, and the media loved it. I saw to that—Samantha was the heroine one-eyed panther who had been lovingly cared for by the ailing but no less heroic Lenora. When I played Lenora into the story like a skilled publicist, donations and cards and letters came in so fast Lenora had to hire the two Episcopalian nuns to count the money, write the thank-you cards, and be her bookkeepers.

And, not only did Samantha rescue us, but she was rescued right back. After killing Rayford, the big cat had hidden from the storm under Josey's big truck. Adam got there quickly with his tranquilizer gun and a small army of panther lovers, and she ended up getting a nice nap, courtesy of modern chemistry, and then a huge, natural, new cage—actually just a hell of a fence around an acre of Lenora's land—paid for by Mrs. Sherilyn Moody, who told me in a ceremony honoring her for the generous gift that it was the least she could do to help the cat that killed the man who had killed her beloved husband.

Generous among the money that flowed into the wildlife preserve was a huge infusion of cash from an anonymous source, aka Delvon. Lenora is making regular payments on her mortgage and medical bills, and, not incidentally, helping Delvon launder his money.

Under the prayerful care of Delvon and the two nuns, Lenora is recovering, and though she still wears the wig of Delvon's red hair, she's shown me where her own is now growing back. And it's curly, she says, and giggles.

Delvon the faithful keeps watch, waiting for Lenora to get over Angus enough to maybe love him back.

Though I am not at all certain how having my crazy brother living nearby is going to play out, I figure, oh, what the heck, at least Dolly won't be stealing his affections and moving him in with her.